2018 最新題型

NEW TOEIC
新多益一本通

【試題解析】

★ 新多益六度滿分狀元

文之勤 著

★試題最逼真！

採 2018 全新制新多益題型，共三回全真試題，仿正式考題開本大小與編排方式，體驗正式上場的真實感。

★規劃最用心！

六次新多益滿分狀元文之勤老師親自選題，囊括所有出現頻率最高的主題與單字，徹底掌握新多益命題方向。

★解題最有效！

詳盡的試題翻譯與解析，不錯過題目中任何關鍵性單字與文法，精準有效解讀題目，快速找出解題技巧。

★發音最專業！

新多益想拿高分首重聽力，搭配專業外師精心錄製的 MP3，熟悉各國不同發音腔調，提前做好應試準備。

師德

Table of Contents
目錄

Test 1
試題解析

LISTENING TEST

Part I									
1	2	3	4	5	6				
C	B	D	A	B	A				
Part II									
7	8	9	10	11	12	13	14	15	16
B	B	A	A	C	A	A	C	A	B
17	18	19	20	21	22	23	24	25	26
C	C	A	A	B	A	B	A	A	B
27	28	29	30	31					
C	A	B	C	A					
Part III									
32	33	34	35	36	37	38	39	40	41
A	C	B	B	D	A	B	C	D	C
42	43	44	45	46	47	48	49	50	51
A	A	C	B	A	B	C	B	A	B
52	53	54	55	56	57	58	59	60	61
D	A	B	C	A	D	C	A	C	B
62	63	64	65	66	67	68	69	70	
B	C	B	A	B	D	D	A	A	
Part IV									
71	72	73	74	75	76	77	78	79	80
A	B	D	B	C	D	A	A	C	B
81	82	83	84	85	86	87	88	89	90
A	B	C	B	C	A	D	B	A	C
91	92	93	94	95	96	97	98	99	100
A	B	A	C	C	B	B	A	D	B

Part I. ► Photographs

1.

(A) These two people are walking side by side. 兩人並肩而行。
(B) Both of these two people are wearing casual attire.
兩人都穿著休閒服裝。
(C) These two people are shaking hands. 兩人在握手。
(D) Neither of these two people is smiling. 兩人都沒有微笑。

◀ 解析 ▶
1. 照片中兩人穿著正式服裝，面對面微笑握手，故選 (C)。
2. side by side：肩並肩、一起　casual (adj.)：非正式的　attire (n.)：服裝

2.

(A) The woman is fixing a car. 女子在修汽車。

(B) The woman is operating a photocopier. 女子在操作影印機。

(C) The woman is holding a glass of water.
女子手中握著一杯水。

(D) The woman is trying to transfer a call. 女子試著要轉接電話。

◀ 解析 ▶

1. 照片中女子正在操作影印機，故選 (B)。
2. photocopier (n.)：影印機　transfer (v.)：轉接（電話）

3.

(A) The airplane is about to take off. 飛機就快要起飛了。

(B) The train station is full of people. 火車站內滿是人潮。

(C) All check-in counters are closed. 所有的報到櫃檯都關閉著。

(D) Some passengers are waiting in line in front of the counter.
一些旅客在櫃檯前排隊。

◀ 解析 ▶

1. 照片中的場景是機場櫃檯，旅客正在排隊辦理登機手續，故 (D) 最為合適。
2. take off：（飛機）起飛　wait in line：排隊

4.

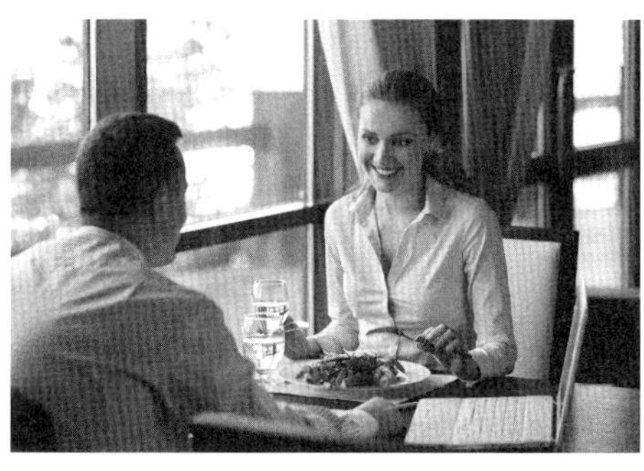

(A) Two people are having a lunch meeting.
兩人在進行午餐會議。

(B) One of them is standing by the table. 其中一人站在桌旁。

(C) The man is carrying a suitcase. 男子提著公事包。

(D) The woman is typing something on the computer.
女子在電腦上打字。

◀ 解析 ▶

1. 照片中兩人面對面坐著，一邊用餐，一邊用筆記型電腦討論事情，故選 (A)。
2. suitcase (n.)：公事包

© Caves Educational Training Co., Ltd.

5.

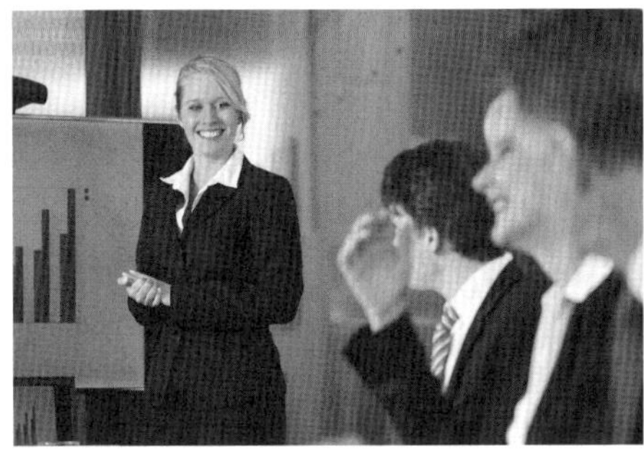

(A) A man is writing some figures on the board.
男子在白板上寫一些數字。
(B) A woman is doing a presentation. 女子在做簡報。
(C) Other team members are about to leave.
其他團隊成員即將離席。
(D) The woman standing is pointing to a man.
站著的女子指向某位男子。

◀ 解析 ▶
1. 照片中的女子，站在會議桌前方，後方有一些圖表，由此推斷女子可能在做簡報，故選 (B)。
2. figure (n.)：數字　presentation (n.)：簡報

6.

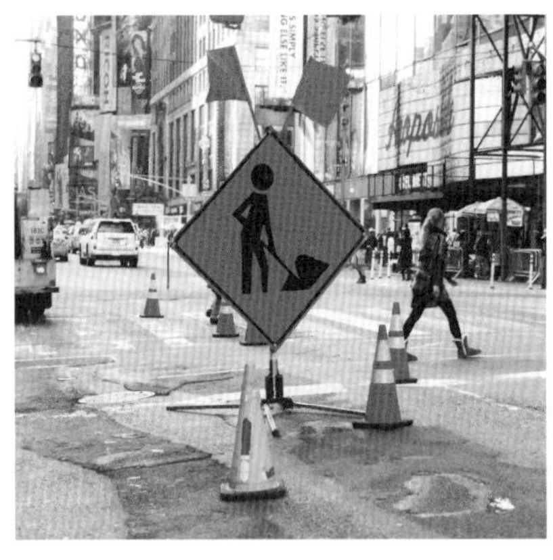

(A) The road is being paved. 馬路在修理中。
(B) The traffic is congested here. 此處塞車嚴重。
(C) A woman is about to remove the sign. 女子將把標誌移開。
(D) Some workers are cleaning the road. 一些工人在清理路面。

◀ 解析 ▶
1. 照片中是一座路面施工的標示牌，看不出有塞車或是清理路面的狀況，故選 (A) 較為合適。
2. pave (v.)：鋪路　congest (v.)：堵塞　remove (v.)：移動

Part II. ▶ Question-Response

7. Are you guys going to have a meeting? 你們要開會嗎？
   (A) The weather is always good in this city, isn't it? 這城市的天氣一直都不錯，不是嗎？
   (B) Yeah, we are planning the product launch schedule. 要啊，我們在計畫產品上市的時程。
   (C) He is the best trainer I've ever had. 他是我遇過最棒的講師。

◀ 解析 ▶
1. 本題是問是否要開會，選項 (B) 與會議主題相關，較為合理。
2. launch (n.)：發行、上市　trainer (n.)：訓練員

8. When will our department meeting be held? 我們的部門會議何時會召開？
   (A) The VP of Sales will also join the discussion. 業務副總也會加入討論。
   (B) According to the notification, it's tomorrow at 10 a.m. 根據通知上的內容，是明早十點。
   (C) We are all flying to Japan tomorrow. 我們明天會飛去日本。

◀ 解析 ▶
1. 本題是問部門會議舉行的時間，故選 (B)。
2. VP：(= vice president) 副總經理、副主席　notification (n.)：通知

9. Did you do anything special yesterday? 你昨天有做什麼特別的事嗎？
   (A) I spent almost all day preparing for the upcoming presentation.
   我花了幾乎一整天準備接下來的簡報。
   (B) Yesterday was a hot day. 昨天天氣很熱。
   (C) I didn't know how to get to Harry's house. 我不知道怎麼去哈利他家。

◀ 解析 ▶
1. 本題是問昨天做了什麼事，故選 (A)。
2. upcoming (adj.)：即將來臨的

10. You know the ABF report is due today, right? 你知道今天要交那份 ABF 報告，對吧？
   (A) I am almost finished. I just need another 10 minutes. 我快完成了，再給我十分鐘。
   (B) Sure, that report is really clear. 當然，那份報告非常清楚。
   (C) We write to each other every week. 我們每週都寫信給對方。

◀ 解析 ▶
1. 本題是提醒報告的繳交期限就在今天，故選 (A)。
2. due (adj.)：到期的

11. Come on, let's have lunch together. 走吧，我們一起去吃午餐。
    (A) There are two women standing on the corner. 有兩名女子站在街角。
    (B) Some people prefer chicken, but I prefer beef. 有些人愛吃雞肉，但我喜歡吃牛肉。
    (C) Sure, just let me send out this email first. 好呀，讓我先寄出這封電子郵件。

◀ 解析 ▶
本題是對方邀請一起用餐，選 (C) 回應較為合理，故本題答案為 (C)。

12. Some difficult customers are really hard to handle. 有些難纏的客戶真的很難搞定。
    (A) Yeah, I totally agree with you. 是呀，我完全同意。
    (B) The customer service department will be dismissed next month. 客服部門下個月就要被解散了。
    (C) The smartphone market seems pretty promising. 智慧型手機的市場看起來頗樂觀。

◀ 解析 ▶
1. 本題在說某些客戶不容易應付，選項 (A) 表示同意對方所說的話，故選 (A)。
2. customer (n.)：顧客　handle (v.)：處理　dismiss (v.)：解散　promising (adj.)：有希望的

13. Have you heard that Jim is leaving the company soon? 你有聽說吉姆就快離開公司了嗎？
    (A) I sure have. There is not much room for him to advance in this company anyway.
    當然，反正他在公司也沒有什麼升遷的機會。
    (B) I have known Jim for more than 20 years. 我認識吉姆已經超過二十年了。
    (C) Jim always speaks with a forked tongue. 吉姆講話總是不太可靠。

◀ 解析 ▶
1. 本題問是否聽聞同事將離職的消息，選項 (A) 回應離職原因，最為合理，故選 (A)。
2. advance (v.)：晉升　speak with a forked tongue：說話不誠實

14. Oh, I need to pull an all-nighter to get this job done. 哎，我要通宵熬夜才能完成這工作了。
    (A) I am sure it's the best solution. 我確定這是最好的辦法了。
    (B) I have to attend a wedding tonight. 我今晚要參加一場婚禮。
    (C) Do you want me to lend you a hand? 你需要我幫忙你嗎？

◀ 解析 ▶
1. 本題對方提到要熬夜完成工作，選項 (C) 表示自己願意幫忙，最為合理，故選 (C)。
2. pull an all-nighter：熬夜工作　solution (n.)：解決方法　attend (v.)：參加

15. Where are you planning for a vacation? 你打算去哪裡渡假？
    (A) Florida is a good choice. 佛羅里達是個不錯的選擇。
    (B) By the end of this year. 今年年底前。
    (C) I will go with my wife and two children. 我會和太太與兩個小孩一起去。

◀ 解析 ▶
本題問的是渡假地點，故本題答案應選 (A)。

16. How do you like Chinese food? 你喜歡中國菜嗎？
    (A) I am a vegetarian. 我吃素。
    (B) Oh sure, it's my favorite food. 當然，那是我最愛的食物。
    (C) Chinese people are always friendly. 中國人都很友善。

◀ 解析 ▶
1. 本題詢問對方是否喜歡中式料理，選項 (A)、(C) 皆答非所問，故選 (B)。
2. vegetarian (n.)：素食者

17. Can you help me move these boxes? 你可以幫我搬這些箱子嗎？
    (A) I don't know what time he is available. 我不知道他何時才有空。
    (B) What's inside the box? 箱子內有什麼？
    (C) Sure. Let's do it together. 當然，我們一起搬吧。

◀ 解析 ▶
1. 本題主要在尋求協助，選項 (C) 表達願意幫忙，較為合理，故選 (C)。
2. available (adj.)：有空的

18. Have you ever worked in an American company? 你有在美商公司工作的經驗嗎？
    (A) They use English to communicate. 他們用英語溝通。
    (B) I've been to the US twice. 我去過美國兩次。
    (C) Yes, around two years ago. 有的，大約兩年前。

◀ 解析 ▶
1. 本題詢問是否有在美商公司工作的經驗，(A) 未直接回答問題，(B) 回答的是去美國的經驗，故選 (C)。
2. communicate (v.)：溝通

19. Whose turn is it to clean the meeting room? 輪到誰整理會議室了？
    (A) It's my turn. 輪到我了。
    (B) You should make a U-turn. 你應該迴轉。
    (C) The meeting is productive, isn't it? 這場會議很有收穫，對嗎？

◀ 解析 ▶
1. 本題重點是 whose turn「輪到誰」，故選 (A)。
2. productive (adj.)：有收穫的

© Caves Educational Training Co., Ltd.

20. Did you turn off the lights yesterday when you left the office? 你昨天離開辦公室時有關燈嗎？
    (A) Of course, I did. 當然有呀！
    (B) Yes, I will be waiting in the office. 是的，我會在辦公室等著。
    (C) That's a very good idea. 那真是個好主意。

◀ 解析 ▶
本題在問昨天離開辦公室的時候是否記得關燈，故選 (A)。

21. Where are all our salespeople? 我們的業務員都跑到哪去了？
    (A) They are my brothers. 他們是我的哥哥。
    (B) They are having a meeting in the conference room. 他們都在會議室開會。
    (C) We need to hire more sales reps. 我們需要招募更多業務員。

◀ 解析 ▶
1. 本題問業務員在哪裡，選項 (B) 回答地點，最為合理，故選 (B)。
2. conference room：會議室　sales rep：(= sales representative) 銷售代表、業務員

22. Have you finished the report yet? 你完成報告了嗎？
    (A) No, I need one more day to get it done. 還沒，我還要一天的時間才能完成。
    (B) He is a good reporter, isn't he? 他是位好記者，對嗎？
    (C) I like to write reports. 我喜歡寫報告。

◀ 解析 ▶
本題問是否已完成報告，選項 (B) 提到 reporter（記者），與題目無關，(C) 則答非所問，故選 (A)。

23. Will James take on that new project? 詹姆士會負責那個新專案嗎？
    (A) James really works his butt off. 詹姆士真的很認真工作。
    (B) Yes, he thinks it's a wonderful opportunity for him. 會呀，他認為對他來說是個好機會。
    (C) Don't you worry, he will be fine. 你不用擔心，他會沒事的。

◀ 解析 ▶
1. 本題問詹姆士是否會負責新專案，選項 (A) 說的是工作態度，(C) 則未回答問題，故本題選 (B)。
2. work one's butt off：某人非常努力工作　opportunity (n.)：機會

24. Can I reserve a table for two, please? 請問我可以訂一張兩人座的桌位嗎？
    (A) Sure, please tell me your name and phone number. 當然，請告知您的姓名和電話。
    (B) That table is broken. 那張桌子壞掉了。
    (C) We do not need to place a table here. 我們不需要在這裡放張桌子。

◀ 解析 ▶

1. 本題是打電話到餐廳訂位時，常見的對話內容，選項 (A) 請對方留下訂位名字與電話，最為合理，故本題選 (A)。
2. reserve (v.)：預約

25. What do you usually do on the weekends? 你週末通常都做些什麼？
    (A) I regularly attend yoga classes on Sundays. 我週日固定去上瑜珈課。
    (B) I love working in such a friendly environment. 我很愛在這種友善的環境下工作。
    (C) We celebrated my mother's birthday last Saturday. 上週六我們幫媽媽慶生。

◀ 解析 ▶

1. 本題是問平常週末的休閒娛樂，故選 (A)。
2. regularly (adv.)：定期地　environment (n.)：環境

26. What time will the Japanese delegates arrive? 日本代表何時會抵達？
    (A) It's around 30 minutes driving. 開車大約要三十分鐘。
    (B) They are supposed to be here by 3 p.m. 他們應該下午三點前會到。
    (C) I visit Japan about twice a year. 我一年大概去日本兩次。

◀ 解析 ▶

1. 本題是問日本代表到達的時間。選項 (A) 說明所需的時間長短，(C) 則答非所問。選項 (B) 回答了明確的時間，故選 (B)。
2. delegate (n.)：代表

27. How was your trip to Belgium? 你的比利時之旅如何？
    (A) People in Belgium speak French and Dutch. 比利時的人講法語和荷蘭語。
    (B) I don't like to travel by plane. 我不喜歡搭機旅行。
    (C) Pretty fantastic, I would say. 我覺得真的很棒。

◀ 解析 ▶

1. 本題是問對旅行的感想，選項 (C) 的回應最為合理，故選 (C)。
2. fantastic (adj.)：極好的

28. Should we go over these sales figures before the meeting? 開會前我們要確認一下這些銷售數字嗎？
    (A) Okay, I will be right with you. 好的，我馬上過去。
    (B) Just give me a ballpark figure, please. 請給我個大略數字就好。
    (C) Come on, don't think too much. 好啦，別想太多了。

© Caves Educational Training Co., Ltd.

◀ 解析 ▶
1. 本題重點在於提到了 go over（確認），表示兩人要一起確認數字，必須互相討論，故選 (A)。
2. a ballpark figure：約略數字

29. Have you got any plans after work? 你下班後有任何計畫嗎？
   (A) That's an interesting question. 那個問題真有趣。
   (B) Not really, why? 沒耶，怎麼了？
   (C) You should go home right after work. 你一下班就應該馬上回家。

◀ 解析 ▶
本題是問下班後的計畫，故選 (B) 最為合理。

30. Can I get you something to drink? 你想喝點什麼嗎？
   (A) That sounds really wonderful. 那聽起來很棒。
   (B) I need a salad and sandwich, please. 請給我一份沙拉和三明治。
   (C) Oh, a cup of coffee would be good. 噢，來杯咖啡應該不錯。

◀ 解析 ▶
本題問是否需要喝點什麼，選項 (A) 未回答問題，(B) 回答的是食物，並非飲料，故選 (C)。

31. Why are you late again? 你怎麼又遲到了？
   (A) Sorry, I missed the early train this morning. 不好意思，我今早錯過早班火車了。
   (B) It's getting late outside, so we'd better stay home. 外面有點晚了，我們最好待在家。
   (C) I bought a new alarm clock yesterday. 我昨天買了一個新鬧鐘。

◀ 解析 ▶
本題是問遲到的原因，選項 (A) 回答未趕上火車，最為合理，故本題答案為 (A)。

Part III. ▶ Conversations

Questions 32 - 34 refer to the following conversation.

[CA] M / [AU] W

M: Rose Hotel. This is Jack King. How may I help you?

W: Good morning. This is Rosa Chen calling from Taipei. I would like to book a conference room while I am there in Singapore on Monday, May 15th.

M: Sure, no problem, Ms. Chen. Can you tell me the name of your company, so I can put it on the reservation list?

W: OK, the name of my company is East-Asia International. And I need a conference room for up to 30 people, please. We will be using it for a training session, so if you could provide a projector, that would be great.

男：玫瑰飯店，我是傑克金恩。很高興為您服務。
女：早安。我是陳羅莎，我是從台北打來的。我五月十五日週一會在新加坡，我想要訂一間會議室。
男：當然沒問題，陳小姐。請告知 貴公司寶號，讓我登記在預約表上。
女：好的，公司的名字是東亞國際。我們需要一間可以容納三十個人的會議室。我們會在這裡舉辦教育訓練，因此，如果你們能夠提供投影機會更好。

training (n.)：訓練　session (n.)：會議　provide (v.)：提供　projector (n.)：投影機

32. What is most likely the man's job? 男子的工作最有可能是什麼？
   (A) A hotel employee 飯店員工
   (B) A sales manager 業務經理
   (C) A conference attendee 會議與會者
   (D) A hotel customer 飯店客戶

◀ 解析 ▶
1. 對話第一句男子說出飯店名稱與自己姓名，以及後續提供的服務，可知男子為飯店員工，故選 (A)。
2. employee (n.)：員工　attendee (n.)：與會者

33. Why does the woman call? 女子打電話的目的為何？
   (A) To reserve a double room 訂雙人房
   (B) To make an appointment 安排會面
   (C) To reserve a meeting venue 訂會議場地
   (D) To cancel a reservation 取消預約

◀ 解析 ▶
1. 對話第二句，女子即表示要預訂會議室，故選 (C)。
2. double room：雙人房　venue (n.)：地點　cancel (v.)：取消

34. What does the woman need the room for? 女子需要會議室的用途為何？
   (A) Job interview 工作面談
   (B) Training session 教育訓練
   (C) Marketing meeting 行銷會議
   (D) Technical discussion 技術討論

◀ 解析 ▶
1. 對話最後，女子表示會議室是用來舉辦教育訓練，故選 (B)。
2. marketing (n.)：行銷　technical (adj.)：技術性的

Questions 35 - 37 refer to the following conversation.

[UK] M / [US] W

M: Judy, are you attending this year's sales meeting in Japan next month? I've heard that all sales reps from branches worldwide will attend.

W: Definitely. I really look forward to the annual sales conference. I think it's a great opportunity for us to meet colleagues from other offices and old friends who've moved to other jobs.

M: Yeah, you are right about that. I still remember last year's sales meeting in Barcelona, Spain. I had such a great opportunity to meet the Sales Director, Mr. William Legg, at Spanish branch. We talked about different sales strategies and… you know, everything. I think he inspired me a lot.

W: That's wonderful, Jack! Well, I excahgned emails with some sales counterparts in Japan but haven't actually seen them. I'd love to meet them in person and exchange some creative ideas.

M: Exactly. But just be aware that hotels will be all booked very soon, you'd better arrange your trip itinerary early.

W: Oh yeah, thanks for reminding me. I will call the event coordinator right away.

男：茱蒂，你會去參加下個月在日本舉辦的年度業務會議嗎？我聽說全球各分部的業務代表都會去參加耶。

女：當然。我非常期待這場年度業務會議。我想那是個很棒的機會，可以讓我們跟其他分部的同事見面，或看看調去其他部門的老朋友們。

男：是呀，你說得很對。我還記得去年在西班牙巴塞隆納的業務會議。我有幸與西班牙分公司的業務總監威廉雷格見面。我們討論了不同的業務策略，還有…你知道的，就是很多事情。我認為他大大地鼓舞了我。

女：那很棒呀，傑克。像我呀，跟日本的業務同仁用電子郵件往來，但沒真的見過面。我很想親自跟他們見個面，並交換一些創新的點子。

男：的確是如此。但你要注意飯店很快就會被訂滿囉。你最好早點安排行程。

女：對喔，謝謝你提醒我。我馬上就跟活動聯絡人接洽。

branch (n.)：分店、分部　annual (adj.)：一年一次的　colleague (n.)：同事　strategy (n.)：策略
exchange (v.)：交換　arrange (v.)：安排　itinerary (n.)：旅行計畫　coordinator (n.)：協調者

35. Where does the conversation most likely take place? 此對話最有可能出現在何處？
(A) In a hotel 在飯店
(B) In an office 在辦公室
(C) At an airport 在機場
(D) In Japan 在日本

◀ 解析 ▶
從對話內容可得知，兩人應為同事關係，且尚未前往日本參加會議，故選 (B)。

36. What does the woman think of the conference? 女子如何看待這場會議？
(A) It is a good opportunity to make new friends. 那是可以交新朋友的好機會。
(B) It is a waste of time. 那根本是浪費時間。
(C) It is a perfect way to communicate with clients. 那是可以跟客戶溝通的好時機。
(D) It is a wonderful opportunity to see old colleagues. 那是可以看到老同事的好機會。

◀ 解析 ▶
對話第二句，女子提到參加會議可以跟其他分部的同事見面，或看看調去其他部門的老同事，故選 (D)。

37. What suggestion does the man give to the woman? 男子提供給女子什麼建議？
 (A) To make a hotel reservation as soon as possible 要儘早預約飯店
 (B) To call colleagues in other branches 打電話給其他分部的同事
 (C) To meet old friends more often 經常跟老朋友見面
 (D) To visit Japan again soon 很快再去日本看看

◀ 解析 ▶
對話最後，男子提醒女子當地飯店可能會很快被訂滿，建議她提早安排，故選 (A)。

Questions 38 - 40 refer to the following conversation.

[CA] M / [AU] W

M: Ms. Hart, some of our clients are interested in knowing more about your IT Service products and solutions. So we would like to propose that we be your agent here in Taiwan and distribute your products to the local customers.

W: Well, I think your idea is really interesting. We should talk about this some more.

M: Sure, I'd be happy to. I am sure we could do some pretty profitable business together.

W: How about arranging a meeting to talk about this issue further? I will also invite our partnership managers to join.

男：哈特小姐。我們有些客戶對 貴公司提供的 IT 服務產品與解決方案有興趣。所以我們想向您提案，由我們擔任 貴公司在台灣的代表，代理您的產品，銷售給本地客戶。

女：您的意見聽起來不錯。我們可以更進一步討論。

男：當然，我很樂意。我很確定我們的合作可以共創佳績。

女：我們約個時間開會討論此案的細節，好嗎？我也會邀請我們的合作廠商經理來參與。

client (n.)：客戶　propose (v.)：提案　agent (n.)：代理人　distribute (v.)：分配、配銷
profitable (adj.)：有獲利的　partnership (n.)：合夥關係

38. What is most likely the relationship between the two speakers? 兩人的關係最有可能是什麼？
 (A) Professor and student 教授和學生
 (B) Vendor and distributor 廠商和代理商
 (C) Supervisor and subordinate 老闆和員工
 (D) CEO and secretary 執行長和祕書

◀ 解析 ▶
對話第一句，男子即表明希望成為台灣的產品代理商。由此可知兩人關係應為廠商和代理商，故選 (B)。

39. What does the woman think of the man's suggestion? 女子如何看待男子的提議？
    (A) She hopes he could reconsider. 她希望他可以再考慮一下。
    (B) She needs some time to think more thoroughly. 她需要點時間徹底想一想。
    (C) She thinks the idea is worth discussing further. 她認為這個想法值得進一步討論。
    (D) She will consult with her boss first. 她要先請示她的老闆。

◀ 解析 ▶
對話第二句，女子表示這個想法很不錯，並希望進一步討論，由此可推斷答案為 (C)。

40. What will the two speakers probably do next? 兩人接下來可能會做什麼？
    (A) Develop new products 開發新產品
    (B) Attend a presentation 出席一場簡報會議
    (C) Sign an agreement 簽訂合約
    (D) Arrange a further meeting 安排下一次會議

◀ 解析 ▶
對話最後，女子建議約個時間討論細節，可推斷兩人接下來會安排下一次會議，故選 (D)。

Questions 41 - 43 refer to the following conversation.

[UK] M / [AU]W

M: So Mandy, what changes do you think we need to make in advertising in the future?

W: Well, one thing I am certain is that TV advertising is getting less important, so we should not invest too much on that.

M: Good point. But are there any media which are becoming more important?

W: Yeah, one growth area is online advertising, you know, things like banners and pop-up ads on web pages. And if we look at how much is spent on Internet advertising, the figure is increasing by at least 10% a year.

男：曼蒂，你認為未來我們在廣告方面，應該有什麼改變呢？

女：這個嘛，有件事我很確定，就是電視廣告的重要性應該會降低，所以我們不應該花太多錢在這方面。

男：有道理。但是，有什麼新的媒體變得相形重要的嗎？

女：有呀，線上廣告就成長頗多。你知道的，像網頁上的橫幅廣告、視窗跳出廣告等。如果我們觀察花在網路廣告的金額，數據是以至少每年百分之十在成長呢。

advertising (n.)：廣告　invest (v.)：投資　media (n.)：媒體　banner (n.)：橫幅廣告
pop-up (n.)：彈出式廣告

41. What department do the speakers probably work in? 兩人可能是在哪個部門工作？

(A) Administration 管理部

(B) Engineering 工程部

(C) Marketing 行銷部

(D) Research & Development 研發部

◀ 解析 ▶

1. 對話內容討論的是廣告及媒體運用，可以推論兩人的工作應該和宣傳及行銷相關，故選 (C)。

2. administration (n.)：管理、行政

42. What does the man want to know? 男子想知道的資訊為何？

(A) What advertising methods are more effective 更有效的廣告方式為何

(B) How the company can make more profits 公司如何能賺更多錢

(C) Where the meeting should be held 會議應該在何處舉行

(D) Why they can't invest more in advertising 他們為何不能投資更多在廣告上

◀ 解析 ▶

對話當中，男子想知道哪些廣告媒介較為重要，可以更有效地利用，故選 (A)。

43. What does the woman say about online ads? 女子對網路廣告的看法是？

(A) Its popularity is growing. 正日益流行。

(B) It is old-fashioned. 很老套。

(C) Customers don't like it. 客戶並不喜歡。

(D) It will be replaced by other media. 將會被其他媒體取代。

◀ 解析 ▶

對話最後，女子提到線上廣告大幅成長，更提出相關數據，故可知女子對網路廣告的看法為 (A)。

Questions 44 - 46 refer to the following conversation.

[UK] M1 / [US] W / [CA] M2

M1: Guys, do you know what I need to do if I want to order some office supplies?

W: Yeah, Mark... you should get the order book kept in the top drawer first, and then you fill in the top form with the items you need, say like stationery.

M2: And then the order needs to be authorized by your supervisor, right?

W: Yeah, Jerry is right. The order form should be approved by your manager.

M1: Okay, that's it? I mean what else needs to be done after my order comes?

W: Well, that part... I'm not too sure...

M2: After the order comes, you should write "goods received" on the invoice and give it to the accounting department so they can process the payment.

男一：兩位，如果我想訂購一些辦公室用品，你們知道要如何辦理嗎？

女：知道呀，馬克…你要先去拿那本在最上層抽屜裡的訂購本，然後將你所需的項目，像文具之類的，寫在

上面的訂貨單裡。
男二：然後將訂單呈給你的主管批准，沒錯吧？
女：是，傑瑞說對了。訂單要經過你的經理核准。
男一：好，就這樣嗎？我是說貨到之後還需要做什麼嗎？
女：嗯，關於那部分…我不是很確定…。
男二：貨到之後，你就要在發票上寫「貨已收到」，並將發票交給會計部，由他們處理後續付款。

supply (n.)：用品　fill in：填寫　stationery (n.)：文具　authorize (v.)：批准、授權
supervisor (n.)：主管　approve (v.)：同意、認可　receive (v.)：收到　invoice (n.)：發票
process (v.)：處理　payment (n.)：付款

44. What are they talking about? 三人在討論什麼？
(A) Marketing activities 行銷活動
(B) Meeting agenda 會議議程
(C) Ordering processes 訂貨程序
(D) Sales strategies 業務策略

◀ 解析 ▶
對話第一句，男子問另外兩人要如何訂購辦公室用品，女子與另一男子進而解釋辦理流程，故選 (C)。

45. Who should approve the order? 訂貨單需要由誰批准？
(A) The vendor 廠商
(B) The supervisor 主管
(C) The accountant 會計師
(D) The CFO 財務長

◀ 解析 ▶
第二位男子（傑瑞）在對話中提到，填完訂購單後，要交由主管批准，故選 (B)。

46. What action should the accounting department take? 會計部門要做什麼？
(A) Pay for the order 付貨款
(B) Keep the invoice in the drawer 將發票放抽屜裡
(C) Write “goods received” on the invoice 在發票上寫「貨已收到」
(D) Call the supplier 打電話給廠商

◀ 解析 ▶
對話最後，第二位男子（傑瑞）說明貨到之後，要將發票交給會計部，會計部將處理後續付款，故選 (A)。

Questions 47 - 49 refer to the following conversation.

[CA] M / [US] W

M: Hello, my name is Mark Willis. I am calling from Choice Consulting to make some enquiries about the communication training courses you offer. And this is for some newly hired employees we have.

W: Yes, we do have standard courses, which are three hours a week for six weeks. Or if you want us to offer you tailor-made courses adapted for your employees, we are happy to do that too.

M: Right, that sounds like it fits our needs more.

W: Well, how about this. I will transfer you to one of our course coordinators and he will do an analysis of your needs and then we can design a course to suit you and provide you with a quotation of how much it would cost, OK?

男：你好，我是馬克威利斯。我從喬伊斯顧問公司打電話來，主要想詢問你們所提供的溝通訓練課程，是要針對我們新進員工所安排的課程。

女：是的，我們有標準課程，就是每週三小時，為期六週。若您想要我們為您的員工規劃客製化的課程，我們也很樂意協助您。

男：好，這聽起來更符合我們的需求。

女：這樣好了，我會將您的電話轉接給一位課程規劃員，他會分析您的需求，然後我們就能針對您的要求設計課程，並且跟您報價，這樣可以嗎？

enquiry (n.)：詢問　offer (v.)：提供　employee (n.)：員工　tailor-made (adj.)：客製化的
adapt (v.)：適應、適合　transfer (v.)：轉換　analysis (n.)：分析　quotation (n.)：報價

47. What business is the man most likely in? 男子最有可能從事什麼行業？
   (A) Car manufacturing 汽車製造業
   (B) Consulting 顧問公司
   (C) Education 教育業
   (D) Engineering 工程業

◀ 解析 ▶
1. 對話第一句，男子表明自己任職於顧問公司，故選 (B)。
2. manufacturing (n.)：製造業

48. What information does the man want to know? 男子想知道的是什麼資訊？
   (A) New software systems 新軟體系統
   (B) Job interview strategies 工作面試策略
   (C) Custom-made communication courses 客製化溝通課程
   (D) Company meeting schedules 公司會議排程

◀ 解析 ▶
1. 對話第一句，男子說希望了解溝通課程，接著又表示客製化課程較為合適，故選 (C)。
2. custom-made (adj.)：客製化的

49. What will the woman most likely do next? 女子接下來最有可能會做什麼？
    (A) Provide the man a quotation 提供報價給男子
    (B) Transfer the call to a course coordinator 將電話轉接給課程規劃員
    (C) Design a new course 設計一套新課程
    (D) Fax the man an agreement 將同意書傳真給男子

◀ 解析 ▶
對話最後，女子說會將電話轉接給課程規劃員，才能根據課程提供報價，因此應該選 (B)。

Questions 50 - 52 refer to the following conversation.

[UK] M / [AU] W

M: What do you think of this new proposal, Jean? The company will offer us an option to work four days a week instead of five.

W: Well, I think it's a great idea. I would like to take some time off anyway. I always want to have a break from spending all five days with figures, balance sheets, cash flow, and you know stuff like that. If I choose to work four days a week, then I will have more time to be with my kids.

M: Yeah, I know what you are getting at.

W: And this new proposal might just give me that chance.

男：珍，你覺得新的提案如何？公司給我們選擇一週上班四天的權益耶。

女：嗯，我認為太棒了。我也想喘口氣。我工作滿滿的五天都是在看數據、損益表、現金流那類的東西，真想休息一下呢！若我選擇一週工作四天，那我就有多點時間可以陪小孩了。

男：是呀，我瞭解你的心情。

女：這個新提案正好給我這樣的機會。

proposal (n.)：提案　option (n.)：選擇　balance sheet：資產負債表　cash flow：現金流
stuff (n.)：物品、東西

50. What are the speakers talking about? 兩人在討論什麼？
    (A) A new company policy 公司內的新政策
    (B) A new product 新產品
    (C) A newly formed team 新成立的團隊
    (D) A new accounting system 新會計系統

◀ 解析 ▶
對話第一句，男子提到公司有新的提案，並說明其內容，故選 (A)。

51. How does the woman react to the proposal? 女子對於新提案的反應為何？

(A) She doesn't care that much. 她不是很在乎。

(B) She is all in favor of it. 她非常贊同。

(C) She thinks it doesn't make any sense. 她認為不合理。

(D) She hopes her kids really like it. 她希望小孩會喜歡。

◀ 解析 ▶

1. 對話第二句，女子認為此提案很棒，可以讓她充分獲得休息，故選 (B)。
2. react (v.)：反應　in favor of：贊成、支持　make sense：合理、有意義

52. What is most likely the woman's job? 女子的工作最有可能是什麼？

(A) HR director 人資經理

(B) Janitor 清潔工

(C) Engineer 工程師

(D) Accountant 會計

◀ 解析 ▶

1. 對話中女子提到自己的工作，要注意許多數字、資產負債表、現金流等，故可推論其工作與財務或會計相關，故選 (D)。
2. HR：(= human resources) 人力資源　janitor (n.)：清潔工

Questions 53 - 55 refer to the following conversation.

[CA] M / [AU] W

M: Lily, could you see if you could change my train on Friday?

W: Good morning, Mr. Jones. Your train schedule to Stony Brook this Friday... Let me see. The train will leave at 11 in the morning, and now you'd like to change...?

M: Well, the thing is that I've got a meeting with my clients at 10 a.m., so I am afraid I won't be able to leave until 11:30 a.m.

W: I see, Mr. Jones. So what time do you have to get to Stony Brook?

M: Well, I'd like to be there by 5 p.m. if it's possible, since I will have a dinner meeting with one of our partners.

W: Yeah, I understand. That's the dinner with Ms. Smith and her team members at 6 p.m. Let me just check. Oh okay. I can get you onto the 3 p.m. train and you will arrive at Stony Brook by 4:30 p.m. Is that okay, Mr. Jones?

M: Sounds great, Lily. Thank you very much.

男：莉莉，請你幫我看看，週五的火車能不能改時間？

女：早安，瓊斯先生。你週五要前往石溪的火車時間…我看看。火車早上十一點開，那您現在是要改成…？

男：是這樣的，我早上十點跟客戶開會，恐怕要到上午十一點半才有辦法離開。

女：我瞭解了，瓊斯先生。那您打算幾點到達石溪呢？

男：可能的話，我想下午五點前到達，因為我要跟一位合夥人共進晚餐。

女：我知道，是晚上六點與史密斯小姐和她的團隊同仁一起用餐。我看看。嗯，可以的。我可以幫您訂下午三

點的火車，您下午四點半前就會抵達石溪了。這樣可以嗎，瓊斯先生？

男：聽起來很好，莉莉。非常謝謝你。

53. What's the man's problem? 男子遇到什麼問題？

(A) He needs to change his train schedule. 他需要更改搭火車的時間。

(B) He needs to take sick leave. 他需要請病假。

(C) He needs to cancel his trip. 他需要取消旅行。

(D) He needs to relocate to Stony Brook. 他要搬家到石溪。

◀ 解析 ▶

1. 對話第一句，男子請女子幫忙確認，是否可以改搭其他班次的火車，故選 (A)。

2. sick leave：病假　relocate (v.)：重新安置、搬遷

54. Who is most likely the woman? 女子最有可能是誰？

(A) The man's student 男子的學生

(B) The man's assistant 男子的助理

(C) The man's lawyer 男子的律師

(D) The man's client 男子的客戶

◀ 解析 ▶

依據對話內容，女子的工作為協助男子確認行程，可推論應該是男子的助理或秘書，故選 (B)。

55. When will the man take the train? 男子會搭幾點的火車？

(A) At 10 a.m. 早上十點

(B) At 11:30 a.m. 早上十一點半

(C) At 3 p.m. 下午三點

(D) At 5 p.m. 下午五點

◀ 解析 ▶

對話最後，女子表示可以幫男子訂下午三點的火車票，可以趕得及五點前到達目的地，故選 (C)。

Questions 56 - 58 refer to the following conversation.

[UK] M / [US] W

M: Good afternoon. My name is Jack Benson. One of my friends suggested I call you because she told me that you might have an opening for a sales representative position.

W: Yes, that's right. Although we haven't advertised it yet, we will need to recruit somebody soon.

M: Good. Is it okay if I ask you some questions about the job?

W: Sure, no problem. Please just give me a second while I get the details of the job. Hang on. Oh, here it is. Now, what would you like to know?

男：午安，我是傑克班森。我的一個朋友建議我跟您們聯絡，因為她跟我說 貴公司可能有個業務代表的工作職缺。

女：是的，沒錯。雖然我們尚未登出廣告，我們的確急需招募新人。
男：好。那我可以跟您請教一些關於這份工作的問題嗎？
女：當然，沒問題。請給我一點時間，我將工作細項的列表拿出來。稍等一下，噢，在這裡。那麼，您想知道什麼細節呢？

opening (n.)：（職位的）空缺　position (n.)：職位　recruit (v.)：招募

56. Why does the man call? 男子打電話的目的為何？
(A) To ask about a job opening 詢問工作職缺
(B) To set up an interview 約面談時間
(C) To file a complaint 投訴抱怨
(D) To promote a product 推廣產品

◀ 解析 ▶
對話第一句，男子即表明想詢問業務代表的工作職缺，故選 (A)。

57. What does the woman say about the job? 女子提到關於工作的什麼事？
(A) It has been filled. 此職缺已找到人。
(B) It is a management level position. 此職缺是高階管理職。
(C) It requires a lot of traveling. 此職缺需常出差。
(D) It is still open. 此職位還有空缺。

◀ 解析 ▶
對話第二句，女子說雖未刊登廣告，但此職務的確需要招募新人，故可知答案為 (D)。

58. What will the man most likely do next? 男子接下來最有可能會做什麼？
(A) Fax the woman his application form 將申請表傳真給女子
(B) Double check with his friend 跟他朋友再度確認
(C) Ask more details about the position 詢問更多關於職缺的細節
(D) Go visit the woman's company himself 親自到女子公司拜訪

◀ 解析 ▶
1. 對話最後，男子表示想詢問關於此工作的問題，女子也準備了工作項目列表，等待男子提問，故選 (C)。
2. application form：申請表

Questions 59 - 61 refer to the following conversation.

[CA] M / [AU] W

M: Linda, Mr. Smith's plane arrives at twenty past three, so is it okay if you drive to the airport after the meeting and pick him up, please?

W: Let me check my schedule first. Hmm… one problem though. I am meeting Ms. Brook at three to discuss the advertising campaign. Do you think Mr. Smith could get a taxi here? Or maybe we could

arrange a limo to pick him up?
M: Well, I am sure Mr. Smith must have a heavy bag, so I think we'd better send a limo to drive him here.
W: Okay, I'm going to call Stacy and she will take care of it.

男：琳達，史密斯先生的班機將在三點二十分抵達，你可以在會議之後開車到機場接他嗎？
女：先讓我看看時間表。嗯，有點問題耶。我三點要跟布魯克小姐討論廣告活動事宜。你認為史密斯先生可以搭計程車來嗎？還是我們可以安排轎車去接他？
男：我確定史密斯先生一定提著很重的行李，因此我們最好還是派輛車去接他吧。
女：好的，我來打電話給史黛西，她會處理後續事宜的。

campaign (n.)：活動　limo (n.)：(= limousine) 轎車

59. What are the speakers talking about? 兩人在討論什麼？
(A) The way to pick up Mr. Smith 去接史密斯先生的方法
(B) Mr. Smith's travel arrangement 史密斯先生的旅遊行程
(C) Linda's performance review 琳達的績效評核
(D) Stacy's job responsibilities 史黛西的工作職責

◀ 解析 ▶
1. 對話第一句，男子原本想請女子去接史密斯先生，但女子時間無法配合，故可知本題答案為 (A)。
2. performance (n.)：表現、績效　responsibility (n.)：責任、職責

60. How will Mr. Smith be picked up? 史密斯先生會如何被接送？
(A) By a taxi 搭計程車
(B) By a shuttle bus 搭接駁車
(C) By a limo 搭轎車
(D) By Stacy 史黛西去接他

◀ 解析 ▶
對話最後，男子認為還是派轎車接送比較好，故選 (C)。

61. What will the woman probably do next? 女子接下來可能會做什麼？
(A) Write Mr. Smith an email 寫電子郵件給史密斯先生
(B) Call Stacy to arrange transportation details 打電話給史黛西安排接送細節
(C) Drive to the airport to pick up her client 開車去機場接客戶
(D) Cancel the meeting with Ms. Brook 取消與布魯克小姐的會議

◀ 解析 ▶
對話最後，女子說要打電話給史黛西，由她安排後續事宜，故選 (B)。

Questions 62 - 64 refer to the following conversation and chart.

[CA] M / [US] W

M: Hello! We're Eco-Paper, and as you can see, we are an office supply company. We provide all sorts of stationery products. And I'm Kevin Lin.

W: Thank you. I'd just like to have a look at some of these recycled notebooks here.

M: So you're interested in recycled products?

W: Yeah, exactly. Well, the thing is that we're looking at making our working environment greener. And that's why I'm here at this Green-Goods Trade Fair.

M: All right, I see. A lot more manufacturers are moving that way too. So environmental responsibility is one of your company's core values, right?

W: Yeah, for sure. It's quite important for us.

男：您好，我們是環保紙公司，您可以看到，我們販售辦公室用品。我們提供各種辦公類用品。我的名字是林凱文。

女：謝謝。我只是想看看這些再生紙記事本。

男：所以您是對再生系列產品有興趣囉？

女：的確是。是這樣的，我們想把工作環境弄得更綠化環保一點。這也就是我來這裡參觀「環保商品展覽」的原因。

男：好的，我瞭解。有很多製造商也都轉型製作環保商品了。所以說環保責任是 貴公司的核心價值之一，對吧？

女：是呀，當然。這對我們來說很重要。

62. Who is most likely the man? 男子最有可能是誰？
    (A) A truck driver 卡車司機
    (B) A sales representative 業務代表
    (C) An English teacher 英文老師
    (D) A dancer 舞者

◀ 解析 ▶
對話第一句，可知男子在展場向客戶介紹公司產品，所以男子應為業務，故選 (B)。

63. Where are most likely the speakers? 兩人最有可能在何處？
    (A) In a restaurant 餐廳
    (B) At an airport 機場
    (C) In an exhibition center 展覽會場
    (D) At home 家裡

◀ 解析 ▶
女子在對話中提到，自己來參觀展覽的原因，所以兩人是在展覽會場，故選 (C)。

64. Please look at the chart. What product is the woman probably not interested in?
請看表格。女子可能對何項產品不感興趣？

Product	Note
Notebooks	Recycled paper
Pens	Eco-certified
Staplers	n/a
Folders	Biodegradable plastic

產品	備註
記事本	再生紙
筆	環保標章
訂書機	無
文件夾	可分解塑膠

(A) Notebooks 記事本
(B) Staplers 訂書機
(C) Pens 筆
(D) Folders 文件夾

◀ 解析 ▶
依據對話內容，女子想要找環保用品，再看到表格內容，只有訂書機沒有標「環保」備註，故選 (B)。

Questions 65 - 67 refer to the following conversation and table.
[UK] M / [AU] W
M: I'd like to check out, please. Here is my room key.
W: Sure, sir. I hope you've enjoyed your stay with us.
M: Yes, it was lovely. Well, but the room cost 250 US dollars, which seems a bit expensive. Last year I also stayed here, and I remember I only paid $200.
W: Right, I'm sorry, sir. We had to increase our prices considerably this year. But $250 is actually a discounted price as you're a regular guest. This type of room would normally be US$280.
M: Well, it sounds like the price has increased sharply. Anyway, please charge this amount on my plastic.
W: Thank you, sir. Here is the discount voucher for your next stay.

男：我想要退房，這是我的鑰匙。
女：好的，先生。希望您住得還滿意。
男：是的，很愉快。嗯，但是價格要兩百五十美元，似乎有點貴。去年我也是住這飯店，記得那時候的價格才兩百元。
女：很不好意思，先生。今年我們不得不大幅調漲價格。但事實上，因為您是常客才有兩百五十元的折扣價。這個房型通常是一晚兩百八十美元。
男：嗯，聽起來價格調高了不少。不管怎樣，請用我的信用卡付款吧。
女：謝謝您，先生。這是下次住宿時可以使用的優惠券。

65. What is the woman probably doing? 女子可能正在做什麼？
(A) Helping a guest to check out 協助客戶退房
(B) Giving a lecture 演講
(C) Playing with kids 跟小孩玩
(D) Presenting a product 介紹產品

◀ 解析 ▶
對話第一句，男子表示要退房，所以女子接下來的動作應該是協助男子退房，故選 (A)。

66. What is the man's major concern? 男子主要在意的事情為何？
(A) Bad service 惡劣服務
(B) High hotel rate 房間價格高
(C) Lousy weather condition 氣候狀況不佳
(D) Small room 房間過小

◀ 解析 ▶
男子在對話中提到，認為房間價格太貴，比去年入住時還高，故選 (B)。

67. Please look at the table. What type of room did the man most likely live in?
請看表格。男子最有可能入住哪一個房型？

Type of Room	List Price	Discounted Price
Family Fun	US$300	US$280
Standard	US$200	US$185
Ocean View	US$230	US$200
Cozy Suite	US$280	US$250

房型	標價	優惠價
歡樂家庭	300 美元	280 美元
標準房	200 美元	185 美元
海景房	230 美元	200 美元
舒適套房	280 美元	250 美元

(A) Standard 標準房
(B) Ocean View 海景房
(C) Family Fun 歡樂家庭
(D) Cozy Suite 舒適套房

◀ 解析 ▶
女子在對話中提到，因為男子是常客才會有折扣價兩百五十元，再看到表格內容，故選 (D)。

Questions 68 - 70 refer to the following conversation and CV.

[UK] M / [US] W

M: All right, Ms. Lee. According to your CV, you are able to speak multiple languages, right?

W: Yeah, exactly. I was born in Taiwan and my family immigrated to the US when I was around 12, so I'm fluent in both Chinese and English. I also worked in Japan for a couple of years after I graduated from college, so I can communicate in Japanese without problems.

M: I see. So you also had experience working in Japan… that sounds wonderful. But your longest employment so far has been in the US, if I'm not mistaken?

W: You're right. I've been working as a designer at Rose Advertising in New York for more than six years.

M: Then you must be a pretty experienced ad designer. Why do you plan to change jobs now?

W: Actually, I'm thinking to move into the area of marketing. I've been interested in marketing, and it was my major at university.

男：好的，李小姐。看你的履歷表，你似乎會講多種語言，對嗎？

女：是的，沒錯。我在台灣出生，大約十二歲時隨父母移民到美國，所以中英文都很流利。大學畢業後，我也在日本工作過兩年，因此用日文溝通沒有問題。

男：瞭解。所以你有在日本的工作經驗…，聽起來很棒。但如果我沒看錯的話，你目前做最久的工作是在美國吧？

女：是的。我在紐約的「玫瑰廣告公司」當設計師已超過六年了。

男：那你一定是經驗很豐富的廣告設計師。為何現在會想要換工作呢？

女：事實上，我想進入行銷領域。我一直對行銷很有興趣，而且那也是我大學時的主修項目。

68. What is the man doing? 男子正在做什麼？
    (A) Opening a baseball game 為棒球賽開場
    (B) Hosting a sales meeting 主持業務會議
    (C) Preparing reports for the woman 幫女子準備報告
    (D) Interviewing a job applicant 跟一位求職者面談

◀ 解析 ▶
依據對話內容，男子詢問「會講的語言」、「工作經驗」及「換工作的原因」，可知男子在與女子面談，故選 (D)。

69. Who is most likely the woman? 女子最有可能是誰？
    (A) An interviewee 面談應試者
    (B) An English teacher 英文老師
    (C) An HR specialist 人資專員
    (D) A Japanese artist 日本畫家

◀ 解析 ▶
女子在對話中回答自己會的語言、工作經歷等，可知女子應為面談受訪者，故選 (A)。

70. Please look at the CV. Where did the woman stay in 2006?
請看履歷表。女子 2006 年時待在何處？

Jenny Lee
Work Experience
2002-2004 Sales Assistant, Best Software Inc., NJ, USA
2005-2007 Specialist, Yamaha Co., Tokyo, Japan
2007-2008 Marketing Coordinator, PSG Corp., Taipei, Taiwan
2008-2015 Designer, Rose Advertising, NY, USA

李珍妮
工作經驗
2002-2004 最佳軟體公司業務助理，美國紐澤西
2005-2007 山葉公司專員，日本東京
2007-2008 PSG 集團行銷聯絡人，台灣台北
2008-2015 玫瑰廣告公司設計師，美國紐約

(A) Tokyo, Japan 日本東京
(B) Taipei, Taiwan 台灣台北
(C) New York, USA 美國紐約
(D) New Jersey, USA 美國紐澤西

◀ 解析 ▶
根據對話和履歷表內容，女子從 2005 年至 2007 年都待在日本，故選 (A)。

Part IV. ▶ Talks

Questions 71 - 73 refer to the following talk.
[CA] M
Good morning and welcome to the TTC radio program. Today we will talk about some local company owners who are both successful businessmen, and who are also deeply concerned with the welfare of their employees. One of the examples I would like to talk about is Mr. Oliver Jenkins. You might know the name, as Jenkins' one-bite cookies are very popular these days. Mr. Jenkins is not just a director of a successful company, but he is also concerned with finding ways to reduce poverty. He provides free education for workers under twenty, and he used USD10,000 of the company's profits to set up a pension fund for his workers. Before we discover more about Mr. Jenkins, let's listen to the weather forecast now. Stay tuned.

早安，歡迎收聽 TTC 電台，今天我們將討論一些地方企業老闆，他們是成功的商人，同時也關心員工的福利。其中一位要討論的就是奧利佛詹金斯先生。您或許聽過這個名字，因為詹金斯的「一口餅乾」在你我生活中隨處可見。詹金斯先生不只是一家成功公司的主管，而且他也想盡辦法解決貧窮問題。他提供給二十歲以下員工免費教育，他還運用公司一萬美元的獲利，為員工設立退休基金。在我們了解更多關於詹金斯先生的事蹟之前，讓我們先聽一下氣象報告。敬請期待，不要轉台喔！

welfare (n.)：福利　commonly (adv.)：通常　reduce (v.)：減少　poverty (n.)：貧窮　profit (n.)：利潤
pension fund：退休基金　forecast (n.)：預測、預報

71. Who is most likely the speaker? 說話者最有可能是誰？
(A) A radio program host 廣播節目主持人
(B) A local company owner 地方企業老闆
(C) A university professor 大學教授
(D) Mr. Oliver Jenkins 奧利佛詹金斯先生

◀ 解析 ▶
從第一句話的介紹中，說話者即報出電台名稱，由此可推斷是廣播節目主持人，故選 (A)。

72. Who is Mr. Oliver Jenkins? 奧利佛詹金斯先生是誰？
(A) A factory worker 工廠員工
(B) A director of a cookie company 餅乾公司的主管
(C) A weather forecaster 氣象播報員
(D) A civil servant 公務員

◀ 解析 ▶
1. 本題問的是詹金斯先生的身分，他的產品為「一口餅乾」，且後續又說明他是主管，故選 (B)。
2. civil servant：公務員

73. Besides managing a company, what else is Mr. Jenkins concerned about?
除了管理公司，詹金斯先生還關心什麼事？
(A) The climate change issue 氣候變化的議題
(B) The radio program quality 廣播節目的品質
(C) The compulsory education 義務教育
(D) The welfare of employees 員工的福利

◀ 解析 ▶
1. 前段即提到今天要討論的是關心員工福利的老闆，中段也提到詹金斯先生設立退休基金等事蹟，故選 (D)。
2. climate (n.)：氣候　quality (n.)：品質　compulsory (adj.)：義務的

Questions 74 - 76 refer to the following talk.

[AU] W

Hello Paul, it's Jean. Sorry about the late call. I've just received an email from Mr. Nolan saying that he's missed his connecting flight from Hong Kong, so he is not arriving in Taipei tomorrow. He will be arriving next Monday, the 18th at 10 a.m. instead. His flight number is HK3978. Do you know which hotel he is staying? Could you please let the hotel know and also book a limo for the 18th? Could you please also call the restaurant to cancel the booking for tomorrow and rebook for next Monday, the same time at 7:30 p.m., all right? I am going to change our meeting schedule now and inform all the other participants as soon as possible. Anyway, call me back if there are any problems. Thank you and bye.

哈囉，保羅。我是琴，不好意思這麼晚才打電話過來。我剛接到諾倫先生的一封電子郵件，信裡提到他剛錯過從香港來的轉乘班機，所以他明天無法到達台北。他將會於下週一，也就是十八號早上十點到達，他的班機號碼是 HK3978，你知道他將會下榻哪家飯店嗎？可以請你通知飯店並幫忙在十八號預約一輛豪華轎車嗎？還要請你幫忙打電話取消明天的餐廳預約，並重新預約下週一晚上七點半的時間，好嗎？我現在要去重新安排我們的會議時間，並以最快的速度告訴所有的與會人員。無論如何，有任何問題的話，請再打電話給我。謝謝，再見。

inform (v.)：通知　participant (n.)：參與者

74. Why can't Mr. Nolan arrive in Taipei on time? 為什麼諾倫先生無法準時抵達台北？
(A) Because of the bad weather condition 因為氣候狀況不佳
(B) Because he missed his flight 因為他錯過班機
(C) Because he canceled the trip 因為他取消行程
(D) Because he doesn't know which hotel he will stay 因為他不知道要住哪間飯店

◀ 解析 ▶
1. 前段即提到因為他錯過轉機的班機，因此明天無法抵達台北，故選 (B)。
2. condition (n.)：狀況

75. When will Mr. Nolan arrive in Taipei? 諾倫先生將於何時抵達台北？
(A) Wednesday, the 20th at 11 a.m. 二十號，週三早上十一點
(B) Tuesday, the 19th at 4 p.m. 十九號，週二下午四點
(C) Monday, the 18th at 10 a.m. 十八號，週一早上十點
(D) Friday, the 15th at 3 p.m. 十五號，週五下午三點

◀ 解析 ▶
本題是問實際抵達的時間，因此可知答案為 (C)。

76. What will the woman probably do next? 女子接下來可能會做什麼？
(A) Fax Mr. Nolan's meeting agenda to the man 將諾倫先生的會議議程傳真給男子
(B) Call the hotel to reschedule room reservation 打電話給飯店改期
(C) Cancel the restaurant reservation 取消餐廳訂位
(D) Reschedule the meeting and inform the others 將會議改期並通知他人

◀ 解析 ▶
後段女子提及，希望男子代為聯絡飯店與餐廳，女子自己則要重新安排會議時間，並通知所有與會者，故選 (D)。

Questions 77 - 79 refer to the following talk.

[UK] M

Good afternoon, ladies and gentlemen. Welcome to our 15th annual marketing conference. As we all know, promoting a product or service these days has become more challenging and exciting than ever with the usage of so many social networking tools. So we have decided to share our experience and take "social media" as the conference theme this year. Our first speaker, Ms. Jane Legg, will be talking about online social media trends we can all look forward to in 2018. Ms. Legg is a professor at AHOY University teaching Strategic Marketing, and is also the author of the best seller "Social Media and You" published last year. Now I'd like to hand you over to Ms. Legg. Once again thank you all for coming here today.

午安，各位女士先生，歡迎參加我們十五週年的年度行銷大會。我們都知道，由於各種社群網路工具的使用，要推廣一個產品或服務，遠比以前更加具有挑戰性與刺激性。所以我們決定要分享我們的經驗並以「社群媒體」為今年的大會主題。我們的第一位演講者為珍雷格女士，她將討論我們在 2018 年所將面對的線上社群媒體趨勢。雷格女士是 AHOY 大學策略行銷學的教授，同時也是去年出版的暢銷書「社群媒體與你」的作者。現在，我要將時間交給雷格女士，再次感謝您今天的參加！

challenging (adj.)：有挑戰性的　trend (n.)：趨勢　author (n.)：作者　publish (v.)：出版

77. What's the purpose of the conference? 大會的目的為何？
    (A) To talk about marketing approaches 討論行銷方式
    (B) To recruit more employees 招募更多員工
    (C) To plan a company trip 規劃員工旅遊
    (D) To sell new books 銷售新書

◀ 解析 ▶
前段即談到商品推廣與社群媒體的關連，由此可推知大會的目的，是想要討論行銷方式，故選 (A)。

78. What will be a marketing focus in 2018? 2018 年的行銷重點會是什麼？
    (A) Online social media 線上社群媒體
    (B) TV commercial 電視廣告
    (C) Advertising 平面廣告
    (D) Online banners 網頁橫幅廣告

◀ 解析 ▶
由於演講者將討論的是 2018 年的線上社群媒體趨勢，故選 (A)。

79. Besides teaching at university, what else does Ms. Legg do? 除了在大學教書，雷格女士還做些什麼？
    (A) Sell advertising 賣廣告
    (B) Work as a part-time consultant 當兼職顧問
    (C) Write books 寫書
    (D) Write blog articles 寫部落格文章

◀ 解析 ▶
1. 後段提及雷格女士去年曾出版新書，由此可知她除了擔任大學教授，也投入寫作，故選 (C)。
2. consultant (n.)：顧問　article (n.)：文章

Questions 80 - 82 refer to the following talk.

[US] W

Hi everyone, thank you for attending today's company meeting. Before going over our agenda, I am pleased to report very impressive results of our financial performance for last year, or I should say – great results – despite the problems in the world economy. I think we have confidence to predict that we are going into next year in a very strong position. The turnover for last year was NTD30 million and we've continued to enjoy a high rate of profitability. In addition, the customer satisfaction rate has also gone up by 15%. All our colleagues work hard together to make these happen, so thank you very much.

嗨，各位，謝謝你們參加今天的公司會議。在開始我們今天的議程之前，我很高興向你們報告，去年儘管全世界景氣發生許多問題，我們仍然有非常理想的財務表現，或許我應該說是極佳的表現。我想我有信心預測，我們會繼續佔有優勢，邁向下一個年度。去年的營業額為三千萬台幣，且我們已經持續擁有高獲利率。除此之外，客戶滿意度也提高 15%，這是我們所有同仁一起努力的成果，我在此由衷地感謝各位。

predict (v.)：預測　turnover (n.)：營業額　profitability (n.)：收益　colleague (n.)：同事

80. According to the speaker, how is the company doing? 根據說話者所言，公司營收如何？
(A) It's weak. 營收不佳。
(B) It's doing a roaring trade. 公司賺不少錢。
(C) It's in the red this year. 今年公司負債。
(D) As good as last year's performance. 跟去年表現一樣好。

◀ 解析 ▶
1. 前段提及公司的財務表現十分理想，故選 (B)。
2. do a roaring trade：暢銷、生意興隆　in the red：出現赤字、負債

81. How does the speaker predict the company performance for next year?
說話者預期明年公司表現如何？
(A) Continue to rise 持續成長
(B) Start to decline 開始下跌
(C) Drop by 15% 下滑百分之十五
(D) Boost by 50% 暴增百分之五十

◀ 解析 ▶
1. 根據女子的預測，進入下一個年度仍能佔有優勢，表示看好業績會持續成長，故選 (A)。
2. decline (v.)：下降　boost (v.)：增加

82. What does the speaker say about the customer satisfaction rate? 說話者提到客戶滿意度如何？
   (A) It declines by 25%. 下跌百分之二十五。
   (B) It increases by 15%. 上升百分之十五。
   (C) It remains unchanged. 維持不變。
   (D) It reaches its record low. 達到有史以來新低點。

◀ 解析 ▶
1. 後段提到 customer satisfaction rate「客戶滿意度」為增加 15%，故選 (B)。
2. increase (v.)：增加　remain (v.)：維持

Questions 83 - 85 refer to the following talk.

[CA] M

For those of you who are planning some outdoor activities tomorrow, I have good news for you. The sky will be clear tomorrow with high temperature of at least 26 degrees C. And for the day after tomorrow, you can expect fair skies with temperatures in the high 30's. However, things might change by Friday evening with a storm front moving in. We can expect light scattered showers over the northern part of Taiwan bringing slightly cooler temperatures in the 20's. By Sunday morning, it will be partly cloudy, but these clouds should move out by mid-afternoon. And that's all for today's weather. Thank you for tuning in.

對於明天已經規劃戶外活動的人，我有好消息要告訴你們。明天將會晴朗無雲又高溫，最低也會有攝氏 26 度。至於後天，也可以預期將是晴朗的天氣，氣溫最高在 30 度。然而，星期五晚上可能由於暴風雨前緣接近而變天，台灣北部將有短暫陣雨，氣溫也會變得較低，大約在 20 度左右。直到星期日早上，都是局部多雲的天氣，但午後就會恢復晴朗無雲的天氣型態。以上是今日的氣象報告，謝謝您的收聽。

temperature (n.)：溫度　degree C：(= degree Celsius) 攝氏溫度　scattered shower：陣雨

83. What is this talk about? 此段談話主要關於什麼？
   (A) Environmental issues 環境議題
   (B) Outdoor events 戶外活動
   (C) Weather forecast 氣象報告
   (D) Traffic condition 交通狀況

◀ 解析 ▶
前段即提到天氣晴朗又高溫等內容，故可知答案為 (C)。

84. What will the weather be like tomorrow? 明日天氣將會如何？
   (A) It will be raining. 會是下雨天。
   (B) It will be clear. 會是晴天。
   (C) It will be cloudy. 會是陰天。
   (D) It will be humid. 會很潮溼。

◀ 解析 ▶
1. 說話者提到明天天氣將會晴朗無雲且高溫，故選 (B)。
2. humid (adj.)：潮濕的

85. What will happen on Friday? 週五會發生什麼事？
(A) The temperature will drop below zero. 氣溫會降到零下。
(B) There will be a lot of snow. 會降下大雪。
(C) There will be light scattered showers. 會有短暫陣雨。
(D) The weather will be hot and sunny. 天氣會炎熱又晴朗。

◀ 解析 ▶
說話者也提到，週五由於暴風雨接近，會轉變為短暫陣雨的天氣，故選 (C)。

Questions 86 - 88 refer to the following talk.

[AU] W

Good morning, passengers. This is the pre-boarding announcement for flight EVA209 to Taipei. We are now inviting passengers with small children, and passengers needing special assistance to begin boarding at this time. Next we will invite passengers with Gold-Fly VIP cards to board. Please have your boarding pass and passport ready. Regular boarding will begin in approximately twenty minutes. Thank you for your attention.

早安，各位乘客，現在宣佈飛往台北的 EVA209 班機開放優先登機。現在先請帶著幼兒的乘客與需要特殊協助的旅客，開始登機。接下來，請持有 Gold-Fly 貴賓卡的乘客開始登機。請將您的登機證與護照準備好。一般旅客登機約在二十分鐘後開始。謝謝您。

passenger (n.)：乘客　boarding (n.)：登機、登船、上車等　approximately (adv.)：大約

86. What is the purpose of this announcement? 此段廣播的目的為何？
(A) To invite passengers to board the plane 邀請旅客登機
(B) To announce a delayed departure information 宣佈延後起飛的訊息
(C) To invite passengers to board the train 邀請旅客登上火車
(D) To inform passengers of a gate change 通知旅客更改登機門

◀ 解析 ▶
1. 廣播第一句，即說明此廣播的目的是要邀請旅客優先登機，故選 (A)。
2. purpose (n.)：目的　departure (n.)：出發、起飛　gate (n.)：大門、登機門

87. Who is invited to board the plane first? 誰受邀優先登機？
   (A) Passengers flying to Taipei 要飛往台北的旅客
   (B) Passengers with credit cards 有信用卡的乘客
   (C) Passengers with large suitcases 有大型行李的乘客
   (D) Passengers with small children 有幼兒的乘客

◀ 解析 ▶
廣播中提到，先請帶著幼兒的乘客與需要特殊協助的旅客登機，故選 (D)。

88. When will the regular boarding begin? 一般登機何時會開始？
   (A) In 10 minutes 十分鐘後
   (B) In 20 minutes 二十分鐘後
   (C) In 30 minutes 三十分鐘後
   (D) In 40 minutes 四十分鐘後

◀ 解析 ▶
廣播最後提到，一般旅客登機約在二十分鐘後開始，故選 (B)。

Questions 89 - 91 refer to the following talk.
[UK] M
Train service on the West Line has been delayed by an average of 30 minutes in both directions. The cause of the initial delay has been traced to a fault in the traction power system at 10 in the morning. At about 2:30 in the afternoon, a new fault in the signaling system was discovered. That resulted in a further delay in train services. Our engineers are currently working to repair this fault to ensure that service delays are minimized. We deeply apologize to all affected passengers for the inconvenience caused.

西部幹線列車服務，雙向平均皆誤點三十分鐘，最初造成延遲的原因已經查出，起因為早上十點牽引供電系統的故障。下午兩點三十分左右，發現另外一個號誌系統的故障，造成各列車班次再度延遲。我們的工程師目前正在進行搶修，以確保列車延誤的時間降低至最少。對於所有受到影響的乘客，造成您的不便，我們感到萬分抱歉。

average (n.)：平均　initial(adj.)：最初的　traction (n.)：牽引　ensure (v.)：保證
minimize (v.)：減到最少　affect (v.)：影響　inconvenience (n.)：不便

89. What's the problem with the train services? 列車服務發生什麼問題？
   (A) They have been delayed by 30 minutes. 誤點了三十分鐘。
   (B) The platform is undergoing renovation. 月台正在進行整修。
   (C) All train tickets are sold out. 所有車票都賣光了。
   (D) Train conductors are on strike. 列車長正在罷工。

◀ 解析 ▶
1. 廣播開頭即提到，雙向列車皆誤點三十分鐘，故選 (A)。
2. renovation (n.)：修理、重建　conductor (n.)：火車列車長　on strike：罷工

90. What time did the signaling problem happen? 號誌系統幾點發生問題？
(A) 10 a.m. 早上十點
(B) 2 p.m. 下午兩點
(C) 2:30 p.m. 下午兩點半
(D) 10:30 a.m. 早上十點半

◀ 解析 ▶
本題問的是後來發生的號誌系統問題，時間為下午兩點半，答案為 (C)。

91. What are engineers doing now? 工程師現在都在做什麼？
(A) Fixing problems 解決問題
(B) Going on vacations 渡假中
(C) Selling train tickets 販售火車票
(D) Apologizing to passengers 向旅客道歉

◀ 解析 ▶
廣播最後提到，工程師正在修復系統故障，也就是設法解決問題，故選 (A)。

Questions 92 - 94 refer to the following talk.

[US] W

Hello, this is Winnie Chen of Blueway Jeans, with a message for Ms. Kelly Hung, please. Ms. Hung, as you know, Blueway is planning a new range of jeans, and we are commissioning you to do the designs for it. There are several points I'd like to discuss with Ms. Hung. We need to define our target market first, and we hope you can create an image that will have wide appeal. Oh and the launch schedule has been brought forward, so we need to talk to you about the change to the deadline that we originally discussed. Okay, please call me back, Ms. Hung. You've got my number.

哈囉，我是 Blueway 牛仔褲的陳溫妮，我要留言給洪凱莉小姐。洪小姐，如您所知，Blueway 規劃了一個新的牛仔褲產品線，我們正委託您幫忙設計，有許多要點我想與洪小姐討論。我們必須先定義我們的目標市場，而且我們希望您可以建立一個具廣泛感染力的形象。推出的時程已經提前，所以我們必須與您討論，更改當初我們約定的期限。洪小姐，請再打電話給我。您有我的電話號碼。

commission (v.)：委託　define (v.)：定義　target (n.)：目標　appeal (n.)：吸引力、感染力
launch (n.)：發行、上市　originally (adv.)：原本

92. What kind of product is Winnie Chen selling? 陳溫妮賣的是什麼產品？
    (A) Snacks 點心
    (B) Jeans 牛仔褲
    (C) Books 書籍
    (D) Interior design 室內設計

◀ 解析 ▶
留言開頭即提到，溫妮任職於 Blueway 牛仔褲，故選 (B)。

93. Who is most likely Ms. Kelly Hung? 洪凱莉小姐最有可能是誰？
    (A) A fashion designer 時尚設計師
    (B) A doctor 醫生
    (C) A shoe vendor 鞋子供應商
    (D) An event planner 活動規劃人員

◀ 解析 ▶
溫妮委託洪凱莉小姐設計新牛仔褲，由此可知其為設計師，故選 (A)。

94. What is Ms. Hung asked to do next? 洪小姐接下來被要求做什麼？
    (A) Fax Winnie the design draft 將設計草稿傳真給溫妮
    (B) Email Winnie the contract 將合約寄電子郵件給溫妮
    (C) Call Winnie back to discuss details 打電話給溫妮討論細節
    (D) Look for Winnie's number in the White Pages 在公共電話簿中找溫妮的號碼

◀ 解析 ▶
留言最後，溫妮請洪小姐打電話給她，且洪小姐已有溫妮的電話，不需翻找公共電話簿，故選 (C)。

Questions 95 - 97 refer to the following talk and table.

[CA] M

Good morning, and welcome to the Good-Deed Hotel. Thank you very much for staying with us. I know some of you have traveled a long way from South America, and I hope you've all had good journeys. So let me introduce myself first. My name is Jack Galli, and I am the customer manager of the Hotel. Now I'd like to give you a brief introduction of our hotel. Our stunning 30-story complex features 200 lavishly appointed guest rooms. This 5-star hotel was created by the world-famous interior designer, Mr. Paul Parker, and combines comfort and style with exceptional services in a spacious and elegant environment. Once again welcome and I hope you all enjoy your stay here at Good-Deed Hotel.

早安，歡迎來到古迪飯店，謝謝您入住本飯店，我知道有些人是從南美洲長途旅行到此，我希望各位都有愉快的旅程。讓我先自我介紹，我的名字是傑克蓋里，我是飯店的客服經理。現在讓我為您簡單地介紹我們的飯店，這座令人驚嘆的飯店是三十層樓高的複合式建築，共有兩百間豪華客房。這座五星級飯店，是由全世界著名的室內設計師保羅帕克所設計，結合舒適性與風格性，不僅有寬敞的空間與優雅的環境，更具備卓越的服務。再次歡迎您，並期望各位都能享受古迪飯店的住宿時光。

introduce (v.)：介紹　stunning (adj.)：驚人的　complex (n.)：綜合體　lavishly (adv.)：豐富地
appointed (adj.)：有裝飾的　exceptional (adj.)：優秀的　spacious (adj.)：寬廣的　elegant (adj.)：優雅的

95. Who is most likely the speaker? 說話者最有可能是誰？
(A) An interior designer 室內設計師
(B) A hotel guest 飯店客人
(C) A hotel customer manager 飯店客服經理
(D) A business manager 企業經理人

◀ 解析 ▶
男子的自我介紹中提到，自己是飯店的客服經理，故選 (C)。

96. Please look at the table. Which hotel is also the work of Good-Deed Hotel's designer?
請看表格。哪間飯店也是古迪飯店設計師的作品？

5-Star Hotel	Designer
Venus Hotel	Tom Walker
Grand Central Inn	James Williams
Hotel Grace	Grace Bush
Great View Resort	Paul Parker

五星級飯店	設計師
維納斯飯店	湯姆沃克
豪美中城飯店	詹姆士威廉斯
優雅飯店	葛瑞絲布希
好景飯店	保羅帕克

(A) Grand Central Inn 豪美中城飯店
(B) Great View Resort 好景飯店
(C) Hotel Grace 優雅飯店
(D) Venus Hotel 維納斯飯店

◀ 解析 ▶
男子介紹古迪飯店的設計師為保羅帕克，再看到表格內容，該名設計師的作品還有好景飯店，故選 (B)。

97. What's Mr. Parker's design style? 帕克先生的設計風格如何？
(A) Crowded and dark 擁擠又黑暗
(B) Spacious and elegant 寬敞又高雅
(C) Expensive and luxurious 昂貴又奢華
(D) Simple and modern 簡單又現代

◀ 解析 ▶
1. 後段提到飯店的設計，使得整體環境寬敞又高雅，故選 (B)。
2. luxurious (adj.)：豪華的、奢華的

Questions 98 - 100 refer to the following talk and table.

[AU] W

Hello, thank you for calling Yellow Dock Consultancy. Our business hours are Monday through Friday, 9 a.m. to 6 p.m., and Saturday, 10 a.m. to 2 p.m. If you want to leave a message, please wait for the tone. If you want to leave your name and number, please press the pound key, then dial your name, then press 6 and dial your number. If you want to make an appointment, please dial extension 4373 to leave a message, and one of our consultants will get back to you as soon as possible. Thank you.

哈囉，謝謝您來電耶羅達克顧問公司。我們的服務時間是星期一到星期五，早上九點到下午六點，以及星期六的早上十點到下午兩點。如果您想要留言，請在嘟聲後留言。如果您想要留下姓名與電話，請按下 # 字鍵，再輸入您的姓名，最後按 6 並輸入您的電話號碼。如果您想要預約，請撥分機號碼 4373 並留言，我們的顧問將會以最快的速度回覆您。謝謝。

consultancy (n.)：顧問公司　tone (n.)：音調　pound key：電話上的 # 字鍵　extension (n.)：電話分機

98. Where does the announcement most likely appear? 這段訊息最有可能出現在何處？
(A) On a telephone answering machine 電話答錄機內
(B) In a radio program 廣播節目中
(C) In a weather forecast 氣象預報中
(D) In an electronics store 電子用品店裡

◀ 解析 ▶
1. 一開始提到謝謝對方來電，又說明如何留言及預約，由此可推斷應是電話答錄機，故選 (A)。
2. electronics (n.)：電子產品

99. Please look at the table. When does the listener probably hear this message?
請看表格。聽者何時有可能聽到這則訊息？

Day	Time
Monday – Friday	9 a.m. – 6 p.m.
Saturday	10 a.m. – 2 p.m.
Sunday	Closed

星期	時間
週一至週五	早上九點至下午六點
週六	早上十點至下午二點
週日	未營業

(A) Tuesday 4 p.m. 週二下午四點
(B) Saturday 12 noon 週六中午十二點
(C) Friday 5 p.m. 週五下午五點
(D) Saturday 9 a.m. 週六上午九點

◀ 解析 ▶
根據表格所列出的服務時間，應該要選「服務時間以外」的選項較為合理，故選 (D)。

100. What should the person who wants to make an appointment do? 想預約的人該怎麼做？

(A) Call again tomorrow 明天再打一次

(B) Dial 4373 and leave a message 撥 4373 並留言

(C) Wait for the tone 等候嘟聲

(D) Press the pound key 按 # 字鍵

◀ 解析 ▶

選項 (C) 為留言的作法，選項 (D) 則是留下姓名的作法。最後提到的預約方式，是撥分機號碼 4373 並留言，故選 (B)。

READING TEST

Part V									
101	102	103	104	105	106	107	108	109	110
A	C	A	B	D	B	C	B	C	B
111	112	113	114	115	116	117	118	119	120
D	A	B	C	A	A	A	C	B	D
121	122	123	124	125	126	127	128	129	130
A	B	D	A	B	C	C	A	D	B
Part VI									
131	132	133	134	135	136	137	138	139	140
A	B	D	B	D	C	A	C	A	D
141	142	143	144	145	146				
B	B	B	D	C	B				
Part VII									
147	148	149	150	151	152	153	154	155	156
A	B	A	C	D	B	C	A	C	A
157	158	159	160	161	162	163	164	165	166
B	A	B	B	C	B	D	A	A	B
167	168	169	170	171	172	173	174	175	176
A	B	A	A	A	B	C	A	D	B
177	178	179	180	181	182	183	184	185	186
C	C	D	C	B	A	D	D	D	C
187	188	189	190	191	192	193	194	195	196
B	A	A	B	C	D	A	A	B	A
197	198	199	200						
D	C	B	B						

Part V. ► Incomplete Sentences

101. Production applications are at the foundation of all processes ___________ with doing business.
產能應用程式是跟企業營運相關的所有程序的基礎。
(A) associated
(B) association
(C) associating
(D) associate

◀ 解析 ▶
本題重點在「與…有關聯的」，句子後半段原本應該是 all processes which are associated with doing business，此處省略了 which are，故選 (A)。

102. A presenter can reasonably assume that the audience arrives with a desire to know __________ the presenter is going to tell them.
一個演講者可以很合理地假設，聽眾來聽演講就是想知道講者會傳遞什麼訊息。
(A) why 為何
(B) which 哪個
(C) what 什麼
(D) that 那個

◀ 解析 ▶
根據句意可推斷，聽眾想知道講者會傳遞「什麼訊息」，故選 (C)。

103. Organizations today __________ challenged with the implementation of cost effective information security solutions.
現今企業正面臨的挑戰，是要採用符合成本效益的資訊安全解決方案。
(A) are
(B) were
(C) will
(D) being

◀ 解析 ▶
從前面的 organizations today，可見是敘述一般企業目前面臨的狀況，且空格後接的是過去分詞 challenged，可推斷其為被動語態，故選 (A)。

104. We have been responsible __________ the ongoing support of Information Technology for over ten years.
我們負責提供不間斷的資訊科技服務，已經超過十年的時間了。
(A) of
(B) for
(C) at
(D) in

◀ 解析 ▶
本題的重點在於是否熟悉 be responsible for 的用法，故選 (B)。

105. Just as the speaker said, "A presentation is an exercise in __________ ."
誠如講者所言：「做簡報的目的就是要傳遞訊息以說服他人。」
(A) persuaded 說服（過去式）
(B) persuasive 有說服力的
(C) persuade 說服
(D) persuasion 說服力

◀ 解析 ▶
空格的前面為介系詞 in，可以推斷答案應該是名詞或動名詞，故選 (D)。

106. Creative people see __________ as creative and give themselves the freedom to create.
想像力豐富的人會認為自己富有創造力，且給自己自由發揮的空間。
(A) them 他們
(B) themselves 他們自己
(C) their 他們的
(D) they 他們

◀ 解析 ▶
空格前為動詞 see，後為連接詞 as，故不可填入 their 或 they，再根據句子內容，答案應該是反身代名詞 (B)。

107. Brainstorming provides a freewheeling environment __________ everyone is encouraged to participate and contribute good ideas.
集思廣益就是要提供無拘無束的環境，讓每個人可以勇於參與並貢獻好點子。
(A) in that
(B) who
(C) in which
(D) when

◀ 解析 ▶
此句用到關係代名詞，合併兩個語意相關的句子，適用於主詞 environment 的關係代名詞為 which 或 that，that 前不加 in，故答案為 (C)。

108. __________ I brainstorm on my own, I usually tend to produce a wider range of good ideas.
當我獨自發想點子時，我通常會想到更多的好點子。
(A) Because 因為
(B) When 當…時
(C) Only 僅僅
(D) If 假如

◀ 解析 ▶
本題重點在選擇適合的連接詞，從全句的意思來看，選 (B) 最為合適。

109. ITCO provides a cost __________ solution for delivering risk management and knowledge management.

ITCO 公司提供一個划算的解決方案，為企業客戶進行風險管理和知識管理。

(A) effect 影響

(B) efficiency 效能

(C) effective 有效的

(D) effectively 有效地

◀ 解析 ▶

本題選項詞性各有不同，意義也有所區別，而 cost effective 意思為「划算的」，故選 (C)。

110. I ask for your opinion __________ I am investigating the different partnership options we can have in place.

我想詢問你的意見，因為我正在研究我們以何種方式來合作較適當。

(A) however 然而

(B) because 因為

(C) only if 假使

(D) although 雖然

◀ 解析 ▶

從前後文意來看，可發現後句是說明詢問對方意見的原因，兩句為因果關係，因此 (B) 為正確答案。

111. This is to inform you that the contract __________ received and I have sent it to the manager for final approval.

我是想告知你，合約已經收到了，而且也已經傳給經理做最後的批示。

(A) has had

(B) has being

(C) have been

(D) has been

◀ 解析 ▶

本題以 contract「合約」為動作的對象，動詞部分應該用被動語態 be + p.p.，且動作已經完成，所以用現在完成式 have / has + p.p.。兩者結合可知動詞部分為 has been received，故選 (D)。

112. A one-year free license for internal use can be __________ to partners only after they started to sell the solutions.

可於公司內部使用的一年期免費授權，僅提供給已開始銷售解決方案的合作夥伴。

(A) provided 提供

(B) provides 提供

(C) provider 提供者

(D) providing 提供

◀ 解析 ▶
本題以 license「授權」為動作的對象，動詞部分應該用被動語態 be + p.p.，故選 (A) provided。

113. When individual group members get stuck on an idea, __________ member's creativity and experience can take the idea to the next stage.
當團隊內的成員陷入繞著同一個想法打轉的困境時，另一位成員的創意和經驗可以讓此想法更進一步。
(A) each other 互相
(B) another 另一
(C) others 其他的（人事物）
(D) the other 另一

◀ 解析 ▶
another 和 the other 都有「另一」之意，但 the other 為限定用法，多半用於 one... the other... 的句型。another 則可泛指「另一」或「另外的」，故本題選 (B)。

114. You will be __________ receiving an email with the details to log into our Sales portal.
你很快就會收到一封電子郵件，內容會有告知如何登入到我們業務主頁的所有細節資訊。
(A) shorten 縮短
(B) short 短的
(C) shortly 立即
(D) short of 短少

◀ 解析 ▶
本題主要的動詞為 receive an email，要修飾動詞必須使用副詞，故選 (C)。

115. The chair should make it clear that the __________ of the meeting is to generate as many ideas as possible.
主席應該清楚地告知，會議的目的就是要員工盡可能發想點子，越多越好。
(A) objective 目標
(B) objection 異議
(C) objects 物體
(D) objected 反對

◀ 解析 ▶
根據前後文來看，空格內應該填入名詞，故不選 (D)，再從句意推斷，答案應為 (A)。

116. Royal Network, the region's leading media network, is __________ exceptional candidates to join our Corporate Development Team.
皇家網路公司，此領域最具領導地位的媒體網路，正在尋找傑出人士加入我們的企業發展部門。
(A) seeking 尋找
(B) looking 看
(C) searching 搜尋
(D) asking 詢問

◀ 解析 ▶
本題從句意推斷，應該是「尋找」之意。若是選項 (B) 或 (C)，則應該用 looking for 或 searching for，故選 (A)。

117. We need to sign an agreement with you __________ proceeding further, clarifying intentions and vision on both sides.
在進一步討論之前，我們要跟您簽個合約，以確認雙方的目標和期望。
(A) before 在…之前
(B) since 自從
(C) when 當…時
(D) once 一旦

◀ 解析 ▶
本題從句意來看，應該是在進一步討論「之前」，先簽定合約，故選 (A)。

118. The chairman should ask people to give their ideas during a meeting, making sure to give everyone a fair opportunity to __________ .
主席在會議中應要求大家說出看法，也要確定有給每個人公平的機會貢獻意見。
(A) contributing 貢獻
(B) contribution 貢獻（物）
(C) contribute 貢獻
(D) contributor 貢獻者

◀ 解析 ▶
本題考的是不定詞的用法，to 後面應接原形動詞，故選 (C)。

119. Nowadays businesses are faced with the __________ of analyzing a growing landslide of data flowing into their organizations.
現今企業面臨的挑戰，是要分析流入企業系統的大量資料。
(A) integration 整合
(B) challenge 挑戰
(C) damage 損害
(D) deployment 部署

© Caves Educational Training Co., Ltd.

◀ 解析 ▶
本題的動詞是 face「面臨」，依照句意推斷，應選 (B) 較為適當。

120. Unlike traditional email systems, Cloud-Mail __________ full advantage of cloud technology, which makes Could-Mail unique in the market.
跟傳統電子郵件系統不同的是，「雲端信件」可充分利用雲端科技，在市場上無可取代。
(A) gets
(B) does
(C) makes
(D) takes

◀ 解析 ▶
本題考的是片語 take advantage of「利用」，加上形容詞 full 為加強修飾，故選 (D)。

121. With our risk management solution, you can eliminate surprises by identifying risks before __________ become problems.
透過我們的風險管理解決方案，您可以辨識風險，並在它們成為問題之前就提早排除。
(A) they 他們
(B) their 他們的
(C) theirs 他們的
(D) them 他們（受格）

◀ 解析 ▶
在連接詞 before 之後，應該加上代名詞主格 they，替代前面的 risks，故選 (A)。

122. You are cordially invited to __________ a Rosman MBA Class on March 18th at 6:30 p.m. at our downtown Toronto campus.
我們誠摯地邀請您在三月十八日晚上六點半，到多倫多市中心校區來體驗一堂羅斯曼商管學院的課程。
(A) guarantee 保證
(B) sample 體驗
(C) register 註冊
(D) request 請求

◀ 解析 ▶
本題考的是 sample 當作動詞，有「體驗」的意思，跟上下文意思最合，所以本題選 (B)。

123. In today's __________ environment, reputation risk is the number one risk factor organizations face.
在現今競爭激烈的環境中，信譽風險是企業面臨的第一大挑戰。
(A) competent 有能力的
(B) compete 競爭
(C) competition 競爭
(D) competitive 競爭性的

◀ 解析 ▶
名詞 environment 前面應該放形容詞，所以不選 (B)、(C)。再依照句意推斷，「競爭性的」意思最為符合，故選 (D)。

124. Thanks to the increasing __________ of modern life, people have more opportunities to travel abroad.
由於現代生活的日益富足，人們有更多機會可以出國旅遊。
(A) affluence 富裕
(B) affluent 富裕的
(C) affluently 富裕地
(D) afflux 流入

◀ 解析 ▶
increasing「逐漸增加的」後面應該接名詞，再按照本題句意，故選 (A)。

125. I wanted to let you know that your email was well-received this morning, __________ as I am leaving for Japan later today, I won't have time to reply for another two days or so.
我想通知你，你寄的電子郵件我今早已經收到了。但我今天稍晚要前往日本，因此可能要兩三天之後才能回覆你了。
(A) or 或者
(B) but 但是
(C) therefore 因此
(D) if 如果

◀ 解析 ▶
根據句意推斷，雖然已經收信，但要兩三天後才能回信，故選語氣轉折的連接詞 (B) but。

126. This is your chance to experience first-hand __________ it is like to be a student at Singapore's top business school.
這是你的機會，可以去親身體驗在新加坡一流商業學院學習是什麼感覺。
(A) where
(B) in which
(C) what
(D) why

◀ 解析 ▶
本題重點在 it is like「像是…」，這裡指「當學生是什麼感覺」，所以選 (C) what。

127. Would you be willing to provide any advice about how I can raise __________ in the Sales Department?
你可以提供一些建議，告訴我該如何提升業務部門的士氣嗎？
(A) expense 費用
(B) thought 想法
(C) morale 士氣
(D) innovation 創新

◀ 解析 ▶
raise 意思為「提升」，再根據句意推斷，選項 (C) morale 最為適當。

128. __________ can overseas travel broaden our views, but it can also provide us with an opportunity to experience foreign cultures.
出國旅遊不僅可以讓我們增加見識，也讓我們有機會可以體驗異國文化。
(A) Not only 不僅
(B) Furthermore 此外
(C) However 然而
(D) In addition 除此之外

◀ 解析 ▶
本題前句出現了倒裝句型 (... can overseas travel broaden our views)，後句則有 but also，由此可推斷空格內應為 (A) Not only。

129. Thank you for your email of October 21st telling us __________ the unfortunate remark made by one of our sales reps.
謝謝您於 10 月 21 日來信的電子郵件中，告知我們關於您受到某位業務員的不當評論一事。
(A) on 在…上
(B) in 在…裡
(C) of …的
(D) about 關於

◀ 解析 ▶

本題的重點為 tell sb. about sth. 的用法，故答案為 (D)。

130. While many schools offer scholarships, for most students, business school is a __________ financial investment.

雖說很多學校有提供獎學金，但對大多數學生來說，唸商學院還是一項重大的財務投資。

(A) heavy 重的

(B) significant 重大的

(C) configurable 可設定的

(D) valuable 有價值的

◀ 解析 ▶

financial investment「財務投資」前面應加上形容詞，且從句意來看，選項 (B) 較為符合。

Part VI. ▶ Text Completion

Questions 131 - 134 refer to the following article.

Many business leaders realize that __________ oneself from the competition is one of the persistent

131. (A) differentiating
(B) scheduling
(C) trapping
(D) satisfying

challenges in the business. Nothing works quite as well as having superior answers to __________ the customers' needs.

132. (A) respond
(B) meet
(C) answer
(D) reply

__________, even when one can achieve product superiority there remains the problem in service

133. (A) While
(B) Furthermore
(C) If
(D) However

businesses of making sure that the difference __________ recognized and applauded.

134. (A) were
(B) is
(C) are
(D) be

許多企業領袖都知道，如何在競爭當中達到差異化，是商業界持續面臨的挑戰之一。最有效的方法當然是提出最佳解決方案來符合客戶的需求。然而，即使一個企業可以做出最優良的產品，服務產業也無法全然確定，產品的差異點是能被客戶辨識出來且受到客戶歡迎的。

131.
(A) differentiating 區別
(B) scheduling 安排
(C) trapping 設置陷阱
(D) satisfying 滿足

◀ 解析 ▶
根據前後文意推斷，應該是說明如何在競爭中脫穎而出，所以必須做出與其他產品的區隔，故選 (A)。

132.
(A) respond 回應
(B) meet 符合
(C) answer 回答
(D) reply 回覆

◀ 解析 ▶
空格後是 the customers' needs「客戶的需求」，我們通常用 meet one's needs 表示「符合、滿足某人的需求」，故選 (B)。

133.
(A) While 當…時
(B) Furthermore 此外
(C) If 假使
(D) However 然而

◀ 解析 ▶
從空格後的 even「即使、儘管」，可以推論空格內應填入語氣轉折詞，故選 (D)。

134.
(A) were
(B) is
(C) are
(D) be

◀ 解析 ▶
此處為被動語態 be + p.p. 的用法，由於主詞是 the difference，be 動詞要用單數，故選 (B)。

Questions 135 - 138 refer to the following article.

A resume is the most important job-search __________ by far.

135. (A) letter
(B) sheet
(C) paper
(D) document

Your resume presents and introduces your most significant experiences, skills, __________

136. (A) but
(B) also
(C) and
(D) or

academic training to potential employers.

Your resume usually meets interviewers before you do, so it's the first __________ an interviewer

137. (A) impression
(B) impressive
(C) impress
(D) impressible

gets of you.

Your resume serves as your personal advertisement. It can be a good tool to get you an interview opportunity. __________, you should identify your major selling points in your resume.

138. (A) However
(B) Besides
(C) Therefore
(D) If

目前為止，履歷表是找工作時最重要的文件。你的履歷表代表你個人，且將你最出眾的經驗、技能與學術訓練，介紹給潛在的雇主。通常在你跟面試官見面之前，你的履歷表就已經交到他手中，所以履歷表就是面試官對你的第一印象。履歷表就像你的個人廣告。它可以是為你爭取面試機會的好工具。因此，你應該在履歷表中列出你的主要競爭優勢。

135.
(A) letter 信件
(B) sheet 單子
(C) paper 紙張
(D) document 文件

◀ 解析 ▶
從本句句意來推斷，履歷表應為求職時最重要的「文件」，故選 (D)。

136.
(A) but 但
(B) also 也
(C) and 和
(D) or 或

◀ 解析 ▶
空格前後為同類型的詞列舉，需用對等連接詞相互連結，且語意承接無轉折，故選 (C)。

137.
(A) impression 印象
(B) impressive 印象深的
(C) impress 給…很深的印象
(D) impressible 易感動的

◀ 解析 ▶
空格前為形容詞 the first「第一的」，可推斷空格中應該為名詞，故選 (A)。

138.
(A) However 但是
(B) Besides 除此之外
(C) Therefore 因此，所以
(D) If 如果

◀ 解析 ▶
前段說明了履歷表的重要性，依照文意推斷，最後一句的空格中應該是「所以、因此」，故本題選 (C)。

Questions 139 - 142 refer to the following notice.

If you are attending the Professional Secretary Meeting in Tokyo, Japan, please join Reality experts for informal discussions __________ the future direction of Reality Inc.

139. (A) about
(B) refer
(C) whether
(D) from

What: Open House
When: Tuesday, February 26 – between 9 a.m. and 11 a.m. (come by anytime)
Where: Reality Inc. suite (for __________ location, stop by booth #333)

140. (A) concise
(B) correct
(C) prefect
(D) exact

Come early to get the best size selection of our newest T-shirt!

Refreshments will be __________ throughout the morning.

141. (A) serving
(B) served
(C) serves
(D) serve

Please let us know if you plan to attend by signing up here: www.reality.com/meeting.

We will notify you with the exact location. If you can't make it to the open house, please visit us in the exhibit hall booth #333.

We look forward to __________ you in Tokyo.

142. (A) sees
(B) seeing
(C) saw
(D) see

若您正計畫參與在日本東京舉辦的專業秘書會議，請參加實境公司專家的非正式討論會，以瞭解實境公司的未來方向。
事件：開放參觀活動
時間：2 月 26 日週二，早上九點到早上十一點（任何時間都可加入）
地點：實境公司教室（確切的地點，請至第 333 號攤位詢問）
提早抵達可獲得合身的新款設計 T 恤！

上午全程供應茶點。
若您有意參加，請至 www.reality.com/meeting 網站報名。
我們將會通知您確切的地點。若您無法參加當日的開放參觀活動，請到展覽館內的第 333 號攤位參觀。
我們期待在東京與您見面。

139.
(A) about 關於
(B) refer 歸因於
(C) whether 是否
(D) from 來自

◀ 解析 ▶
本題的空格前是 discussion「討論」，後面則是討論的主題，用介系詞 about 可說明兩者之間的關連，故選 (A)。

140.
(A) concise 簡明的
(B) correct 正確的
(C) prefect 完美的
(D) exact 確切的

◀ 解析 ▶
此處應該是要補充說明活動的「確切」地點，可以至攤位上詢問，故選 (D)。

141.
(A) serving
(B) served
(C) serves
(D) serve

◀ 解析 ▶
本句的主詞為 refreshments「茶點」，要用被動語態 be + p.p.，句子時態為未來式，所以用 wiil be + p.p.，故本題為 (B)。

142.
(A) sees
(B) seeing
(C) saw
(D) see

◀ 解析 ▶

look forward to 為「期待」之意，後面接名詞或動名詞，故本題答案為 (B)。

Questions 143 - 146 refer to the following article.

Nowadays, one way technology influences global cultures is __________ media globalization.

143. (A) thought
(B) through
(C) thorough
(D) though

With the advent of the Internet, people in different parts of the world have been seamlessly connected. Since the 1990s, an increasing amount of Korean pop cultural contents including Korean dramas, songs and celebrities have __________ immense popularity across most Asian countries.

144. (A) gains
(B) gain
(C) gaining
(D) gained

Young people are able to share schedules of Korean concerts and movies, news of Korean celebrities __________ all related information about Korea on the Internet.

145. (A) of
(B) but
(C) and
(D) as

Some people in the U.S. even form a Korean POP fan page on the Facebook that allows people from different countries to share their favorite Korean stars. Thus, we can clearly see that the Internet and media do have a huge __________ on culture distribution in the world.

146. (A) application
(B) impact
(C) setback
(D) difference

如今，科技影響全球文化的其一方法是媒體全球化。隨著網際網路的出現，世界各地的人們已被無縫地連接在一起了。自 1990 年代以來，越來越多的韓國流行文化，包括韓劇、韓樂和韓星，都在多數亞洲國家受到廣泛歡迎。年輕人能夠在網路上分享韓國演唱會和電影上映的時間表，以及韓國藝人的動態消息與所有跟韓國有關的訊息。有些住在美國的人，甚至在臉書上組了一個韓國 POP 粉絲專頁，讓來自不同國家的人都能分享他們最喜愛的韓國明星。由此，我們可以清楚地看到網際網路和媒體，在世界文化傳播中確實發揮巨大的影響力。

© Caves Educational Training Co., Ltd.

143.
(A) thought 想法
(B) through 透過
(C) thorough 徹底的
(D) though 雖然

◀ 解析 ▶
根據前後文語意，應是「透過」較為合理，且其他選項代入句中都不合理，故選 (B)。

144.
(A) gains
(B) gain
(C) gaining
(D) gained

◀ 解析 ▶
此題空格之前看到 have，可判斷是現在完成式用法，所以空格內應為過去分詞，故選 (D)。

145.
(A) of 屬於
(B) but 但是
(C) and 還有
(D) as 如同

◀ 解析 ▶
此題空格之前已有數個名詞，空格之後也是名詞，可判斷空格中應為連接詞 and ，故選 (C)。

146.
(A) application 應用
(B) impact 影響
(C) setback 挫折
(D) difference 差異

◀ 解析 ▶
根據前後文語意，應是「有很大的影響」較為合理，且其他選項代入句中都不合理，故選 (B)。

Part VII. ► Reading Comprehension

Questions 147 - 148 refer to the following letter.

從「最佳叢書」贏得「優買」壹佰元禮券

親愛的客戶您好，

謝謝您購買我們的商品。

我們想更瞭解您的需求，以便持續提供您真正需要並喜歡的商品。

請花一點時間完成這份關於您最近一次消費的簡短問卷，只需幾分鐘的時間，完成後您還有機會可以獲得「優買」壹佰元禮券喔。

我們非常重視您的寶貴意見。

http://www.customer-survey.com

非常感謝您。

最佳叢書

purchase (n.)：購買　complete (v.)：完成　survey (n.)：調查　recent (adj.)：最近的

147. What's the purpose of this email message? 此電子郵件目的為何？
   (A) To get customers' feedback 取得客戶意見
   (B) To propose solutions 提供解決辦法
   (C) To schedule an appointment 安排會議
   (D) To recruit new employees 招募新員工

◀ 解析 ▶
從第三句可知，此公司希望多了解客戶，最後也提到非常重視客戶意見，所以本題選 (A)。

148. What are customers asked to do? 客戶被要求要做什麼？
   (A) Purchase more books 購買更多書籍
   (B) Provide opinions online 線上提供意見
   (C) Enter a contest 參加比賽
   (D) Check the latest prices online 線上確認最新價格

◀ 解析 ▶
從第四句可知，客戶要花一點時間完成問卷，郵件最後也提供了網址，可見是採取線上填寫問卷的方式，故選 (B)。

Questions 149 - 151 refer to the following advertisement.

客戶經理招募

工作地點：馬尼拉
副理和經理的職務是要引領客戶服務，協助做出更快更好的資訊導向決策。他們要將公司最高指導原則的理念應用到解決商業問題上。

工作內容：
- 與在現場的同仁合作，共同瞭解客戶的需求
- 整合現場及自電話中與客戶端收集到的資訊，並協助團隊成員瞭解資訊內容
- 事先預想可能的問題瓶頸，同時決定處理方式
- 與團隊成員開會以瞭解他們的問題，並讓成員們保持熱情。我們主張開放的工作文化，並鼓勵大家可以分享意見。

資格需求：
- 有將模糊資訊具體化的能力：將團隊自混沌不明的困境中帶領出來，並在過程中保持高昂的鬥志
- 我們喜歡的人，必須相信自己有能力可以影響他人或事情發展的過程，將環境塑造成對完成團體目標有利的情況
- 要有能力運用基本原則與結構化的方法來解決問題，而不能只是過度依賴過去的產業經驗
- 要有開放的心胸和令人喜歡的個性，有能力跟不同背景的人互動和相互激勵

福利：
- 在具挑戰性又富有變化的環境中工作，我們總是將「學習」視為生活的一部分
- 跟一流團隊成員共事，更有機會激勵自己拓展潛力
- 開放的企業文化，同儕間士氣高昂，強調互相合作學習的重要性

經驗：三年以上
教育背景需求：工程 / 商管 / 統計 / 經濟學系之大學畢業生

請將求職信與個人簡歷寄到 jobs.singapore@systemtech.com。

client engagement：客戶服務　counterpart (n.)：拍檔　requirement (n.)：需求　synthesize (v.)：綜合
deadlock (n.)：僵局　enthuse (n.)：使…充滿熱忱　ambiguity (n.)：不明確的事物　influence (v.)：影響
expertise (n.)：專業知識　diverse (adj.)：不同的　top-notch (adj.)：頂尖的　emphasis (n.)：強調
collaborative (adj.)：合作的

149. Where will the employees who are hired for the advertised positions work?
此職缺錄取的員工會在何處工作？
(A) The Philippines 菲律賓
(B) Singapore 新加坡
(C) Malaysia 馬來西亞
(D) Thailand 泰國

◀ 解析 ▶
從第一句可知，工作地點在馬尼拉，可推知國家為菲律賓，故選 (A)。

150. What job responsibility is mentioned in the advertisement? 廣告中提及哪一項工作職責？
(A) Have a meeting with the CEO once a week 每週跟執行長開會
(B) Make decisions all alone 全然按照自己的意思做決定
(C) Talk to colleagues openly about their concerns 跟同事開誠佈公地討論他們的問題
(D) Ignore customers' requirements 忽略客戶的需求

◀ 解析 ▶
從第二段「工作內容」當中，最後一點提到需與團隊成員開會，討論他們的問題，故選 (C)。

151. What benefit is NOT mentioned in the advertisement? 哪項福利沒有在廣告中提及？
(A) Keep learning while working 在工作中不斷學習
(B) Work with brilliant colleagues 跟出色的同事一起工作
(C) Opportunity to realize your own potential 有機會發展自己的潛能
(D) Paid training programs 付費的教育訓練

◀ 解析 ▶
需注意本題是問「未提及」的項目，在第四段「福利」當中，並未提到教育訓練，故選 (D)。

Questions 152 - 153 refer to the following online messages.

潔西 10:20 a.m.
你好，傑克。你在忙些什麼？[1]

林傑克 10:21 a.m.
嗨，潔西。[2] 我在為週五的業務會議準備簡報檔呀。我的進度其實有點慢了。

潔西 10:22 a.m.
喔，這樣的話，我就不要麻煩你了。我本來想請你協助我寫業務報告。[3]

林傑克 10:24 a.m.
沒問題，我很樂意幫忙。你知道的，我在做業務簡報時，也對如何增加業績想到很多好點子。我很願意跟你分享我的想法。

潔西 10:27 a.m.
那真是太棒了，傑克。好，那麼我們要不要一起吃午餐，再進一步討論細節呢？

林傑克 10:28 a.m.
當然好呀。那我們就中午十二點半，在樓下的西達小館見囉！[4]

152. What does Jessie ask Jack to do? 潔西請傑克做什麼？
(A) Buy her some lunch 幫她買午餐
(B) Help with her sales report 協助她寫業務報告
(C) Finish his slides as soon as possible 儘速完成他的簡報檔
(D) Attend the meeting on time 準時出席會議

◀ 解析 ▶
根據潔西傳的第二則訊息，可知道她想請傑克協助她寫業務報告，故選 (B)。

153. In which of the positions marked [1], [2], [3], and [4] does the following sentence best belong?
"I really need to come up with effective sales strategies to include in my report."
下面句子最適合放在文章中 [1] [2] [3] [4] 哪個位置？
「我得要想些有效的業務策略放進我的報告裡。」
(A) [1]
(B) [2]
(C) [3]
(D) [4]

◀ 解析 ▶
此題要放入的句子是有關「將業務策略放進報告」的內容，再比對四個位置，只有 [3] 跟潔西提到的業務報告相關，故選 (C)。

Questions 154 - 156 refer to the following article.

遠亞航空與東方航空兩家航空公司的合併消息，將於明日 12 月 13 日宣佈。兩家公司的董事會針對合併協議已達成共識，並於週一晚間通過該交易內容。兩家航空公司在合併完成後，預計將保留遠亞航空的名稱，而這個嶄新的航空公司，將成為亞洲地區規模最大的航空業者。

對於旅客而言，暫時不會有任何重大改變。這類規模龐大的合併，平均皆須耗費一年以上的時間才能完成，因此旅客不會立即感受到任何改變。但仍有部分民眾感到擔憂：「這是否代表未來旅客們將必須支付更高的票價？」某些分析師認為，由於兩家航空業者在許多航道上已經不再需要彼此競爭，票價暫時不會受到重大影響。而兩家航空公司將會對各自的飛行常客計畫進行整合，旅客也不需要擔心自己既有的里程數會失效。

目前兩家航空公司所要面對的最大挑戰，是要如何合併所有員工與其合約。飛行員、空服人員、技術人員的合約條件皆已談妥，以確保兩家航空公司的合併更加順利。

merger (n.)：合併　board of directors：董事會　retain (v.)：保留　complicated (adj.)：複雜的
accomplish (v.)：完成　eventually (adv.)：最後　route (n.)：路線　hurdle (n.)：障礙、困難

154. What is the purpose of this article? 此文章的目的為何？
(A) To announce the merger of two airlines 宣佈兩家航空公司的合併案
(B) To inform passengers of changed gates 通知旅客登機門異動
(C) To describe renovation details at an airport 描述機場整修的細節
(D) To attract foreign investment 吸引外商投資

◀ 解析 ▶
1. 最前面兩句話即清楚說明，此段文章是關於兩家航空公司的合併案，故選 (A)。
2. renovation (n.)：整修、更新

155. How long will the merger take? 合併案會耗時多久？
(A) More than a decade 超過十年
(B) Several years 好幾年
(C) More than a year 超過一年
(D) Less than a year 一年以內

◀ 解析 ▶
第二段提到，規模龐大的合併案需耗時一年以上，故選 (C)。

156. What might be a potential problem for the merged airlines? 合併後的航空公司可能會面臨什麼問題？
(A) Combining crew members of two airlines 整合兩家航空公司的機組人員
(B) Dealing with customer complaints 處理客戶抱怨
(C) Integrating computer systems 整合電腦系統
(D) Planning more air routes 規劃更多航線

◀ 解析 ▶
最後一段提到合併的最大挑戰，就是員工的整合與存續，故選 (A)。

Questions 157 - 159 refer to the following advertisement.

貝斯特管理訓練

目標

- 提升您銷售與行銷管理的技能：成功的基礎
- 實用的研習課程內容，將完整地探討銷售生命週期，並建立起有關行銷管理知識、技術、工具等的紮實基礎。

概論

隨著商務世界競爭日益激烈，企業組織開始意識到增加銷售專案數量的必要性。在這次的訓練當中，您將學習並熟悉各種關鍵工具與技巧，經證實這些是成功管理銷售的必備資源。本課程針對各種概念的實際應用而設計。您將帶著各種必要的知識與工具回到工作崗位，以正確的方式開始進行銷售專案，並圓滿達成目標。

費用

- 3 天：$2,999 非會員
- 3 天：$1,999 貝斯特訓練會員
- 3 天：$999 合作夥伴

時程

日期	地點	期間
2017. 3. 8 – 2017. 3. 10	日本東京	3 天
2017. 3. 11 – 2017. 3. 13	韓國首爾	3 天
2017. 3. 14 – 2017. 3. 16	台灣台北	3 天
2017. 3. 17 – 2017. 3. 19	中國香港	3 天
2017. 3. 20 – 2017. 3. 22	澳洲伯斯	3 天
2017. 3. 23 – 2017. 3. 25	西班牙巴塞隆納	3 天
2017. 3. 26 – 2017. 3. 28	美國紐約	3 天
2017. 4. 1 – 2017. 4. 3	加拿大多倫多	3 天
2017. 4. 4 – 2017. 4. 6	美國伊利諾州芝加哥	3 天

註冊

請撥打 1-383-7483-4762（分機 122）聯絡安娜史密斯小姐，或是造訪我們的網站：http://www.besttrainings.com，以取得更多資訊。

foundation (n.)：基礎　hands-on (adj.)：實用的　critical (adj.)：關鍵性的　concept (n.)：概念

157. What is the main topic of this message? 此訊息的主題為何？
   (A) Notify employees of a meeting schedule change 通知員工更改會議時間
   (B) Inform sales and marketing personnel of a training 通知行銷業務人員訓練課程資訊
   (C) Invite managers to attend a conference 邀請經理出席研討會
   (D) Ask customers to place orders as soon as possible 要求客戶儘早下訂單

◀ 解析 ▶
本訊息內容提及訓練課程對象、主題、費用、日期等資訊，可知答案為 (B)。

158. What benefit can a Best Training partner receive? 貝斯特訓練的合作夥伴可享有的好處為何？
   (A) A discount 優惠折扣
   (B) A free training session 免費訓練課程
   (C) Some rebate 金額回饋
   (D) A job offer 工作機會

◀ 解析 ▶
需注意本題問的是 partner「合作夥伴」所享有的好處，從費用列表當中可知，合作夥伴所需支付的課程費用較低，故選 (A)。

159. What should a person do if he needs more course information?
   想得到更多課程資訊的人應該怎麼做？
   (A) Visit Anna Smith in person 親自拜訪安娜史密斯
   (B) Visit Best Training website 上貝斯特訓練公司網站
   (C) Call a toll-free number 打免付費電話
   (D) Write Best Training a letter 寫信給貝斯特訓練公司

◀ 解析 ▶
最後一段註明聯絡方式為撥打電話或至網站查詢，選項 (C) 雖然有部分符合，但訊息中並未說明此為免付費電話，故本題選 (B)。

Questions 160 - 161 refer to the following advertisement.

GO-GYM 健身中心會員資格

GO-GYM 健身中心並非只是一間普通的健身房。在這裡，您將能夠在放鬆且舒適的氣氛當中，獲得充滿歡樂與笑容的健身體驗。同時，我們有多位友善且熱心的健身教練，會主動地隨時關心您的進度。

健身中心提供了多種不同的會員方案，來滿足每一位顧客的需求：
- GO-GYM 健身中心會員資格
- 健康每月通行證
- 輕鬆無負擔的入班體驗

GO-GYM 健身中心會員費用

類型	4 個月	8 個月	1 年
一般費用	$2,199	$4,099	$8,199
非尖峰時段	$1,599	$2,999	$5,999
基本費用	$1,299	$2,399	$5,499

GO-GYM 健身中心營業時間

開放時間	一般 / 基本	非尖峰時段
週一至週五	早上 6 點至晚上 11 點	早上 8 點至下午 5 點
週末與國定假日	早上 7 點至晚上 11 點	早上 7 點至下午 3 點

設施
- 健身房
- 室內／室外游泳池
- 三溫暖房
- 瑜珈教室
- 美容護膚室

ordinary (adj.)：平凡的　encounter (v.)：遇見　atmosphere (n.)：氣氛　instructor (n.)：教練
progress (n.)：進展　scheme (n.)：方案　peak (n.)：尖峰

160. What is the main purpose of this advertisement? 此廣告的主要目的為何？
(A) To announce a training schedule 公告訓練時間
(B) To attract membership application for a gym 吸引顧客成為健身房會員
(C) To promote a community event 推廣社區活動
(D) To fund community activities 贊助社區活動

◀ 解析 ▶
廣告中說明了健身中心會員資格、費用、開放時間等資訊，更強調各種會員方案，由此可推斷答案為 (B)。

161. Which facility is NOT included in the gym? 健身房中不包括哪種設施？
(A) Yoga room 瑜珈教室
(B) Swimming pool 游泳池
(C) Cafeteria 自助餐廳
(D) Spa room 美容護膚室

◀ 解析 ▶
需注意本題問的是「不包括」哪項設施，由最後一段可知，其中不包括自助餐廳，故選 (C)。

Questions 162 - 164 refer to the following advertisement.

系統科技股份有限公司經銷合作夥伴計畫

拓廣解決方案並提升企業成長的良好機會

系統科技經銷合作夥伴計畫，專為協助您的企業成長、創造全新機會、提升獲利，以及加速完成交易而設計。

合作夥伴優勢

- 與領先業界且成長最為快速的 ERP 軟體公司合作
- 隨著合作夥伴層級晉升，將可獲得更有利的價差
- 當您的客戶購買系統科技商品時，您將有機會為客戶提供各種專業服務
- 可登入系統科技合作夥伴資源中心，包含一系列銷售與行銷工具的使用權限
- 免費的每月合作夥伴教育網路研討會與證照訓練計畫
- 參與每三個月舉行一次的合作夥伴討論會，與合作夥伴專屬的活動邀請
- 列名於系統科技合作夥伴頁面的公司名單

若要取得更多資訊，請造訪我們的網站：http://www.systemtech.com 或利用電話聯絡我們：1-204-3728-7493。

reseller (n.)：經銷商　generate (v.)：產生　association (n.)：結合　favorable (adj.)：有利的
margin (n.)：利潤　tier (n.)：等級　access (n.)：進入、使用　webinar (n.)：網路研討會
certification (n.)：證明、證照　exclusive (adj.)：獨有的

162. For whom is this advertisement most likely intended? 此篇廣告主要讀者是誰？

(A) Software developers 軟體開發人員

(B) Potential business partners 潛在商務夥伴

(C) Famous university professors 知名大學教授

(D) Computer network experts 電腦網路專家

◀ 解析 ▶

廣告主題為「經銷合作夥伴計畫」，內容也強調成為經銷合作夥伴的好處，故可知答案為 (B)。

163. What is NOT mentioned as a benefit to partners? 合作夥伴可享有的好處不包括哪一項？

(A) High profit margins 高獲利

(B) Opportunities to attend partner events 參與夥伴活動的機會

(C) Free training programs 免費教育訓練

(D) Free ERP software products 免費 ERP 軟體

◀ 解析 ▶

需注意本題是問「不包括」哪一項好處，廣告中未提及免費軟體，故選 (D)。

164. What is indicated about the System Tech Inc.? 由文中可知關於系統科技公司的什麼事？

(A) It's a company selling ERP solutions. 它是一間銷售 ERP 解決方案的公司。

(B) The company provides 24 / 7 technical services. 此公司提供全年無休的技術支援。

(C) Some employees will be laid off soon. 部分員工很快會被裁撤。

(D) They have branches around the world. 他們在世界各地都有辦公室。

◀ 解析 ▶

由合作夥伴優勢第一項可知，系統科技與 ERP 軟體公司合作，故選 (A)。

Questions 165 - 167 refer to the following letter.

親愛的史考特先生：

上次於新加坡會面時，我們聊到有關獨家經銷權的話題。[1] 我希望能將本公司在新加坡市場所採取的商業策略及銷售途徑，彙整完整資訊提供給您，並參考您的意見與建議，回答所有相關問題。

我們了解在特定地域內建立「主要合作夥伴」的價值（雖然此項關係並不絕對等於建立獨家經銷商的合作關係）。基本上，本公司希望在當地實行銷售的「生態系統」，讓多個擁有不同優勢的瑪可羅經銷商互相合作，以利市場的推廣與行銷。[2]

市場推廣：
我們以遠景顧問股份有限公司為例子，這是一間專門進行 CMMI 評鑑的小規模顧問公司。該公司的主要客戶是我們想要接觸的高級 IT 主管人員，但是遠景顧問公司並沒有傳統的行銷能力。希望藉由與該公司合作，對其既有客戶取得銷售線索，並為瑪可羅的電子報、網路研討會與討論會提供當地內容。他們將會進行促銷推廣，並協力拓展新加坡市場。[3]

進行銷售：
如同上述所言，瑪可羅目前於新加坡並未與任何經銷商或行銷組織簽署任何契約。[4] 我個人認為，擁有我們所需的行銷與分銷能力的 IT-Tech 公司，是最具有優勢的合作人選。

我希望能夠聽聽您對這件事的看法，並期盼星期五再次與您會面。

誠摯地，

派翠克葛瑞金，瑪可羅股份有限公司亞太地區總裁
辦公室：123-581-9215
行動電話：0947-609-4279

distributorship (n.)：經銷權　principal (adj.)：主要的　territory (n.)：區域　implement (v.)：實行
specialty (n.)：專長　appraisal (n.)：評價　traditional (adj.)：傳統的　currently (adv.)：現在
contender (n.)：競爭者

165. What is the purpose of this letter? 此信的主要目的為何？
(A) To clarify some partnership details 釐清一些合作計畫的細節
(B) To explain some communication techniques 解釋一些溝通技巧
(C) To recruit some new employees 招募一些新進員工
(D) To enroll for a training class 登記參加訓練課程

◀ 解析 ▶
信件前兩段即提到經銷權、合作夥伴等內容，由此可推斷答案為 (A)。

166. What is indicated in the letter about Vision Consulting? 信中提到關於遠景顧問公司的什麼事？

(A) They are good at organizing international conferences. 他們專長在舉辦國際會議。

(B) They are not familiar with marketing approaches. 他們對行銷方法不是很熟悉。

(C) They are the only distributor in Singapore. 他們是新加坡的唯一代理商。

(D) They will meet with Patrick Gragen on Friday. 他們會在週五跟派翠克葛瑞金會面。

◀ 解析 ▶

在「市場推廣」部分，提到遠景顧問公司沒有傳統的行銷能力，故選 (B)。

167. In which of the positions marked [1], [2], [3], and [4] does the following sentence best belong?

"I want to follow up on this subject further."

下面的句子最適合放在文章中 [1] [2] [3] [4] 哪個位置？

「我想更進一步討論此話題。」

(A) [1]

(B) [2]

(C) [3]

(D) [4]

◀ 解析 ▶

此題要放入的句子是有關「進一步討論某個主題」的內容，通常置於段落中間，不適合放在段落末尾。再比對四個位置，只有 [1] 前面的句子有提到關鍵字 "subject"，可與這個句子銜接，故選 (A)。

Questions 168 - 171 refer to the following advertisement.

絕佳體驗餐廳

地點： 陽光城市豪華大飯店
泰國芭達雅春天街 180 號

營業時間： 每日下午 5:30 至晚上 10:30

訂位方式： 請撥打電話 123-363-7030 或線上訂位 www.best-ever.com

服裝要求： 請來賓以高標準的正式穿著入場

停車需求： 前來陽光城市豪華大飯店絕佳體驗餐廳用餐的來賓，用餐當日可享有本飯店所提供的免費代客泊車服務。

每人 170 元

套裝行程內含：

- 下列服務任選一項（1 小時）：招牌按摩、招牌臉部按摩、溫牛奶與檀香足療，或溫牛奶與檀香美甲護手
- 兩道菜餚晚宴，包含絕佳體驗餐廳獨家的亞洲、太平洋，與傳統歐式風味的綜合料理（可從指定菜單上選擇前菜與主餐或是主餐與甜點）
- 陽光城市豪華大飯店的免費代客泊車服務

本優惠於週一至週五提供，來賓必須在晚上 6:30 之前於絕佳體驗餐廳入座。需事先訂位。請撥打絕佳美容中心電話 0987-363-7050。提供團體訂位與禮券服務。本項優惠時間有限，售完為止。套裝內容必須當日使用完畢。

complimentary (adj.)：贈送的、免費的　valet (n.)：泊車人員　treatment (n.)：款待
sandalwood (n.)：檀香　pedicure (n.)：修腳趾甲、足療　manicure (n.)：修（手）指甲
cuisine (n.)：菜餚　entrée (n.)：前菜　essential (adj.)：必要的　gift voucher：禮券
be subject to...：受限於…　redeem (v.)：兌換、履行

168. Where is the Best-Ever Restaurant located? 絕佳體驗餐廳位於何處？

(A) In Singapore 新加坡

(B) In Thailand 泰國

(C) In China 中國

(D) In Japan 日本

◀ 解析 ▶

廣告開頭「地點」一欄，即註明餐廳位於泰國的陽光城市豪華大飯店，故選 (B)。

169. What is NOT true about the dress code? 關於服裝規定何者為非？

(A) Flip-flops are allowed. 可以穿人字拖鞋。

(B) Business suits are allowed. 可以穿商務套裝。

(C) Evening gowns are allowed. 可以穿晚禮服。

(D) Formal dresses are allowed. 可以穿正式裙裝。

◀ 解析 ▶

服裝規定是以「正式服裝」為標準，穿人字拖鞋並不適合，故選 (A)。

170. How much would a group of four people cost? 一組四位賓客共需花費多少錢？

(A) $680 680 元

(B) $860 860 元

(C) $570 570 元

(D) $340 340 元

◀ 解析 ▶

每位賓客需花 170 元，且無任何折價方案，故四位賓客共需 680 元，答案為 (A)。

171. Which of the following is true? 以下敘述何者正確？

(A) The offer is valid during weekdays. 此優惠在週間有效。

(B) Guests can go without a reservation. 賓客不用先預約亦可進入。

(C) The voucher is good for two years. 優惠券在兩年內有效。

(D) There is no parking space available. 不開放使用停車位。

◀ 解析 ▶

內容提及需事先預約，故 (B) 不正確。敘述中未提及禮券期限，故不選 (C)。餐廳提供代客泊車服務，故 (D) 不正確。最後一段第一句，說明優惠僅於週一至週五提供，故選 (A)。

Questions 172 - 175 refer to the following letter.

親愛的史密斯小姐：

本信是為了回覆我們於 5 日（週二）關於軟體銷售管理職位的電話會談內容。

我本身在軟體銷售上有相當優秀的記錄，身為業務經理，我認為自己非常適合我們先前商談的職位。就如同在電話面試時所提到的，我從基層開始做起，並逐步晉升至目前的職位。我認為自己在銷售流程的不同層級學習到的經驗，使我有能力面對挑戰，並肩負起您所提出的領導責任。

我是個相當具有競爭力的人。身為業務經理，我運用自身的特長與技能，超越銷售目標並創下紀錄。我一直相信，成果才是衡量績效表現的最佳方法。

希望您能夠考慮撥冗與我會面，讓我能夠向您詳述我的銷售與管理能力。若您方便的話，請打電話給我安排面試時間。您可以撥打電話號碼 (283) 3728-4783 或透過電子郵件 jackbeta@outlook.com 與我聯繫。

誠摯地，

傑克貝塔

regarding (prep.)：關於　track record：過去的業績、記錄　exposure (n.)：接觸、暴露
display (v.)：表現、展示　exceed (v.)：超出　appreciate (v.)：感謝　convenience (n.)：方便

172. Who is most likely Jack Beta? 傑克貝塔最有可能是誰？
(A) A tour guide 導遊
(B) A job candidate 求職者
(C) A human resources manager 人資經理
(D) A company CEO 公司執行長

◀ 解析 ▶
信件一開頭提及軟體行銷管理職位，後續並說明自己的求職優勢，故選 (B)。

173. What is most likely Mr. Beta's job? 貝塔先生的工作最有可能為何？
(A) Sports coach 運動教練
(B) Personal tutor 私人家教
(C) Software sales manager 軟體業務經理
(D) Magazine publisher 雜誌出版商

◀ 解析 ▶
第二段的第一句中，提到他在軟體行銷業擔任業務經理，故選 (C)。

174. What is NOT true about Mr. Beta? 關於貝塔先生何者為非？
(A) He has no passion about software. 他對軟體業沒有熱情。
(B) He is a competitive person. 他是有競爭力的人。
(C) He has leadership quality. 他有領袖特質。
(D) He has good sales records. 他有亮麗的業績記錄。

◀ 解析 ▶
需注意本題問的是「不正確」的敘述。從第二、三段當中，可知其對軟體業有相當熱忱，故選 (A)。

175. Why does Mr. Beta write to Ms. Smith? 貝塔先生寫信給史密斯小姐的目的為何？
(A) To sign up for a training class 報名教育訓練課程
(B) To apply for business school 申請商業管理學校
(C) To request some product information 要求產品資訊
(D) To request a meeting opportunity 要求會面機會

◀ 解析 ▶
最後一段貝塔先生提出想與史密斯小姐見面的請求，故選 (D)。

Questions 176 - 180 refer to the following form and advertisement.

大樹旅舍訂房表

** 請將這份表格直接交給旅舍 **
傳真：預約訂房 (123) 886-2902
或撥打電話：(123) 886-1234 或 1-800-BIGTREE
或造訪網站：www.BIG-TREE.com

姓名 ______________________________
住址 ______________________________
城市 ______________ 州 ________ 郵遞區號 ________ 國家 ____________
電話（住家）________ / ______________（公司）________ / ______________
（傳真）________________ 電子郵件信箱 ______________________

抵達時間：日期 / 時間 / 航空公司 / 班機號碼 ______ / ______ / ________ / ________
離開時間：日期 / 時間 / 航空公司 / 班機號碼 ______ / ______ / ________ / ________

住宿：
住宿天數 ______
149 元 / 每晚：花園 / 高爾夫球場 / 山景 ______
169 元 / 每晚：部分景觀 ______
199 元 / 每晚：豪華景觀 ______

- 提供單人或雙人住宿
- 額外住宿人數，每人加收 35 元。每間房間住宿人數上限為：3 名成人，或 2 名成人與 2 名孩童。
- 由父母陪同的 12 歲以下孩童無需付費。

與誰同住？______________________________
請填寫個別姓名（若為孩童，請填寫姓名與年齡）

特殊要求（視情況而定）：______ 雙人加大 1 床 或 ______ 標準雙人 2 床
______ 抽菸 或 ______不抽菸

來賓姓名：（請正楷書寫）______________________________

occupancy (n.)：居住

地點：北非
住宿類型：旅舍
舒適程度：奢華

簡介

獲獎無數的大樹旅舍，位於蘇吉私人禁獵區的岩石河河岸，共有 6 間套房，是享受豪華度假體驗的最佳選擇。這間極具代表性的旅舍，提供眺望蘇吉國家公園廣大砂石河岸的絕佳景色。

在這裡可以體驗刺激的野生動物觀賞，或是來趟迷人的叢林步行。導覽車內皆附有鳥類書籍與望遠鏡。若是早晨搭車，車上也將提供毛毯與熱水壺，為您驅趕寒意。

最新消息

- 建於蘇吉私人禁獵區，提供各種專屬體驗
- 精緻奢華的旅舍，小而溫馨，充滿現代風格
- 私密且量身訂做的服務，非常適合蜜月假期的新人
- 寬廣到令人無法置信的生態觀賞別墅，每間套房都擁有獨立的無邊際泳池與管家服務
- 在您的私人套房內，享受絕佳的 spa 服務
- 充滿野外風味，以新鮮食材烹煮而成的高級美食饗宴

reserve (n.)：保留地、保護區　iconic (adj.)：指標性的　opt (v.)：選擇　equip (v.)：配備
binoculars (n.)：望遠鏡　concession (n.)：營業場所　exquisite (adj.)：精緻的　intimate (adj.)：溫馨的
contemporary (adj.)：現代的　tailored (adj.)：訂做的　safari (n.)：野生動物觀賞旅行　butler (n.)：管家

176. What is indicated about the hotel? 由文中可知關於此飯店的什麼事？
(A) It is the cheapest one in the area. 它是在當地最便宜的。
(B) It won some awards before. 它之前得過獎項。
(C) It is located in Asia. 它位於亞洲。
(D) It is currently under construction. 它目前在整修中。

◀ 解析 ▶

選項 (A)、(D) 未被提及。此飯店位於北非，故 (C) 不正確。簡介一開頭，就提到這間飯店獲獎無數，故本題選 (B)。

177. What activity is NOT available to guests? 賓客不會參與到什麼活動？
(A) Viewing wild animals 看野生動物
(B) Visiting Sugi National Park 參觀蘇吉國家公園
(C) Shopping in a mall 在購物中心買東西
(D) Walking in the bush 到樹叢中散步

© Caves Educational Training Co., Ltd.

◀ 解析 ▶
需注意本題是問「不會參與到」的活動，其中並未提及任何購物行程，故選 (C)。

178. Whom is the “tailored service” designed for? 「客製化的服務」是為誰設計的？
(A) Business travelers 商務旅客
(B) Corporate executives 企業執行長
(C) Newlyweds 新婚夫婦
(D) Homemakers 家庭主夫／婦

◀ 解析 ▶
在「最新消息」中，提到客製化的服務，是給 honeymooner（度蜜月的人），故選意思相同的 (C)。

179. What is NOT indicated as a way to contact the hotel? 由文中可知何者不是飯店的聯絡方式？
(A) Telephone 電話
(B) Fax 傳真
(C) Website 網站
(D) Email 電子郵件

◀ 解析 ▶
訂房表格上載明了電話號碼、傳真號碼以及網址，並沒有電子郵件信箱，故選 (D)。

180. Who might live in this hotel free of charge? 誰有可能可以免費入住飯店？
(A) A 73-year-old grandpa 七十三歲的祖父
(B) A university professor 大學教授
(C) A 10-year-old child 十歲孩童
(D) A middle-aged mother 中年母親

◀ 解析 ▶
訂房表格上提及，由父母陪同的 12 歲以下兒童可免費入住，故選 (C)。

Questions 181 - 185 refer to the following article and form.

慈善募款基金會

對於許多孩童而言，位於高山村莊內的「慈軒」是使他們免於在街上挨餓受凍的溫暖家園。為了讓十名年紀最長的孩子繼續接受教育，我們必須募集更多的資金。這些孩子還需要歷時三年的職業訓練，才能擁有更完整的自立與工作能力。他們都是優秀的學生，一直很努力用功，希望獲得更美好的人生。請大家幫幫忙！

困境

高山村莊內有超過一半的居民不識字，女孩子的狀況尤其嚴重，因為她們普遍被認為不該接受教育。藉由接受教育並取得謀生能力，有益於這些孩子，進而能夠正面地影響整個村莊。

可能的解決辦法

我們想要尋求您的協助。一直以來，我們致力於教育這些孩子，使他們能夠自力更生並回饋故鄉。大部分的孩子都想學習實用的職業技能，如旅館管理、護理，與專業醫療。

今天起請踴躍捐款，一起改變世界！

charity (n.)：慈善　donation (n.)：捐獻　fund (n.)：基金　self-sufficient (adj.)：自足的
employable (adj.)：適宜雇用的　vocational (adj.)：職業的　prevalent (adj.)：普遍的

付款方式

☐ 個人支票 或 ☐ 公司支票 或 ☐ 信用卡

信用卡類型：☐ Visa ☐ MasterCard ☐ American Express ☐ 其他信用卡 ____________________

信用卡卡號：____

有效日期：_____ _____ / 20 _____ _____ （月／年）

信用卡持有人：____（請以正楷填寫）

持卡人簽名：____

日期：____

我們也接受手機和電匯捐款。

exp. (n.)：(= expiration) 到期、期滿　wire transfer：電匯

181. What is the main purpose of the first article? 第一篇文章的主要目的為何？
(A) Ask people to join the foundation's workforce 請大眾加入基金會的工作團隊
(B) Encourage people to donate so children can receive education
鼓勵大眾捐款讓孩童有機會接受教育
(C) Ask foundation employees to work overtime during the weekend 要求基金會員工在週末加班
(D) Inform customers to pay by their credit cards 通知客戶以信用卡付款

◀ 解析 ▶
第一段即提及，需要募集更多款項讓孩子完成教育，故選 (B)。

182. What can be inferred from the article about the Mountain Village?
自文中可推論出高山村莊是怎麼樣的地方？
(A) Most females are illiterate. 大多數女性是不識字的。
(B) People there are good at math. 那裡的人數學很強。
(C) It has a highly developed transportation system. 那裡有高度發展的交通系統。
(D) It is a prosperous city. 那是個繁榮的都市。

◀ 解析 ▶
第二段即提及，村莊內有超過一半的人不識字，尤其是女性，故選 (A)。

183. What would most children in the Mountain Village like to study? 高山村莊的多數孩童都想學什麼？
(A) Company regulations 公司法規
(B) Successful case studies 成功的案例討論
(C) Deep theories 深奧的理論
(D) Practical vocations 實用的職業技能

◀ 解析 ▶
最後一段提到，孩童多半想學習實用的職業技能，故選 (D)。

184. What is NOT required on the payment form? 付款單上沒有要求填寫什麼？
(A) Credit card number 信用卡號碼
(B) Cardholder's name 持卡人姓名
(C) Type of credit card 信用卡類型
(D) Cardholder's birthday 持卡人的生日

◀ 解析 ▶
需注意本題問的是「沒有要求」填寫的項目，根據表格內容，可知不需填寫的是 (D)。

185. What is NOT mentioned as an alternative donation method? 文中沒有提到哪種捐款方式？

(A) Wire transfer 電匯

(B) Check 支票

(C) Mobile device 行動裝置

(D) Cash 現金

◀ **解析** ▶

根據付款單的內容，可使用的付款方式為信用卡、支票、手機、電匯，並不包含現金，故選 (D)。

Questions 186 - 190 refer to the following advertisement, form, and letter.

專屬於您的財富銀行 VISA 金融卡

若您想要一張既安全，又具備消費靈活性的卡片，由財富銀行所發行的 Visa 卡就是您的最佳選擇。

- 使用您的 Visa 卡，讓購物流程更迅速！進行購物時，只要出示您的卡片並在收據上簽名，馬上輕鬆完成消費。
- 您每次消費後都會取得一張收據，而您的帳戶明細表上也會有每一筆交易的詳細資訊。
- 無論身在何處，皆可以使用本卡於商家進行消費，也可使用世界各地的提款機，自個人或公司的支票帳戶及儲蓄帳戶內提領現金。
- 比起隨身攜帶支票或現金，攜帶 Visa 卡安全得多。
- 您的 Visa 卡通行於世界各地超過百萬個消費店家，同時也非常適用於網路或電話購物。

輕鬆填寫下列申請表格，就能立即申請。

flexibility (n.)：靈活性　transaction (n.)：交易

財富銀行 Visa 卡

說明：填妥以下表格。填寫完成並簽名之後，將表格交給離您最近的財富銀行任一分行。

申請者

姓名：　琳達瓊斯
地址：　西達街 229 號
地址（第二行）
城市：　茶頸市
州名：　紐澤西
郵遞區號：　47739
手機：　573-4388-5882
生日：　1987
服務機構：　最佳軟體公司

副卡申請者

姓名：
地址：
地址（第二行）
城市：
州名：
郵遞區號：
手機：
生日：
服務機構：

簽名：完成簽名後即代表保證所有資訊的真實與完整性。簽署者同意財富銀行有審查信用記錄和工作記錄與／或自相關單位取得信用報告的權利。

申請者簽名：　琳達瓊斯　　日期：2018 年 6 月 4 日
副卡申請者簽名：　　日期：

herein (adv.)：在此　authorize (v.)：授權　verify (v.)：核對、查證　obtain (v.)：獲得

日期：2018 年 7 月 1 日
主旨：Visa 卡申請通過確認函

親愛的瓊斯小姐，您好：

謝謝您申請財富銀行 Visa 卡。

財富銀行已複審您的 Visa 卡申請書，很榮幸通知您卡片申請已通過。

在此同時，我們向您推薦超凡信用卡。這是我們特別為重要客戶所推行的信用卡。若您想要了解更多相關資訊，歡迎隨時與我們聯繫。

感謝您選擇財富銀行來滿足您各方面的財務交易需求。

客戶經裡
馬克威廉斯

approval (n.)：核准、通過　approve (v.)：批准、認可

186. What is the purpose of the first message? 第一篇訊息的目的為何？
(A) Recruit new financial advisors 招募新的理財顧問
(B) Announce a merger between two banks 宣佈兩家銀行合併的消息
(C) Attract people to apply for Rich Bank's charge cards 吸引大眾申請財富銀行的簽帳卡
(D) Encourage foreign investments 鼓勵外商投資

◀ 解析 ▶
第一篇訊息的內容，說明了使用財富銀行 Visa 卡的好處，最後也提及填寫申請表就能立即申請，由此可知答案為 (C)。

187. What is mentioned about a Rich Bank Visa Card? 文中提到關於財富銀行 Visa 卡的什麼事？
(A) It's accepted only in some limited places. 僅在幾個有限的地方可使用。
(B) Carrying a Visa card is safer than carrying cash. 攜帶 Visa 卡比攜帶現金安全。
(C) The application process is very time-consuming. 申請手續非常耗時。
(D) It's not used for purchasing products online. 不適用於網路購物。

◀ 解析 ▶
文中提到，財富銀行 Visa 卡不僅可在世界各地的商家內使用，也適用於網路或電話購物，且申辦手續簡單，故 (A)、(C)、(D) 皆不正確，本題答案為 (B)。

188. What should interested applicants do with the application form?
有興趣申請的人應如何處理申請表格？
(A) Complete it and bring it to a Rich Bank branch 填妥之後交到財富銀行分行
(B) Sign it and scan it 簽名並掃瞄成檔案
(C) Email it to the Rich Bank's main office 寄電子郵件到財富銀行總部
(D) Fax it to other relatives 傳真給其他親戚

◀ 解析 ▶
由申請表開頭的說明可知，申請者填寫完成後，只要拿到離家最近的財富銀行分行即可，故選 (A)。

189. In the form, the word "verify" in paragraph 3, line 2, is closest in meaning to
表格中，第三段第二行的 "verify" 一字意思最接近於
(A) check out 檢驗
(B) opt to 選擇
(C) talk about 談論
(D) wait on 伺候

◀ 解析 ▶
verify 一字意思為「核對、證實」，與 check out 意思最接近，故選 (A)。

190. What is the main purpose of Mr. Williams' letter? 威廉斯先生寫信的主要目的為何？
(A) To decline Ms. Jones' job application 婉拒瓊斯小姐的求職申請
(B) To inform Ms. Jones that her credit card application has been approved
通知瓊斯小姐信用卡申請已通過
(C) To ask Ms. Jones to provide extra credit history information 要求瓊斯小姐提供更多歷史信用紀錄
(D) To recruit Ms. Jones to work at the Rich Bank 招募瓊斯小姐到財富銀行上班

◀ 解析 ▶
信件主旨為「Visa 卡申請通過確認函」，表示寫信的目的是為了通知瓊斯小姐卡片已通過申請，故選 (B)。

Questions 191 - 195 refer to the following letter, notice, and testimonial.

您已受邀參加即將於 USC 大學的傑克森管理學院舉辦的活動。請您參閱下列資訊，由於下列活動的座位有限，請您儘快向商管學院招募主任莉蒂亞高登 (lydiag@usc.edu) 回覆是否出席。在您的出席回覆內，請註明您的姓名（名字與姓氏）、目前的職位，與所任職的公司行號名稱。入場報到將於活動開始前 30 分鐘於學院前門入口進行。

我與我的同事們都非常期待您的到來。

莉蒂亞高登
商管學院招募主任
傑克森管理學院
USC 大學
電子郵件：lydiag@usc.edu

RSVP：(= répondez s'il vous plait) **敬請回覆**

活動訊息

三月十九日，下午四點整至六點，古迪中庭（一樓），USC 大學傑克森管理學院

誠摯邀請您參與這場由傑克森國際貿易學院所舉辦的圓桌會議。傑克森資產管理國際中心主任 馬克薛漢教授，將會負責帶領進行討論。

本場圓桌會議由傑克森資產管理國際中心協力贊助。本次活動將會由傑克森國際貿易學院院長 珍妮吉布森教授負責主持。

歡迎您於三月十九日前來與會。本活動為免費入場。若您有任何可能對本活動有興趣的非傑克森學院的同事，請將他們登記為您的來賓，或是將這封邀請函轉寄給他們。

著裝標準為商務便裝。地下停車場將開放使用。

欲參加當日活動者請務必預先登記：
參與活動者請務必完成登記。請將您的姓名、職務名稱，與公司行號名稱（連同您的邀請來賓資料），於三月九日下午五點前，以電子郵件傳送至：event@usc.edu。請注意，完成登記後將不會收到確認郵件。

institute (n.)：**學院、研究所**　co-sponsor：**共同贊助**　session (n.)：**會議、講習**

心得分享：陳光君，台灣，2017 年

我決定進修商管碩士學位的主要原因是，我想在全職工作的同時也學習商管知識，以便我可以立即將我在課堂上學到的東西應用到工作上。我查找了一些課程，並參加過課程說明會。最終我決定在 USC 大學修習商管碩士課程，正因為我愛上了這所大學提供的高品質教學。對於那些正在考慮進修商管碩士的同學，我一定會推薦 USC 大學的商管碩士課程。透過進修該課程，你將瞭解到自己不僅可以向頂尖的教授學習，還可以與來自不同國家和產業的同學進行討論。你也將深刻感受到，當你有效應用所學知識到實際工作上的那一刻。最重要的是，與 USC 大學內的同學建立關係，肯定會對你未來的職業生涯有莫大助益。

191. What event is being arranged? 文章提及的活動安排為何？
   (A) A hands-on workshop 實作講習
   (B) A job fair 就業博覽會
   (C) An MBA information session 商管學院說明會
   (D) A technical meeting 技術會議

◀ 解析 ▶
活動訊息當中提到，此為商管學院圓桌會議，故選 (C)。

192. What is NOT mentioned as an element when registering for the event?
   登記參加活動時，不需要提供下列哪一項資訊？
   (A) Position 職稱
   (B) Name 姓名
   (C) Organization 公司名稱
   (D) Birthday 生日

◀ 解析 ▶
活動訊息最後一段提到，註冊需要姓名、職稱、公司名稱，不需要提供生日，故選 (D)。

193. How long will the event last? 此活動會進行多久時間？
   (A) 2 hours 兩小時
   (B) 4 hours 四小時
   (C) 6 hours 六小時
   (D) 7 hours 七小時

◀ 解析 ▶
從活動訊息開頭即可得知，活動時間為下午四點到六點，共兩小時，故選 (A)。

194. About the event, which of the following is true? 關於此活動，下列敘述何者正確？

(A) It's free of charge. 它是免費活動。

(B) Attendees can pay for the enrollment by cash. 與會者可以用現金支付報名費用。

(C) This event is only open to Jackson School students. 此活動僅限傑克森學院學生參加。

(D) The event is usually held in summer. 此活動通常是在夏天舉辦。

◀ 解析 ▶

活動訊息當中提到，此活動為免費入場，且可邀請非傑克森學院的來賓參加，故選 (A)。

195. What is true about Kuan-Chun Chen? 關於陳光君的敘述何者正確？

(A) He is a professor teaching at University of USC. 他是在 USC 大學教書的教授。

(B) He had excellent studying experience at University of USC. 他在 USC 大學有絕佳的學習經驗。

(C) He just graduated from college and has no work experience at all.
他剛從大學畢業且沒有任何工作經驗。

(D) He only talked to Taiwanese students when he studied abroad.
當他在國外留學時，只跟台灣學生講話。

◀ 解析 ▶

根據第三篇文章所敘述的內容，可看出他對 USC 大學是讚賞有加的，故選 (B)。

© Caves Educational Training Co., Ltd.

Questions 196 - 200 refer to the following letters and comments.

2018 年 2 月 8 日
史提夫布希先生
房號：883

布希先生您好，

歡迎來到格蘭大飯店。謹代表飯店全體員工，希望您和您的家人在此能度過愉快的假期。

我們期望帶給您格蘭大飯店獨特的服務，本飯店提供高級餐飲、休閒 spa、商務中心和健身俱樂部等設施，以滿足客人的需求。我們致力於給您最貼心及最周到的服務。

若您在住宿期間需要任何協助或資訊，請隨時聯繫我們的大廳服務人員，或自客房撥打分機號碼 11 聯絡櫃檯。方便的話，請提供您的回饋意見給我們，有任何問題也可告訴我們，您的想法將對我們有很大的幫助。

藉此機會再次感謝您入住格蘭大飯店。

誠摯地，
陳琳達
格蘭大飯店總經理

on behalf of：代表　look forward to：期待　attentive (adj.)：體貼的

客戶意見：

我們最近在格蘭大飯店住宿，很高興在此住了三個晚上。所有服務人員都很關心我們，也樂於提供協助。我認為他們是我們遇到過最好的服務人員。他們竭盡所能確保所有人都有美好的住宿經驗。飯店的地理位置便利，距離著名的水上廣場僅有幾步之遙。我太太和我也有相同想法，她覺得格蘭大飯店是春城市最好的飯店之一。毫無疑問，我們一定會再回來。

史提夫布希，2018 年 2 月 12 日

encounter (v.)：遇到、遭遇　confirm (v.)：確認、證實　definitely (adv.)：肯定地

2018年 3 月 1 日
史提夫布希先生

布希先生您好，

謝謝您給予格蘭大飯店正面的評價。為了表達我們的感謝之意，將提供給您下次住宿使用的八五折優惠券。

期待不久的將來可以再度為您服務。

陳琳達
格蘭大飯店總經理

格蘭大飯店

八五折優惠券

住宿期間適用於
2017 年 9 月 1 日至 2018 年 12 月 31 日
（優惠券使用限於住宿三十天前預訂飯店房間）
https://www.grand-inn.com
info@grand-inn.com
聯絡電話：383-4399-4882

appreciation (n.)：感謝、感激　arrival (n.)：到達

196. What is the purpose of Linda Chen's first letter to Steve Bush?
陳琳達寫給史提夫布希的第一封信目的為何？
(A) To welcome hotel guests 歡迎飯店賓客
(B) To file a complaint 提出抱怨申訴
(C) To invite seminar attendees 邀請研討會來賓
(D) To enlist soldiers 招募士兵

◀ 解析 ▶
根據第一封信的內容，可看出此信目的是歡迎飯店賓客，故選 (A)。

197. In Linda's first letter, the word "distinctive" in paragraph 2, line 1, is closest in meaning to
在琳達的第一封信裡，第二段第一行的 "distinctive" 一字意思最接近於
(A) tedious 沉悶的
(B) ordinary 普通的
(C) usual 一般的
(D) unique 特殊的

◀ 解析 ▶
distinctive 一字意思為「有特色的、特殊的」，與 unique 意思最相近，故選 (D)。

198. What can be inferred about Mr. Steve Bush? 由文中可推論關於史提夫布希的何事？
(A) His stay in Grand Inn was for business purposes. 他入住格蘭大飯店是因為出公差。
(B) He has been working in Grand Inn for quite a long time. 他在格蘭大飯店工作很久了。
(C) He is satisfied with the service in Grand Inn. 他對格蘭大飯店的服務感到很滿意。
(D) He is still a single man. 他仍然保持單身。

◀ 解析 ▶
根據第二篇文章所敘述的內容，可看出他很滿意飯店的服務，故選 (C)。

199. What is NOT true about Grand Inn? 關於格蘭大飯店何者為非？
(A) It's located in Spring City. 位於春城市。
(B) It's one of the oldest hotels in the world. 是世界上最古老的飯店之一。
(C) It has business amenities. 具備商務設施。
(D) It is near Water Square. 靠近水上廣場。

◀ 解析 ▶
從三篇文章看來，沒有任何資訊提到格蘭大飯店是古老的飯店，故選 (B)。

200. According to the coupon, if Mr. Bush reserves a $200 room for a night, how much will he need to pay?
根據優惠券內容，若布希先生訂了一晚兩百美元的房間，他應該要付多少錢？
(A) $190 一百九十美元
(B) $170 一百七十美元
(C) $200 兩百美元
(D) $150 一百五十美元

◀ 解析 ▶
根據優惠券的說明，下次入住時可以打八五折，而一晚兩百美元經過折扣後應為一百七十美元，故選 (B)。

Test 2

試題解析

LISTENING TEST

Part I									
1	2	3	4	5	6				
A	C	B	B	D	C				
Part II									
7	8	9	10	11	12	13	14	15	16
B	A	B	A	B	C	A	B	C	B
17	18	19	20	21	22	23	24	25	26
B	A	B	C	B	A	C	A	B	A
27	28	29	30	31					
B	C	B	A	B					
Part III									
32	33	34	35	36	37	38	39	40	41
B	A	C	A	D	B	B	B	C	C
42	43	44	45	46	47	48	49	50	51
A	B	A	C	D	A	C	D	A	B
52	53	54	55	56	57	58	59	60	61
C	A	B	B	D	C	D	A	B	A
62	63	64	65	66	67	68	69	70	
B	D	B	B	D	C	C	A	B	
Part IV									
71	72	73	74	75	76	77	78	79	80
A	B	C	B	C	A	B	A	C	D
81	82	83	84	85	86	87	88	89	90
B	A	A	B	D	B	A	C	A	C
91	92	93	94	95	96	97	98	99	100
B	B	A	C	C	B	A	B	D	B

Part I. ► Photographs

1.

(A) The man is painting the wall. 男子正在漆牆壁。
(B) The man is not wearing a helmet. 男子沒戴安全帽。
(C) The man is working on a computer. 男子正在電腦前工作。
(D) The man is carrying a walking stick. 男子拿著拐杖。

◀ 解析 ▶

1. 照片中男子頭戴工程帽，拿著油漆刷，正在粉刷牆壁，故選 (A)。
2. walking stick：拐杖、手杖

2.

(A) The woman is pointing to the computer. 女子正指著電腦。
(B) These four people are having lunch. 這四個人正在吃午餐。
(C) The group is having a discussion. 這個團隊正在討論事情。
(D) One of the men is drinking coffee. 其中一位男子正在喝咖啡。

◀ 解析 ▶

照片中四人利用筆記型電腦，正在聚精會神討論事情，其中指著電腦的是男子，故正確敘述為 (C)。

3.

(A) The flower market is very clean. 花市非常乾淨。
(B) Products are on display. 產品陳列展示著。
(C) Customers are standing in line. 顧客正在排隊。
(D) This luxurious merchandise is very expensive.
這裡的高檔產品很昂貴。

◀ 解析 ▶

1. 此照片地點為量販店的酒品陳列架，此處商品價格應不至於太高，且照片中並無任何顧客，故本題選 (B)。
2. luxurious (adj.)：奢華的　merchandise (n.)：商品

4.

(A) The traffic is not bad at this time of the day.
每天此時的交通狀況還不算太壞。
(B) The traffic is gridlocked. 路上交通阻塞。
(C) Pedestrians are trying to cross the road. 行人試著要穿越馬路。
(D) The road is full of trucks and buses. 路上擠滿了卡車和公車。

◀ 解析 ▶

1. 此照片為市區道路交通阻塞的情形，可見四線道車輛並行，並無行人穿越道，且車輛以小客車與公車為主，故本題選 (B)。
2. gridlock (v.)：交通阻塞　pedestrian (n.)：行人

5.

(A) A lady is helping travelers to check in.
女子正在協助旅客報到。
(B) The airport is full of travelers. 機場擠滿了旅客。
(C) Travelers are waiting at Gate 3. 旅客都在三號登機門等候。
(D) Travelers stop here for a security check.
旅客在此接受安全檢查。

◀ 解析 ▶

此照片為機場海關 (customs) 進行安檢通關的過程，故本題選 (D)。

6.

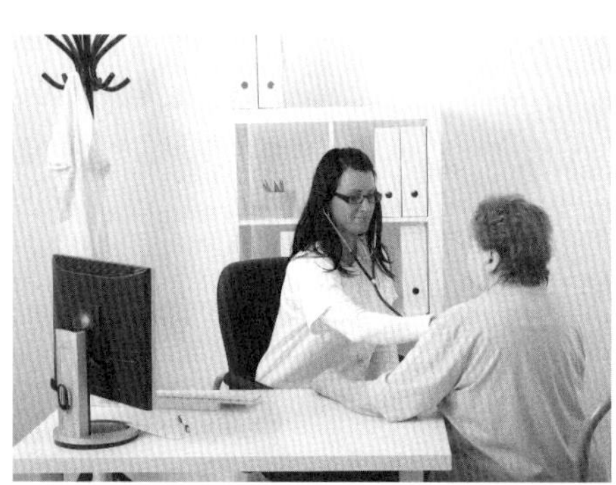

(A) The doctor is on the phone. 醫生正在講電話。
(B) The patient is standing next to a nurse.
病人正站在護士旁邊。
(C) The doctor is checking her patient. 醫生正在為病人檢查。
(D) The doctor is injecting the patient with a new drug.
醫生正在幫病人注射一種新藥。

◀ 解析 ▶

1. 照片地點為醫院或診所的診療室，而醫生正在幫病人看診，故本題選 (C)。
2. patient (n.)：病人　inject (v.)：注射

Part II. ▶ Question-Response

7. Can you handle this situation? 你可以應付這狀況嗎？
   (A) I want to be like you. 我想跟你一樣。
   (B) It's a piece of cake. 簡單得很！
   (C) I don't know how to handle the machine. 我不知道如何操作這台機器。

◀ 解析 ▶
1. 本題是問能否應付某種狀況，回答中應該表達是否能夠應付，雖然選項 (C) 也有 handle 一字出現，但答非所問，故選 (B)。
2. a piece of cake：容易的事

8. It's $30.99. How would you like to pay, sir? 先生，總共是 30.99 元，您想怎麼付款？
   (A) Please charge that amount on my plastic. 請用我的信用卡結帳。
   (B) It's cheaper than I expected. 比我想像中的還要便宜。
   (C) How much do I have to pay? 我應該付多少錢？

◀ 解析 ▶
1. 本題問的是付錢的方法 (how)，故應該回答用現金 (in cash) 或是刷卡 (by credit card) 等方式。選項 (A) 當中的 plastic 也有「信用卡」之意，故選 (A)。
2. charge (v.)：收費

9. It's raining cats and dogs out there. Why don't we just stay home? 外面下著大雨，我們何不待在家？
   (A) Sorry, I'm allergic to cats. 對不起，我對貓過敏。
   (B) Yeah, it might be a good idea. 好啊，這或許是個好主意。
   (C) I like spring because it sometimes rains. 我喜歡春天，因為有時會下雨。

◀ 解析 ▶
1. 本題的 It rains cats and dogs. 為「下著滂沱大雨」之意，與貓狗無關。對方提議下雨天待在家，故選 (B) 較為合理。
2. allergic (adj.)：過敏的

10. Excuse me. Do you have the time? 不好意思，請問現在幾點呢？
   (A) It's ten to four. 現在是三點五十分。（再十分鐘就四點了。）
   (B) I like to read novels when I have spare time. 我喜歡在空閒時看小說。
   (C) Sure, here you go. 當然，拿去吧。

◀ 解析 ▶
1. 本題的 Do you have the time? 問的是「現在幾點？」，故選 (A)。
2. spare (adj.)：空閒的

11. Does the boss like your new ideas? 老闆喜歡你的新點子嗎？
    (A) Well, she seems to hate me. 嗯，她好像討厭我。
    (B) Yeah, I think so. 對，我想是吧。
    (C) All team members need to contribute new ideas. 所有的團隊成員都應該貢獻新點子。

◀ 解析 ▶
1. 本題問的是老闆是否喜歡新的想法，選項 (A) 回答的是對人的好惡，(C) 則答非所問，故選 (B)。
2. contribute (v.)：貢獻

12. Have you heard that Kevin is leaving the company and joining the competitor?
    你有聽説凱文要離職，而且跳槽到我們的競爭公司嗎？
    (A) I think the SamTung Co. is our chief rival. 我認為三通公司是我們的主要對手。
    (B) I know our competitor will launch a similar product soon.
    我知道我們的競爭對手很快會推出類似的產品。
    (C) Really? That's too bad. 真的嗎？那可不妙！

◀ 解析 ▶
1. 本題討論的是同事跳槽的消息，選項 (A)、(B) 雖與競爭對手有關，但未回答問題，故選 (C) 較為合理。
2. competitor (n.)：競爭者　rival (n.)：競爭者

13. How did the presentation go? 簡報做得如何？
    (A) Pretty good. The customer will place an order soon. 不錯呀。客戶很快就會下單了。
    (B) The presentation has been scheduled for next Monday. 簡報訂在下週一舉行。
    (C) How do you know that? 你怎麼知道的？

◀ 解析 ▶
本題是問簡報做得如何，選項 (B)、(C) 皆答非所問，故選 (A)。

14. Do you know what Jason's extension number is? 你知道傑森的分機是幾號嗎？
    (A) Sure, I will be right with you. 當然，我馬上過去。
    (B) I think it's 1254. 我想是分機 1254。
    (C) It comes to $9.87. 總共是 9.87 元。

◀ 解析 ▶
本題問的是傑森的分機號碼，若是知道的話，通常就會直接回答號碼，故選 (B)。

15. What time shall we meet at the airport? 我們幾點在機場集合？

(A) I need to check with her assistant. 我得跟她的助理確認。

(B) How about next month? 下個月如何？

(C) Let's meet at 4 p.m. sharp, OK? 我們四點整見，可以嗎？

◀ 解析 ▶

1. 本題問的是 what time「幾點」，回答中應說明時間，故選 (C)。
2. sharp (adv.)：整點（表示時間）

16. Can you give me a discount on this? 你可以給我打個折嗎？

(A) You can count me in. 你可以把我算進去。

(B) I am afraid not, since there is only one price. 恐怕沒辦法，因為那是不二價。

(C) We accept cash and check. 我們收現金和支票。

◀ 解析 ▶

本題是問價錢能否打折，也就是殺價時的問法，選項 (A) 答非所問，(C) 則是回答支付費用的方法，故選 (B)。

17. Will I have to wait long to see the doctor? 我要等很久才能見到醫生嗎？

(A) Yeah, long time no see. 是呀，好久不見了。

(B) No, you will be next. 不用，下一位就輪到你了。

(C) Dr. White is a very patient man. 懷特醫師是個很有耐心的人。

◀ 解析 ▶

本題是問還要多久才能看到醫生，選項 (A) 是問候語，選項 (C) 則答非所問，故選 (B)。

18. What's the fastest way to get to the train station? 我要如何才能最快到達火車站呢？

(A) At this time of the day, you should take the MRT. 在這種時間，你應該搭捷運。

(B) The train station is near the Summit Bank. 火車站在高峰銀行附近。

(C) Oh, the traffic conditions are certainly bad. 嗯，交通狀況的確很糟。

◀ 解析 ▶

本題是問到達火車站最快的方法，選項 (B) 回答的是火車站的位置，(C) 則答非所問，故選 (A)。

19. How soon can you finish the sales report? 你多快可以完成業務報告？

(A) We are doing better than we expected. 我們做得比預期還要好。

(B) I probably need one more day to get it done. 我可能還要一天才能完成。

(C) He is still working on the CBS project. 他還在處理 CBS 的案子。

© Caves Educational Training Co., Ltd.

◀ 解析 ▶
本題是問 how soon「時間多快…」，回答應說明預期完成的時間，故選 (B)。

20. Mary, you will join Mr. King's retirement party, won't you? 瑪莉，你會去參加金先生的退休派對吧？
   (A) It is time for us to head home. 是我們該回家的時間了。
   (B) I will retire in 3 years myself. 我自己會在三年後退休。
   (C) Sure, I am looking forward to it. 當然，我很期待。

◀ 解析 ▶
1. 本題問是否會參加退休派對，選項 (A)、(B) 皆答非所問，故選 (C)。
2. retirement (n.)：退休

21. Should we order pizza for our lunch meeting? 我們午餐會議訂比薩好嗎？
   (A) I eat pizza at least twice a week. 我一週至少吃兩次比薩。
   (B) Good idea. Let's call Pizza House now. 好主意。我們現在就打電話給「比薩屋」。
   (C) The meeting agenda is on my desk. 會議議程在我桌上。

◀ 解析 ▶
本題是提議中午開會吃比薩，選項 (A)、(C) 雖然也有關鍵字 pizza 或 meeting，但答非所問，故本題答案為 (B)。

22. Would you like this red blouse or that black one? 你想要這件紅色的襯衫還是那件黑色的？
   (A) I will take both. 我兩件都要買。
   (B) Let's paint the wall red. 讓我們將牆漆成紅色。
   (C) You really look good with that white hat. 你戴那頂白色帽子很好看。

◀ 解析 ▶
本題是詢問對方想買哪件襯衫，答案通常會是其中之一，或兩件都要，亦或兩件都不要，故本題選 (A)。

23. Is Mr. Tim still on the phone? 提姆先生還在電話中嗎？
   (A) Sorry, but I don't know his phone number. 抱歉，我不知道他的電話號碼。
   (B) Maybe he will call you tomorrow. 他可能明天打電話給你。
   (C) Yes. May I take your number and have him call you back?
   是的。我可以記下你的電話號碼，再請他回電給你嗎？

◀ 解析 ▶
當對方要找的人正在電話中，接電話者通常會幫忙留言 take a message，或是留電話號碼 take the number，故本題答案為 (C)。

24. Are you ready to order, sir? 先生，您準備好要點餐了嗎？

(A) Can I have a glass of iced water first, please? 請問可以先給我一杯冰水嗎？

(B) Sure, I will place the order within three days. 當然，我三天內會下訂單。

(C) No, I am not ready to be a father yet. 不，我還沒準備好要當爸爸。

◀ 解析 ▶

本題通常是餐廳服務生會問的問題，選項 (B) 當中也有 order，但此處是「訂單」之意，選項 (C) 則答非所問，故選 (A)。

25. What's the matter with Mr. Anderson? He looks sad. 安德森先生怎麼了？他看起來很難過。

(A) He is always on the go. 他總是很忙。

(B) He just lost a big case. 他剛剛失去一個大案子。

(C) He is nearly 50 years old. 他已經快 50 歲了。

◀ 解析 ▶

本題是問安德森先生難過的原因，選項 (A)、(C) 僅為個人狀態的敘述，並非造成心情不好的原因，故本題選 (B) 較為合理。

26. Where did you put the meeting minutes I gave you yesterday? 你把我昨天給你的會議記錄放在哪裡？

(A) I put them back on your desk already. 我已經放回你桌上了。

(B) That meeting was really boring. 那會議真的很無聊。

(C) The annual meeting will be held in Japan this year. 今年的年會將在日本舉行。

◀ 解析 ▶

本題是問會議記錄放在「哪裡」，選項 (B) 是對會議的感想，(C) 是年會舉行的地點，故本題答案為 (A)。

27. I am calling to make a room reservation for this coming weekend.

我打電話來是想要預訂本週末的房間。

(A) Enjoy your stay here. 祝您在這裡玩得愉快。

(B) Sorry, but all rooms are booked already. 不好意思，所有的房間都訂滿了。

(C) Sure, do you prefer a window seat or an aisle seat? 當然，您想要靠窗還是靠走道的座位？

◀ 解析 ▶

本題是顧客訂房的來電，選項 (A) 是服務人員對造訪飯店的客人所說的話，(C) 則會出現在預訂機位時，故本題選 (B) 較為合理。

28. Who is going to cover for Jane when she is on vacation? 當珍休假時，誰會代理她的工作呢？

(A) I am afraid I don't have time then. 恐怕我到時候會沒空。

(B) I think she is going to Thailand for her vacation. 我想她是要去泰國渡假。

(C) Don't worry, I will do it. 別擔心，我會代理她的工作。

◀ 解析 ▶

1. 本題是問珍休假時的代理人是誰，選項 (A) 並未回答問題，選項 (B) 則是說明渡假的地點，故本題答案應選 (C)。
2. cover (v.)：代替

29. Can you put me through to Ms. Joy at extension 45, please?
請問可以幫我轉接分機 45 的喬依小姐嗎？
(A) Sorry, I don't know her extension number. 不好意思，我不知道她的分機號碼。
(B) No problem. Please hold on a second. 沒問題，請稍等。
(C) Sure, can I take a message? 當然，您要留言嗎？

◀ 解析 ▶

本題是對方請求幫忙轉接分機，選項 (A) 用在對方詢問分機號碼時，(C) 則用於喬依小姐不在的時候，故本題選 (B)。

30. How much is this T-shirt? 這件 T 恤多少錢？
(A) It's $5.99, and you can get 20% off if you buy two. 一件是 5.99 元，如果你買兩件可以打八折。
(B) It's really a nice T-shirt, isn't it? 那件 T 恤很好看，不是嗎？
(C) If you can get the price down to 5, I will buy it right away. 若你可以降價只賣 5 元，我立刻買。

◀ 解析 ▶

本題是詢問衣服的價錢，回答當中應說出確切的金額，選項 (A) 不但說明單件衣服的金額，更提出買兩件打八折的優惠價，故本題選 (A) 較為合理。

31. Did you have any trouble finding my office? 你找得到我的辦公室嗎？
(A) I need a map of the city, please. 請給我一張這座城市的地圖。
(B) No, not at all. 完全沒問題。
(C) As you know, I am in big trouble now. 你知道的，我現在麻煩大了。

◀ 解析 ▶

本題是問對方是否能順利找到辦公室，選項 (A) 指涉的範圍太大，(C) 則答非所問，故本題答案應為 (B)。

Part III. ▶ Conversations

Questions 32 - 34 refer to the following conversation.

[CA] M / [AU] W

M: Sorry for being late. This meeting venue is a bit off the beaten track. I thought I'd never find it.

W: Yeah, I know exactly what you are talking about. It took me a while to find this place too. But you don't have an in-car GPS system, do you?

M: You mean the Global Positioning System? No, I don't, but I suppose I should invest in one, right? I often have trouble finding roads, you know. Well, I know the price is going down, so I am going to buy one soon.

W: I am sure you will like it. In fact, I couldn't live without my GPS system now. I am happy that I never have to ask for directions again.

男：不好意思，我遲到了。這個會議地點有點偏遠，我還以為我會找不到。
女：是呀，我完全瞭解。我也花了點時間才找到的。但你車上沒有 GPS 嗎？
男：你是指衛星定位導航系統嗎？我沒有，但我在想我應該花錢買一台，對吧？你知道我在找路方面不是很靈光。反正現在的價格一直在降，我很快就會去買一台。
女：我保證你會喜歡它。事實上我現在完全離不開 GPS。我很高興我不用再一直跟人家問路了。

off the beaten track：人跡罕至之處

32. Why is the man late? 男子為什麼遲到？
(A) His car is broken. 他的車壞了。
(B) He has difficulty finding the location. 他找尋地點時遇到困難。
(C) He misses the train. 他錯過火車。
(D) He forgets to bring his GPS. 他忘了帶 GPS 衛星導航。

◀ 解析 ▶
對話第一句，男子提到因為會議地點偏遠不好找，導致他遲到，故本題選 (B)。

33. What does the man say about the GPS system? 男子提到關於 GPS 衛星導航的什麼事？
(A) He is interested in buying one. 他有興趣要買一台。
(B) He thinks it's too expensive. 他認為那太貴了。
(C) He has one already, but it's not working. 他已經有一台，但是壞了。
(D) He will borrow one from the woman. 他會向女子借一台。

◀ 解析 ▶
對話中男子表示，雖然他目前沒有 GPS，但因為相當實用且價格下降，他應該很快就會買一台，故本題答案為 (A)。

34. What does the woman suggest the man do? 女子建議男子做何事？
(A) Ask for directions next time 下次向人問路
(B) Bring a map with him 隨身帶一張地圖
(C) Purchase a GPS system 買一台 GPS 衛星導航
(D) Leave earlier and be on time 早點出門並準時

◀ 解析 ▶
對話最後，女子提到購買 GPS 的好處，可知她意在推薦男子也買一台，故選 (C)。

Questions 35 - 37 refer to the following conversation.

[UK] M / [US] W

M: Excuse me, Ms. Laurent, is it okay for you to answer a couple of questions before the conference?

W: Okay, but as you know, the conference will commence in ten minutes, so please make it really brief.

M: Sure. You are always identified as a "customer care" expert. What suggestions do you have for customer service representatives when they need to deal with difficult customers? How can they handle the situation?

W: Well, first of all I do suggest customer service representatives listen carefully to what the customer has to say and what his problems are, and then they should work with the customer and focus on providing workable solutions.

M: That's a wonderful suggestion. The goal for the majority of organizations is to fulfill customers' needs, isn't it?

W: You are definitely right. Well, now I have to get ready for my presentation session. If you would like to discuss this further, I'm available after the conference, okay?

男：不好意思，蘿蘭特小姐。在會議開始之前，可以先問您幾個問題嗎？

女：好的，但你也知道，會議十分鐘後就要開始了，所以請盡量簡短些。

男：當然。您是眾所皆知的「客戶服務」專家，對於客服人員需要處理難纏客戶時，有什麼建議？他們要如何處理這種情況？

女：首先，我會建議客服人員仔細傾聽客戶想說什麼，以及問題點為何，接著就要跟客戶合作，把重點放在提供可行的解決方法上。

男：真是個好建議！對多數企業而言，滿足客戶需求不正是最主要的目標嗎？

女：你說得沒錯。嗯，現在我要去準備演講簡報了。若你還想多聊聊，我在研討會結束後有空，好嗎？

commence (v.)：開始

35. Who is most likely the woman? 女子最有可能是誰？
   (A) A customer service manager 客服經理
   (B) An event host 活動主持人
   (C) A sales manager 業務經理
   (D) A literature professor 文學教授

◀ 解析 ▶
對話當中，男子稱呼女子為「客戶服務專家」，由此可知女子應該是擔任客服工作，故本題答案為 (A)。

36. Where is the conversation most likely taking place? 此對話最有可能發生在何處？
   (A) In an office 在辦公室
   (B) In a library 在圖書館
   (C) At an airport 在機場
   (D) In a conference room 在會議室

◀ 解析 ▶
對話一開頭即顯示，男子是利用會議前的十分鐘訪問女子，可推斷兩人是在會議舉行的場地，故選 (D)。

37. What does the woman suggest doing first when dealing with an upset customer?
女子建議在處理生氣的客戶時應先做什麼？
(A) Yell at him 對客戶大吼
(B) Listen to him 傾聽客戶的心聲
(C) Ask him to calm down 請客戶冷靜下來
(D) Attend the conference 參加會議

◀ 解析 ▶
對話最後，女子在回答中，建議客服人員首先應該傾聽客戶的心聲，再一起解決問題，故本題答案為 (B)。

Questions 38 - 40 refer to the following conversation.

[CA] M / [AU] W

M: Hi. What time is your next flight to LA? I need to get there for a meeting this afternoon.

W: Just a moment, let me check. 1:35. Flight 837 to LA. There is still space available. And the fare for round trip is $102.30 with the tax.

M: Good, that's a perfect time for me. And okay, here you are. Please charge the amount on my Fly Club card.

W: All right, sir. Here is your boarding pass and the flight will leave from Gate 74 at 1:35.

男：你好，下一班去洛杉磯的班機是幾點？我下午要飛過去參加會議。
女：請稍等，讓我查查看。一點三十五分，837 航班到洛杉磯還有位置。來回票價是 102.30 元含稅。
男：很好，這時間對我來說剛好。這給你，請用我的飛航俱樂部卡付款。
女：好的，先生。這是您的登機證，飛機將在一點三十五分由 74 號登機門起飛。

38. What is the man doing? 男子在做什麼？
(A) Applying for the driver's license 申請駕照
(B) Checking the flight schedule 確認班機時刻
(C) Signing a contract 簽合約
(D) Rescheduling his meeting 將會議改期

◀ 解析 ▶
對話第一句，男子詢問前往洛杉磯的班機時間，可知他在確認班機時刻，故選 (B)。

39. When will the flight leave? 班機何時會起飛？
    (A) 10:30 十點半
    (B) 1:35 一點三十五分
    (C) 8:37 八點三十七分
    (D) 2:30 兩點半

◀ 解析 ▶
女子為男子查詢到的班機時間為一點三十五分，男子也認為搭此班飛機時間剛好，故本題答案為 (B)。

40. What will the man probably do next? 男子接下來可能會做什麼？
    (A) Pay by cash 以現金付款
    (B) Cancel the meeting 取消會議
    (C) Go to Gate 74 前往 74 號登機門
    (D) Stay in LA for good 永遠留在洛杉磯

◀ 解析 ▶
1. 從對話最後一句可知，從女子手中拿到登機證後，男子應該會前往班機起飛的登機門等待，故選 (C)。
2. for good：永遠

Questions 41 - 43 refer to the following conversation.

[UK] M / [AU] W

M: You have no record of my car reservation? I can't believe this. What can I do now?

W: Don't worry, sir. We still have several cars available. Let's fill out this form first, all right? Are you here on business or for pleasure? And how long will you need the car?

M: Well, I am here on business, and I still don't know for sure how long I'll need it. Please put down two days. My company might pay for more.

W: No problem, sir. Now please let me see your driver's license and a major credit card.

男：你沒有我的訂車記錄？真難以置信，現在我該怎麼辦？

女：先生，別擔心。我們還有其他車輛可以使用。我們先填寫這張表格，好嗎？您到此是為了洽公還是休閒？您需要用車幾天？

男：我到此是為了洽公，但目前還不確定要用車幾天。請先寫兩天，我的公司可能會付更多天的費用。

女：沒問題，先生。現在，請讓我看看您的駕照和信用卡。

41. What is the man trying to do? 男子想做什麼？
    (A) Buy a van 買台貨車
    (B) Apply for a new credit card 申請新信用卡
    (C) Rent a car 租車
    (D) Make a hotel reservation 飯店訂房

◀ 解析 ▶
對話當中，男子需要短期用車，女子也說填寫表格即可申請用車，可推斷此對話的目的較可能為租車，故答案應選 (C)。

42. What does the woman ask the man to do? 女子要求男子做什麼？
(A) Complete the form 填妥表格
(B) Sign an agreement 簽同意書
(C) Pay a deposit 支付押金
(D) Renew the driver's license 換新駕照

◀ 解析 ▶
1. 對話第二句，女子請男子先填寫表格，故本題答案為 (A)。
2. deposit (n.)：保證金、押金

43. What does the man need a car for? 男子需要用車的目的為何？
(A) Vacation 渡假
(B) Business 業務
(C) Pleasure 休閒
(D) Personal issue 個人因素

◀ 解析 ▶
女子詢問男子租車的用途，男子回答是為了洽公，屬於業務需求，故本題答案為 (B)。

Questions 44 - 46 refer to the following conversation.
[CA] M / [AU] W1 / [US] W2

M: Gina, what are you doing this weekend? Ed Mendoza is playing at the Baronet Club, and Julie and I are going. Would you like to join us?
W1: Yeah, I can't wait to go this weekend. Come on, Gina, join us!
W2: You mean the pop singer, Ed Mendoza? Oh, my… he's one of my favorites. Great! I'd love to go with you guys. Then I'd better finish the CPI project by Friday then.
M: The CPI project? Isn't that project due next Wednesday? You're supposed to finish all reports by then, aren't you?
W2: You're right. I've been working hard on it for three weeks and hope to wrap things up soon.
W1: Yeah, I understand. Hey, but don't worry. I am good with numbers so I will give you a hand.
W2: It's very nice of you, Julie, and thank you.

男：吉娜，你這週末有什麼計畫？艾迪門多薩要在巴羅奈特俱樂部表演，茱莉和我要去聽，你要來嗎？
女一：是呀，我等不及週末要去聽了。來嘛，吉娜，跟我們一起去。
女二：你是說流行歌手艾迪門多薩？天呀，他是我最喜歡的歌手之一。太棒了！我很想跟你們一起去。那我最好在週五前完成 CPI 專案。
男：CPI 專案？那不是下週三截止的案子嗎？你應該要在那之前完成所有報告，對吧？

女二：沒錯。我過去三週已花了很多心力在這專案上，希望趕緊結案。
女一：是呀，我瞭解。但別擔心！我對數字很在行，我會協助你。
女二：你真好，茱莉，謝謝你！

44. What are the three speakers talking about? 三人在討論什麼？
(A) Attending a concert on the weekend 週末要去參加演唱會
(B) Listening to a radio program 收聽廣播節目
(C) Inviting Julie to come along 邀請茱莉共同前往
(D) Finding a new job 找個新工作

◀ 解析 ▶
對話第一句，男子表示自己要去聽艾迪門多薩的表演，並邀請女子一起去，故選 (A)。

45. Why is Gina eager to join her colleagues? 吉娜為何熱切地想跟同事們一起前往？
(A) She has nothing to do on the weekend. 她週末沒事做。
(B) She has finished the project already. 她已經完成專案了。
(C) She likes Ed Mendoza very much. 她很喜歡艾迪門多薩。
(D) She likes to help others. 她喜歡幫助他人。

◀ 解析 ▶
對話第三句，吉娜說艾迪門多薩是自己最喜歡的歌手之一，因此她非常想去聽演唱會，故選 (C)。

46. What does Julie offer to do for Gina? 茱莉可以提供吉娜什麼協助？
(A) Buy her a lunch 幫她買午餐
(B) Introduce her to Ed Mendoza 將她介紹給艾迪門多薩
(C) Provide her with a free ticket 給她一張免費門票
(D) Help with her project 協助她完成專案

◀ 解析 ▶
吉娜提到要在週五前完成專案，茱莉表示自己對數字很在行，可以協助她，故選 (D)。

Questions 47 - 49 refer to the following conversation.
[UK] M / [US] W

M: Good morning. I'd like to speak to the manager. I bought this radio here, and look, it doesn't work well. You turn it on and nothing happens.
W: All right, sir. I am the manager. Do you have any proof of purchase – the receipt, for example? We need to know the exact date of purchase.
M: Right, here you go. I purchased it only three days ago.
W: Okay, let me check the product. Hmm… you see this little switch here on the back? It's on "AC" now and it should be on "DC". Now, it's working fine.

男：早安。我想找你們經理。我在這裡買了這台收音機，但你看，根本無法正常運作。開啟之後完全沒反應。

女：好的，先生。我就是經理。您有帶任何購買證明－比方說像發票之類的？我們要知道您確切的購買日期。
男：沒問題，這給你。我三天前才買的。
女：好的，我檢查一下產品。嗯…您有看到後面這個小開關嗎？現在是在 “AC” 這邊，應該要調到 “DC” 才對。現在，收音機可以正常運作了。

proof (n.)：證明

47. Where is the conversation most likely taking place? 此對話最有可能發生在何處？
(A) In an electronics shop 在電子用品店
(B) In a classroom 在教室
(C) In an office 在辦公室
(D) In a restaurant 在餐廳

◀ 解析 ▶
對話第一句，男子提到自己在此處購買了收音機，故本題選 (A) 較為合理。

48. What is the man's problem? 男子遇到的問題為何？
(A) He lost the receipt. 他把發票搞丟了。
(B) He doesn't know where the switch is. 他不知道開關鈕在哪裡。
(C) His newly purchased radio doesn't work. 他新買的收音機無法運作。
(D) He doesn't know what “AC” means. 他不知道 “AC” 是什麼。

◀ 解析 ▶
對話中，男子表示新買的收音機無法正常運作，按下開關卻毫無反應，故本題答案為 (C)。

49. How long ago did the man buy the radio? 男子是多久之前買的收音機？
(A) This morning 今天早上
(B) Three weeks ago 三週前
(C) Last week 上週
(D) Three days ago 三天前

◀ 解析 ▶
男子隨後出示發票，並表示自己是三天前購買收音機的，故本題答案為 (D)。

Questions 50 - 52 refer to the following conversation.
[CA] M / [AU] W
M: Hey, Tina, there is a job in Singapore in today's paper, did you see it? You've been looking for a job in a foreign country, right?
W: Didn't I tell you? It was in last Sunday's paper too, so I called them yesterday and had a phone interview already.
M: Then how was it? Do you think you will get it?

W: Well, they seemed very interested. I think it will be hard work, and I probably won't go unless they offer me a good salary.

男：嗨，蒂娜，今天報上有刊登一則新加坡的工作機會，你有看到嗎？你不是一直在找海外的工作機會嗎？
女：我沒告訴你嗎？這一篇也出現在上週日的報紙上，所以我昨天就打電話去並已經跟他們透過電話面試了。
男：結果如何？你認為你會得到這份工作嗎？
女：嗯，他們似乎很有興趣。我認為那是份辛苦的工作，因此除非他們給我高薪，不然我可能不會過去。

50. What are the two speakers talking about? 兩人在討論什麼？
(A) A job opening 一個工作機會
(B) A trip to Asia 一趟亞洲之旅
(C) A high-paying job 一份高薪的工作
(D) A telephone interview 一個電話面試

◀ 解析 ▶
對話一開始，男子便詢問女子是否注意到一個新加坡的工作機會，女子也回應自己已經透過電話面試了，故選 (A)。

51. Where does the man find out about the job? 男子在何處發現此工作機會？
(A) In a magazine 雜誌上
(B) In a newspaper 報紙上
(C) On a radio program 廣播節目中
(D) At a job fair 就業博覽會上

◀ 解析 ▶
男子第一句提到，工作機會是刊登於今天的報紙上 (today's paper)，故本題選 (B)。

52. What does the woman think of the opportunity? 女子對此機會的看法為何？
(A) It's an easy job. 那是個輕鬆的工作。
(B) The salary is good enough. 薪水已經夠好了。
(C) She expects to get a good pay. 她期望會獲得高薪。
(D) She doesn't want to work abroad. 她不想在海外工作。

◀ 解析 ▶
1. 最後一句女子提到，她認為這會是一份辛苦的工作，所以高薪才能打動她，由此可知答案為 (C)。
2. abroad (adv.)：在國外

Questions 53 - 55 refer to the following conversation.
[UK] M / [US] W
M: Peggy, did you type this letter or did Grace do it?
W: I did, Mr. Connie. Why? Is there something wrong with it?
M: Take a look. This should be US$40,000, and you typed NT$400,000.

W: Let me take a close look. Oh, I'm sorry about that. I'm gonna modify it immediately.
M: And that is not all. You also misspelled the client's name. It should be "Blitz," not "Rlitz." See here?
W: I am really sorry, Mr. Connie. If you hadn't noticed these mistakes, we could have lost the order.
M: Listen, this case is really important to us. I want everything in all documents to be perfectly accurate.
W: Sure, I totally understand. I'm going to re-type the letter right away. And after that, I'll also check everything in the contract and other papers.

男：佩姬，這封信是你打的還是葛蕾絲打的？
女：是我，康尼先生，怎麼了嗎？有什麼問題嗎？
男：你看，這應該是美金四萬，你打成台幣四十萬了。
女：讓我仔細看看。啊，很不好意思，我馬上修改。
男：還不只這樣。你也將客戶名字拼錯了。應該是 "Blitz"，而不是 "Rlitz"。有看到這裡嗎？
女：非常抱歉，康尼先生。如果不是您發現了這些錯誤，我們可能就拿不到訂單了。
男：聽著，這個案子對我們來說非常重要。我要所有文件內容都很精確才行。
女：是的，我完全瞭解。我馬上將信重打一次！我還會將合約與其他文件內容都再檢查一次。

53. Who is most likely the man? 男子最有可能是誰？
(A) A manager 經理
(B) An engineer 工程師
(C) A secretary 秘書
(D) A janitor 清潔工

◀ 解析 ▶
男子首先向女子確認工作狀況，女子負責信件的打字工作，由此可知女子可能為秘書，而男子可能是女子的主管，故選 (A) 較為合理。

54. What is the woman's problem? 女子的問題為何？
(A) She lost a case. 她失去了一個案子。
(B) She made some typing mistakes. 她犯了些打字的錯誤。
(C) She is leaving the company soon. 她即將離開公司。
(D) She should have consulted with Grace first. 她應該先詢問葛蕾絲。

◀ 解析 ▶
對話第三句和第五句中，男子提到女子將金額和客戶名字打錯，故選 (B)。

55. What will the woman probably do next? 女子接下來可能會做什麼？
(A) Call Grace's cell phone 打葛蕾絲的手機
(B) Type the letter over again 將信件重打一次
(C) Apologize to Mr. Connie 跟康尼先生道歉
(D) Call the client and say sorry 打電話跟客戶道歉

◀ 解析 ▶
對話最後，女子表示會立即將信件重打一次，故選 (B)。

Questions 56 - 58 refer to the following conversation.

[CA] M / [AU] W

M: Central Station Lost and Found Department. This is Andy, how can I help you?

W: Oh, hello. I left my purse on the MRT this afternoon. I wondered if it has been turned in by other passengers. It's a small-sized, brown leather purse.

M: Well, we have quite a few that fit your description. Did it have your name on it?

W: No, but it does have my initials: Y. W. H. Please take a look.

男：中央車站失物招領中心，我是安迪，有什麼可以幫您的嗎？

女：是，你好。我今天下午將手提包忘在捷運上了。我想知道是否有其他乘客撿到並送過來呢？那是個小的咖啡色皮製包包。

男：我們有好幾個包包跟您的描述一樣。包包上面有您的名字嗎？

女：沒有，但倒是有我名字的首字母縮寫 Y. W. H.，麻煩幫我看一下。

56. Why does the woman make this call? 女子打此電話的目的為何？
   (A) To file a complaint 投訴抱怨
   (B) To place an order 訂購貨品
   (C) To apply for a job 申請工作
   (D) To retrieve her lost item 取回遺失物

◀ 解析 ▶
對話第二句，女子表示自己將手提包忘在捷運上，希望能透過失物招領中心找回來，故選 (D)。

57. What color is the woman's purse? 女子的皮包是什麼顏色？
   (A) Mauve 淡紫色
   (B) Scarlet 鮮紅色
   (C) Brown 咖啡色
   (D) Beige 米黃色

◀ 解析 ▶
承上題，女子進一步形容皮包的特徵，提及皮包為咖啡色的，故選 (C)。

58. What's written on the woman's purse? 女子的皮包上寫了什麼？
   (A) Her full name 她的全名
   (B) Her company's name 她的公司名稱
   (C) Her ID number 她的身分證號碼
   (D) Her initials 她的姓名首字母縮寫

◀ 解析 ▶
對話最後，女子提到皮包上有自己名字的首字母縮寫，故本題答案為 (D)。

Questions 59 - 61 refer to the following conversation.

[UK] M / [AU] W

M: Mrs. Smith, I am really impressed by all the work you've done on your house. How long have you been working on it?

W: Well, my husband and I first became interested in do-it-yourself a couple of years ago. And we had a rather tight budget and couldn't afford to pay to have it done. So we had to learn to do it ourselves.

M: Sounds really interesting. Did you have any practical skills?

W: Well, we went to a vocational school at night to learn cabinetmaking, and general carpentry too.

男：史密斯太太，我對你們將家裡裝潢得這麼好，感到印象深刻。你們花了多少時間呢？

女：我先生和我是在幾年前開始對 DIY 產生興趣。另外也因為我們的預算很有限，無法請人來做，所以我們就自己學著做了。

男：聽起來很有趣。你們有任何實務技術嗎？

女：其實我們是利用晚上去職業學校學做傢俱，還學了一般的木工技術。

afford (v.)：負擔得起　vocational school：職業學校　cabinetmaking (n.)：傢俱製造
carpentry (n.)：木工

59. What is the man impressed with? 男子對什麼印象深刻？
  (A) The woman's house 女子的房子
  (B) The woman's office 女子的辦公室
  (C) The woman's car 女子的車子
  (D) The woman's sales skills 女子的業務技巧

◀ 解析 ▶
對話第一句，男子即表示對女子的房屋裝潢精美，感到印象深刻，故本題答案為 (A)。

60. Why do Mr. and Mrs. Smith do the house by themselves? 史密斯夫婦為何要自己整修房子？
  (A) They have a deep pocket. 他們有很多錢可花。
  (B) They are short of funds. 他們的資金不足。
  (C) They are architects. 他們是建築師。
  (D) They want to make more money. 他們想多賺點錢。

◀ 解析 ▶
1. 女子提到整修房子的原因，一方面是對 DIY 有興趣，一方面也是因為資金有限，故本題答案為 (B)。
2. deep pocket：口袋很深，意指有很多錢　be short of...：缺乏⋯　architect (n.)：建築師

61. How does the woman learn cabinetmaking skills? 女子如何學到製作傢俱的手藝？
   (A) By attending a vocational school 在職業學校學的
   (B) By reading books 看書學的
   (C) By asking her husband 向她丈夫問來的
   (D) By listening to radio programs 聽廣播節目學來的

◀ 解析 ▶
對話最後，女子提到她和丈夫去職業學校學做傢俱，故本題答案為 (A)。

Questions 62 - 64 refer to the following conversation and table.

[CA] M / [US] W

M: I'm trying to organize a company party and I'm wondering if your hotel has a room we can use?

W: Certainly, sir. We do have several function rooms. Small-sized rooms can accommodate approximately 20 to 50 people, and large-sized rooms can accommodate more than 100 people.

M: I see. I just need a room for 40 attendees.

W: Sure, no problem. What date do you have in mind for the party then? Let me check here… it seems like the first available date I've got is August 15th.

M: August 15th… all right, that's a Friday. Yeah, that's not a problem.

W: Good, then please fill out this form and I'll do the rest for you, sir.

男：我想辦個公司派對，所以想知道你們飯店是否有我們可以使用的場地？

女：當然，先生。我們有不同功能的場地，小場地可容納大約二十到五十人，而大場地可容納超過一百人。

男：瞭解，我僅需要可容納四十人的場地。

女：好的，沒問題。您的派對想辦在哪一天？我看看…目前看起來最快有場地的時間是八月十五號。

男：八月十五日…好的，那天是週五。可以呀，那天沒問題。

女：很好，那麼請填寫這張表格，其他的我來幫您處理。

62. Who is most likely the woman? 女子最有可能是誰？
   (A) The man's sister 男子的妹妹
   (B) A hotel manager 飯店經理人
   (C) A program designer 程式設計師
   (D) A wedding attendee 婚禮賓客

◀ 解析 ▶
對話第二句，女子向男子介紹飯店場地，所以推斷女子應是飯店人員較為合理，故選 (B)。

63. What is the man planning to do? 男子打算要做什麼？
   (A) Reserve a table for two people 預訂兩人座的桌位
   (B) Reserve a conference room for a meeting 預訂開會用的會議室
   (C) Hold a birthday party for his father 幫他爸爸辦慶生會
   (D) Arrange a company event 安排公司活動

◀ 解析 ▶
對話第一句，男子提到要辦一場公司的活動，故本題答案為 (D)。

64. Look at the table. Which room will the man most likely reserve?
請看表格。男子最有可能預訂哪個場地？

Venue	Capacity	Availability
Sunshine Room	35-45 attendees	July, August
Ocean Room	100+ attendees	August, October
Moonlight Room	40 attendees	September
Polar Star Room	50-70 attendees	July, August, September

場地	大小	檔期
陽光廳	35-45 人	七月、八月
海洋廳	100 人以上	八月、十月
月光廳	40 人	九月
北極星廳	50-70 人	七月、八月、九月

(A) Moonlight Room 月光廳
(B) Sunshine Room 陽光廳
(C) Ocean Room 海洋廳
(D) Polar Star Room 北極星廳

◀ 解析 ▶
對話當中，男子說僅需可容納 40 人的場地，且活動將辦在八月，再對照表格內容，故選 (B)。

Questions 65 - 67 refer to the following conversation and list.
[UK] M / [AU] W
M: Hi, Liz. Have you got time to discuss our group project?
W: Certainly, John. I've got a few minutes before my next class. So we need to choose a topic based on the theme of environment protection, right?
M: That's right. Do you have any preferences?
W: Well, recently I read some good materials about conserving water resources, and I think it's a good theme. What do you think?
M: That's a good idea. I think we'd be better off looking online.
W: Sure, I've got a list of website references here. Let's take a look.

男：嗨，麗茲。你有空討論一下我們的團體專案嗎？
女：當然可以，約翰。下一堂課開始前我還有幾分鐘。所以我們要根據環境保護來規劃主題，對吧？
男：是的。你有什麼想做的主題嗎？
女：嗯，最近我讀到一些不錯的資料，跟節約用水有關，我認為那是個好主題。你覺得呢？

男：好主意呀。我想我們可以從網路上開始找資料。
女：沒問題，我有參考網站的列表。我們一起看看。

65. Who are most likely the speakers? 兩人的關係最有可能是什麼？
(A) Strangers 陌生人
(B) Group members 團隊成員
(C) Relatives 親戚
(D) Parents 父母

◀ 解析 ▶
對話第一句，男子說要討論團體專案，所以兩人應是團隊組員較為合理，故選 (B)。

66. What are the speakers discussing? 兩人在討論什麼？
(A) Fixing their laptop computers 修理手提電腦
(B) Discussing marketing strategies 討論行銷策略
(C) Planning a company party 規劃公司活動
(D) Choosing a theme for the project 選擇專案主題

◀ 解析 ▶
對話第二句，女子提到要規劃專案主題，所以本題答案應選 (D)。

67. Please look at the list. Which website would the speakers like to look at?
請看列表。兩人會想看哪一個網站？

1	http://www.waters-save-easy.com
2	http://www.wild-life.net
3	http://www.polar-world.com
4	http://www.eco-products.com

(A) 4
(B) 2
(C) 1
(D) 3

◀ 解析 ▶
對話當中，兩人決定要用「節省水資源」作為研究主題，所以應會參考相關網站，故選 (C)。

Questions 68 - 70 refer to the following conversation and table.

[CA] M / [AU] W

M: Hi, my name is Mark Ford. I'm calling about the small business conference next month.

W: Okay, sir. So would you like to buy a ticket for the conference?

M: Well, the thing is that I'm interested in buying a ticket for this event, but I'm not sure it will be useful for me.

W: All right, I see. This year we plan to focus on sales and marketing strategies specifically for small businesses as well as some successful case studies. There will be sales representatives and marketing specialists from around 300 small companies.

M: That should be interesting and valuable then. All right, I'd like to purchase six tickets for all my team members.

W: Great decision, sir. You can also get a discount then. Now please tell me your credit card number.

男：你好，我是馬克福特。我打來是要問有關下個月的小型企業研討會。

女：好的，先生。所以您想要購票參加嗎？

男：是這樣的，我有興趣參加，但不確定這活動對我實用。

女：我明白了。今年的研討會，我們計畫以小型企業為重點對象，聚焦在業務與行銷策略，以及一些成功案例。大概會有三百個小型企業的業務代表與行銷專員，參加本次活動。

男：這樣應該會滿有趣，也很有用。好吧，我想幫我們部門所有人買票，要六張。

女：很好的決定，先生。您還可以獲得折扣優惠喔。現在請您提供一下信用卡號碼。

68. Why is the man calling? 男子打電話的目的為何？

(A) To invite the woman to a meeting 邀請女子參加會議

(B) To arrange an international conference 安排國際研討會

(C) To enquire more about a business event 詢問更多關於商業活動的資訊

(D) To reserve hotel accommodations 預訂飯店房間

◀ 解析 ▶

對話第一句，男子主動表明打電話的目的，是要詢問有關研討會的資訊，故選 (C)。

69. According to the woman, what's the main theme for the conference?

根據女子所說，研討會的主題為何？

(A) Sales and marketing 業務與行銷

(B) Engineering 工程學

(C) Human resources 人力資源

(D) Accounting 會計學

◀ 解析 ▶

對話當中，女子提到今年研討會將以業務和行銷策略為主，故選 (A)。

70. Please look at the table. What discount rate will the man probably receive?
請看表格。男子可能會獲得什麼折扣？

Number of Tickets	Discount Rate
1 ticket	n/a
2-3 tickets	5% off
4-8 tickets	10% off
9+ tickets	15% off

票數	折扣
1 張	無
2-3 張	95 折
4-8 張	9 折
9 張以上	85 折

(A) None 無折扣
(B) 10% off 9 折
(C) 5% off 95 折
(D) 15% off 85 折

◀ 解析 ▶
對話最後，男子說要購買六張票，再看到表格內容，故本題答案應選 (B)。

Part IV. ▶ Talks

Questions 71 - 73 refer to the following talk.

[CA] M

Attention please, everyone. Before we start our city tour, I want to give you a short presentation – basically an introduction to one of our great buildings, the Golden Museum in local Springfield. My talk will last about five minutes. I will divide the talk into three parts and I begin with an overview of the background. Secondly, I'll talk about the architecture of the building and the architect, Terrance Legg. Finally, I want to describe the impact of the museum on our local city. I am going to talk for about five minutes and later there will be time for you to ask questions.

各位請注意，在我們的城市導覽開始之前，我將做一個簡短的報告，基本上會介紹我們偉大的建築物之一，也就是春田本地的「黃金博物館」。我的報告大約是五分鐘，將分成三個部分。首先我會從概略的背景說起。第二，我將說明建築物的結構與介紹設計師泰倫斯雷格。最後，我要說明博物館對於本地城市的影響。我的五分鐘講解結束之後，將留時間讓各位發問。

architecture (n.)：建築結構

71. Who is most likely the man? 男子最有可能是誰？
(A) A tour guide 導遊
(B) A professor 教授
(C) An administrator 經理
(D) An architect 建築師

◀ 解析 ▶
男子的工作包括城市導覽，以及博物館的介紹講解，可推斷他應該是一名導遊，故選 (A)。

72. What's the speaker's main subject? 說話者所講的主題為何？
(A) A historic city 古蹟城市
(B) A great museum building 偉大的博物館建築
(C) A famous skyscraper 有名的摩天大樓
(D) A beautiful garden 美麗的花園

◀ 解析 ▶
男子的講解內容，主要是對當地「黃金博物館」的介紹，故本題答案為 (B)。

73. What will happen after the speaker's five-minute presentation? 說話者的五分鐘簡報後會發生什麼事？
(A) Another two-hour speech 另一場二小時的演講
(B) A brief introduction to the city 關於城市的簡短介紹
(C) A question and answer session 問答時間
(D) An interview with Terrance Legg 和泰倫斯雷格的訪談

◀ 解析 ▶
最後一句提到，在簡報結束之後，會留時間讓在場的聽眾發問，故選 (C)。

Questions 74 - 76 refer to the following talk.

[AU] W

All right, so let's start our monthly company meeting. First of all, as you all know, we introduced a new sales system last month, but it has never worked well. So far we find that the main problem concerns the information flow, so we've already made some changes to the system and are in the middle of upgrading the software. Next, we plan to recruit and train more sales staff. We also want to introduce more staff training. In the coming months, we will plan a lot more training seminars and workshops.

好，讓我們開始每月例會。首先，如你們所知，我們上個月引進了新的業務系統，但是尚未順利運作。目前我們所看到最主要的問題在於資訊流程，所以我們已經做了一些系統的變更，並且正在進行軟體更新。接下來，我們計畫聘請並訓練更多業務人員。我們也希望帶來更多的員工訓練課程。在往後幾個月，我們將規劃更多的職訓研討會與專題討論。

74. Where does the announcement probably take place? 這段話可能出現在何處？
(A) At an airport 在機場
(B) In a meeting room 在會議室
(C) At a university 在大學
(D) In a restaurant 在餐廳

◀ 解析 ▶
女子第一句即提到，此為公司的例行月會，可推斷開會地點應為會議室，故選 (B)。

75. What's the problem with the newly installed system? 新安裝的系統有何問題？
(A) Hardware 硬體
(B) License 授權
(C) Information flow 資訊流程
(D) Installation 安裝

◀ 解析 ▶
1. 女子提到新業務系統至今尚未順利運作，問題是出在資訊流程，故選 (C)。
2. install (v.)：安裝

76. What will happen in the coming months? 接下來幾個月會發生什麼事？
(A) More training sessions will be arranged. 安排更多訓練課程。
(B) More staff will be laid off. 解雇更多員工。
(C) More meetings will be held. 召開更多會議。
(D) More new systems will be installed. 安裝更多新系統。

◀ 解析 ▶
1. 最後一句提到，接下來幾個月將會有更多職訓研討會與專題討論，故選 (A)。
2. lay off：解雇

Questions 77 - 79 refer to the following talk.

[UK] M

All right, everyone, thank you for attending our weekly sales meeting. As you can see from the chart, the number of customer complaints decreased significantly last month. It's mainly due to our increased focus on after-sales service. So we should be happy that the investment in sales rep training has resulted in more satisfied customers. However, sales figures are not as good as we originally anticipated. We expect sales results will improve next month. Oh, and our new focus on the Asian market will lead to a lot of new business next quarter, so we should go forward with confidence. Thank you.

好的，各位，謝謝你們參加每週的業務會議。你們可以從圖表上看到，上個月客訴次數減少了許多。主要是因為我們更加重視售後服務。我們在業務代表訓練上所做的投資，最終的成果是讓更多客戶滿意，對此我們應該感到高興。然而，銷售數字並不如原先預期。我們期待下個月業績可以上升。還有，我們在亞洲市場的新佈局，將帶領我們在下一季有更多新的商機，所以我們應該更有信心的往前衝。謝謝各位！

77. Who is the speaker probably talking to? 說話者可能在跟誰講話？
   (A) Students 學生
   (B) Sales representatives 業務代表
   (C) Customers 客戶
   (D) Investors 投資人

◀ 解析 ▶
男子一開始便提到，此為業務會議，內容也與業務人員的工作表現相關，可推測與會者為公司的業務代表，故選 (B)。

78. What does the speaker mention about customer complaints? 說話者提到客訴的狀況如何？
   (A) Its rate decreases. 其比例下滑。
   (B) Its rate increases. 其比例上揚。
   (C) Its rate remains unchanged. 其比例維持不變。
   (D) Its rate will fall. 其比例將會下降。

◀ 解析 ▶
第二句提到，客訴的次數減少了許多，故本題答案為 (A)。

79. What will happen next quarter? 下一季會發生什麼事？
   (A) Sales figures will not be good. 業績數字將不盡理想。
   (B) More sales training courses will be arranged. 將安排更多訓練課程。
   (C) New businesses will be expanded in Asia. 亞洲的新商機將蓬勃發展。
   (D) Investors will have more confidence. 投資人將更具信心。

◀ 解析 ▶
男子最後提到，下一季公司在亞洲的佈局，將帶來更多新的商機，故本題答案為 (C)。

Questions 80 - 82 refer to the following talk.
[US] W
Hello and welcome everyone. Thank you for attending today's new employee orientation. My name is Mary Fidelity and I work in the HR department as an HR specialist. I am in charge of external communication, so please ask me if you have any questions. All right, so as you can see from the agenda, we have a tour of the production area with our production manager, Mr. Kim Crabtree, from 10:30 a.m. to 12 noon, and then lunch at 12. After lunch, we have a meeting with the marketing director. All right, does anyone have any questions before the tour? No? Good, now I am going to hand you over to Kim.

哈囉，歡迎各位。謝謝你們參加今天的新進員工訓練。我的名字是瑪莉費德樂蒂，我在人資部門擔任人資專員。我負責對外的溝通，所以如果你有任何問題都可以問我。好，各位可以從流程表中看到，我們有一個與生產部經理金瑰柏翠先生，一起參觀生產區域的行程，時間是從早上 10 點半到中午 12 點。接著在中午 12 點用餐。午餐之後，我們有一個與行銷部主管的會議。好，在我們的行程開始前有任何問題嗎？沒有？好，現在我將時間交給金。

80. Who is Mary Fidelity? 瑪莉費德樂蒂是誰？
  (A) An HR director 人資部主管
  (B) A new employee 新進員工
  (C) A production manager 生產部經理
  (D) An HR specialist 人資專員

◀ 解析 ▶
女子一開頭的自我介紹當中，提到自己是人資部門的人資專員，故本題答案為 (D)。

81. What will the people do after lunch? 大家在午餐之後會做什麼？
  (A) Have a meeting with clients 與客戶開會
  (B) Have a meeting with the marketing director 與行銷部主管開會
  (C) Have a meeting with the production manager 與生產部經理開會
  (D) Have a meeting with the HR specialist 與人資專員開會

◀ 解析 ▶
女子提到在中午用餐之後，將有一個與行銷主管的會議，故本題答案為 (B)。

82. Who will most likely speak next? 接下來最有可能是誰發言？
  (A) The production manager 生產部經理
  (B) The VP of engineering 工程部副理
  (C) The marketing director 行銷部主管
  (D) The chief financial officer 財務長

◀ 解析 ▶
最後一句，女子說要把時間交給金，也就是生產部經理金瑰柏翠先生，故選 (A)。

Questions 83 - 85 refer to the following talk.

[CA] M

Welcome to Taipei everyone. I am your tour guide, Paul Chang. I have to say that Taipei is one of Asia's most exciting cities. Taipei is this island's center of political, commercial and cultural activities. It is famous for its bustling business centers, energetic nightlife and colorful marketplaces. For example, the well-known Taipei 101 building is one of the tallest buildings in the world and the shopping center inside it is equally fantastic! In addition, night markets are my favorite places for traditional Taiwanese food. The combination of both modern and traditional sides makes Taipei a really attractive city. Now, let's all get on the bus please.

歡迎各位來到台北，我是您的導遊張保羅。我必須說，台北是亞洲最刺激的城市之一。台北是台灣的政治、商業與文化活動的中心。它最著名的就是繁榮的商業中心，充滿活力的夜生活和多采多姿的市場。例如：著名的台北 101 大樓是世界上最高的建築物之一，其中的購物中心也是同樣的出色。另外，夜市也是我最愛享用台灣傳統美食的地方。結合現代與傳統，讓台北成為非常吸引人的城市。現在，請讓我們一起坐上巴士吧！

bustling (adj.)：活躍的　attractive (adj.)：有吸引力的

83. Where does the speaker probably work? 說話者可能在哪裡上班？
(A) In a travel agency 在旅行社
(B) In the Taipei 101 building 在台北 101 大樓
(C) In a shopping center 在購物中心
(D) In a night market 在夜市

◀ 解析 ▶
男子一開頭即提到，他是一位導遊，可推斷其工作地點為旅行社，故本題選 (A)。

84. What is special about the Taipei 101 building? 台北 101 大樓有何特殊之處？
(A) It is surrounded by night markets. 它的周邊都是夜市。
(B) It is one of the tallest buildings in the world. 它是世界最高的大樓之一。
(C) It has the largest shopping center inside. 它裡面有最大的購物中心。
(D) It is one of the oldest buildings in the world. 它是世界最古老的建築物之一。

◀ 解析 ▶
男子介紹台北的特點，並舉台北 101 大樓為例，它是世界上最高的大樓之一，故選 (B)。

85. What will travelers probably do next? 旅客接下來可能會做什麼？
(A) Go back to the hotel 回飯店
(B) Board a plane 搭飛機
(C) Shop in Taipei 101 在台北 101 購物
(D) Board a bus 坐巴士

◀ 解析 ▶
最後一句，男子要大家都坐上巴士，前往目的地，故本題答案為 (D)。

Questions 86 - 88 refer to the following talk.

[US] W

All right, welcome back to our radio program. I am Joan Back. Well, for the hundred thousand or more people in New York who buy every issue, *New York Walker* is an invaluable guide to what's going on in the city. In its lists, people can find everything from films, plays, concerts to exhibitions, sports, shows, dance, and special events. Now, I am talking to our special guest for today, Ms. Andrea Parker, the woman who started the magazine back in 1980. Ms. Parker, so tell us, what gave you the idea? And did you have any publishing experience before that?

好，歡迎回到我們的節目，我是瓊安貝克。在紐約，有十萬人甚至更多人，固定購買每期的 *New York Walker* 雜誌，它是一本城市生活的珍貴指南。從雜誌的列表當中，讀者可以找到從電影、戲劇、音樂會到展覽、運動賽事、表演、舞蹈與特殊活動等訊息。現在，我將與我們今天的特別來賓安潔雅派克女士談談，她在 1980 年首度創辦這本雜誌。派克女士，請告訴我們，是什麼讓您有這樣的點子？在此之前，您是否有任何與出版相關的經驗呢？

invaluable (adj.)：無價的　exhibition (n.)：展覽　publishing (n.)：出版業

86. Who is most likely the speaker? 説話者最有可能是誰？
   (A) A magazine publisher 雜誌出版商
   (B) A radio program host 廣播節目主持人
   (C) A city tour guide 都市旅行導遊
   (D) A radio program guest 廣播節目來賓

◀ 解析 ▶
從第一句的 welcome back to our radio program，可以推測女子為廣播節目主持人，故選 (B)。

87. When was the magazine first published? 雜誌最初是在何時出版的？
   (A) In 1980　在 1980 年
   (B) In 1897　在 1897 年
   (C) In 1998　在 1998 年
   (D) In 1889　在 1889 年

◀ 解析 ▶
在介紹雜誌創辦人時，提到她在 1980 年創辦此雜誌，故本題答案為 (A)。

88. What will probably happen next? 接下來可能會發生什麼事？
   (A) A tour guide will talk. 導遊會説些話。
   (B) Joan Back will answer questions. 瓊安貝克會回答問題。
   (C) Ms. Andrea Parker will speak. 安潔雅派克女士會講話。
   (D) A special guest will sing. 特別來賓會唱歌。

◀ 解析 ▶
簡短的介紹後，主持人問了安潔雅派克女士幾個問題，可知接下來安潔雅派克女士會開始回答問題，故選 (C) 較為合理。

Questions 89 - 91 refer to the following talk.
[UK] M
Thank you for tuning in. Here is the 4 p.m. weather forecast. We have a warm and windy night on the way. Temperatures will stay in the 20s the entire night, so you might want to leave your windows open and turn off the air conditioner. While the mild air is welcome, the wind is going to become a problem overnight. Winds will increase and could be strong enough to cause some minor damage and power outages. I will be updating the forecast every hour on the hour, so stay tuned.

謝謝收聽本節目。現在為您播報下午四點的氣象報告。今晚的天氣會是溫暖且有風。整晚的氣溫大約維持在 20 度左右，您可能會想把窗戶打開，不用開冷氣。雖說有點溫和的微風是不錯，但今晚過後強風會是個問題。風力會增強且強度大到可能造成些微損害或停電。我在每個整點會為您更新一次氣象報告，請持續收聽。

tune in：收看或收聽某節目　entire (adj.)：全部的、整個的　outage (n.)：（水、電等）中斷供應

89. What will the weather be like at night? 晚上天氣會如何？
   (A) Warm and windy 溫暖且有風
   (B) Hot and windy 炎熱且有風
   (C) Warm and humid 溫暖且潮濕
   (D) Stuffy and rainy 悶熱且下雨

◀ 解析 ▶
1. 氣象報告一開始即提到，整晚會是溫暖且有風的天氣，故選 (A)。
2. stuffy (adj.)：悶熱的

90. What might be the problem overnight? 晚上過後可能會有什麼狀況？
   (A) High temperature 高溫
   (B) Mild wind 微風
   (C) Strong wind 強風
   (D) Heavy rain 大雨

◀ 解析 ▶
氣象預報中提到，今晚過後最大的問題將是逐漸增強的風勢，故本題答案為 (C)。

91. What time will the next forecast update be? 下一次氣象預測更新會是幾點？
   (A) 4 p.m. 下午四點
   (B) 5 p.m. 下午五點
   (C) 5 a.m. 早上五點
   (D) 3 p.m. 下午三點

◀ 解析 ▶
最後男子提到，自己將會在每個整點播報最新氣象預報，而現在是下午四點，可推測下次播報時間為下午五點，故選 (B)。

Questions 92 - 94 refer to the following talk.

[CA] M

Welcome aboard Pacific Air flight 879 from Tokyo to Seattle. This is Captain Andrew Ross. Our flight time is approximately eight hours and twenty minutes, and we will be arriving at the Tacoma International Airport at 10 a.m. local time. The weather in Seattle is rainy and the temperature is around 20 degrees Celsius. Our flight attendants will be serving beverages shortly and we wish you a pleasant flight with us. Now please fasten your seat belts and prepare for take-off. Thank you once again for flying with Pacific Air.

歡迎搭乘太平洋航空 879 號班機自東京飛往西雅圖。我是機長安德魯羅斯。本班機飛行時間大約是八小時二十分鐘，我們會在當地時間上午十點抵達塔科馬國際機場。西雅圖的天氣是下雨，溫度大約是攝氏二十度。空服員馬上會為您提供飲料服務，希望您有個美好的旅程。現在，請繫好您的安全帶並準備起飛。再度謝謝您搭乘太平洋航空的班機。

flight attendant：空服員　beverage (n.)：飲料　fasten (v.)：繫緊

92. Where does the announcement probably take place? 此廣播可能出現在何處？
   (A) In a conference room 在會議室
   (B) On an airplane 在飛機上
   (C) On a ship 在船上
   (D) In an office 在辦公室

◀ 解析 ▶
廣播一開頭即說明班機資訊，且後續提到飛行時間等細節，故本題選 (B)。

93. What time will passengers arrive in Seattle? 旅客幾點會到達西雅圖？
   (A) 10 a.m. 早上十點
   (B) 10 p.m. 晚上十點
   (C) 8 a.m. 早上八點
   (D) 2 p.m. 下午兩點

◀ 解析 ▶
廣播中提到，班機將會在當地時間上午十點抵達，故本題選 (A)。

94. What will flight attendants do next? 空服員接下來會做什麼？
   (A) Ask passengers to fill out forms 請旅客填表格
   (B) Make another announcement 做另一次廣播
   (C) Serve beverages 提供飲料服務
   (D) Fasten seat belts 繫好安全帶

◀ 解析 ▶
依據廣播內容，空服員接下來將會提供飲料服務，故本題答案為 (C)。

Questions 95 - 97 refer to the following talk and chart.

[UK] W

Your attention please. All passengers traveling to Wellington, please note that due to the construction of a new track, the train will stop at platform 2A instead of 3B. The train will leave in around fifteen minutes. Please proceed to the platform 2A immediately. Once again, the train to Wellington will stop at platform 2A. If you need any assistance, please contact a customer service representative in the information booth, or you may use courtesy phones on the platform to call an assistant. Sorry for the inconvenience and we wish you a nice trip.

請注意。所有要前往威靈頓的乘客請留意，因為新軌道的施工，火車將不會停靠 3B 月台，而會改停在 2A 月台。這班火車將大約在十五分鐘後出發，請您馬上前往 2A 月台搭車。再次注意，前往威靈頓的火車將停靠在 2A 月台。若您需要任何協助，請找詢問處的客服人員，或使用月台上的免費服務電話尋求協助。很抱歉對您造成困擾，希望您有個愉快的旅程。

construction (n.)：建築工程　information booth：詢問台　courtesy (adj.)：免費的

95. Who is probably the audience of this announcement? 此廣播的聽眾可能是誰？
(A) Overseas travelers 海外旅客
(B) Wellington residents 威靈頓居民
(C) Train passengers 火車乘客
(D) Customer service representatives 客服人員

◀ 解析 ▶
廣播內容提及火車時間、停靠月台等資訊，可知此廣播是在火車站內，針對乘客而做的廣播，故選 (C)。

96. Where will the train stop? 火車會停靠在何處？
(A) It won't stop. 火車不會停站
(B) At platform 2A 在 2A 月台
(C) In the information booth 在詢問處
(D) At platform 3B 在 3B 月台

◀ 解析 ▶
廣播一開頭，即為列車更改停靠月台的訊息，女子提到列車將改停 2A 月台，故選 (B)。

97. Please look at the chart. What number should a passenger dial if he lost his luggage?
請看表格。若有乘客遺失行李，應該打哪個號碼尋求協助？

Questions regarding:	Dial extension:
Train Schedules	779
Lost and Found	473
Tickets	398
Wheel Chair Assistance	273

問題類別：	撥打分機：
火車時刻表	779
失物招領	473
票務問題	398
輪椅協助	273

(A) 473
(B) 273
(C) 398
(D) 779

◀ 解析 ▶
對照表格內容，乘客遺失行李應是與 "Lost and Found"（失物招領）較為相關，故選 (A)。

Questions 98 - 100 refer to the following talk and table.
[US] W
This is a message for Mr. Gary Hill please. Hello Mr. Hill, this is Lily Bennett calling from Dr. Dean's office and this is regarding your dental appointment. We are afraid that we might need to reschedule your appointment from this Friday at 4 p.m. to early next week. Since Dr. Dean is flying to Boston for a conference this Thursday and won't be back until next Monday, is it okay if you come next Tuesday in the morning, say, at 10? If it's also a good time for you, please return my call tomorrow to confirm. Our number is (123) 472-3739, and this is Lily Bennett. Thank you.

這是給蓋瑞西爾先生的留言。西爾先生您好，我是莉莉班尼特，從迪恩醫生辦公室打來的。我是想確認關於您的牙科約診。我們恐怕得要更改您的約診日期，從本週五下午四點改到下週初。因為迪恩醫生要飛去波士頓參加會議，本週四出發，要到下週一才會回來。因此您下週二早上大約 10 點過來，可以嗎？若這個時間您可以，請明天回電給我確認。我們的號碼是 (123) 472-3739，我是莉莉班尼特。謝謝您！

dental (adj.)：牙齒的

98. Who is most likely the caller? 打電話者最有可能是誰？
(A) Dr. Dean's sister 迪恩醫生的妹妹
(B) Dr. Dean's assistant 迪恩醫生的助理
(C) Dr. Dean himself 迪恩醫生自己
(D) Dr. Dean's patient 迪恩醫生的病人

◀ 解析 ▶
打電話來的女子首先自我介紹，是從迪恩醫生辦公室打來，並且要確認約診日期，由此推斷她可能是迪恩醫生的助理，故選 (B)。

99. Please look at the table. On what date will Gary Hill most likely meet Dr. Dean?
請看表格。蓋瑞西爾最有可能在哪一天去見迪恩醫生？

Date	Time	Dr. Dean's Availability
10/4, Thursday	3 p.m.	Meeting at Boston
10/5, Friday	Whole Day	Meeting at Boston
10/8, Monday	5 p.m.	Jerry Smith
10/9, Tuesday	10 a.m.	Available

日期	時間	迪恩醫生的行程安排
10/4（週四）	下午 3 點	在波士頓開會
10/5（週五）	整日	在波士頓開會
10/8（週一）	下午 5 點	和傑瑞史密斯有約
10/9（週二）	上午 10 點	有空

(A) 10/4
(B) 10/8
(C) 10/5
(D) 10/9

◀ 解析 ▶
女子在留言中提到，想幫蓋瑞西爾先生將預約時間改到下週二的早上 10 點，再對照表格內容，故本題答案應選 (D)。

100. What is Mr. Gary Hill asked to do next? 蓋瑞西爾先生被要求接下來要做什麼？
(A) Go to see Dr. Dean tomorrow 明天給迪恩醫生看診
(B) Return Lily's call tomorrow 明天回電給莉莉
(C) Call Dr. Dean next Tuesday 下週二打電話給迪恩醫生
(D) Email Lily a new schedule 將新的時程表寄電子郵件給莉莉

◀ 解析 ▶
留言最後，莉莉請蓋瑞西爾先生明天回電，跟她確認時間是否可以，故本題答案為 (B)。

READING TEST

Part V									
101	102	103	104	105	106	107	108	109	110
B	A	C	A	B	B	B	C	D	B
111	112	113	114	115	116	117	118	119	120
C	D	B	A	A	C	B	D	A	B
121	122	123	124	125	126	127	128	129	130
A	B	B	D	B	B	B	B	C	B
Part VI									
131	132	133	134	135	136	137	138	139	140
A	C	D	B	A	D	B	A	C	A
141	142	143	144	145	146				
C	D	D	A	C	C				
Part VII									
147	148	149	150	151	152	153	154	155	156
C	A	A	A	D	C	C	A	B	C
157	158	159	160	161	162	163	164	165	166
D	B	A	B	A	A	B	C	A	C
167	168	169	170	171	172	173	174	175	176
D	C	D	B	A	B	D	C	A	B
177	178	179	180	181	182	183	184	185	186
A	D	A	A	B	B	D	A	A	B
187	188	189	190	191	192	193	194	195	196
C	A	D	B	C	A	B	B	A	C
197	198	199	200						
A	B	D	A						

Part V. ► Incomplete Sentences

101. I am pleased to announce that the last quarter's sales figures ___________ a record for us.
我很高興宣佈我們上一季的業績數字創下記錄了。
(A) configure 設定、安裝
(B) constitute 構成、組成
(C) combine 綜合、結合
(D) combat 戰鬥、反抗

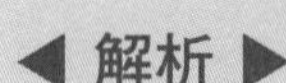

本題考的是相似單字的意思，依照句意，應選 (B) constitute 最合理。

102. A third of the employees __________ passed the qualification exam.

三分之一的員工都通過資格測試了。

(A) have

(B) has

(C) had

(D) had been

◀ 解析 ▶

依照空格後的動詞 passed 與句意來看，此句是用現在完成式 (have / has + p.p.)。句子主詞為 A third of the employees，故本題選 (A)。

103. He works so hard __________ his doctor often tells him to take it easy.

他工作如此勤奮，連醫生都常常要他放輕鬆。

(A) but 但是

(B) then 然後

(C) that 導致

(D) because 因為

◀ 解析 ▶

本題重點在於是否熟悉 so...that...（如此…以致於…）的用法，故本題選 (C)。

104. ITNet is looking for professionals with strategic vision, __________ proven capacity to generate results.

資科網公司在找的專業人才，要具備策略願景和足以達成目標的實力。

(A) and 和

(B) or 或

(C) also 也

(D) but 但

◀ 解析 ▶

1. 本題是列舉專業人才應有的特質，兩種特質之間用 and 互相連結即可，故選 (A)。
2. proven (adj.)：經過證明的　capacity (n.)：能力　generate (v.)：產生、造成

105. Where are you considering __________ for vacation? 你考慮要去哪裡渡假？

(A) travels

(B) traveling

(C) traveler

(D) to travel

◀ 解析 ▶

本題的空格前為 consider，後面可接名詞或動名詞，所以 (A)、(D) 不符，而 (C) traveler 表「旅客」之意，不符合本題句意，故本題答案應選 (B)。

© Caves Educational Training Co., Ltd.

106. I decided to speak __________ the manager after the presentation. 我決定在簡報後跟經理談談。

(A) at 在

(B) to 向

(C) about 關於…

(D) together 一起

◀ 解析 ▶

本題考的是 speak 的用法，「跟某人談談」可用 speak to sb.，故本題答案為 (B)。

107. Our company offers a competitive __________ and benefits package to our employees.
我們公司提供員工優渥的薪資和福利制度。

(A) money 金錢

(B) remuneration 薪資

(C) loan 貸款

(D) penalty 罰款

◀ 解析 ▶

本題選項皆是與金錢相關的單字，依句意來看，本題答案為 (B) 最合理。

108. People like eating sweet food, __________ chocolate, cake, and other sugar-based items.
人們都喜歡吃甜食，像是巧克力、蛋糕和其他含糖的食品。

(A) such like

(B) such that

(C) such as

(D) such

◀ 解析 ▶

本題考的是「像是…」的用法，空格中可以填入 like 或是 such as，故本題選 (C)。

109. He is such a __________ member of the staff that no one in the company would contradict him.
他是一位如此受人敬重的團隊成員，公司內沒有人會跟他唱反調。

(A) respective 各自的

(B) respecting 關於…

(C) respect 尊敬

(D) respected 受尊敬的

◀ 解析 ▶

1. 本題考的是相似單字的意思區別，依照前後句意，本題正確答案為 (D)。
2. contradict (v.)：反駁

110. We are not attending the conference, __________ a few people from the sales department are.

我們不會去參加會議，但一些業務部的人會去參加。

(A) and 和

(B) but 但是

(C) so 因此

(D) due to 因為

◀ 解析 ▶

前半句是 we are not...，後半句則是 a few people are，可見是意思相對的兩個句子，連接詞應有「但是、不過」的意思，故選連接詞 (B) but 最合理。

111. We use __________ huge quantities of pens each month but also oceans of ink.

我們每個月不僅使用大量的筆，還有大量的墨水。

(A) only 僅僅

(B) only if 只要

(C) not only 不僅

(D) only just 剛剛

◀ 解析 ▶

本題考的是 not only... but also...（不僅…而且…）的用法，從句子後半段的 but also，可以推測出空格裡缺少的是 not only，故選 (C)。

112. You should take a rest. You've kept __________ for 12 hours.

你應該休息一下了。你已經連續工作 12 小時了。

(A) to work

(B) worked

(C) work

(D) working

◀ 解析 ▶

本題考的是 keep + Ving（持續進行某事）的用法，故答案為 (D)。

113. A good sales plan should __________ an executive summary, a customer analysis, and a market forecast.

一份好的銷售計畫應包括執行摘要、客戶分析和市場預測。

(A) possess 擁有

(B) contain 包含

(C) deliver 傳遞

(D) exclude 排除

◀ 解析 ▶

本題依照句意，空格中的單字應有「包含、包括」之意，故答案為 (B)。

114. We have six team members: one is an assistant, another is a marketing specialist, and __________ are all sales reps.
我們的團隊有六個成員：一個是助理，另一位是行銷專員，其他的都是業務員。
(A) the others
(B) the other
(C) others
(D) all the other

◀ 解析 ▶
本題考的是三者以上的代名詞用法。當對象有三個以上且限定指稱範圍時，我們可以用 one..., another..., and the others...（其中一個…，另一個…，剩下其他的…），故本題選 (A)。

115. __________ candidates should have excellent leadership skills, and can lead teams from different culture backgrounds.
對此工作有興趣的人應該要有優秀的領導能力，並能領導來自不同文化背景的成員。
(A) Interested 有興趣的
(B) Interests 興趣
(C) Interesting 有趣的
(D) Interestingly 有趣地

◀ 解析 ▶
由於空格後為名詞，可推斷空格內應填入形容詞，故不選 (B)、(D)。依照句意，此形容詞意思應該為「對此工作感興趣的」，故選 (A)。

116. When the CEO entered the meeting room, everybody __________ talking.
當執行長進入會議室時，每個人都安靜了下來。
(A) will stop 將停止
(B) ended 終止
(C) stopped 停止（stop + Ving 表「停止做…」）
(D) stopped to 停止（stop to + V 表「停下來去做…」）

◀ 解析 ▶
根據句子時態一致性的原則，故不選未來式 (A)。依照句意，應為「停止原本在講話的狀態」，故選 (C)。

117. We plan __________ a technical seminar next month. 我們計畫要在下個月安排一場技術研討會。
(A) to arranging
(B) to arrange
(C) arrangement
(D) to have arranged

◀ 解析 ▶
本題考的是 plan to + V（計畫做某事）的用法，故本題選 (B)。

118. Our goal is to help our clients build a useful system __________ fits each client's unique situation.
我們的目標是協助客戶建構實用的系統，可以符合每個客戶的獨特需求。
(A) when
(B) who
(C) where
(D) that

◀ 解析 ▶
本題考的是關係代名詞的用法，空格前的先行詞為 a useful system，可以用關係代名詞 which 或 that，故本題選 (D)。

119. Hawaii has many interesting tropical trees, flowers, __________ beautiful beaches.
夏威夷有很多有趣的熱帶樹木、花和美麗的沙灘。
(A) and 和
(B) also 也
(C) additional 額外的
(D) or 或

◀ 解析 ▶
本題列舉夏威夷的景物，三者以上時，彼此用逗號分開，最後一個名詞前則加上 and，故本題選 (A)。

120. The best and most direct way for companies to get the right person for the job is to get a __________ from a trusted friend.
對公司來說，最好也最直接找到合適員工的方式，就是靠可信賴的朋友推薦。
(A) reputation 名譽
(B) recommendation 推薦
(C) resignation 辭職
(D) rotation 輪替

◀ 解析 ▶
本題考的是相似單字的意思區別，依照前後句意來看，尋找合適員工的方式可以透過「推薦」，故本題答案應選 (B)。

121. The weather wasn't good yesterday but it's __________ today.
昨天的天氣不好，但今天天氣比較好。
(A) better 較好的
(B) best 最好的
(C) goods 商品
(D) worst 最壞的

◀ 解析 ▶
本題重點在於比較級的概念。今天天氣比昨天好，應該用 good 的比較級 better，故選 (A)。

122. Business leaders around the world __________ Mason Business School their preferred choice for advanced education.
全世界的商務領導人士都選擇梅森商業學校做為他們的進修首選。
(A) have make
(B) have made
(C) had making
(D) has been making

◀ 解析 ▶
本題考的是完成式的用法。從句意推斷，空格內應該用現在完成式 have / has + p.p.，又主詞為 business leaders，故選 (B) have made。

123. The CEO and his secretary __________ going to attend that conference.
執行長和他的秘書都會參加會議。
(A) is
(B) are
(C) will
(D) was

◀ 解析 ▶
本題考的是未來式 be going to + V 的用法。句子主詞為複數 the CEO and his secretary，故本題選 (B)。

124. Of the two people, one is from China and __________ is from Japan.
兩個人當中，一個來自中國，另一個來自日本。
(A) the others 其他的（人事物）
(B) another 另一（用於指稱對象為三者以上時）
(C) others 其他的（人事物）
(D) the other 另一

◀ 解析 ▶
本題考的是代名詞的用法。當指稱對象為受到限定的兩者時，我們可以用 one..., and the other...（一個…，另一個…），故本題選 (D)。

125. Our Marketing and Sales departments are working together on a ___________ plan for the new software product.
我們的行銷和業務部門，正在共同合作一個新軟體產品的促銷計畫。
(A) procedural 程序上的
(B) promotional 促銷的
(C) primary 基礎的
(D) protective 保護的

◀ 解析 ▶
本題考的是相似單字的意思區別，依照前後句意來看，新產品所需要的是促銷的計畫，故本題選 (B)。

126. The city ___________ the conference will be held is beautiful. 舉行會議的都市是一個很漂亮的地方。
(A) who
(B) in which
(C) what
(D) why

◀ 解析 ▶
本題考的是關係代名詞的用法，先行詞 the city 是一個地點，關係代名詞可以用 where 或是 in which，故本題選 (B)。

127. Anyone can learn how to operate this machine ___________ he wants to.
只要有心，任何人都可以學會如何操作這台機器。
(A) since 因為
(B) if 如果
(C) although 雖然
(D) but 但是

◀ 解析 ▶
本題重點在於不同連接詞所代表的意義。依照句意來看，空格內應該是「假如、只要」，故本題選 (B) if。

128. A smile on your face can make a big difference in your interview success, because it will make you appear more ___________ and confident.
臉上掛著微笑會讓你的面試大大加分，因為微笑會讓你看起來平易近人又有自信。
(A) articulate 說話清楚的
(B) approachable 易親近的
(C) strict 嚴格的
(D) diligent 勤奮的

◀ 解析 ▶
本題重點是在描述微笑帶給人的感覺。依照句意來看，最合適的答案為 (B)。

129. Susan didn't get a promotion, __________ disappointed her a lot.
蘇珊沒有獲得升遷，這件事讓她很失望。
(A) that
(B) what
(C) which
(D) who

◀ 解析 ▶
本題空格中需填入關係代名詞，依照句意來看，蘇珊是對沒獲得升遷的「這件事」失望，which 可用來代表前面整句話或整件事，此時 which 前要逗號，且不可用 that 代替，故本題選 (C) which。

130. There are many online price comparison tools __________ people to get quotes from different resellers on the Internet today.
現在網路上有很多線上比價工具可供利用，可以讓人們拿到不同經銷商的報價。
(A) used to 用於…
(B) available for 可供…利用
(C) popular with 受…歡迎
(D) interested in 對…有興趣

◀ 解析 ▶
本題考的是形容詞片語的用法，依照句意來看，比價工具是「可供人們利用的」，故選 (B)。

Part VI. ▶ Text Completion

Questions 131 - 134 refer to the following article.

In order to help our students fully prepare the university admission, I would like to __________ a few

131. (A) share
(B) lecture
(C) tell
(D) inform

tips on how to put your best foot forward in the interview process.

- **Be yourself.** This sounds obvious, but many applicants get tripped up trying to get inside interviewers' heads. Don't __________ matters further. Tell interviewers about what you care

132. (A) standardize
(B) satisfy
(C) complicate
(D) compromise

about, not what you think interviewers want to hear.

- **Don't ignore your weaknesses.** There's no such thing as a perfect applicant. Everyone has weaknesses. Interviewers will see them, __________ you're better off acknowledging them and

133. (A) in addition
(B) if
(C) but
(D) so

incorporating them into your application instead of hoping interviewers will miss them.

- **Don't stress about grades.** Grades matter. Test scores matter. Essays matter. Everything in the application is important. Do a good job and take everything __________.

134. (A) overwhelmingly
(B) seriously
(C) anxiously
(D) surprisingly

為了協助我們的學生充分準備申請學校，我想要分享幾個如何在面談時跨出成功第一步的技巧。

- **做你自己。**這聽起來理所當然，但很多申請人會困在試圖揣測面試官在想什麼的關卡。不要將事情複雜化。直接告訴面試官你真正在乎的是什麼，而不是講那些你認為面試官想聽的。
- **不要忽略自己的弱點。**沒有完美的申請人。每個人都有弱點。面試官會看得出來，因此你最好認清自己的弱點，並將它放在你的申請表內，而不是希望面試官最好會忽略。
- **不要只強調成績。**成績很重要、考試分數很重要、論文很重要。申請表中的每件事都很重要。將事情做好，並對每件事認真以待。

© Caves Educational Training Co., Ltd.

applicant (n.)：（全職／考大學的）申請人　trip up：絆倒、犯錯　weakness (n.)：缺點、弱點

131.
(A) share 分享
(B) lecture 演說
(C) tell 告訴
(D) inform 通知

◀ 解析 ▶
從前後句意來推斷，是要分享面談時的技巧，若要用 tell 則後面必須接 you，故本題只能選 (A)。

132.
(A) standardize 使標準化
(B) satisfy 使滿意
(C) complicate 使複雜
(D) compromise 妥協

◀ 解析 ▶
依照前後句意，應是「不要把事情想得太複雜」，直接誠實的告訴面試官自己真正的想法。故本題選 (C) complicate 最合適。

133.
(A) in addition 除…之外
(B) if 如果
(C) but 但是
(D) so 所以

◀ 解析 ▶
空格前後兩句有因果關係，前句是因，後句是果，此處應該用連接詞 so（所以），故選 (D)。

134.
(A) overwhelmingly 壓倒性地
(B) seriously 認真地
(C) anxiously 急切地
(D) surprisingly 令人訝異地

◀ 解析 ▶
依照文意推斷，最後是要提醒學生，對每件事都認真看待，故選 (B)。

Questions 135 - 138 refer to the following article.

When done properly, a computer network virtualization project can save enterprises money, and it can make company network management far __________, more secure, and more effective.

135. (A) easier
(B) easy
(C) easily
(D) more easily

Please note that the key words here __________ "when done properly".

136. (A) was
(B) is
(C) should
(D) are

Without proper planning, execution, and post-virtualization monitoring, your company's virtualization dream will quickly __________ an expensive nightmare.

137. (A) have become
(B) become
(C) became
(D) becomes

Fortunately, there are steps enterprises can take to __________ a smooth virtualization project.

138. (A) ensure
(B) manufacture
(C) happen
(D) admit

Step 1: Prepare for your company's virtualization well
Step 2: Execute your company's virtualization project fully
Step 3: Manage your company's virtualization infrastructure wisely

若能適當執行，電腦網路虛擬化是可以幫企業省錢的，且可以讓公司的網路管理更容易、更安全和更有效。請注意，此處的關鍵點是「適當執行」。若不能適當的規劃、執行以及監控虛擬化後的狀況，公司的虛擬化夢想很快就會成為昂貴的惡夢。

所幸，企業還是可以採取以下步驟來確保虛擬化計畫順利進行。
步驟一：善加規劃公司的虛擬環境
步驟二：徹底執行公司的虛擬計畫
步驟三：用聰明的方式管理公司的虛擬化基礎建設

virtualization (n.)：虛擬化　enterprise (n.)：企業　execution (n.)：執行　infrastructure (n.)：基礎建設

135.
(A) easier
(B) easy
(C) easily
(D) more easily

◀ 解析 ▶
從本句結構來看，空格後是 , more secure, and more effective，可以推斷空格中應該也是形容詞比較級的用法，故選 (A)。

136.
(A) was
(B) is
(C) should
(D) are

◀ 解析 ▶
依照句意，此處空格中應填入現在簡單式的 be 動詞，而主詞為 the key words，故本題應選 (D) are。

137.
(A) have become
(B) become
(C) became
(D) becomes

◀ 解析 ▶
句中空格前已經出現 will 表示未來式，可知其後應該接原形動詞，故本題應選 (B)。

138.
(A) ensure 確保
(B) manufacture 製造
(C) happen 發生
(D) admit 承認

◀ 解析 ▶
依照前後句意推斷，採取三個步驟可以「確保」虛擬化計畫的進行，故本題應選 (A)。

Questions 139 - 142 refer to the following article.

Hi, everyone. This is a pretty simple article __________ a very innovative sales technique – leveraging

139. (A) saying
(B) relative
(C) about
(D) around

our customers to sell.

In our class, we'll cover several models about this. One of __________ will be

140. (A) these
(B) it
(C) him
(D) this

a method that combines "online group-coupon" with customer sales. I hope you can ask good questions to draw out data and ideas that the class can use to propose suggestions.

__________ the process, I will teach some methods for "hypothesis-driven" and "model-driven"

141. (A) When
(B) While
(C) During
(D) At

questioning – which are methods I first learned at Macro Consulting.

I hope you enjoy this exploration of our real-life, innovative case. Perhaps you'll even discover some excellent suggestions I have not yet __________. I deeply look forward to this, our final session.

142. (A) considers
(B) considering
(C) consideration
(D) considered

大家好，這是一篇十分簡單的文章，內容關於創新的銷售技巧——運用客戶的銷售力。在課堂上，我們會討論到關於此主題的幾個典型模式。其中一個模式會是結合「線上團購券」與客戶銷售。我希望大家盡可能提出好問題，整理出資訊和想法，讓班上同學可以對此提供意見。在過程中，我會教幾個「假設導向」和「模型導向」的提問法，這些都是我在瑪克羅顧問公司首度學到的。我希望你們針對這個實際又創新的案件，盡情參與討論。或許你們會發現一些我沒想到的好點子。我非常期待我們最後的討論會。

innovative (adj.)：創新的　leverage (v.)：運用　draw out：提出、說出　hypothesis (n.)：假設

139.
(A) saying 敘述
(B) relative 相關的
(C) about 關於…
(D) around 在…周圍

◀ 解析 ▶
依照句意推斷，空格中應該填入「關於…」，故不選 (A)、(D)。(B) relative 無法單獨使用於此，故選 (C)。

140.
(A) these 這些
(B) it 它
(C) him 他
(D) this 這

◀ 解析 ▶
此空格中的代名詞，替代的是前一句的 several models，故本題選 (A) these。

141.
(A) When 當…
(B) While 當…
(C) During 在…期間
(D) At 在

◀ 解析 ▶
本句的意思為「在討論過程當中」，也就是在討論的期間內，故本題選 (C)。

142.
(A) considers
(B) considering
(C) consideration
(D) considered

◀ 解析 ▶
空格處的句子為 I have not yet...，可知本句用的是現在完成式，故應該選擇過去分詞 (D) considered。

Questions 143 - 146 refer to the following article.

In the search for helpful or __________ visual aids, it is all too easy for a presenter to forget the value

143. (A) memories
(B) memory
(C) memorized
(D) memorable

of a small object fished out of the pocket, or a larger one from under the desk. It is worth __________ that if there is any object, or part of any object, which could be interesting and

144. (A) noting
(B) note
(C) noted
(D) notes

reasonably relevant to display.

For example, a presenter is quite familiar __________ the inside of a smartphone, and he forgets

145. (A) of
(B) about
(C) with
(D) for

that his audience has possibly never __________ one. Simply producing something and holding it

146. (A) sees
(B) saw
(C) seen
(D) seeing

up lifts the presentation for a couple of reasons: 1. It turns an abstract idea into a physical object, and 2. It substitutes a memorable picture for a forgettable word.

在尋找實用或有記憶點的視覺輔助物品時，演講者很容易忘記，從口袋裡掏出的小物件或從桌子底下拿出來大一點的東西，都是有利用價值的。可以注意是否有任何有趣的且和演講內容相關的（部分）物品，可以拿來展示。例如，演講者對智慧型手機的內部結構非常熟悉，但是忘了聽眾可能從未見過。只要拿些物件，高舉展示給聽眾看，對於演講有加分效果，原因如下：一、可以將抽象的想法變成有形的物件。二、可用好記的圖像代替容易忘記的字彙。

visual (adj.)：視覺的　relevant (adj.)：有關的、切題的　abstract (adj.)：抽象的、純概念的
substitute (v.)：用…取代、代替

143.
(A) memories 回憶（名詞）
(B) memory 記憶（名詞）
(C) memorized 記憶、記住（動詞）
(D) memorable 易記的（形容詞）

◀ 解析 ▶
連接詞 or 用來連接相同詞性的單字，前面已有形容詞 helpful，空格後為名詞 visual aids，由此可判斷空格內應為形容詞，故選 (D)。

144.
(A) noting
(B) note
(C) noted
(D) notes

◀ 解析 ▶
此空格之前看到 "It is worth..."，便可判斷其後應為 Ving 形式，故選 (A)。

145.
(A) of 屬於
(B) about 關於
(C) with 與
(D) for 為

◀ 解析 ▶
此題空格之前看到 "is quite familiar..."，便可判斷是要考 "be familiar with" 片語，故選 (C) with。

146.
(A) sees 看
(B) saw 看
(C) seen 看過
(D) seeing 在看

◀ 解析 ▶
此題空格之前看到 "has possibly never..."，便可判斷空格中的動詞變化應為過去分詞，故選 (C)。

Part VII. ▶ Reading Comprehension

Questions 147 - 148 refer to the following memo.

致：羅利安德森小姐
來自：詹姆士雷格先生
日期 / 時間：2018 年 11 月 15 日 / 下午 4 點

訊息：
雷格先生想要謝謝您，讓他有一趟愉快且充實的參訪行程。他很高興能夠認識所有的行銷人員，並且感謝您撥冗和他一起討論有關在香港做生意的機會。對於您協助召開顧問會議，他也想要致上謝意。他獲得了許多非常有用的資訊，他十分感激。

他非常期待 2019 年是成功的一年。您在工作上若遇到任何需要協助或其他需要討論的事項，雷格先生歡迎您隨時與他聯繫。

訊息記錄人員：雪莉摩根

147. Why did Mr. Legg call Ms. Anderson? 雷格先生打電話給安德森小姐的目的為何？
(A) To arrange a visit next month 安排下個月的拜訪
(B) To reschedule an appointment 將會議改期
(C) To express appreciation 表達感謝之意
(D) To make a hotel reservation in HK 預訂香港的飯店

◀ 解析 ▶
從第一句可知，雷格先生是想感謝安德森小姐，在他參訪香港的期間與他見面，故選 (C)。

148. Who is most likely Sherry Morgan? 雪莉摩根最有可能是誰？
(A) Ms. Anderson's personal assistant 安德森小姐的個人助理
(B) Mr. Legg's secretary 雷格先生的秘書
(C) Ms. Anderson's client 安德森小姐的客戶
(D) Mr. Legg's accountant 雷格先生的會計師

◀ 解析 ▶
雪莉摩根協助記錄給安德森小姐的留言訊息，由此可推斷她可能是安德森小姐的助理或秘書，故選 (A)。

© Caves Educational Training Co., Ltd.

Questions 149 - 151 refer to the following email.

親愛的辛小姐，

請您撥冗參加 2018 年 5 月 25 日至 26 日第 15 屆資訊科技年度會議。

主題：
數個具有大規模導入科技的開發與工具等實務經驗的企業組織，將於當日發表演說，某些與會者及演講者已有超過十年的產業經驗。別錯過他們的故事！

洛克威大飯店
紐約州高登市
位於科里爾河谷附近的洛克威大飯店，提供商務和渡假旅客一個最為放鬆的休憩環境。來賓將能夠體驗最專業的會議場所，並同時享受最完美的渡假時光。您將能夠使用最先進的健身中心，在餐廳與酒吧享用美味的雞尾酒，並沉浸於幽靜客房所帶來的舒適感受。

本會議將是您與各個企業的精英們認識與聯繫的最佳機會。請務必抽空於 5 月 25 日、26 日，與我們在洛克威大飯店相會。

誠摯地，
鍾麥克

總裁
資訊科技股份有限公司

implement (v.)：實行　state-of-the-art (adj.)：最先進的　indulge (v.)：沉浸於…

149. How long does the conference last? 此會議為期多久？
    (A) Two days 兩天
    (B) Two weeks 兩週
    (C) Twelve days 十二天
    (D) One day 一天

◀ 解析 ▶
從第一句可知，會議日期為 5 月 25 日至 26 日，為期兩天，故選 (A)。

150. What is indicated about the conference speakers? 由文中可知關於會議演說者的什麼事？

(A) They are well seasoned. 他們都經驗豐富。

(B) They are new in the industry. 他們都是剛進入此產業的菜鳥。

(C) They all work at Rockware Grand Hotel. 他們都在洛克威大飯店工作。

(D) They also teach in universities. 他們也在大學教課。

◀ 解析 ▶

在「主題」當中提到，參與會議的某些演講者，已經有超過十年的產業經驗，第一個選項中的形容詞 seasoned，為「經驗豐富的」之意，故選 (A)。

151. Which hotel facility is NOT mentioned in the article? 哪一項飯店設施沒有在文中被提及？

(A) Guestrooms 客房

(B) Fitness center 健身中心

(C) Restaurants 餐廳

(D) ATM machines 提款機

◀ 解析 ▶

注意本題是問「未提及」的設施。文中提及的飯店設施，包括會議場所、健身中心、餐廳、酒吧，以及客房，只有提款機未提到，故本題選 (D)。

Questions 152 - 153 refer to the following message chain.

客戶詢問 下午 3:05	你好！我想瞭解更多關於你們在網站上刊登要出租的單人臥室套房。我叫林傑瑞。[1]
客服人員 下午 3:06	好的。傑瑞，有什麼我能為您服務的嗎？
客戶詢問 下午 3:07	那間套房租出去了嗎？
客服人員 下午 3:08	很抱歉，那間單人臥室套房今天早上剛租出去了。
客戶詢問 下午 3:08	噢，真是不巧。[2]
客服人員 下午 3:09	我們還有其他房型可以租。您想看看嗎？
客戶詢問 下午 3:11	好，我們要約個時間嗎？還是…？[3]
客服人員 下午 3:12	沒問題。我們「最佳出租公司」的營業時間是週一到週五，早上十點到下午五點。我們要不要約今天下午的時間？
客戶詢問 下午 3:13	沒關係。我想我明天早上大約十一點會過去。[4]
客服人員 下午 3:15	好的。我會等您，傑瑞。對了，我的名字是愛蜜莉史密斯。

152. What is Jerry trying to do? 傑瑞想要做什麼？
(A) Apply for a new job 申請新工作
(B) Purchase a new smartphone 購買新的智慧型手機
(C) Rent an apartment 租賃公寓
(D) File a complaint 提出客訴

◀ 解析 ▶
從首句即可看出，林傑瑞想要租一間單人臥室套房，故本題選 (C)。

153. In which of the positions marked [1], [2], [3], and [4] does the following sentence best belong?

"What are your business hours?"

下面的句子最適合放在文章中 [1] [2] [3] [4] 哪個位置？

「你們的營業時間是幾點到幾點？」

(A) [1]

(B) [2]

(C) [3]

(D) [4]

◀ 解析 ▶

訊息內容中，僅 [3] 的位置之後提到營業時間，可見此問題應是在提出營業時間之前所問的較為合理，故本題選 (C)。

Questions 154 - 156 refer to the following article.

來自招生辦事處
2018 年 1 月 23 日

各位親愛的學生：

研究並申請進入商學院就讀，可能是一段非常耗費時間的過程。在做出這項決定的同時，考慮未來要如何支付 MBA 課程的學費，也是一項非常重要的課題。下列提示能夠協助你提前了解助學貸款的程序與管道：

- **檢查你的信用報告**－沒人想要在申請貸款時出現任何驚喜，所以提前向信用評等機構了解你的信用狀況是很重要的。
- **了解聯邦及私人貸款等不同選擇**－市面上充斥著各種不同的貸款方案，所以請務必花時間尋找一個能夠提供最佳利率並且最適合你的方案。若你有其他關於助學貸款選擇的問題，請造訪我們的網站。
- **了解獎學金與特定產業助學計畫**－有許多獎學金搜尋引擎，能夠協助你尋找願意資助你完成 MBA 學位的企業組織。

希望這些資訊能夠對你有所幫助。下個月的電子報中，我們將討論有關招生面談的主題。

招生辦事處
林登管理學院
招生辦事處：123-489-3327
訪客中心：123-489-2326
傳真：123-489-7004
電子郵件：mba@linden.edu

154. Whom is this message intended for? 此訊息的主要讀者是誰？

(A) Business students 商學院學生

(B) Accountants 會計師

(C) Fundraisers 募款者

(D) Website designers 網頁設計者

◀ 解析 ▶

此訊息主要是 MBA 課程的助學貸款資訊，可知此訊息的讀者應該是想要申請就讀 MBA 的商學院學生，故選 (A)。

155. How can interested students find out more about scholarship programs?
有興趣的同學如何找到更多關於獎學金計畫的資訊？

(A) Visit the Admissions Office in person 親自拜訪招生辦事處

(B) Take advantage of scholarship search engines 善用獎學金搜尋引擎

(C) Ask professors to provide more information 請教授提供更多資訊

(D) Check credit reports first 先檢視信用報告

◀ 解析 ▶

第三點提示當中提到，可以利用獎學金搜尋引擎來尋找獎學金的相關資訊，故選 (B)。

156. What is most likely the topic for next month's newsletter? 下個月的電子報主題最有可能是什麼？

(A) MBA outlooks MBA 商學院的展望

(B) Future trends 未來的趨勢

(C) Successful interviews 成功的面談

(D) Correct investments 正確的投資

◀ 解析 ▶

文中最後提到，下個月將討論與招生面談相關的主題，故本題選 (C)。

Questions 157 - 158 refer to the following letter.

史密斯先生，您好：

我們相當感謝您展現出與資訊工程公司合作的興趣。資訊工程公司提供兩種類型的合作夥伴計畫：推薦人（系統整合）與經銷商（加值經銷商），請參閱隨信附上的詳細計畫書。請注意，所有新的合作夥伴只能選擇推薦人計畫，即以系統整合夥伴的身分簽訂合約。我們會根據績效制度，邀請一些優秀合作夥伴加入經銷商計畫，並成為加值經銷商。加值經銷商將繼續支援其他系統整合的夥伴，並完整地管理行銷、預售、銷售，以及資訊工程公司針對個別地區的業務支援。

在我們探討與您建立合作關係的可能性時，您或者您的團隊也必須評估本公司及本公司的產品，是否符合您的客戶與產業。最簡單的方式為下載本公司軟體解決方案的試用版本。請參閱以下資源，以協助您了解更多有關資訊工程公司的訊息。

資源：

+ 下載資訊工程公司的試用版本：http://www.info-works.com/trial
+ 即時隨選的訓練程式庫：http://www.info-works.com/training
+ 資訊工程公司的產品示範：http://www.info-works.com/product-demo
+ 資訊工程公司的相關支援，包含產品手冊、問答集、知識庫與提示：http://www.info-works.com/support

若您有任何其他問題，歡迎聯繫：

莉莉錢斯
亞太通路經理
電話：123-6736-7464
電子郵件：lilyc@Info-Works.com

referral (n.)：推薦　reseller (n.)：代理商、經銷商　metrics (n.)：公制　fellow (adj.)：夥伴的
respective (adj.)：各自的　evaluate (v.)：評估　manual (n.)：手冊

157. What can be inferred about Mr. Smith? 此文中可推論出關於史密斯先生的什麼事？
(A) He wants to know where to download the software. 他想知道哪裡可以下載軟體。
(B) He will visit Ms. Chance in person next month. 他將會在下個月親自拜訪錢斯小姐。
(C) He would like Info-Works to distribute his products. 他想請資訊工程公司代理他的產品。
(D) He is interested in Info-Works' partnership program. 他對資訊工程公司的合作夥伴計畫有興趣。

◀ 解析 ▶
文中第一段即提到，史密斯先生對資訊工程公司的合作夥伴計畫有興趣，故本題選 (D)。

© Caves Educational Training Co., Ltd.

158. The word “evaluate” in paragraph 2, line 1, is closest in meaning to
第二段第一行的 “evaluate” 一字意思最接近於
(A) simplify 簡化
(B) assess 評估
(C) perform 表現
(D) participate 參與

◀ 解析 ▶
evaluate 一字意思為「評估」，與 assess 意思最相近，故本題選 (B)。

Questions 159 - 161 refer to the following letter.

親愛的金傑克：

Well-CAD 於 2018 年 7 月 10 日正式發表了全新的入口網站「CAD」，使 Well-CAD 廠商能夠註冊本公司的服務並進行線上查詢。您可以在我們的新聞稿中取得相關的詳細資訊，新聞稿名稱為「Well-CAD 於 7 月 10 日發布 CAD」。

藉由此入口網站，我們同時也可以讓通路合作夥伴，對其公司的基本資料進行線上檢閱。我們鼓勵您登入 CAD 並在完成安全認證後，將您公司的資訊更新至最正確的版本。您的基本資料將會提供給超過三千個，對於拓展亞太地區合作關係版圖具有高度熱情的 IT 廠商進行瀏覽。本公司敬祝您的企業生意興隆。

最誠心的祝福，

藍斯利金恩
總經理

portal (n.)：入口　query (n.)：詢問　press release：新聞稿　validation (n.)：確認

159. What is the main topic of this message? 此訊息的主題為何？
(A) The announcement of a new portal for vendors 針對廠商新入口網站的公告
(B) The invitation to a press conference 記者會的邀請函
(C) The news of a company acquisition 公司併購案的新聞
(D) The release of a new software product 新軟體產品推出的消息

◀ 解析 ▶
此訊息的第一句即公告，針對合作廠商發表全新的入口網站，故本題選 (A)。

160. Who is most likely Jack Kim? 金傑克最有可能是誰？

(A) Lancely King's close friends 藍斯利金恩的好朋友

(B) Lancely King's business partner 藍斯利金恩的生意夥伴

(C) Lancely King's attorney 藍斯利金恩的律師

(D) Lancely King's relative 藍斯利金恩的親戚

◀ 解析 ▶

由於本訊息的讀者對象，應該是 Well-CAD 的合作廠商，故本題選 (B)。

161. What is the benefit for vendors to log on to CAD portal? 廠商登入 CAD 入口網站有何好處？

(A) Other vendors can find them easily online. 其他的廠商可透過網路找到他們。

(B) They can post their product release online. 他們可以在網路上公布產品上市訊息。

(C) They can compare prices online. 他們可以在線上比較價格。

(D) Clients in the US can place orders online. 在美國的客戶可以透過網路下單。

◀ 解析 ▶

此訊息的第二段提到，合作廠商的基本資料，會提供給有意拓展亞太地區合作關係的廠商進行瀏覽，故本題應選 (A)。

Questions 162 - 164 refer to the following letter.

哈囉，潔咪：

由於我們將在明天討論行銷活動的效益，我將下列備忘錄寄給你作參考，讓你能夠有一些初步的想法。

卡特公司工作備忘錄：塑造我們獨特的定位

I. 目標：我們希望公司三至五年後，在市場上的定位為何？
   A. 市場滲透目標
   B. 公司收益目標

II. 我們的目標客戶為？
   A. 他們購買我們的產品是為了解決何種問題？
   B. 他們決定購買的首要考量為何？
   （價格、方便性、易於取得、易於使用、耐用度等。）
   C. 我們產品最特殊的賣點為何？
   D. 我們獨特的定位為何？

III. 我們主要的競爭對手為？
   A. 為什麼我們的目標客戶群目前選擇購買對手的產品？
   B. 別人的產品有提供什麼功能，是我們所沒有的？
   C. 我們提供什麼功能，是別人所沒有的？

IV. 與我們的客戶接觸並發展關係？
   A. 針對感興趣的產品，他們習慣如何做進一步的了解？
   B. 針對我們的產品，他們習慣支付多少的價位？

我很期待與你在明天的會議上交換彼此的意見。

祝事事順心，
凱莉羅莎

penetration (n.)：滲透　revenue (n.)：收益　durability (n.)：耐久性　be accustomed to...：習慣於…

162. According to the letter, what can be inferred about Jamie?
根據信件內容，可以推論出關於潔咪的什麼事？
(A) She will have a meeting with Kelly tomorrow. 她明天會和凱莉開會。
(B) She will fly to Japan for a conference next week. 她下週會搭飛機去日本開會。
(C) She doesn't know about their chief rival that much. 她不是很瞭解她們的主要競爭對手。
(D) She is in charge of arranging seminars. 她負責安排研討會。

◀ 解析 ▶
信中第一句提到，潔咪和凱莉即將在明天開會，故本題選 (A)。

163. What is most likely Kelly Rosa's job? 凱莉羅莎最有可能是做何種工作？
(A) Developing new product lines 開發新產品線
(B) Planning new marketing strategies 規劃新行銷策略
(C) Dealing with customer complaints 處理客訴
(D) Directing company employees 帶領公司員工

◀ 解析 ▶
凱莉和潔咪討論的是行銷活動的效益，由此推斷凱莉可能是負責產品的行銷策略規劃，故本題選 (B)。

164. What does Kelly Rosa want to know about customers? 凱莉羅莎想知道關於客戶的什麼事？
(A) How customers would like to pay for products 客戶喜歡用什麼方式付款
(B) Where customers usually do their shopping 客戶通常在哪裡購物
(C) The ways customers find products to fulfill their needs 客戶如何尋找符合需求的產品
(D) Why customers are not satisfied with their products 客戶不滿意他們產品的理由

◀ 解析 ▶
從備忘錄中列舉的事項，可看出凱莉羅莎想了解的面向，只有選項 (C) 的敘述包含在備忘錄中，故選 (C)。

© Caves Educational Training Co., Ltd.

Questions 165 - 167 refer to the following advertisement.

為進入商學院做準備

進入商學院只是最基本的條件。踏進這裡你就必須成功。

[1] 禾豐商業學苑指導上千名學生如何在商學院中獲得成功。我們在台灣各大城市，提供為期一週的夏季密集預備課程。[2] 在過去 8 年，經問卷調查結果顯示超過 90% 的學生，會推薦禾豐商業學苑給其他即將進入商學院就讀的學生。

立即就讀禾豐商業學苑
* 由全國一流的商學系教授進行超過 30 小時的密集指導 [3]
* 熟練我們獨特的解題方法並運用在商學院的測驗當中
* 學習由最成功的商學系學生所使用的學術策略
* 享受書籍與輔助學習教材的獨家優惠價格

[4] 若要線上註冊，請至 www.business-horizon.com.tw 或撥打 1-800-3728-3847。

excel (v.)：勝出　intensive (adj.)：密集的　academic (adj.)：學術的　exclusive (adj.)：獨有的

165. What is the purpose of this message? 此訊息的主要目的為何？
(A) To recruit business students 招收商學院學生
(B) To enlist new soldiers 招募新兵
(C) To promote a new product 推廣新產品
(D) To inform students of a course change 通知學生課程異動

◀ 解析 ▶
從第一段可發現，禾豐商業學苑是針對商學院學生所設置的學習機構，故本題選 (A)。

166. The word “intensive” in paragraph 2, line 2, is closest in meaning to
第二段第二行的 “intensive” 一字意思最接近於
(A) renewed 重新的
(B) customized 量身訂做的
(C) concentrated 集中的、密集的
(D) attentive 留意的、體貼的

◀ 解析 ▶
intensive 一字意思為「密集的」，與 concentrated 意思最相近，故本題選 (C)。

167. In which of the positions marked [1], [2], [3], and [4] does the following sentence best belong?

"For further information, feel free to contact Carol Kelly at ck@good-mail.com."

下面的句子最適合放在文章中 [1] [2] [3] [4] 哪個位置？

「如要索取更多資訊，歡迎隨時寄電郵至 ck@good-mail.com 與卡蘿凱莉聯絡。」

(A) [1]

(B) [2]

(C) [3]

(D) [4]

◀ 解析 ▶

此句是表示有問題的話可聯絡該電郵的連絡人，再對照內文，只有 [4] 的位置為提供後續聯絡方式，故本題應選 (D)。

Questions 168 - 170 refer to the following article.

艾博米爾頓撰寫之餐廳評論

泰斯堤燒烤
第 2 大街 182 號，電話：3282-3849
適用各大銀行信用卡
營業時間：早上 11 點至晚上 10 點，週一公休
建議提前預約

這間開幕僅兩個月的餐廳，已藉由網路好評口碑，成功吸引眾人的目光。室內的裝潢設計充滿了美國鄉村風格的魅力與溫暖。菜單內容也非常多樣化，且充滿道地的美式風味。

我們所嘗試的主菜中，最美味的是一道內含馬鈴薯、胡蘿蔔、洋菇，以及香嫩牛肉的鄉野燉肉。由於使用高品質的牛肉作為食材，這道菜的美味的確令人驚豔。另一道精心烹煮的主菜是炸雞，口感非常的新鮮香脆。主菜所附上的蔬菜雖然很新鮮，但是卻有點煮得太久。

因為主菜的份量相當充足，真的沒有必要再多點開胃菜或湯品。針對食量較大的人，我推薦綜合沙拉。如果在吃完全部之後，還想要吃一點甜點的話，請試試他們的蘋果派，裡面的蘋果既多汁又鮮脆，餅皮則非常的清爽。

當我晚上 7 點前往用餐時，整家餐廳因為客滿而導致服務速度變得有點慢。預約系統似乎出了一點問題。先前已經有人登記了我們的晚餐預約，但我們抵達時，系統上卻沒有我們的預約記錄。就算餐點再如何美味，這類的狀況仍然會嚴重影響到餐廳的商譽。

168. What kind of food does the restaurant serve? 此餐廳提供哪一種餐點？
(A) Italian food 義式餐點
(B) Japanese food 日式餐點
(C) American food 美式餐點
(D) Chinese food 中式餐點

◀ 解析 ▶
第一段當中提到，此餐廳的菜單充滿道地美式風味，故本題選 (C)。

169. How old is the Tasty Grill? 泰斯堤燒烤開幕多久了？
(A) Two years old 兩年
(B) Two and half months old 兩個半月
(C) Three weeks old 三週
(D) Two months old 兩個月

◀ 解析 ▶
從開頭的 the two-month-old restaurant 可知，此餐廳開幕僅兩個月，故本題選 (D)。

170. What does the reviewer say about the main courses? 評論者提到關於主菜的什麼事？
(A) They are overcooked. 主菜煮得太老了。
(B) They are large meals. 主菜份量很大。
(C) They are not as delicious as salad. 主菜沒有沙拉好吃。
(D) They are not recommended. 主菜不值得推薦。

◀ 解析 ▶
第三段開頭提到，因主菜份量充足，不需再點開胃菜或甜品。另外，文中提到煮得太老的，是主菜附上的蔬菜，而非主菜本身，故本題選 (B)。

Questions 171 - 175 refer to the following article.

要成為春田市的計程車司機並非一件容易的事。若要取得春田市計程車的駕駛執照，申請者必須通過一場複雜的測驗。他們不單單需要了解街道、地標，以及旅館的地點，還需要知道抵達目的地的最佳路線。申請者不僅要接受各種路線的測驗，還需要熟知一天內不同時段的最佳交通路線。春田市的計程車並沒有安裝計費錶。司機將依照整趟路程所穿越的區域數目來對乘客進行收費。因此申請者必須瞭解所有的區域與費率。想要通過測驗的人，必須花費許多時間在春田市四處駕駛、研究地圖，並將所有街道的門牌地址都熟記在腦海中。

hackie (n.)：計程車司機　route (n.)：路線　meter (n.)：計量器　directory (n.)：姓名地址簿

171. What should candidates do to receive a taxi license in Springfield?
申請者要做什麼才能在春田市取得計程車駕照？
(A) Pass a comprehensive exam 通過一項綜合考試
(B) Buy a taxi 買一台計程車
(C) Memorize all traffic rules 將交通規則都背下來
(D) Fill out an application form 填申請書

◀ 解析 ▶
第二句提到，想取得春田市計程車駕駛執照，必須通過測驗，故本題選 (A)。

172. What is indicated about becoming a taxi driver in Springfield? 文中提及在春田市開計程車的什麼事？
(A) It's a dangerous job. 是一項危險的工作。
(B) It's not as simple as expected. 不如想像中的簡單。
(C) It's rather easy. 是輕而易舉的事。
(D) It takes more than two years to apply. 要花兩年以上去申請。

◀ 解析 ▶
依照文中敘述，春田市計程車司機需具備許多知識和能力，可知此工作並不簡單，故本題選 (B)。

173. What is NOT mentioned as an element for taxi drivers to learn?
哪一項不是計程車司機要學習的項目？
(A) Street names 街道名稱
(B) The best way to get to the destination 到達目的地的最佳方式
(C) Major landmarks 主要路標
(D) Various payment methods 各種付款方式

◀ 解析 ▶
需注意本題問的是「不用」學習的項目，文中並未提到付款方式，故本題選 (D)。

174. According to the article, how are passengers being charged? 根據文章內容，車資如何計算？
(A) Based on cab meters 根據計程車跳錶
(B) Based on driver's experience 根據司機的經驗
(C) Based on the number of zones 根據經過的區域數量
(D) Based on the size of the cab 根據計程車的大小

◀ 解析 ▶
文中提到車上並不安裝計費錶，而是以整趟路程所經過的區域來計費，故本題選 (C)。

175. What should candidates do in order to pass the exam? 申請者要如何才能通過考試？
    (A) Get familiar wlth roads in Springfield 熟悉春出市的道路
    (B) Call the city government to apply 打電話到市政府申請
    (C) Participate in a seminar 參與研討會
    (D) Discuss routes with passengers 跟乘客討論路線

◀ 解析 ▶
依照文章敘述，申請者必須熟知所有春田市的道路，才可能通過考試，故本題選 (A)。

Questions 176 - 180 refer to the following letters.

艾恩街 113 號
115 台灣台北市

2018 年 1 月 21 日

蘿絲瓦特旅館客戶經理
新加坡艾巷 383 號

親愛的經理：

這封信是關於我之前入住貴旅館時，遺失及損壞的代洗衣物。我的衣物於去年 12 月 16 日（我退房當日）被送回來時，我發現有 2 隻襪子（一隻褐色、一隻黑色）不見了。同時，有一件白色的襯衫，被洗成了難看的藍色。我有向清潔人員抱怨這件事，而她向我保證，將會把遺失的襪子連同一張美金 50 元的支票寄還給我，以補償那件我幾天前才剛買的襯衫。

現在已經超過一個月的時間了，我卻仍然沒有收到任何東西。

感謝您幫忙處理這項問題。

誠摯地，
林提姆

蘿絲瓦特旅館
新加坡艾巷 383 號
123-2840-3828

2018 年 2 月 10 日

林提姆先生
艾恩街 113 號
115 台灣台北市

親愛的林先生：

感謝您於 1 月 21 日的來信。您在裡面提到您在本旅館住宿時，代洗衣物出現了遺失及受損的情況。

很抱歉，我們並沒有追蹤到您遺失物品的下落。與您交談的清潔人員目前已經不在本旅館工作。我們誠摯地提醒您，在委託清洗衣物的表格中，有清楚提到本旅館對於代洗衣物所發生的遺失或損害均不負責。用來收納您衣物的塑膠袋上，一樣也有相同的警告，以粗體字印製在上方。

造成您的不便，我們致上歉意，並期望不久的將來，還有再次為您服務的機會。

誠摯地，
安姬葛列德

176. Why does Tim Lin write to Rosewater Motel? 林提姆寫信到蘿絲瓦特旅館的目的為何？

(A) To suggest a partnership formation 提議建立合作關係
(B) To file a complaint 提出客訴
(C) To thank for their good service 感謝他們的優良服務
(D) To make a reservation 預約訂房

◀ 解析 ▶
第一封信中林提姆提到，自己入住旅館時，送洗的衣物有損害和遺失的情形，信件的目的應該是為了抱怨此事，故選 (B)。

177. What was the original color of Tim's shirt? 提姆的襯衫原本是什麼顏色？

(A) White 白色
(B) Blue 藍色
(C) Black 黑色
(D) Brown 棕色

◀ 解析 ▶
依照文中所敘述，他的襯衫原本是白色，卻被洗成了藍色，故本題選 (A)。

178. What did the housekeeper claim? 清潔人員聲稱會怎麼做？
(A) A thank-you note will be sent to Tim. 會寄給提姆一張感謝狀。
(B) A new pair of socks will be sent to Tim. 會寄給提姆一雙新襪子。
(C) A hotel voucher will be sent to Tim. 會寄給提姆一張旅館住宿券。
(D) A $50 check will be sent to Tim. 會寄給提姆一張 50 元支票。

◀ 解析 ▶
清潔人員聲稱，會將遺失的襪子寄回去，連同一張 50 元支票作為補償，故本題選 (D)。

179. Who is most likely Angie Glad? 安姬葛列德最有可能是誰？
(A) Rosewater Motel customer care manager 蘿絲瓦特旅館的客服經理
(B) Mr. Tim Lin's secretary 林提姆先生的秘書
(C) Rosewater Motel housekeeper 蘿絲瓦特旅館的清潔人員
(D) Mr. Tim Lin's housekeeper 林提姆先生家中的清潔人員

◀ 解析 ▶
安姬葛列德負責回覆客戶林提姆的抱怨信件，由此可推斷她應該是旅館的客服經理，故本題選 (A)。

180. What does Angie Glad claim? 安姬葛列德的主張為何？
(A) The motel is not responsible for the loss. 旅館不需負責客戶所遺失的物品。
(B) The motel will send a new shirt to Mr. Lin soon. 旅館會儘快寄給林先生一件新襯衫。
(C) The motel is happy to offer Mr. Lin a discount for his next stay.
旅館很樂意在林先生下次入住時提供他折扣。
(D) The motel will keep looking for Mr. Lin's socks. 旅館會持續幫林先生找襪子。

◀ 解析 ▶
第二封信件中，安姬葛列德認為旅館於送洗衣物的申請單與收納袋上，都有註明旅館對代洗衣物的遺失或損害均不負責，客戶應自行負責。故本題選 (A)。

Questions 181 - 185 refer to the following emails.

收件人：劉潔西
寄件人：張保羅
副本：陳傑克
日期：2018 年 4 月 14 日
主旨：訓練課程問題

親愛的潔西：

我想要寫信告知你，我下午的軟體訓練課狀況非常地糟糕。因為緊急召開的業務會議，我和傑克被從 A 大會議室移至 B 小會議室。但整個 B 會議室的空間卻有很大的問題。有兩張桌子不見了，而且最糟糕的是投影機故障了，所以我沒辦法投影我的簡報。那間會議室內的一些燈泡也早就壞掉、需要更換了。針對這些問題，你知道我應該向誰反映嗎？感謝你。

保羅

收件人：張保羅
寄件人：劉潔西
日期：2018 年 4 月 15 日
主旨：回覆：訓練課程問題

親愛的保羅：

聽到這項消息，我真是感到抱歉！根據公司的規定，任何損壞的設備，都需要填寫維修需求表回報。請你填寫完之後，將它交給技術支援人員。我們的設備技術人員亞當威利目前正在休假，他要 28 日才會回到公司。在此同時，請你將表格交給暫時協助支援的馬克派克。我了解 B 會議室的空間比較小，但是它應該要有相同數量的桌子才對。我會親自上去做一次檢查，確保該會議室內有足夠的桌子。

潔西

disaster (n.)：災難　maintenance (n.)：維修　in the meantime：同時

181. What is true about Paul Chang? 關於張保羅的敘述何者正確？
(A) Paul was trying to arrange a meeting with Jack. 保羅試著要跟傑克約開會時間。
(B) His training session did not go well at all. 他的訓練課程進行得很不順利。
(C) He liked the environment in meeting room B. 他很喜歡 B 會議室的環境。
(D) He liked the performance of the new projector. 他很喜歡新投影機的效能。

◀ 解析 ▶
第一封信件的第一句中，張保羅就表示他的訓練課程狀況非常糟糕，且 B 會議室的設備有些問題。故本題選 (B)。

182. What is wrong with lights in meeting room B? 在 B 會議室內的燈有何問題？
(A) Some lights are missing. 有些燈不見了。
(B) Some light bulbs need to be changed. 有一些燈泡需要更換。
(C) Some lights are not energy efficient. 有一些燈不是節能省電燈具。
(D) Some lights are moved to meeting room A. 有些燈被移到 A 會議室去了。

◀ 解析 ▶
第一封信件提到，B 會議室內的兩張桌子不見了，投影機也故障，還有一些燈泡需要更換。故本題選 (B)。

183. Whom should Paul give the maintenance request form to? 保羅應該將維修需求表交給誰？
(A) Jessie Liu 劉潔西
(B) Jack Chen 陳傑克
(C) Adam Willy 亞當威利
(D) Mark Parker 馬克派克

◀ 解析 ▶
依照第二封信件的回覆，由於設備技術人員亞當威利正在休假，保羅應該將維修需求表先交給協助支援的馬克派克。故選 (D)。

184. What does Jessie offer to do? 潔西會提供什麼協助？
(A) Check the number of desks in meeting room B 查看 B 會議室內桌子的數量
(B) Call Adam Willy to come back soon 打電話請亞當威利儘速趕回來
(C) Reschedule Paul Chang's presentation 將張保羅的簡報會議改期
(D) Buy a new projector 買一台新的投影機

◀ 解析 ▶
第二封信件的最後一句，潔西提到她會親自去確認 B 會議室的桌子數量。故本題選 (A)。

185. In the second email, the word "maintenance" in paragraph 1, line 2, is closest in meaning to
第二封信件內，第一段第二行的 "maintenance" 一字意思最接近於
(A) upkeep 保養、維修
(B) distribution 分配、散佈
(C) development 發展
(D) establishment 創辦、建立

◀ 解析 ▶
maintenance 一字意思為「維修、保養」，與 upkeep 意思最相近，故本題選 (A)。

Questions 186 - 190 refer to the following press release and letters.

慶祝數位科技公司二十週年！

2018 年 5 月 10 日，來自新墨西哥州古德鎮消息——數位科技公司自豪地宣布，在會計軟體開發所居的領導地位已邁入第二十個年頭。這二十年來，數位科技公司持續創新並穩定成長。數位科技公司早期的成功來自於 @Easy 軟體的開發，這說明了使用者對容易操作的會計軟體工具，需求上有不斷增加的趨勢。最近公司更推出了@Efficient軟體，功能將會更加強大。

數位科技公司對現有產品的不斷提升，反映出該公司在會計應用方面，持續致力於提供創新又強大的解決方案。銷售部副總裁傑克傑佛森如此說道：「數位科技公司的成功和永續經營之道，部分就在於我們不間斷地力求改進產品。」

數位科技公司將展開週年慶活動，並於 6 月 18 日（星期五）舉辦一場慶祝餐會。欲了解詳細資訊，請至數位科技公司網站查詢：www.digitech.com，或致電公關專員陳依娃：800-333-9483。

2018 年 5 月 15 日

大衛克拉克
谷德衛路 1138 號
83817 新墨西哥州谷德鎮

克拉克先生，您好：

數位科技公司將於 6 月 18 日星期五，舉辦 20 週年慶祝餐會。因為您是我們尊貴的客戶，我們非常希望您能蒞臨參加。您的參與是我們至高的榮幸。

餐會地點定在綠樹飯店，位於第四街和第五大道路口東南方。晚上六點可進場享用茶點，並於八點開始享用晚餐。

期待您能夠參加。請您儘早撥空回覆是否出席。

謝謝您，我們期待您的蒞臨。

祝安好，
莫莉裴瑞茲
數位科技公司

2018 年 5 月 20 日

莫莉裴瑞茲
數位科技公司
工商路 4732 號
83817 新墨西哥州谷德鎮

裴瑞茲小姐，您好：

謝謝您邀請我參加 貴公司的慶祝餐會。我相信 貴公司的餐會活動將會相當有趣，也是一個可以跟其他商務人士交流的好機會，但因我屆時要去新加坡參加會議，故無法出席 貴公司的活動。

再次謝謝您的邀請，預祝數位科技公司業績蒸蒸日上。

誠摯地祝福，
大衛克拉克

186. According to the press, which of the following statements about Digi-Tech is NOT true?
根據報導，下列關於數位科技公司的敘述何者為非？
(A) It started its business twenty years ago. 公司在二十年前成立。
(B) It has only a few employees. 公司僅有數位員工。
(C) It's a software development company. 公司是軟體開發公司。
(D) It releases new products continuously. 公司持續推出新產品。

◀ 解析 ▶
根據首篇報導內容，並沒有看到「此公司僅有幾位員工」的資訊，故選 (B) It has only a few employees. 為答案。

187. Why does Molly Perez write to David Clark? 莫莉裴瑞茲寫信給大衛克拉克的原因為何？
(A) To invite him to attend a webinar 邀請他出席線上研討會
(B) To place an order 為了要下訂單
(C) To invite him to attend a company celebration 邀請他出席公司的慶祝活動
(D) To inform him of a job opening 要告知他一個職缺訊息

◀ 解析 ▶
從第一封信可知，莫莉裴瑞茲代表數位科技公司，邀請大衛克拉克參加公司 20 週年的慶祝活動，故選 (C)。

188. What does Molly Perez ask David Clark to do next? 莫莉裴瑞茲要求大衛克拉克接下來做什麼事？

(A) Confirm his attendance 確認出席狀況

(B) Submit an application form 繳交申請表

(C) Return her call tomorrow 明天回她電話

(D) Arrange a meeting at the Green Tree Inn 安排在綠樹飯店開會

◀ 解析 ▶

第一封信件結尾，莫莉裴瑞茲請大衛克拉克回覆是否出席活動，故選 (A)。

189. What does David Clark think of the party? 大衛克拉克認為餐會活動如何？

(A) The cost is too high. 價格太高了。

(B) It's not fun at all. 一點也不好玩。

(C) Party food is not that delicious. 活動餐點不是那麼好吃。

(D) People can socialize with other business counterparts. 可以跟其他同業交流。

◀ 解析 ▶

1. 第二封信當中，大衛克拉克認為活動會相當有趣，也是一個跟其他商務人士交流的好機會，故選 (D)。

2. counterpart (n.)：同業、職務相當的人

190. Why can't David Clark attend the event? 大衛克拉克為何無法出席活動？

(A) Because he is too tired to go. 他因為太累而無法參加。

(B) Because he will be traveling then. 因為屆時他要出差。

(C) Because his wife won't allow it. 因為他太太不准他去。

(D) Because he doesn't know where the party will be held. 因為他不知道活動舉辦的地點。

◀ 解析 ▶

第二封信當中，大衛克拉克表示自己要前往新加坡開會，無法參與餐會活動，故選 (B)。

Questions 191 - 195 refer to the following memo, document, and email.

辦公室備忘錄

致：葛蕾絲依凡思、馬克伍德、蒂娜迪亞茲、梅貝莉
發自：威爾尼爾森，行銷業務部副總
主旨：公司整體發展策略會議

此為通知各位，我們將於 2018 年 6 月 13 日星期三舉行每月檢討會議。除了將討論上次會議的工作分配外，我們也會討論更多獲得潛在客戶名單的方法，以求在競爭激烈的市場上使公司茁壯。因此，我要求各位都務必參與會議。我也希望大家都要報告自己的計畫，還有提出幫助公司與團隊成長的想法。若有任何疑問，請在兩個工作天內聯絡我的助理。

comprehensive (adj.)：綜合的　conduct (v.)：實施　assignment (n.)：分派的工作

五塔公司
會議記錄

日期：2018 年 6 月 13 日，星期三

出席者
- 葛蕾絲依凡思（行銷專員）
- 馬克伍德（客戶業務代表）
- 蒂娜迪亞茲（技術支援工程師）
- 梅貝莉（客戶服務代表）

會議地點
- 大樓：東方大樓 B 棟
- 會議室：A372 室

會議開始
- 預定開始時間：6 月 13 日星期三，下午 3 點
- 實際開始時間：6 月 13 日星期三，下午 3 點 15 分
- 會議記錄：琳達卡特

議程
- 檢討上次五月份會議工作分配
- 檢討上週業務狀況並確認潛在業務機會
- 計畫第三季的行銷活動以獲得潛在客戶名單
- 檢視客戶調查的結果

會議結束
- 預定結束時間：下午 4 點 30 分
- 實際結束時間：下午 4 點 15 分

收件者：葛蕾絲依凡思、蒂娜迪亞茲、梅貝莉、威爾尼爾森
發信者：馬克伍德
日期： 2018年 6 月 15 日

大家好：

我們星期三開了一個相當有效率的業務會議。以下是我想出來的一些銷售策略，想跟大家分享一下。

1. 我認為我們應該更明確地定義出我們的目標市場，因為這對於我們的銷售成功與否，至關重要。所以，為了再次創造新商機，找出一個新產業來主打，對我們而言非常重要。

2. 為了更迅速完成交易，我建議業務代表和真正的採購決策者坐下來好好談一談。我們應該要根據採購決策者的喜好，調整銷售話術。

3. 根據我的經驗，客戶可以在銷售過程中，確實感受到業務代表的真誠與否。因此，向我們的客戶傳達「我們很在乎他們的營運」這件事，極其重要。

我們下個季度的主要目標之一是增加公司收入，而我真的覺得，縮短銷售週期應該可以讓業績成長。因此，上述的這些方法可能有助於我們的業務代表更快速地達成交易。

馬克伍德

critical (adj.)：關鍵性的、緊要的　momentum (n.)：（推）動力　customize (v.)：（按顧客要求）訂製
genuine (adj.)：真誠的　convey (v.)：傳達、表達

191. What's the purpose of the scheduled meeting? 此會議排定的目的為何？
(A) To review customers' feedback 檢視客戶的意見回饋
(B) To brainstorm new product ideas 腦力激盪出新產品點子
(C) To discuss company's future development 討論公司未來發展
(D) To interview some applicants 跟一些應徵者面談

◀ **解析** ▶
從第一則備忘錄的主旨 (subject) 當中，清楚寫明會議的目的是討論公司未來發展策略，故本題選 (C)。

192. What will NOT be discussed at the meeting? 會議中不會討論到什麼事？
(A) Training workshops for customers 為客戶舉辦的訓練講習
(B) Opinions from each attendee 每個與會者的意見
(C) The assignments from last meeting 上次會議的工作分配
(D) Ways to generate sales leads 獲得銷售線索的方法

◀ 解析 ▶
需注意本題是問「不會」討論的事，議程當中並未提及訓練講習，故本題選 (A)。

193. What are the attendees required to do in the meeting? 會議中與會者被要求做什麼？
(A) Call and invite customers to join the meeting 打電話請客戶來參加會議
(B) Contribute good ideas 貢獻好的意見
(C) Bring lunch to share with others 帶午餐來跟大家分享
(D) Print out PPT files 將簡報檔案列印出來

◀ 解析 ▶
第一則備忘錄內容當中，威爾尼爾森要求與會者必須針對公司發展，提供好的意見，故選 (B)。

194. What is most likely Grace Evans' job responsibility? 葛蕾絲依凡思的工作內容最有可能是下列何者？
(A) Answer technical phone calls 接聽詢問技術問題的電話
(B) Plan marketing activities 規劃行銷活動
(C) Deal with angry customers 安撫生氣的客戶
(D) Hire new employees 招募新進員工

◀ 解析 ▶
從葛蕾絲依凡思的職位為行銷專員，可推測其工作內容應包括規劃行銷活動，故本題選 (B)。

195. What does Mark Wood mean when he says, "We should customize sales pitch"?
當馬克伍德提及「我們應該要調整銷售話術」，他意指為何？
(A) In order to raise the points that decision makers really care about
為了要提及採購決策者真正關心的話題
(B) In order to attract more new customers from worldwide 為了吸引更多來自世界各地的新客戶
(C) In order to come up with more marketing strategies 為了想出更多行銷策略
(D) In order to increase the meeting efficiency 為了增加會議效率

◀ 解析 ▶
根據馬克伍德在信中建議，要根據採購決策者的喜好，來調整銷售話術，講些他們真正關心的議題，如此才有機會快速結案，故選 (A)。

Questions 196 - 200 refer to the following advertisement and letters.

歡迎光臨海濱酒店

海濱酒店距離海灘僅一個街區之隔，距離迷人的市區也只需十分鐘的車程。這裡位於中心位置，無論是上街購物、大啖美食，還是從事各種戶外活動，都很便利。

辦理入住手續即可享用現烤餅乾，入住後還有豪華歐陸早餐，所有賓客都可享受海濱酒店無微不至的服務。酒店內備有室內溫水游泳池，還有優秀的餐旅專家團隊，致力於滿足您所有的住宿需求。

海濱酒店裡的 50 間寬敞客房和套房，均設有無線網路、冰箱和咖啡機。還提供免費的電影租借服務。海濱酒店會是您放鬆度過海岸假期的最佳住宿選擇。

服務項目：免費歐陸早餐、無線上網、現烤餅乾、商務中心、乾洗中心、報紙、停車場。

線上訂房請至：http://www.seaside-hotel.com 或來電：800-383-5555。

deluxe (adj.)：豪華的、高檔的　hospitality (n.)：餐旅、款待　complimentary (adj.)：免費的
destination (n.)：目的地、終點

你好，

我是傑克詹姆士，我正在規劃和家人前往濱海城市渡假，而我碰巧在網路上看到你們酒店的網站。海濱酒店似乎是我們家庭假期不錯的選擇。

我想知道是否有四人的家庭套房可以預訂，日期從 2018 年 8 月 4 日起，為期七天。此外，若可以訂到一間面向海灘的套房，就再好不過了。因為 8 月 5 日是我兒子的生日，我們會需要一個生日蛋糕。另外，我想知道你們是否有提供機場接送服務。

請回信確認上述事項和相關費用。我想儘早確認訂房，以便規劃家庭旅遊的其他部分。

非常感謝你。

傑克詹姆士

availability (n.)：可獲得性、可利用性　confirmation (n.)：確認

親愛的傑克詹姆士先生，您好：

感謝您選擇濱海城市的海濱酒店。我們很高興與您確認訂房細節，內容如下：

抵　　達：2018 年 8 月 4 日
時　　間：15:00
離　　開：2018 年 8 月 11 日
時　　間：12:00
房客人數：4 人
房間類型：家庭豪華套房，含兩張加大雙人床
內　　含：免費早餐、生日蛋糕、機場接送服務
價　　格：每晚兩百美元
訂房編號：83872

訂房規定：
✓ 酒店入住時間為下午三點，退房時間則為中午十二點。
✓ 住宿費用餘額請於辦理入住登記時付清。
✓ 最晚須於到達日前兩天取消訂房。若於到達日前 48 小時內取消，將收取保留一晚的住宿費。如若未入住，將不提供退款。
✓ 退房時將收取電話費、餐飲費等額外費用或其他附帶費用。
✓ 海濱酒店內所有房間皆一律「禁煙」。

海濱酒店期待您的蒞臨！

祝順心，
莉莉安瓊斯
海濱酒店訂房服務團隊

cancellation (n.)：取消　retention (n.)：保留　refund (n.)：退款　incidental (adj.)：附帶的、次要的

196. What is true about Seaside Hotel? 關於海濱酒店的敘述何者正確？
(A) It's located on the high mountain. 位於高山上。
(B) It's a famous historical site. 是個著名古蹟。
(C) It's near the beach. 靠近海灘。
(D) It's a 2-star hotel. 是二星級飯店。

◀ 解析 ▶
從第一篇廣告內容的一開頭，可以知道這家酒店是靠近海灘的，故選 (C)。

197. What's the purpose of Jack James' letter? 傑克詹姆士寫信的目的為何？

(A) To make a hotel reservation 預訂飯店房間

(B) To request product samples 索取產品試用

(C) To cancel his restaurant reservation 取消餐廳訂位

(D) To arrange a birthday party 安排生日派對

◀ 解析 ▶

根據傑克詹姆士在信中所表達的意思，以及詢問是否能預訂四人的家庭套房，可知他是要預訂飯店房間，故選 (A)。

198. How does Jack James learn about the Seaside Hotel? 傑克詹姆士是如何得知有關海濱酒店的訊息？

(A) Through friend recommendations 透過朋友推薦

(B) On the web 從網路上得知

(C) In the newspaper 在報紙上看到

(D) From one of his relatives 從某位親戚那裡聽到

◀ 解析 ▶

根據傑克在信中所說，他是碰巧在網路上看到酒店的網站，故選 (B)。

199. How much does Jack James need to pay for the hotel accommodation in total?
傑克詹姆士總共要付給海濱酒店多少錢？

(A) US$1,200 一千二百美元

(B) US$1,700 一千七百美元

(C) US$2,000 兩千美元

(D) US$1,400 一千四百美元

◀ 解析 ▶

由海濱酒店的回信內容可看出，一晚房價是兩百美元，而傑克一家要住七天便是一千四百美元，故選 (D)。

200. In the letter from Lilian Jones, the word "incidental" in paragraph 3, line 6, is closest in meaning to
在莉莉安瓊斯的信中，第三段第六行的 "incidental" 一字意思最接近於

(A) related 相關的

(B) inevitable 不可避免的

(C) attractive 吸引人的

(D) impossible 不可能的

◀ 解析 ▶

incidental 一字意思為「附帶的、次要的」，與 related 意思最相近，故選 (A)。

Test 3
試題解析

LISTENING TEST

Part I									
1	2	3	4	5	6				
A	B	A	B	D	C				
Part II									
7	8	9	10	11	12	13	14	15	16
A	C	C	B	A	A	B	A	A	A
17	18	19	20	21	22	23	24	25	26
C	A	C	A	A	C	B	B	A	A
27	28	29	30	31					
A	C	A	B	A					
Part III									
32	33	34	35	36	37	38	39	40	41
D	B	D	A	B	B	C	A	B	B
42	43	44	45	46	47	48	49	50	51
B	C	A	A	B	A	C	D	D	A
52	53	54	55	56	57	58	59	60	61
C	B	C	A	A	B	C	D	A	C
62	63	64	65	66	67	68	69	70	
B	D	C	A	D	B	B	A	B	
Part IV									
71	72	73	74	75	76	77	78	79	80
A	C	B	C	B	D	A	B	C	A
81	82	83	84	85	86	87	88	89	90
C	B	B	D	B	C	A	C	B	C
91	92	93	94	95	96	97	98	99	100
D	A	C	B	B	C	A	C	A	B

Part I. ► Photographs

1.

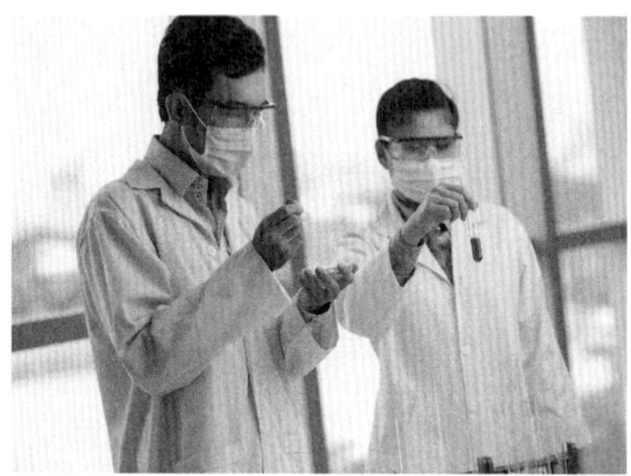

(A) They are doing some experiments. 他們在做實驗。
(B) They are writing a report. 他們在寫報告。
(C) One of them is recording notes. 其中一人在做記錄。
(D) The doctor is performing surgery. 醫生在動手術。

◀ 解析 ▶
1. 照片中兩人在研究室裡，正在進行實驗，故選 (A)。
2. experiment (n.)：實驗　surgery (n.)：手術

2.

(A) Some waiters are serving customers. 一些侍者在服務客人。
(B) The tables are all set. 桌面都擺設好了。
(C) Several pictures are hanging on the wall. 牆上掛了好幾幅畫。
(D) Customers are ready to order. 客人準備好要點餐了。

◀ 解析 ▶
1. 由照片可看出此為餐廳，桌子已經擺設完成，尚無任何客人入席，牆上則以擺飾為主，故本題選 (B)。
2. order (v.)：點餐

3.

(A) The bed has been made. 床已經鋪整齊了。
(B) A maid is cleaning the room. 一個女傭在整理房間。
(C) The single bed is narrow and small. 這張單人床又窄又小。
(D) Some towels are on the floor. 地上有些毛巾。

◀ 解析 ▶
1. 此為飯店房間，房內為雙人床 (double bed)，床是鋪整齊的，房內沒有人，故選 (A)。
2. make one's bed：為某人鋪床　maid (n.)：女傭、女僕　single bed：單人床

4.

(A) The chef is cutting a piece of meat. 主廚在切肉片。
(B) The chef is preparing some food. 主廚在準備食物。
(C) The chef is writing his recipe. 主廚在寫食譜。
(D) The chef is serving customers. 主廚在服務客人。

◀ 解析 ▶

1. 從照片中主角的衣著，可知為一位廚師，他正在攪拌某些食材原料，故選 (B) 最為合適。
2. chef (n.)：主廚　recipe (n.)：食譜

5.

(A) Some sheep are eating grass. 有一些羊在吃草。
(B) Some people are milking the cows. 有一些人在擠牛奶。
(C) The cattle are in the shed. 牛關在棚子內。
(D) The cattle are in the field. 牛在平原上。

◀ 解析 ▶

1. 照片中為牛群，正在草原上吃草，故選 (D)。
2. milk (v.)：擠奶　cattle (n.)：牛群　shed (n.)：棚子

6.

(A) Two people are riding motorcycles. 兩人在騎機車。
(B) Two people are riding horses in the forest. 兩人在森林裡騎馬。
(C) Two people are riding bikes. 兩人在騎單車。
(D) The street is full of cars and buses. 街上滿是汽車與公車。

◀ 解析 ▶

1. 照片中可見兩人在市區街道上，並肩騎著腳踏車，街道上車輛不多，故選 (C)。
2. be full of...：充滿…

Part II. ▶ Question-Response

7. How long have you been with the company? 你在公司工作多久了？
   (A) I've been working here for three years. 我在這裡工作三年了。
   (B) Yes, I am happy working at this company. 是的，我在這間公司工作很愉快。
   (C) It's just around the corner; you can't miss it. 它就在轉角處，你一定會看到。

◀ 解析 ▶
本題是問 How long「多久…」，回答當中應提及時間，故選 (A)。

8. What time will the performance begin? 表演幾點開始？
   (A) I didn't perform well last year. 我去年表現不盡理想。
   (B) The train leaves in ten minutes. 火車十分鐘後離站。
   (C) It will begin at 7 p.m. So let's go now. 晚上七點開始。我們現在走吧。

◀ 解析 ▶
本題問表演幾點開始，選項 (A) 的 perform 是指「表現」，而選項 (B) 則是指火車出發時間，故本題應選 (C)。

9. Can you offer us a discount if we purchase ten more copies of this software application?
   如果我們多買十套應用軟體，你可以給我們折扣嗎？
   (A) Sure, it's easy-to-use software. 當然，那套軟體很好用。
   (B) Sure, call me when you are ready to see a demo. 當然，您想看操作示範的話再打電話給我。
   (C) Sure, we can offer another 5% off. 當然，我們可以再幫您打九五折。

◀ 解析 ▶
本題的重點在於 discount「折扣」，只有選項 (C) 當中提到了 5% off（九五折），與題目相呼應，故選 (C)。

10. Oh no, the color printer is out of ink. What am I supposed to do now?
    噢不，彩色印表機沒墨水了。我現在該怎麼辦？
    (A) I think you should talk to your boss about it. 我認為你應該跟你老闆談談。
    (B) You should call the maintenance department for assistance. 你應該請維修部門協助。
    (C) You can just purchase a new printer. 你可以買台新的印表機。

◀ 解析 ▶
1. 印表機的墨水用完了，應該請維修部門來協助較為合理，故選 (B)。
2. be supposed to…：應該…

11. Would you like some more coffee? 您還要加點咖啡嗎？
    (A) Oh, thank you, please. 好的，謝謝。
    (B) It's a very rude question. 那是很無禮的問題。
    (C) The doctor said I should drink more water. 醫生說我應該多喝水。

◀ 解析 ▶
1. 本題用 would you like 詢問對方的意願，選項 (B)、(C) 皆答非所問，故選 (A)。
2. rude (adj.)：粗魯的、無禮的

12. Why don't you propose your ideas to the board? 你何不將意見表達給董事會知道？
    (A) Actually, that's what I plan to do next. 事實上，我正打算這麼做。
    (B) I don't because I don't know him well enough. 我沒這麼做，因為我跟他還不夠熟。
    (C) The proposal is on your desk. 企劃書在你桌上。

◀ 解析 ▶
此處需注意 the board 是指「董事會」，從題意來判斷，選項 (B) 指涉對象錯誤，而選項 (C) 則答非所問，故選 (A)。

13. How much is this pair of shoes, please? 請問這雙鞋多少錢？
    (A) It really depends on how you see it. 這完全取決於你如何看待此事。
    (B) They're $29.99. Do you want to try them on? 是 29.99 元。您想試穿看看嗎？
    (C) You can reach Mr. Ruffalo at extension 483. 你可以打分機 483 找盧法洛先生。

◀ 解析 ▶
本題是問 how much「多少錢」，選項 (A)、(C) 皆未直接回答問題，故選 (B)。

14. What do you think we should go over next? 你認為我們接下來要討論什麼？
    (A) How about if we go over these sales figures? 我們就來討論這些銷售數字如何？
    (B) I think we can go there next week. 我認為我們可以下週過去那裡。
    (C) I think we should talk about it later. 我覺得我們應該晚一點再談。

◀ 解析 ▶
本題重點在 go over 的用法，選項 (B) 的 go there 可能混淆作答，需特別注意，故本題應選 (A)。

15. What are you doing after work? 你下班後要做什麼？
    (A) I am going to my Japanese class. 我要去上日文課。
    (B) I am doing great. How about you? 我很好，你呢？
    (C) You can do whatever you want. 你可以做任何你想做的事。

◀ 解析 ▶
本題問下班後要做什麼，選項 (B) 為對方問 How are you? 時可能的回答，而選項 (C) 則答非所問，故選 (A)。

16. I don't see the point of these meetings, do you? 我實在無法理解這些會議的重點為何，你覺得呢？
(A) I don't, either. I think these long meetings are totally meaningless.
我也無法理解。我認為這些冗長的會議完全沒有意義。
(B) I'd like to, but I kind of like what he just proposed. 我想要，但我還滿喜歡他剛才的提議。
(C) I need to go now. My next meeting starts in 5 minutes.
我必須走了，我的下一個會議五分鐘後開始。

◀ 解析 ▶
1. 對方提出對會議的看法，認為會議毫無重點。選項 (A) 表達同樣意見，並表示自己認為這些會議冗長而無意義，為合理之回答，故選 (A)。

17. What would you like to have for lunch? 你午餐想吃什麼？
(A) Yes, let's take a 10-minute break. 是的，讓我們休息十分鐘。
(B) After lunch, let's discuss the CBS project, okay? 午餐後，我們來討論 CBS 專案，好嗎？
(C) Let's have Chinese food. How does that sound? 我們來吃中國菜吧，聽起來如何？

◀ 解析 ▶
本題是問午餐想吃什麼，只有選項 (C) 直接回應了問題，故選 (C)。

18. What should we do to promote our products? 我們應該如何推廣我們的產品？
(A) Maybe we should place an ad in the newspaper. 或許我們應該在報上登廣告。
(B) You got promoted? I am happy for you. 你升遷了？我真替你高興。
(C) Customers reacted positively. 客戶反應良好。

◀ 解析 ▶
本題重點在 promote our products「推廣產品」，注意選項 (B) 的 promote 為「升遷」之意，回應中應提出推廣產品的方法，故正確答案為 (A)。

19. Have you received the email I just sent you? 你收到我剛寄給你的電子郵件了嗎？
(A) You will fax me the agreement, right? 你會將合約傳真給我，是嗎？
(B) Yes, I do like your writing style. 是的，我很喜歡你的寫作風格。
(C) Yes, I have and I will reply this afternoon. 是的，我收到了，我下午會給你回覆。

◀ 解析 ▶
本題問是否收到了電子郵件，選項 (A) 說的是合約，而選項 (B) 則答非所問，故選 (C)。

20. Do you think we should recruit more employees? 你認為我們要再多聘請些員工嗎？
   (A) Maybe wait until the economic conditions improve. 或許等到經濟狀況好轉再說吧。
   (B) Today's job market is really competitive. 現在的就業市場競爭很激烈。
   (C) I know Amy is between jobs. 我知道艾咪現在待業中。

◀ 解析 ▶
1. 本題詢問是否需要增聘員工，選項 (B)、(C) 皆未回應問題，(A) 則提出視經濟狀況而定，故選 (A) 較為合理。
2. economic (adj.)：經濟上的

21. Where is Jason? We need to start our meeting soon. 傑森去哪了？我們馬上就要開會了。
   (A) I don't know. Let me call his cell phone. 不知道耶，我打他手機看看。
   (B) Jason has been awarded the Best Sales Rep of the Year. 傑森獲選為年度最佳業務員。
   (C) Jason was out visiting customers yesterday. 傑森昨天出去拜訪客戶。

◀ 解析 ▶
1. 本題是問傑森為什麼不在場。選項 (C) 雖然解釋了傑森不在的原因，但時間點為昨天，並不正確。依據題意應該是要想辦法找到傑森，故答案為 (A)。
2. award (v.)：授獎

22. Would you like your seat near the aisle or near the exit? 您喜歡靠走道的座位還是靠出口的座位呢？
   (A) I'd like a seat for the 7 p.m. show, please. 我想要七點那場表演的座位，謝謝。
   (B) I would like to reserve a non-smoking room, please. 我想預訂一間禁菸房，謝謝。
   (C) Near the aisle, please. 請安排靠走道的座位，謝謝。

◀ 解析 ▶
1. 本題是訂位時會出現的問題，回答時應說出自己喜歡的座位位置，故選 (C)。
2. aisle (n.)：走道　non-smoking (adj.)：禁止吸菸的

23. Did you buy some snacks for the party? 你買了派對需要的點心嗎？
   (A) No, I forgot to bring money so I didn't eat lunch. 還沒，我忘記帶錢包了，所以沒吃午餐。
   (B) Yes, things were all prepared. 有呀，東西都準備好了。
   (C) They went to the park. 他們去公園了。

◀ 解析 ▶
本題問是否買了派對所需的點心，選項 (A) 回答的是為何沒吃午餐，選項 (C) 答非所問，故選 (B)。

24. When will Mr. James deliver his speech? 詹姆士先生何時會發表演說？
(A) In the park. 在公園。
(B) Next Monday morning. 下週一早上。
(C) I'm looking forward to it. 我很期待。

◀ 解析 ▶
本題重點是在問 when「何時」，回答則應與時間相關，故本題答案為 (B)。

25. Have you read any good books at all recently? 你最近有讀到什麼好書嗎？
(A) I think *The Last Station* is worth reading. 我認為《最後一站》很值得一讀。
(B) I always read storybooks to my children. 我都唸童書給我的孩子聽。
(C) He is not interested in reading. 他對閱讀沒興趣。

◀ 解析 ▶
本題是詢問對方最近有沒有讀到什麼好書，選項 (B)、(C) 皆答非所問，故選 (A)。

26. The cake looks delicious. Who brought it here? 那個蛋糕看起來很美味，是誰帶來的？
(A) Lily did. 是莉莉帶來的。
(B) Our products sell like hot cakes. 我們的產品很熱賣。
(C) No, thank you. I am on a diet. 不了，謝謝。我在節食。

◀ 解析 ▶
1. 本題重點在詢問 who「是誰」。選項 (B) 出現 hot cakes，容易混淆作答。選項 (C) 則答非所問。選項 (A) 清楚地回應了問題，故本題答案應選 (A)。
2. on a diet：節食

27. Are you supposed to join the conference call? 你是不是應該去參與電話會議呀？
(A) I just need to grab my sales report very quickly. 我只是要很快地拿一下我的業務報告。
(B) The conference call will last approximately one hour. 電話會議大約會進行一小時。
(C) Some board members are joining too. 有些董事會成員也會參加。

◀ 解析 ▶
1. 本題其實是要詢問對方此時出現在這裡的原因。選項 (B) 回答的是會議預計多長時間，(C) 回答的是還有哪些人會參加，故本題答案為 (A)。
2. conference call：電話會議 grab (v.)：抓取 approximately (adv.)：大約

28. Do you know what time Mr. Todd will probably return? 你知道陶德先生大約幾點會回來嗎？
(A) I have no idea what he is doing. 我不知道他在做些什麼。
(B) Mr. Todd will go to Singapore for a trade show. 陶德先生會去新加坡參加展售會。
(C) Mr. Todd will come back by 3 p.m. 陶德先生會在下午三點前回來。

◀ 解析 ▶
1. 本題重點在於 what time「幾點」，只有選項 (C) 回答出確切的時間，故本題答案為 (C)。
2. trade show：商展、貿易展覽

29. Would you like sugar in your tea? 你的茶要加糖嗎？
(A) Yes, please. 好的，謝謝。
(B) Drinking tea is good for your health, you know. 你知道的，喝茶對身體有益。
(C) Sure, give me a cup of coffee, please. 好呀，請給我一杯咖啡吧。

◀ 解析 ▶
本題是問對方要不要在茶裡加糖，選項 (B) 並未回答問題，選項 (C) 回答的是想要一杯咖啡，也不正確，故選 (A)。

30. How about catching a movie on the weekend? 週末去看場電影如何？
(A) That's an interesting film. 那是部有趣的電影。
(B) I'd love to, but I can't. 我很想去，但不行。
(C) It's a 3D movie, right? 那部電影是 3D 的，對嗎？

◀ 解析 ▶
本題以 how about + Ving 的句型，提議一起去看電影，應該回答是否能去，故正確答案為 (B)。

31. Will you be able to fix this fax machine? 你有辦法修好這台傳真機嗎？
(A) Not sure, but I will find out. 不確定耶，不過我會想辦法。
(B) This copy machine is certainly very old. 這台影印機真的很舊了。
(C) I used to work as a car repairman. 我以前是修車技師。

◀ 解析 ▶
本題是問能否修好傳真機，選項 (B) 說的是影印機，選項 (C) 則表示自己是修車技師，皆與傳真機無關，故選 (A)。

Part III. ▶ Conversations

Questions 32 - 34 refer to the following conversation.

[UK] M / [AU] W

M: Hello, this is Tim Jackson here. I am just phoning to make an appointment with Mr. Chance tomorrow morning.

W: I am sorry, Mr. Jackson, but Mr. Chance won't be in the office until 2 o'clock in the afternoon tomorrow.

M: Oh, too bad. I need to go visit an important client tomorrow at 4 p.m. Okay, anyway, please check if Mr. Chance will be available at 2:30 p.m. If it's all right, I'd like to meet with him tomorrow afternoon.

W: Sure, let me see. All right, no problem. See you then, Mr. Jackson.

男：你好，我是提姆傑克森。我打電話來是想跟錢斯先生約明天早上見面。

女：很抱歉，傑克森先生，但錢斯先生明天要下午兩點才會進辦公室耶。

男：這樣呀，真不巧，我明天下午四點要去拜訪個重要的客戶。好吧，沒關係，請幫我確認錢斯先生下午兩點半是否有空。如果可以的話，我就明天下午過來跟他見面。

女：當然，讓我看看。好的，時間上沒問題。傑克森先生，那就到時見了。

32. Who is most likely the woman? 女子最有可能是誰？
    (A) Mr. Jackson's assistant 傑克森先生的助理
    (B) Mr. Chance's client 錢斯先生的客戶
    (C) Mr. Jackson's boss 傑克森先生的老闆
    (D) Mr. Chance's secretary 錢斯先生的秘書

◀ 解析 ▶

對話第二句，女子掌握了錢斯先生的行程，最後還幫忙確認錢斯先生有空的時間，可見女子應該是錢斯先生的秘書，故選 (D)。

33. What would the man probably like to do? 男子可能想要做什麼？
    (A) Visit his relatives 拜訪親戚
    (B) Visit his customer 拜訪客戶
    (C) Visit his doctor 去看醫生
    (D) Visit his high school classmates 去看高中同學

◀ 解析 ▶

對話當中，男子透過錢斯先生的秘書約見面的時間，可知並非拜訪親戚或同學。而男子並未表示身體不舒服、需就醫，且第三句有提到 I need to go visit an important client…，可推斷應為拜訪客戶，故選 (B)。

34. When will the man meet with Mr. Chance? 男子何時會跟錢斯先生會面？
    (A) Tomorrow morning at 10 明天早上十點
    (B) This afternoon at 2:30 今天下午兩點半
    (C) Tomorrow afternoon at 4 明天下午四點
    (D) Tomorrow afternoon at 2:30 明天下午兩點半

◀ 解析 ▶
男子最後請秘書確認錢斯先生明天下午兩點半是否有空，女子回答沒問題，所以兩人會在明天下午兩點半見面，故選 (D)。

Questions 35 - 37 refer to the following conversation.

[CA] M / [US] W

M: Excuse me. How do I get to S Avenue and Q Street? I mean, which is the nearest metro station, please? I'm kind of new to this area, so… Uh…

W: It's okay, no problem. Well, here. Take a look at this map. You take the Red Line to Plaza Place, and then you'll have to change to the Green Line. It's the fourth stop.

M: I see. By the way, could I take the Yellow Line to City Hall and change to the Blue Line there? Which way is faster?

W: Yes, you could do that as well. It's about the same distance.

M: Thank you very much. Oh, another question please. Do you know where the nearest bank is? I might need to open an account first.

W: Of course. Look that way, you see a gas station right next to the traffic light, right? Well, you go directly toward the gas station, and then turn left. After two blocks, you'll see a City Bank on your right-hand side. It's a pretty big building, and you won't miss it.

男：不好意思，請問我要如何到 S 大道和 Q 街呢？我的意思是，離那邊最近的捷運站是哪一站呢？我才剛到此處，所以…嗯…。

女：沒關係的。這裡，看這張地圖。你可以搭紅線到廣場站，然後轉綠線。第四站就是了。

男：瞭解。對了，順便問一下，我可以搭黃線到市政府站，然後轉藍線到那裡嗎？哪種方式比較快？

女：是的，你也可以這樣搭。兩條路線差不多距離。

男：非常謝謝你。還有一個問題。你知道最近的銀行在哪嗎？我可能要先開個戶。

女：當然。請看那個方向，你有看到紅綠燈旁邊的加油站吧？你直接往加油站的方向走去，接著左轉。過兩條巷子之後，就會看到都市銀行在你的右手邊了。那棟大樓很大，你一定不會錯過的。

avenue (n.)：大道、大街　plaza (n.)：廣場　distance (n.)：距離

35. Where does the conversation most likely take place? 此對話最有可能出現在何處？
    (A) In a metro station 在捷運站
    (B) On a beach 在海灘上
    (C) In a conference room 在會議室
    (D) In a bank 在銀行

◀ 解析 ▶
對話第一、二句，提到如何搭乘捷運到達目的地，可推測此對話發生在捷運站，故選 (A)。

36. Who is most likely the woman? 女子最有可能是誰？
   (A) An interviewer 面試官
   (B) A customer service representative 服務人員
   (C) A city hall employee 市府員工
   (D) A broadcast announcer 廣播人員

◀ 解析 ▶
女子針對男子的問題，提供詳盡的捷運搭乘路線與站名，由此可推測女子很可能是捷運站的服務人員，故本題應選 (B)。

37. What is the man's major concern? 男子最在意的事情為何？
   (A) How much he needs to pay 他要付多少車資
   (B) How fast he can get to the destination 他如何最快到達目的地
   (C) How far he needs to walk 他需要走多遠
   (D) How often the metro train leaves 捷運車次多久會有一班

◀ 解析 ▶
男子還詢問女子是否可搭乘其他路線，並問哪種方式較快，可知男子最在意的是如何快速到達目的地，故選 (B)。

Questions 38 - 40 refer to the following conversation.

[CA] M / [AU] W

M: Good morning, Rosa. Could you come in for a minute, please? I need you to run through the messages for me from yesterday.

W: Sure. Ms. Judy Smith called from Canada to say she might be in town from the 3rd to the 6th. She said she wanted to see you then and would call again to confirm.

M: Good. I hope she can make it. I need to talk to her about the CAI project. Anything else?

W: Yeah, and Anne Mori called to say that North Systems had to cancel their last order since their customers had changed their minds.

男：蘿莎，早安。你可以進來一下嗎？我需要跟你確認昨天有哪些留言。

女：好的。茱蒂史密斯小姐從加拿大打電話來，説她可能在三號到六號之間來一趟。她説想跟你見個面，而且還會再打來確認。

男：很好。我希望她可以來一趟。我也必須跟她討論一下 CAI 的專案。還有別的嗎？

女：有，安莫莉打電話來説，諾斯系統公司要取消最近這次的訂單，因為他們的客戶改變心意了。

confirm (v.)：確認　cancel (v.)：取消

38. What is most likely the relationship between the two speakers? 兩人的關係最有可能是什麼？
(A) Husband and wife 先生和太太
(B) Professor and student 教授和學生
(C) Administrator and secretary 老闆和秘書
(D) Sales manager and client 業務經理和客戶

◀ 解析 ▶
對話一開頭，男子就請女子到辦公室裡，跟她確認所有的留言內容，由此可推測兩人為老闆和秘書的關係，故選 (C)。

39. What's the purpose of Ms. Smith's call? 史密斯小姐打電話來的目的為何？
(A) To propose a meeting 想約見面
(B) To invite the man to attend a conference in Canada 邀請男子去加拿大參加研討會
(C) To check the CAI project 檢視 CAI 專案
(D) To cancel an order 取消訂單

◀ 解析 ▶
女子提到史密斯小姐來電，主要是想在三號到六號之間來訪，故本題答案為 (A)。

40. Why does North Systems want to cancel the order? 為什麼諾斯系統公司要取消訂單？
(A) Because they lost the CAI case 因為他們失去了 CAI 的案子
(B) Because their customers don't want it anymore 因為他們的客戶不想買了
(C) Because they are short of money 因為他們資金不足
(D) Because their customers are happy with the quality 因為他們的客戶對品質很滿意

◀ 解析 ▶
1. 對話最後提到諾斯系統公司要取消訂單，是因為客戶改變心意，也就是不想買了，故本題答案為 (B)。
2. be short of...：缺少⋯ quality (n.)：品質

Questions 41 - 43 refer to the following conversation.
[UK] M / [US] W
M: Grace, is it possible to arrange a meeting next week? I'd like to discuss some technical problems with our computer network.
W: Sure, Phil, no problem. When are you free then? And should I also invite Tom, the network architect to join the discussion?
M: Well, I am available next Friday at 1:30, right after lunch. And yeah, it's a good idea to listen to Tom's suggestions as well.
W: Good then. I will call Tom right away and inform him about the meeting next Friday.

男：葛蕾絲，我們可以約下週開會嗎？我想要跟你討論一些電腦網路的技術問題。
女：菲爾，當然沒問題。你何時有空呢？我要不要也邀請網路工程師湯姆來加入討論呢？
男：我下週五用完午餐後一點半有空。另外，聽聽湯姆的建議也是個不錯的主意。

女：很好。我馬上打電話給湯姆，通知他下週五開會。

technical (adj.)：技術性的　architect (n.)：設計者、工程師

41. Why does the man want to arrange this meeting? 男子為什麼想要約開會？
(A) To interview some candidates 要跟一些應徵者面談
(B) To discuss some computer network problems 要討論電腦網路問題
(C) To celebrate Tom's promotion 要慶祝湯姆升遷
(D) To review the woman's performance 要檢討女子的表現

◀ 解析 ▶
1. 對話第一句即提到，男子想跟女子討論電腦網路的問題，故本題答案為 (B)。
2. candidate (n.)：應徵者

42. Who is Tom? 湯姆是誰？
(A) The sales manager 業務經理
(B) The network architect 網路工程師
(C) The team leader 團隊領導人
(D) The VP of engineering 工程部副總

◀ 解析 ▶
對話第二句，女子提到是否需邀請網路工程師湯姆一起開會，故本題答案為 (B)。

43. What will the woman probably do next? 女子接下來可能會做什麼？
(A) Email Tom an agreement 將合約寄電子郵件給湯姆
(B) Fax Phil the meeting agenda 將會議議程傳真給菲爾
(C) Call and invite Tom to attend a meeting 打電話給湯姆邀請他參加會議
(D) Reschedule the meeting to next Friday 將會議改期至下週五

◀ 解析 ▶
1. 對話最後，女子說她會馬上打電話給湯姆，通知開會事宜，故本題答案為 (C)。
2. agenda (n.)：議程

Questions 44 - 46 refer to the following conversation.
[CA] M1 / [AU] W / [UK] M2
M1: Hello Anny and John. How are you guys? Thank you for participating in this conference call.
W: Hello, there. So John is calling from Singapore, right?
M2: Yeah, I'm here in Singapore. Nice to join this video conference. So we're gonna discuss some progress of the TDI project today, aren't we?
M1: Yes, John is right. But before that, I'd like to confirm something. I didn't get the minutes from our last conference call. So, Anny, did you send it to all participants via email or fax?

© Caves Educational Training Co., Ltd.

W: Actually, I sent them last week via email right after our last conference call.

M1: Well, I don't think they arrived in my email. Could you please send them to me again?

M2: It seems like I didn't receive the meeting minutes from last time either. Anny, please also resend them to me.

W: Okay. I am sorry about that. I'll do it right after the conference. Inform me if you still haven't received it within today. All right, now let's get down to business.

男一：哈囉，安妮和約翰。你們好嗎？謝謝你們參與這次的線上會議。

女：大家好。所以約翰是從新加坡上線的，對吧？

男二：是呀，我現在在新加坡。很高興參與這場線上會議。所以我們今天要討論 TDI 專案的一些進度，沒錯吧？

男一：是的，約翰說的沒錯。但在開始之前，我想要確認一件事。我沒有收到上次線上會議的會議記錄。安妮，你是用電子郵件還是傳真，寄給所有與會者的呢？

女：事實上，我在上週線上會議之後，馬上就將會議記錄用電子郵件寄給大家了。

男一：我的信箱裡並沒有收到會議記錄的郵件。你可以再寄給我一次嗎？

男二：看起來我也沒收到上次的會議記錄耶。安妮，也請你再寄給我一次。

女：好的，非常不好意思。會議結束後我立刻寄。如果你們今天內還沒有收到的話，請跟我說一聲。好的，現在我們來談正事吧。

participate (v.)：參與　conference call：電話會議　conference (n.)：會議　minutes (n.)：會議記錄
participant (n.)：參與者　via (prep.)：經由　get down to business：開始做正事

44. Where does the conversation probably take place? 此對話可能出現在何處？
    (A) A meeting point on the Internet 在網路的線上會議
    (B) In Singapore 在新加坡
    (C) At an airport 在機場
    (D) In the woman's kitchen 在女子的廚房

◀ 解析 ▶
從對話一開始，可聽出三人是在進行「線上電話會議」，故本題答案為 (A)。

45. What's both men's problem? 兩名男子遇到的問題為何？
    (A) They didn't receive the meeting minutes. 他們沒收到會議記錄。
    (B) They forgot to send out the meeting minutes. 他們忘了寄出會議記錄。
    (C) Their email systems are not working properly. 他們的電子郵件系統都有問題。
    (D) They didn't send the contract to the woman. 他們沒將合約寄給女子。

◀ 解析 ▶
根據對話中兩名男子的回應，都表示自己沒收到上次開會的會議記錄，故選 (A)。

46. How did the woman send out the minutes? 女子是以何種方式寄出會議記錄？
(A) Via fax 透過傳真
(B) Via email 透過電子郵件
(C) Via courier 透過快遞
(D) Via mail 透過信件

◀ 解析 ▶
1. 女子在對話的後半段回應兩名男子，自己是用電子郵件的方式寄出，故本題答案為 (B)。
2. courier (n.)：快遞

Questions 47 - 49 refer to the following conversation.
[US] W / [CA] M
W: Are you ready to order, sir?
M: Yes, I'd like the chicken, but can I have fries instead of salad? Also please give me a glass of water.
W: Sure. Chicken, fries, and water… It will be about ten minutes. Is it okay with you? One of our cooks is off sick today.
M: Oh, don't worry. It's all right.

女：先生，您準備好要點餐了嗎？
男：是的，我要雞肉餐，但可以將沙拉換成薯條嗎？另外，請給我一杯水。
女：好的。雞肉餐、薯條和水。大約要等十分鐘。可以嗎？今天我們一位廚師請病假。
男：無妨，沒關係。

instead of：代替　off (adj.)：休假的

47. Where does the conversation probably take place? 此對話可能出現在何處？
(A) In a restaurant 在餐廳
(B) In a supermarket 在超市
(C) On a street 在街上
(D) In a kitchen 在廚房

◀ 解析 ▶
從女子為男子點餐的情況來看，這段對話最有可能出現在餐廳裡，故選 (A)。

48. Who is most likely the woman? 女子最有可能是誰？
(A) A cook 廚師
(B) A student 學生
(C) A waitress 女侍者
(D) An actress 女演員

◀ 解析 ▶
承上題，女子的身分應該是餐廳的服務生，故本題答案為 (C)。

49. How does the man feel about the 10-minute wait? 男子對於要等十分鐘感覺如何？
 (A) He thinks it is annoying. 他認為很討厭。
 (B) He thinks it is a good idea. 他認為是好主意。
 (C) He will be cooking tonight. 他今晚想自己煮。
 (D) It doesn't bother him that much. 對他來說影響不大。

◀ 解析 ▶
1. 對話最後，女子告知男子需要等十分鐘，而男子的反應是認為「無妨、沒關係」，故可推知答案為 (D)。
2. annoying (adj.)：惱人的　bother (v.)：困擾、煩擾

Questions 50 - 52 refer to the following conversation.
[UK] M / [AU]W
M: Good afternoon, West Coast Hotel. How may I help you?
W: Hello there. I'd like to make a reservation for a single room, if that's possible, from May 15th for a week. And do you have access to the Internet?
M: Okay, let me see. You are in luck because we've got only one single room left during that period. Also, yes, we have an Internet café here, with ten computers. You can send and receive emails for free.
W: Thanks. That sounds good. Now do you need my ID number or anything?

男：午安，西岸飯店。有什麼可以為您服務的嗎？
女：你好。我想要預約一間單人房，如果可以的話，從五月十五日起住宿一週。另外，飯店內可以上網嗎？
男：好的，我看看。您很幸運，那段期間我們剛好只剩下一間單人房。另外，有的，我們這邊有網路咖啡屋，有十台電腦可上網。您可以免費收發電子郵件。
女：謝謝。聽起來很棒。你需要我的身分證號碼或其他資料嗎？

50. Where is the man probably working? 男子可能是在哪裡上班？
 (A) In an Internet café 在網路咖啡屋
 (B) In a computer store 在電腦用品店
 (C) In a travel agency 在旅行社
 (D) In a hotel 在飯店

◀ 解析 ▶
1. 對話一開始，男子主動說出飯店名稱，以及協助女子訂房，由此可推知男子是西岸飯店的客服人員，故本題應選 (D)。
2. travel agency：旅行社

51. Why does the woman call? 女子打電話的目的為何？
   (A) To make a room reservation 預約訂房
   (B) To cancel a meeting 取消會議
   (C) To retrieve her ID number 取得身分證號碼
   (D) To ask about the availability of a conference venue 詢問會議室是否可用

◀ 解析 ▶
1. 女子一開始即表明，自己需要預約一間單人房，故本題答案為 (A)。
2. retrieve：檢索（資訊）

52. When will the woman probably be checking out? 女子可能何時退房？
   (A) May 15th 五月十五日
   (B) May 30th 五月三十日
   (C) May 22nd 五月二十二日
   (D) June 2nd 六月二日

◀ 解析 ▶
1. 女子提到自己將從五月十五日起，住宿一週（共七天），由此可推算退房日期為五月二十二日，故本題應選 (C)。
2. check out：結帳離開

Questions 53 - 55 refer to the following conversation.

[CA] M / [AU] W

M: Do you want to meet sometime next week to discuss the customer research survey?

W: Yeah, sure. The customer research survey is considered one of our most important tasks for this quarter. We definitely should talk about it soon.

M: Good, then I am available on Monday afternoon. How about you, Linda?

W: You mean next Monday? Well, is it possible that we could meet earlier than that?

M: Earlier? So you're available this week? I thought you're busy this week.

W: Well, how about this Thursday or Friday morning? I'm free then. As a matter of fact, I've got a rather tight schedule next week. You know, Mr. Jackson is flying to the UK for the annual marketing briefing next weekeend, and I need to prepare some documents for him.

M: Let me see, this Thursday or Friday morning… Hm… sorry, I can't make either of those. I am in a meeting on both days. How about this Friday afternoon?

W: Well, okay then, let's meet this Friday at 2 p.m., after lunch, all right?

M: Sure, let me write it down on my planner. See you then.

男：你下週想約個時間來討論客戶問卷調查嗎？

女：好呀！客戶問卷調查是我們本季度最重要的任務之一。這是一定要儘早討論的。

男：那好，我週一下午有空。琳達，你呢？

女：你是說下週一？我們可以約早一點嗎？

男：早一點？那你這週有空囉？我以為你這週很忙耶。

女：這個週四或週五的早上如何？我有空。事實上，我下週行程有點滿。你知道的，傑克森先生下週末要前往英國開年度行銷會議，所以我要幫他準備一些文件。

男：讓我看看，本週四或五早上…。嗯…抱歉，我兩個時間都沒辦法。這兩天我都在開會。那麼本週五下午呢？

女：好吧，那我們就約這個週五的下午兩點，午餐過後，可以嗎？

男：好的，我記在行事曆上。到時見囉。

research (n.)：研究、調查　definitely (adv.)：確實、當然　tight (adj.)：緊湊的

53. What are the two speakers talking about? 兩人在討論什麼？
 (A) Customer survey results 客戶問卷調查的結果
 (B) Meeting arrangement 會議安排
 (C) Lunch meeting 午餐會議
 (D) Travel plan 旅遊行程

◀ 解析 ▶
男子一開始即詢問女子，希望約個時間開會討論，故本題答案為 (B)。

54. Why does the woman want to meet earlier? 為什麼女子想將會議提前？
 (A) Since she will be traveling next week 因為她下週要去旅行
 (B) Since the man will visit clients next week 因為男子下週要拜訪客戶
 (C) Since she will be busy next week 因為她下週很忙
 (D) Since the man will have a meeting next week 因為男子下週有會議

◀ 解析 ▶
女子提到她下週的行程比較滿 (got a rather tight schedule)，換言之，她下週會很忙，故本題答案為 (C)。

55. When will the speakers meet? 兩人何時會開會？
 (A) This Friday afternoon 本週五下午
 (B) This Thursday morning 本週四早上
 (C) Next Wednesday afternoon 下週三下午
 (D) This Friday Morning 本週五早上

◀ 解析 ▶
女子雖希望本週四或五早上開會，但男子時間上無法配合。由對話最後兩句可知，兩人最終訂於本週五下午兩點開會，故選 (A)。

Questions 56 - 58 refer to the following conversation.
[UK] M / [US] W

M: Hello, Jessie. It's Mark Kloof here. I am calling to clarify something. It's about this invoice which your company still hasn't paid, and I was wondering when you were intending to pay it.

W: Oh yes, that one. I am really sorry. We are hoping to pay it as soon as we possibly can. The problem is that we're having cash flow difficulties.
M: Well, Jessie, when do you think that might be?
W: Hopefully by the end of this week. Just as soon as we have some cash available.

男：潔西，你好。我是馬克克魯夫。我打電話來是為了確認一件事。關於一張 貴公司還未付清的帳單，我想知道你們打算何時付款呢？
女：是的，那張帳單。我很抱歉。我們希望儘可能早一點付款。問題是我們現在資金周轉有點問題。
男：潔西，你想大約何時能付款呢？
女：希望是這個星期以內。我們一有現金就會付款了。

clarify (v.)：澄清、說明　intend (v.)：想要、打算

56. What's the purpose of the man's call? 男子打電話的目的為何？
(A) To ask about an outstanding invoice 詢問關於未清償的帳單
(B) To request some product information 詢問產品訊息
(C) To invite the woman to attend a seminar 邀請女子參加研討會
(D) To arrange some shipments 安排商品裝運

◀ 解析 ▶
1. 對話開頭，男子即提到要確認一張未付款的帳單，故本題答案為 (A)。
2. outstanding (adj.)：未解決的、未償付的　seminar (n.)：研討會　shipment (n.)：裝運

57. Why does the woman's company delay the payment? 為什麼女子的公司遲遲未付款？
(A) Because the accountant is on vacation 因為會計師去渡假
(B) Because they don't have cash available 因為他們沒有現金可周轉
(C) Because the bank won't lend them any more money 因為銀行不願再借他們錢
(D) Because the woman has maxed out her credit cards 因為女子刷爆了她的信用卡

◀ 解析 ▶
1. 女子回應未付款的原因，是因為遇上現金周轉困難 (cash flow difficulties)，由此可知答案為 (B)。
2. accountant (n.)：會計師　max out：超過最大限度

58. When will the woman's company expect to pay? 女子的公司預計何時付款？
(A) By the end of this month 月底前
(B) By the end of the day 今天內
(C) By the end of the week 本週內
(D) Within three days 三天內

◀ 解析 ▶
對話最後，女子提到希望在本週內支付款項，故本題答案為 (C)。

Questions 59 - 61 refer to the following conversation.

[UK] M / [AU] W

M: So Samantha, let's plan the weekend. How about we go somewhere?

W: Yeah, what about Madison Square? It's a really nice place, and not far from New York. By train it takes about 30 minutes. Or perhaps we could drive there.

M: Well, I'd like to go by train. Where do we catch it?

W: The East Station is quite close. It only takes us about 10 minutes to walk there. Okay, I will purchase two train tickets online.

男：莎曼珊，我們來規劃一下週末吧。我們要去哪裡呢？

女：好呀，去麥迪遜廣場如何？那是個好去處，離紐約也不遠。搭火車大約三十分鐘就到了。或者我們也可以開車去。

男：我想搭火車去。可以在哪裡搭呢？

女：東站離這裡很近。走路大約十分鐘就到了。好，我會上網買兩張火車票。

59. What are the two speakers doing? 兩人在做什麼？

(A) Arranging a conference in Madison 安排一場在麥迪遜的會議

(B) Driving to New York 開車前往紐約

(C) Purchasing plane tickets 購買機票

(D) Planning their weekend 規劃週末活動

◀ 解析 ▶

對話開頭，男子即提到想要規劃週末的活動，故本題答案為 (D)。

60. How far is it from New York to Madison? 從紐約到麥迪遜有多遠？

(A) It takes 30 minutes by train. 搭火車三十分鐘。

(B) It takes 10 minutes by car. 開車十分鐘。

(C) It takes 20 minutes on foot. 走路二十分鐘。

(D) It takes 30 minutes by car. 開車三十分鐘。

◀ 解析 ▶

女子說紐約離麥迪遜不遠，搭火車只要三十分鐘，故本題答案為 (A)。

61. What will the woman probably do next? 女子接下來可能會做什麼？

(A) Plan the weekend with other friends 跟其他朋友規劃週末活動

(B) Drive to New York with the man 跟男子一起開車前往紐約

(C) Go online to buy train tickets 上網購買火車票

(D) Go to the East Station to take a train 到東站去搭火車

◀ 解析 ▶

男子說想搭火車去麥迪遜，因此對話最後一句，女子說自己將要上網購買火車票，故選 (C)。

Questions 62 - 64 refer to the following conversation and map.

[US] W / [CA] M

W: Excuse me. Can you tell me how to get to the supermarket?

M: Sure, let me see here. Okay, so we're now on Rose Street and the supermarket is on Tulip Street.

W: Well, the only street I know is Lily Street. I know my hotel is on the corner there.

M: All right, good. Now just go along Rose Street, and when you see a gas station, turn right. That's Cherry Road.

W: Okay, go this way and turn right. Sure.

M: Then you walk along Cherry Road to the next set of traffic lights, and you'll see Tulip Street. You turn left there and the supermarket is just on your right.

W: Well, that's not too far. Thank you very much.

女：不好意思。請問你知道超市要怎麼走嗎？

男：當然，我看一下。好，我們現在是在玫瑰街，而超市是在鬱金香街上。

女：嗯，我所認識的街道只有百合街。我知道我的飯店就在那條街轉角的地方。

男：很好。現在你就沿著玫瑰街走去，看到加油站時右轉。那裡就是櫻桃路。

女：好，朝這走並右轉。沒問題。

男：接著沿櫻桃路走到下一個紅綠燈，你會看到鬱金香街。然後再左轉，超市就在你的右手邊。

女：嗯，這樣並沒有太遠。非常謝謝你。

62. Where does the conversation most likely take place? 此對話最有可能出現在何處？
   (A) By a beach 在海邊
   (B) On a street 在街上
   (C) At an airport 在機場
   (D) In an office 在辦公室

◀ 解析 ▶

根據對話，可聽出女子在向男子問路，因此應該是在街上或路邊較為合理，故選 (B)。

63. What is the woman doing? 女子在做什麼？
   (A) Attending a seminar 參加研討會
   (B) Taking some photos 拍一些照片
   (C) Driving to a gas station 開車前往加油站
   (D) Asking for directions 向人問路

◀ 解析 ▶

根據對話第一句，女子問男子去超市要怎麼走，可知女子是在問路，故本題答案應選 (D)。

64. Please look at the map. Which hotel does the woman probably live in?
請看地圖。女子可能住在哪一間飯店？

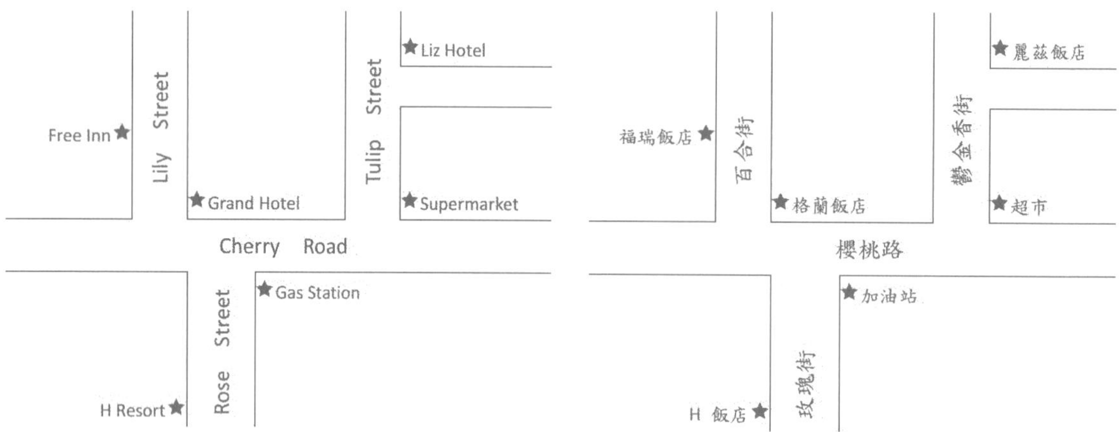

(A) Liz Hotel 麗茲飯店
(B) H Resort H 飯店
(C) Grand Hotel 格蘭飯店
(D) Free Inn 福瑞飯店

◀ 解析 ▶
根據對話第三句，女子表示入住的飯店是在百合街轉角處，再對照地圖內容，故選 (C)。

Questions 65 - 67 refer to the following conversation and table.

[UK] M / [AU] W

M: Excuse me. Could you tell me if flight H889 to Chicago has departed yet? I just arrived from Japan and have to connect to Chicago on that flight.

W: Oh, I'm really sorry, sir. That flight departed 10 minutes ago. But let me check what I can do here.

M: Yes, please do help. Here is my ticket. Oh, and I have one bag to check.

W: All right… let me see. Well, I'm afraid all flights to Chicago today are fully booked. The next available flight is tomorrow morning.

M: Tomorrow morning? That's not good at all. I've got an important meeting tomorrow at 1 in the afternoon. But now I guess that's the only thing I can do.

W: Right, now I need your passport please, sir.

男：不好意思。請問飛往芝加哥的班機 H889 起飛了嗎？我剛從日本抵達，然後要轉搭那班飛機到芝加哥。
女：噢，很抱歉，先生。那班飛機十分鐘前就起飛了。讓我看看可以幫您做些什麼。
男：好，請務必幫忙。這是我的機票。對了，我還有一只皮箱要託運。
女：好的，讓我看看。嗯，恐怕今天要前往芝加哥的班機都滿了。下一班有空位的飛機是明天早上。
男：明天早上？這可不太妙呀！我明天下午一點有個重要會議。但現在看起來也只能這樣了。
女：是的，現在我需要您的護照，先生。

65. What is the man's problem? 男子遇到什麼問題？
(A) He missed the flight. 他錯過班機。
(B) He arrived too early. 他太早抵達。
(C) He lost his passport. 他遺失護照。
(D) He doesn't know which gate to go. 他不知道應前往哪個登機門。

◀ 解析 ▶
根據對話內容，男子表示要轉搭前往芝加哥的航班，但女子回應該班機已起飛，可知男子錯過了他的飛機，故選 (A)。

66. What does the woman suggest the man do? 女子建議男子做何事？
(A) Go to Gate 8 immediately 馬上前往八號登機門
(B) Purchase another ticket 購買另一張機票
(C) Go to Chicago by train instead 改搭火車去芝加哥
(D) Take another flight next day 搭第二天的其他班機

◀ 解析 ▶
對話中，女子表示今天往芝加哥的班機都客滿了，只能搭乘第二天早上的飛機，故本題應選 (D)。

67. Please look at the table. Which flight will the man most likely take?
請看表格。男子最有可能搭乘哪一架班機？

Flight Number	Date	Time	To	Status
A483	10/4	3 p.m.	Singapore	Delayed
H889	10/4	4:15 p.m.	Chicago	Departed
GR937	10/5	10 a.m.	Chicago	---
SI012	10/5	11:30 a.m.	New York	---

班機號碼	日期	時間	前往	狀態
A483	10/4	下午三點	新加坡	誤點
H889	10/4	下午四點十五分	芝加哥	起飛
GR937	10/5	早上十點	芝加哥	---
SI012	10/5	早上十一點半	紐約	---

(A) SI012
(B) GR937
(C) A483
(D) H889

◀ 解析 ▶
承上題，男子錯過了本來要搭的班機 H889，並且要搭隔天早上前往芝加哥的飛機，再對照表格內容，故選 (B)。

Questions 68 - 70 refer to the following conversation and table.

[CA] M / [AU] W

M: Welcome to CBA Rent-a-Car. My name is Jack Wilson. How may I help you?

W: Good morning, Jack. I'd like to rent a car for 2 days to Springfield.

M: Sure. You've come to the right place. We do have a very comprehensive range. So what kind of car would you like?

W: Well, I don't know too much about cars… What's available? Oh, and I'm on a budget.

M: In that case, you can select from these GM compacts and standards. This car includes automatic transmission and air conditioning.

W: Okay, then this one is good enough. Here is my driver's license.

M: Sure. Please sign here and I'll get you fixed up in no time.

男：歡迎來到 CBA 租車公司。我是傑克威爾森。有什麼能為您效勞嗎？

女：早安，傑克。我想租台車到春田市，要用兩天。

男：沒問題。您來對地方了。我們的確是有完整的租車選擇。您想要哪種類型的車呢？

女：嗯，我對車不是很瞭解…。你們有什麼車？對了，我預算有限。

男：這樣的話，您可以選這些 GM 簡約型小車和標準型的車款。這輛車有含自動排檔和空調系統。

女：好呀，這台就夠好了。這是我的駕照。

男：好的。請在此簽名，我馬上幫您處理好。

68. What is the woman going to do? 女子正要做什麼？
    (A) Apply for a job 申請工作
    (B) Rent a car 租一台車
    (C) Reserve a room 訂一間房
    (D) Arrange a meeting 安排會議

◀ 解析 ▶
根據對話第二句，女子表示要租一輛車，故本題答案應選 (B)。

69. What does the man suggest the woman do? 男子建議女子做何事？
    (A) Select a compact model 選擇簡約型小車
    (B) Pay by credit card 用信用卡付款
    (C) Search online first 先上網搜尋
    (D) Renew her driver's license 換發駕照

◀ 解析 ▶
根據對話內容，男子提議女子可從簡約型的小車和標準型的車款中作選擇，故本題答案應選 (A)。

70. Please look at the table. Which car would the woman most likely rent?
請看表格。女子最有可能租哪一台車？

Car Number	Availability	Inclusion	Model
1	O	Automatic transmission, A/C, insurance	Lux
2	O	Automatic transmission, A/C	GM Compact
3	X	Automatic transmission	GM Standard
4	O	A/C	GM Compact

車號	出租狀態	配備	型號
1	O	自排、空調、保險	豪華型
2	O	自排、空調	GM 簡約型
3	X	自排	GM 標準型
4	O	空調	GM 簡約型

(A) 1
(B) 2
(C) 3
(D) 4

◀ 解析 ▶
對話最後，女子表示男子提議的車輛就夠好了，也就是有自排和空調的簡約型小車，再對照表格內容，故選(B)。

Part IV. ▶ Talks

Questions 71 - 73 refer to the following talk.

[AU] W

Thank you for attending today's children's psychology session. As we all know, fear, doubt, and worry arise when a child is continually criticized. Even if the child accomplishes something worthwhile, it never seems enough to gratify his parents. Based on a recent survey result, in many homes in Taiwan, the parents seldom express love or approval, or they tend to withdraw their love and approval if they feel that the child is failing to please them in some way. Therefore, in order to help our children to build confidence, parents should praise children as much as possible. All right, let's move on and talk about when and how parents should praise their children.

謝謝您參加今天的兒童心理課程。我們都知道，當孩子們不斷地被批評，他們會產生恐懼、懷疑與憂慮的情緒。即使孩子們完成某些值得誇讚的事情，似乎也不足以讓他們的父母滿足。根據最近的一份問卷調查，結果顯示在台灣的許多家庭，父母很少表現出對孩子的愛或認同感，或是當他們感覺孩子不順從他們的想法，便傾向於收回他們對孩子的愛與認同感。因此，為了幫助我們的小孩建立自信，父母們要盡最大的努力來稱讚孩子。好，接下來讓我們來談談父母應在何時以及如何稱讚孩子。

psychology (n.)：心理學　continually (adv.)：不停地　criticize (v.)：批評　worthwhile (adj.)：值得做的
gratify (v.)：使滿意　approval (n.)：認可　withdraw (v.)：收回、取消　confidence (n.)：信心
praise (v.)：讚美

71. According to the speaker, what will happen when a child is continually criticized?
根據說話者所言，當孩子不斷地被批評，他們會怎麼樣？
(A) Fear, doubt, and worry will arise. 產生恐懼、懷疑和憂慮。
(B) Children will feel happy and optimistic. 孩子會感到快樂和樂觀。
(C) Their school performance will improve. 他們的在校表現會進步。
(D) They will never feel upset. 他們永遠不會感到沮喪。

◀ 解析 ▶
1. 根據第二句，小孩不斷地被批評，會產生恐懼、懷疑和憂慮，故選 (A)。
2. optimistic (adj.)：樂觀的

72. What is mentioned about parents in Taiwan? 內容提到台灣父母如何？
(A) They tend to spoil their children. 他們會溺愛小孩。
(B) They praise their children a lot. 他們很常讚美小孩。
(C) They seldom express love to their children. 他們鮮少表達對小孩的愛。
(D) They gratify their children's demands. 他們滿足小孩所有的要求。

◀ 解析 ▶
1. 根據問卷調查結果，台灣的父母很少表達對孩子的愛與認同感，故選 (C)。
2. spoil (v.)：寵壞、溺愛　demand (n.)：要求

73. What will the speaker probably talk about next? 說話者接下來可能會討論什麼？
(A) How to gratify parents 如何滿足父母
(B) How and when to praise children 如何和何時讚美孩子
(C) How to build parents' confidence 如何建立父母的信心
(D) When to express love 何時要表達愛

◀ 解析 ▶
最後一句提到，接下來要討論的是何時和如何讚美孩子，故選 (B)。

Questions 74 - 76 refer to the following talk.
[UK] M
Hello, everyone. I am happy to attend today's sharing session. I am Sam and I am head of R&D at ITG Technologies. I am in charge of research and development at our research center located in Singapore. Our laboratories are some of the most innovative in the IT industry, and we have made many new inventions and breakthroughs. I love using scientific knowledge for practical purposes. However, I totally understand that the high-tech products of today may become the low-tech products of tomorrow. So

that's why we need to keep developing up-to-date products and make sure that ITG's products are never obsolete.

哈囉，各位好。我很高興參加今天的分享會。我是山姆，ITG 科技公司研發部主管，我負責位於新加坡研究中心的研發工作。我們是資訊產業界最具有創新精神的實驗室之一，我們更有許多新發明與突破。我喜歡將科學知識應用在實用層面。然而，我完全了解今日的高科技產品，明天可能就會變成低階產品。這也就是為什麼我們必須持續研發更新的產品，確保 ITG 的產品永不過時。

laboratory (n.)：實驗室　innovative (adj.)：創新的　invention (n.)：發明　breakthrough (n.)：突破
scientific (adj.)：科學的　obsolete (adj.)：過時的

74. What is the speaker's job? 說話者的工作是什麼？
(A) A professional speaker 專業演講者
(B) A technology consultant 技術顧問
(C) An R&D manager 研發經理
(D) A product manager 產品經理

◀ 解析 ▶
男子一開始就介紹自己是 ITG 科技公司的研發部主管，故可推測本題答案為 (C)。

75. Where does the speaker most likely live? 說話者最有可能住在哪裡？
(A) In the US 美國
(B) In Singapore 新加坡
(C) In the UK 英國
(D) In China 中國

◀ 解析 ▶
男子說自己是負責新加坡研究中心的研發工作，以常理推斷，男子應該居住於新加坡當地，故選 (B)。

76. What is the speaker's main job responsibility? 說話者的主要工作內容是什麼？
(A) Study more software knowledge 學習更多軟體知識
(B) Manage an IT company 管理資訊科技公司
(C) Invent new cell phones 發明新手機
(D) Develop state-of-the-art products 開發先進的產品

◀ 解析 ▶
1. 演講內容提到高科技產品的研發，以及創新的發明，可見其主要工作是開發先進的產品，故選 (D)。
2. state-of-the-art (adj.)：最先進的

Questions 77 - 79 refer to the following talk.

[CA] M

Okay, I am afraid we are running out of time, so we need to stop here. To go over what's been discussed, there is an agreement about budgets in the advertising department. However, there is a disagreement about our new product launch timeline. I will talk to our general manager about this and consult him for further opinions. I will let you know his decision about the solution to the issue by the end of this week. So now, does anyone have anything else to add? No? Good, and I think that's it. Thank you all for attending today's discussion.

好，我擔心我們會超過時間，所以我們必須在這裡告一段落。我來整理一下已經討論過的內容。一個是廣告部門預算方面的審核通過，另一個則是關於新產品上市時間的不同意見。我將會與總經理討論這個問題，並徵詢他的意見。我也會在這個禮拜結束前，讓各位知道他對於這個問題的解決方法有何決議。那麼，有人有其他意見要補充的嗎？沒有？好，我想就這樣了。謝謝你們參加今天的討論。

budget (n.)：預算　advertising (n.)：廣告　launch (n.)：上市、發行

77. Who is most likely the speaker? 說話者最有可能是誰？
    (A) The chairperson 主席
    (B) A participant 與會者
    (C) The general manager 總經理
    (D) A consultant 顧問

◀ 解析 ▶

1. 從前面的發言裡，可看出男子是擔任掌控時間與統整意見的角色，由此可推測男子應為會議主席，故本題應選 (A)。
2. chairperson (n.)：主席　participant (n.)：參與者

78. What is the problem with the product launch? 產品上市方面有什麼問題？
    (A) The general manager disagrees about the budget. 總經理不同意預算。
    (B) Members disagree about the launch timeline. 成員在上市時間上意見分歧。
    (C) The new product launch will be delayed. 新產品會延後上市。
    (D) The chairperson can't make a final decision. 主席無法做最後決定。

◀ 解析 ▶

男子提到對於新產品上市的時間，與會者有不同的意見 (disagreement)，故本題答案為 (B)。

79. When will the decision be finalized? 最終決定何時會定案？
    (A) Within this quarter 本季內
    (B) Within this month 本月內
    (C) Within this week 本週內
    (D) Within two days 兩天內

◀ 解析 ▶
男子也提到會徵詢總經理的意見，並在本週之內將決議告知所有人，故本題答案為 (C)。

Questions 80 - 82 refer to the following talk.

[US] W

Hello, Jack, this is Wendy calling from Mascull Company. I have received the hotel reservation confirmation you sent me yesterday, but I need you to make some changes for me please. I had planned to check in at the Plaza Hotel on May 21st; however, I have to change my arrival date to May 25th. My checkout date will remain the same on May 30th. Also please make sure that they have the Internet access in the room. Please inform the hotel and make the change. Once it's done, send me confirmation via email. Thank you.

哈囉，傑克。我是馬斯庫爾公司的溫蒂。我已經收到你昨天寄來的飯店預約確認，但我需要請你幫我做一些變更。我先前計畫在五月二十一日入住廣場飯店，然而，我必須將抵達的時間更改為五月二十五日。我的退房日期則保持原來的五月三十日不變。還有，請確認房間內有網際網路連線服務。請通知飯店變更日期。完成之後，用電子郵件將確認信寄給我。謝謝。

80. What was sent to the speaker yesterday by Jack? 傑克昨天寄了什麼給說話者？
 (A) Hotel reservation confirmation 飯店預約確認函
 (B) Plane tickets 飛機票
 (C) Project contract 專案合約
 (D) Hotel list 飯店列表

◀ 解析 ▶
女子一開始，便提及自己已收到傑克寄來的飯店預約確認，故本題答案為 (A)。

81. When will the speaker probably check in? 說話者可能何時會入住？
 (A) On May 21st 五月二十一日
 (B) On May 30th 五月三十日
 (C) On May 25th 五月二十五日
 (D) On May 15th 五月十五日

◀ 解析 ▶
女子想將入住日期從原來的五月二十一日，更改成五月二十五日，可知其正確入住日期為五月二十五日，故選 (C)。

82. How will Jack probably contact the speaker? 傑克可能以何種方式跟說話者聯絡？
 (A) Directly visit the speaker 直接拜訪說話者
 (B) Via email 透過電子郵件
 (C) By returning the call 回電
 (D) Via fax 透過傳真

◀ 解析 ▶
開頭提到傑克寄給女子確認函，最後女子也希望傑克透過電子郵件，將變更之後的確認函寄給她，可推測兩人是以電子郵件互相聯絡，故選 (B)。

Questions 83 - 85 refer to the following talk.

[UK] M

Good evening. I am Tom Brook. Tonight on *Bright Future* we will talk to three women who have started their own businesses. We will talk to each of them about the excitement and risks of starting their own business and find out what it takes to be an owner of a company in today's competitive business world. First of all, let's welcome Lisa Sweeney, Avon Dignen, and Lorrie Flinders. Well, now I'd like to ask you ladies why you started your own businesses in the first place. Lisa, how about you go first? Why did you decide to take the plunge?

各位晚安，我是湯姆布魯克。今晚在「光明未來」節目中，我們將訪問三位自行創業的女性，逐一與她們談談創辦公司的興奮感與風險性，並找出在充滿競爭的商業環境裡，成立自己的公司需要哪些條件。首先，讓我們歡迎莉莎史威尼、雅芳迪南、蘿莉福林德斯。好，現在我想要請問各位女士，為何一開始會創立您自己的公司呢？莉莎，由您開始好嗎？您為何決定冒險投入創業的行列？

risk (n.)：風險　take the plunge：冒險嘗試

83. Who are the guests on the program? 節目來賓有誰？
   (A) Three female professors 三位女教授
   (B) Three female entrepreneurs 三位女性創業家
   (C) Three male directors 三位男性主管
   (D) Three male engineers 三位男性工程師

◀ 解析 ▶
1. 男子一開頭即介紹今天的節目來賓，是三位自行創業的女性，由此可知本題答案為 (B)。
2. entrepreneur (n.)：企業家、事業創辦者

84. What is special about the three guests? 三位來賓的特別之處為何？
   (A) They are all outstanding translators. 他們都是傑出的翻譯員。
   (B) They all won an award. 他們都得過獎。
   (C) They all know how to avoid risks. 他們都知道如何避免風險。
   (D) They all started their own businesses. 他們都自行創業。

◀ 解析 ▶
1. 承上題，三位女性共同的特點為自行創業，故選 (D)。
2. outstanding (adj.)：傑出的　translator (n.)：翻譯員

85. Who will probably speak next? 接下來可能由誰發言？
(A) Tom Brook 湯姆布魯克
(B) Lisa Sweeney 莉莎史威尼
(C) Avon Dignen 雅芳迪南
(D) Lorrie Flinders 蘿莉福林德斯

◀ 解析 ▶
最後，男子開始訪問三位女性，並提議由莉莎先開始回答，故可推斷接下來講話的人應該是莉莎史威尼，故選 (B)。

Questions 86 - 88 refer to the following talk.

[AU] W

After some snow yesterday, this morning finds us mostly sunny and cold for February. Actually, this afternoon's temperatures will still be a bit milder than you might expect, rising into the lower teens. A cold front is to our west right now and I drew a line on the map below to show where this front is located. Like most cold fronts, the weather behind the front gets colder. As the front pushes through the area today, colder air will rush in and by tomorrow morning it will be 20 degrees colder than this morning. I will be updating the forecast frequently, so please stay tuned.

在昨天下了場雪之後，今天早上各地區大多恢復到二月份晴朗而寒冷的天氣。事實上，今天下午的氣溫仍然會比您所預期的溫暖一些，氣溫將提高到十度多一點。冷鋒目前在我們的西邊，我在地圖上畫一條線表示冷鋒的位置。和大部分的冷鋒一樣，鋒面過後的天氣會比較冷。今天鋒面穿過的區域，冷空氣將會被帶進來，而明天早上，氣溫將會比今天早上再低二十度左右。我將會持續地更新氣象報告，所以請您繼續關注。

temperature (n.)：溫度　mild (adj.)：溫和的、溫暖的　cold front：冷鋒

86. What was the weather like yesterday? 昨天天氣如何？
(A) Sunny 晴天
(B) Rainy 雨天
(C) Snowy 下雪
(D) Windy 強風

◀ 解析 ▶
女子第一句即提到 some snow yesterday，也就是昨天有下雪，因此本題答案為 (C)。

87. What will the weather be like tomorrow? 明天天氣會如何？
(A) Colder 更冷
(B) Warmer 更暖
(C) More humid 更濕
(D) Hotter 更熱

◀ 解析 ▶
女子提到冷鋒接近之後，天氣會變冷，倒數第二句更直接說明，明早氣溫會比今早低二十度左右，故選 (A)。

88. What is the audience asked to do? 聽眾被要求做什麼事？
   (A) Get up earlier tomorrow morning 明早早點起床
   (B) Take an umbrella 帶雨傘
   (C) Keep listening to the program 持續聽節目
   (D) Wear a heavy coat 穿厚外套

◀ 解析 ▶
最後一句，女子說自己會持續更新氣象報告，請聽眾繼續關注節目內容，故選 (C)。

Questions 89 - 91 refer to the following talk.
[CA] M
All right, so welcome to today's workshop. The purpose of this workshop is to talk about some of the problems you may have with meetings and to see if we can find the way to solve some of them. We all want to make our working life a little happier and more productive, don't we? Well, first of all I have to say that during the meeting, a good chairperson has to be a good organizer. He should start the meeting on time, without waiting for latecomers. Also the chair should make sure that each participant has the chance to make their points, and should deal with disagreements. Now let's go around the table and get a few ideas from you. Let's start with you, Bob.

好，歡迎參加今天的研討會。這個研討會的目的，是討論關於你在會議中可能遇到的問題，並且看看我們是否能找到方法解決部分問題。我們都希望讓職場生活更快樂、更有收穫，不是嗎？首先我必須說，開會時，一個好的會議主席，必須是一個好的組織者。主席必須讓會議準時開始，而非一直等待遲到的與會人員。主席必須確定所有參加的人，都有機會表達他們的意見，也必須能夠處理意見不同的狀況。現在，我們依照座位順序輪流發表意見，讓各位貢獻一些想法。鮑伯，就從你開始吧。

productive (adj.)：富有成效的　organizer (n.)：組織者　latecomer (n.)：遲到者　deal with：處理

89. What is the workshop all about? 此研討會主題為何？
   (A) How to live more happily 如何更快樂地生活
   (B) How to hold productive meetings 如何提高會議成效
   (C) How to deliver a good speech 如何發表精彩的演講
   (D) How to deal with conflicts 如何處理衝突

◀ 解析 ▶
男子提到此會議的目的，是討論會議中可能遇到的問題，並找出解決方法。由此可推知，主題是與提高會議成效有關，故選 (B)。

90. What's one of the chairperson's duties? 主席的任務包括以下哪一項？
   (A) Disagree with all participants 跟所有與會者意見分歧
   (B) Make a final decision all by himself 自己做最後的決定
   (C) Be a good timekeeper 有效掌控時間
   (D) Start the meeting late 晚點開始會議

◀ 解析 ▶
男子認為主席必須掌握會議開始的時間，確保每個人都有機會發表意見，並能處理意見不同的狀況，故本題答案為 (C)。

91. What will workshop participants do next? 參與研討會的人接下來會做什麼？
   (A) Have lunch together 一起吃午餐
   (B) Have a long sales meeting 開個冗長的業務會議
   (C) Select a chairperson 選出主席
   (D) Contribute their ideas 貢獻自己的想法

◀ 解析 ▶
最後，男子引導所有參加者，開始按照座位順序輪流發表意見，故本題答案為 (D)。

Questions 92 - 94 refer to the following talk.
[US] W
Attention all passengers traveling on flight 938 to Singapore. Boarding will be delayed due to a minor mechanical problem on the plane. We will have this issue solved as soon as possible. We ask that you remain near boarding gate 73 during this time please, so you can hear all related updates. Our staff will have more information for you within twenty minutes. We also encourage passengers to view real-time flight status updates on the display screens located at the airport terminal. If you need any assistance, please feel free to contact our staff.

所有搭乘 938 號班機前往新加坡的乘客請注意，由於飛機出現輕微的機械故障，登機時間將會稍微延遲。我們將以最快的速度解決這個問題。這段期間，敬請您留在 73 號登機門附近，以確保您可以聽到相關的最新通知。我們的工作人員將於二十分鐘內告訴您更多的訊息。我們同時鼓勵乘客，可以在機場航廈的顯示螢幕上，觀看班機的即時狀況更新。如果您需要任何協助，請隨時與我們的工作人員聯繫。

minor (adj.)：較小的　related (adj.)：相關的　encourage (v.)：鼓勵　real-time (adj.)：即時的
terminal (n.)：航空站　staff (n.)：（全體）工作人員

92. What is the problem? 發生什麼問題？
(A) Boarding will be delayed. 延遲登機。
(B) Weather condition is bad. 天候狀況不佳。
(C) Passengers are too tired. 旅客太累了。
(D) Display screens are not working. 顯示螢幕壞了。

◀ 解析 ▶
此為機場的廣播內容，廣播一開始提到，由於飛機的機械故障，登機時間會稍微延遲，故本題答案為 (A)。

93. Where should passengers be waiting? 旅客應在哪裡等候？
(A) Near the check-in counter 在報到櫃檯附近
(B) Inside the aircraft 在飛機內
(C) Near Gate 73 在 73 號登機門附近
(D) Outside the airport 在機場外

◀ 解析 ▶
1. 廣播中提到希望旅客留在靠近 73 號登機門的位置，才能聽到最新的通知，故選 (C)。
2. aircraft (n.)：飛機

94. What should passengers do if they have questions? 若旅客有問題應該怎麼做？
(A) Call their relatives 打電話給親戚
(B) Contact the staff 跟工作人員聯繫
(C) Email the captain 寄電子郵件給機長
(D) Call the airline company 打電話給航空公司

◀ 解析 ▶
1. 廣播最後告知旅客，若有任何問題，可以與工作人員聯繫，故本題答案為 (B)。
2. relative (n.)：親戚　captain (n.)：機長

Questions 95 - 97 refer to the following talk and table.

[UK] M

Hello, Ms. Benchmark. This is Ben Elvis calling from Neo Company. It's now about ten past eight on Monday evening. I am calling regarding the meeting scheduled tomorrow morning. One of our clients will come tomorrow to sign a technical support agreement, so I have to stay in the office. If it's okay with you, I'd like to reschedule for later this week. I am available this Thursday afternoon between 1 and 3, and Friday afternoon after 3. Please call my cell phone at 0917-438-546 or my assistant Tiffany Mok at (02) 4737-3729 tomorrow to confirm. I am looking forward to meeting you soon.

哈囉，班區瑪克女士，這是從尼歐公司打電話來的班艾維斯。現在是星期一晚上約莫八點十分，這通電話是關於明天早上的預定會議行程。我們明天會有一位客戶前來簽署技術支援同意書，所以我必須留在辦公室。如果可以的話，我想要更改會議時間到這個禮拜稍後的其他時間。我本週四下午一點到三點，或本週五下午三點之後有空。明天請撥打我的手機 0917-438-546，或電話聯絡我的助理蒂芬妮莫克 (02) 4737-3729 以便確認。我非常期待很快能夠與您見面！

support (n.)：支援、支持　look forward to：期待…

95. What time is the man leaving the phone message? 此電話留言發生在幾點？
(A) 2 p.m. 下午兩點
(B) 8:10 p.m. 晚上八點十分
(C) 3 a.m. 早上三點
(D) 8:10 a.m. 早上八點十分

◀ 解析 ▶
男子一開頭說明自己身分，接著便確認留言時間為星期一晚上八點十分，故選 (B)。

96. Why does the speaker call Ms. Benchmark? 說話者打電話給班區瑪克女士的目的為何？
(A) He wants to cancel the meeting. 他想要取消會議。
(B) He wants to schedule a con-call. 他想要安排電話會議。
(C) He wants to reschedule the meeting. 他想要將會議改期。
(D) He wants to schedule a visit. 他想要安排拜訪的時間。

◀ 解析 ▶
1. 男子提到因為明早會有其他客戶前來，他必須更改會議時間，故本題答案為 (C)。
2. con-call (n.)：(= conference call) 電話會議

97. Please look at the table. When will they most likely meet? 請看表格。他們最有可能何時開會？

Time	Wednesday	Thursday	Friday
9 a.m.	Sales Meeting	TDI Discussion	Client – Ms. Dan
11 a.m.	Mr. Jackson	Sales Strategies	PM Reports
1 p.m.	Budget Planning	n/a	Lunch Meeting
3 p.m.	Ticket Confirmation	n/a	n/a
5 p.m.	Con-call	Return Emails	n/a

時間	週三	週四	週五
9 a.m.	業務會議	TDI 討論	客戶—丹小姐
11 a.m.	傑克森先生	業務策略	PM 報告
1 p.m.	預算規劃	無	午餐會議
3 p.m.	票務確認	無	無
5 p.m.	電話會議	回覆電郵	無

(A) Friday afternoon at 3:30 週五下午三點半
(B) Thursday afternoon at 5 週四下午五點
(C) Friday morning at 10 週五上午十點
(D) Wednesday afternoon at 2 週三下午兩點

© Caves Educational Training Co., Ltd.

◀ 解析 ▶
男子提供兩個可以開會的時段，再對照表格內容的行程與時間，故本題答案為 (A)。

Questions 98 - 100 refer to the following talk and CV.

[AU] W

Well, thank you for this interview opportunity, Mr. Louis. I think I am the best candidate for this position. As you can see on my resume, I've taken not only the courses in the financial field, but I've also gone beyond by double majoring in technology management. In addition, I've taken some communication-related training courses, such as negotiation skills and presentation skills. I believe the combination makes me a qualified product manager. And by the way, I am proud of my English language ability. I've recently got TOEIC certification to make my resume stand out. Now I am happy to answer any questions you might have for me, Mr. Louis.

謝謝您給我這個面試的機會，路易斯先生。我想我是這個工作的最佳候選人，您可以從我的履歷表中看出，我不僅修過財務領域的課程，同時也雙主修科技管理。除此之外，我還參加了一些與溝通技巧相關的訓練課程，例如：談判技巧與簡報技巧。我相信這些知識的結合，足以讓我勝任產品經理的職位。另外，我對於我的英語能力很有信心。我最近取得了 TOEIC 證書，讓我的履歷更加出色。現在，我非常樂意回答任何您想知道的問題，路易斯先生。

double major：雙主修　negotiation (n.)：談判、協商　combination (n.)：結合
qualified (adj.)：合格的、勝任的

98. When does the talk most likely take place? 此獨白最有可能在什麼時候出現？
(A) During a resume-writing workshop 在撰寫履歷表的研習會中
(B) During a presentation training course 在簡報訓練的課程中
(C) During a job interview 在工作面試中
(D) During a technology conference 在科技會議中

◀ 解析 ▶
第一句女子即提到，謝謝對方給予面試的機會，後來又簡單介紹了自己的履歷，可知女子正在參加面試，故選 (C)。

99. Please look at the CV. What position is the speaker applying for?
請看履歷表。說話者要申請什麼職位？

Lily Chang
Lily.chang@mail.com
Objective: Applying for the Product Manager position
Education: 1st major – Financial Management
2nd major – Technology Management
Training: Communication / Presentation Skills
Language: Fluent in English, Chinese and Japanese

張莉莉
Lily.chang@mail.com
目標：申請產品經理職位
教育：第一主修——財務管理
第二主修——科技管理
訓練：溝通技巧、簡報技巧
語言：精通英、中、日文

(A) Product manager 產品經理
(B) Sales representative 業務代表
(C) TOEIC instructor 多益講師
(D) Communication trainer 溝通訓練員

◀ 解析 ▶
根據履歷表內容，女子遞履歷表的目的是為了要申請 product manager「產品經理」的職位，故本題答案為 (A)。

100. What will the speaker probably do next? 說話者接下來可能會做什麼？
(A) Study technology management 學習科技管理
(B) Answer some interview questions 回答面試問題
(C) Ask the interviewer some questions 問面試官一些問題
(D) Negotiate with Mr. Louis 跟路易斯先生談判

◀ 解析 ▶
最後一句，女子說自己很高興回答路易斯先生的任何問題，由此可知接下來她將回答對方的提問，故選 (B)。

READING TEST

Part V									
101	102	103	104	105	106	107	108	109	110
B	A	B	C	B	C	B	A	B	A
111	112	113	114	115	116	117	118	119	120
D	A	C	B	A	B	B	D	A	C
121	122	123	124	125	126	127	128	129	130
C	B	D	A	C	C	D	D	A	B
Part VI									
131	132	133	134	135	136	137	138	139	140
B	A	B	D	A	C	A	C	B	D
141	142	143	144	145	146				
B	C	B	A	C	D				
Part VII									
147	148	149	150	151	152	153	154	155	156
A	C	A	C	C	B	D	B	B	C
157	158	159	160	161	162	163	164	165	166
C	D	B	A	A	A	C	D	C	B
167	168	169	170	171	172	173	174	175	176
C	C	C	A	B	A	C	D	C	A
177	178	179	180	181	182	183	184	185	186
D	D	A	B	A	C	B	D	A	A
187	188	189	190	191	192	193	194	195	196
B	B	C	A	B	A	D	B	C	B
197	198	199	200						
D	A	C	D						

Part V. ► Incomplete Sentences

101. As people live hectic lives in this modern world, our minds are kept busy ___________ what is going on around us.
在現代化世界中，人們過著忙碌的生活，我們的心思總是忙於解讀發生在周遭的種種事物。
(A) interpretation 解讀（名詞）
(B) interpreting 解讀
(C) interpreter 譯者
(D) interpret 解讀（原形動詞）

◀ 解析 ▶
本題考的是 keep 的用法。我們通常會用 keep + Ving 表示「持續做某件事」，故選 (B)。

102. __________ you are nervous, you should sit somewhere comfortable where you won't be disturbed.
當你緊張時，你應該找個舒適、沒人會打擾的地方坐下來。
(A) When 當…時
(B) Although 雖然
(C) But 但是
(D) However 然而

◀ 解析 ▶
1. 本題考的是哪個連接詞的意思最符合句意。依照句意，應選 (A) When 最合理。
2. disturb (v.)：妨礙、打擾

103. One of our team members, Marian, __________ a collection of framed drawings in her office.
我們的團員之一，瑪莉安，她的辦公室內掛有一系列裱框的素描作品。
(A) have
(B) has
(C) having
(D) hasn't

◀ 解析 ▶
本題的動詞是 have，Marian 是主詞 One of our team members 的同位語，主詞為第三人稱時，動詞應該用 has，故選 (B)。

104. We all know that the balance __________ work and other aspects of our life can have a huge impact on our health.
我們都知道工作與生活上其他方面的平衡，對我們的健康有莫大的影響。
(A) with 與
(B) together 一起
(C) between 在…（兩者）之間
(D) among 在…（三者）當中

◀ 解析 ▶
1. 本題重點在「…的平衡」，而需要取得平衡的事物為 work and other aspects of our life，此為 A and B 兩者之間，故選 (C) between。
2. among (prep.)：在…之中，通常用於三者以上。

105. TakeNote's user-friendly screens allow __________ to analyze project risks and respond to potential problems.
鐵克諾特的易操作螢幕讓客戶容易分析專案風險和回應潛在問題。
(A) customs 習俗
(B) customers 客戶
(C) costumes 服裝
(D) copiers 影印機

◀ 解析 ▶
本題提到 user-friendly 的螢幕，而此處的 user，指的應該就是「客戶」customers，故選 (B)。

106. There are speaking coaches who can teach leaders how to pitch their voice __________ they are able to control the room.
專門教授演說技巧的教練可以教領導階層如何運用聲音，讓他們可以控制全場。
(A) ever since 自從
(B) in spite of 即使
(C) so that 以致於
(D) in order to 為了

◀ 解析 ▶
1. 從前後句語意來看，選項 (C) 和 (D) 意思都符合，但 in order to 後面應該接動詞而非子句，故本題選 (C) so that。
2. pitch (v.)：定調、定音高

107. Studies have shown that constant interruptions are the most __________ element of a manager's day.
研究顯示出，一天當中最讓經理人惱怒的因素就是不間斷的干擾。
(A) annoy 惹惱
(B) annoying 令人惱怒的
(C) annoyed 感到惱怒的
(D) annoyance 惱怒

◀ 解析 ▶
1. 空格後是名詞 element，空格前是最高級 the most…，可知空格內應為形容詞。又 (C) annoyed 是用來形容人的感覺，故本題選 (B)。
2. constant (adj.)：持續的　interruption (n.)：阻礙、干擾

108. When you deal with a __________ customer, treat that customer as if he was a tired, hungry child who is becoming angry.
當你在面對難纏的客戶時，可以把他視為一個又累又餓、即將發怒的小孩子一般對待。
(A) difficult 難相處的
(B) challenging 具挑戰性的
(C) hard 困難的
(D) troubled 為難的

◀ 解析 ▶
依照前後句意來判斷，空格內應該是「棘手的、難纏的」，故本題選 (A)。

109. Working from home one day a week is good for employees, but __________ their home can offer the necessary privacy.

每週在家工作一天，對員工來說是很好，只要他們家裡有隱私的空間可以辦公的話。

(A) only 僅僅

(B) only if 只要

(C) even 甚至

(D) as well as 也

◀ 解析 ▶

1. 根據前後句意判斷，員工在家工作的首要條件，就是「只要」家裡有隱私的空間可以辦公。故本題選 (B)。
2. privacy (n.)：隱私

110. Our goal is to allow our customers to __________ shareholder value and improve end-user satisfaction.

我們的目標是要讓客戶提高股東價值和增加產品使用者的滿意度。

(A) increase 提升

(B) decrease 降低

(C) fluctuate 波動

(D) decline 下降

◀ 解析 ▶

1. 企業經營的目標，通常是在提高股東價值。故本題選 (A)。
2. shareholder value：股東價值　end-user (n.)：直接用戶、終端用戶

111. Because of early childhood criticism, many people grow up __________ fears of rejection.

因為在孩童時期所受的批評，很多人成長過程中都有擔心被拒絕的恐懼。

(A) of …的

(B) for 為了

(C) in 在…裡面

(D) with 有

◀ 解析 ▶

1. 此處的 with，有「伴隨著…」的意思，故本題選 (D)。
2. criticism (n.)：批評　rejection (n.)：拒絕

112. No one who __________ part of a team can work in isolation. 在團隊中沒有人可以獨來獨往。

(A) is

(B) are

(C) were

(D) was

◀ 解析 ▶

1. 本題是敘述一則常理，通常用現在簡單式。而句子的主詞是 no one，動詞應搭配使用第三人稱單數，故本題選 (A)。
2. isolation (n.)：孤立

113. I am afraid we are running out of time, __________ we will have to stop our discussion.
我怕我們的時間不夠，因此我們要先暫停討論了。
(A) or 或
(B) and 和
(C) so 因此
(D) but 但是

◀ 解析 ▶

本題前後句之間有因果關係，前句為因，後句為果，故本題選 (C)。

114. Zenia and Alife had a discussion __________ the possibility of two companies working together.
齊尼亞和亞萊福公司討論了兩家公司合作的可能性。
(A) for 為了
(B) about 關於
(C) of …的
(D) with 和

◀ 解析 ▶

本題重點為說明討論的主題，通常會用 have a discussion about…，故本題選 (B)。

115. If you offer more flexible payment __________ , we will agree to place an order next week.
如果你們可以提供更有彈性的付款條件，我們就會同意下週就下訂單。
(A) conditions 條件
(B) occasions 場合
(C) guarantees 保證
(D) procedures 程序

◀ 解析 ▶

1. 依照前後句意來看，空格中可能是指付款的方式、條件或日期等，再對照各選項的意思，可知本題應選 (A)。
2. flexible (adj.)：有彈性的

116. For over ten years, CoreValue has __________ continuous year-over-year growth.

過去十年中，核心價值公司每年業績都是成長的。

(A) experiences
(B) experienced
(C) experiencing
(D) experience

◀ **解析** ▶

本題的時間為 for over ten years，動詞部分通常會搭配現在完成式 (have / has + p.p.)，此處應該選動詞 experience 的過去分詞，故選 (B)。

117. I am appointed to chair a meeting about the year-end party, but I am incredibly nervous as I've never __________ one before.

我被指派當尾牙活動會議的主席，但因為我以前沒有任何主持會議的經驗，所以相當緊張。

(A) chair 主持
(B) chaired 主持
(C) chairing 主持
(D) chairman 主持人

◀ **解析** ▶

空格部分的句子為 I've never…，可知其為現在完成式 (have / has + p.p.)，故此處應該選動詞 chair 的過去分詞，故選 (B)。

118. __________ faced with a failed conversation, most people are quick to blame others.

當面對溝通不良的狀況時，大多數人都會直接把錯誤推到別人身上。

(A) Since 因為
(B) During 在…期間
(C) Although 雖然
(D) When 當…時

◀ **解析** ▶

依照前後句意推斷，空格中應該是「當狀況發生時」，故本題選 (D)。

119. We need at least three days to __________ the genuineness of their intentions.

我們至少需要三天的時間來評估他們的誠意。

(A) assess
(B) assessing
(C) assessed
(D) assessment

© Caves Educational Training Co., Ltd.

◀ 解析 ▶
句子的動詞是 need，後面通常會接 to + V，空格中應該填入原形動詞，故選 (A)。

120. During difficult times, the tension in people's bodies __________ mounting, making people uptight and exhausted.
在面臨困難時，人們體內的壓力會持續累積，導致我們感到緊張和疲憊。
(A) keeping
(B) keep
(C) keeps
(D) kept

◀ 解析 ▶
1. 需注意句子的主詞是 the tension，動詞應該搭配使用第三人稱單數，故選 (C)。
2. mount (v.)：上升　uptight (adj.)：煩躁的　exhausted (adj.)：精疲力竭的

121. In interpersonal communication, the first rule is to focus on listening to what __________ person wants to say.
在人際溝通中，第一要旨就是要將焦點放在傾聽他人的心聲上。
(A) else 其他
(B) some 有些
(C) the other 其他的
(D) others 其他的（人事物）

◀ 解析 ▶
空格中應該填入的是形容詞。(A) else 為副詞，通常接在代名詞後，如 something else。(D) others 為代名詞。故選 (C)。

122. The first step in keeping customers is finding out __________ we lose customers.
要留住客戶的第一步，就是要先瞭解我們失去客戶的原因何在。
(A) what 什麼
(B) why 為何
(C) who 誰
(D) when 何時

◀ 解析 ▶
依照前後句意來看，應該是要找出失去客戶的原因，故選 (B)。

123. The ideal leader demonstrates extreme professionalism combined __________ a warm humanity.
理想的領導階層展現的是極度的專業，結合平易近人的特質。
(A) to 去
(B) and 和
(C) for 為了
(D) with 和

◀ 解析 ▶
1. 本題重點是在 combine 的用法，通常會用 combine A with B 來表示「將 A 和 B 結合」，故本題選 (D)。
2. extreme (adj.)：極度的　professionalism (n.)：專家氣質、專業精神　humanity (n.)：（人的）特質

124. People tend to choose peace __________ conflict. 人們傾向保持和平，不要衝突。
(A) over 超越
(B) than 比
(C) to 去
(D) of …的

◀ 解析 ▶
1. 本題重點是在 choose A over B 的用法，可用來表示「選擇 A 而非 B」，故本題選 (A)。
2. conflict (n.)：衝突

125. He is __________ for a career in business. 他不適合選擇商業作為終身職業。
(A) impossible 不可能的
(B) inconvenient 不方便的
(C) unfit 不適合的
(D) unclear 不清楚的

◀ 解析 ▶
1. 依照句意來看，選擇終身職業需考慮適不適合，此處應該用 unfit ，故本題選 (C)。
2. be unfit for...：不適合…

126. I'd like to talk to you today about an __________ development.
今天我想跟大家談談一個令人興奮的發展。
(A) excitement 興奮
(B) excited 感到興奮的
(C) exciting 令人興奮的
(D) excite 使…興奮

◀ 解析 ▶
從空格後所接的名詞來看，推斷空格內應為形容詞，故 (A)、(D) 不符合。又 excited 多用來形容人的內心感受，故本題選 (C)。

© Caves Educational Training Co., Ltd.

127. He always does a __________ piece of work. 他做事總是非常細心。
(A) brisk 活潑的
(B) virtuous 有品德的
(C) timid 膽小的
(D) careful 小心的

◀ 解析 ▶
空格裡的形容詞是要形容一個人做事的態度，選項 (A)、(B)、(C) 較常用來形容人的個性，故本題選 (D)。

128. Many scientists believe that global warming is having a negative impact __________ the climate.
很多科學家都相信地球暖化對氣候帶來負面的衝擊。
(A) for 為了
(B) in 在…裡面
(C) of …的
(D) on 在…之上

◀ 解析 ▶
本題的重點在於 have an impact on... 的用法，可用來表示「在…方面造成衝擊」，故本題選 (D)。

129. The secretary had all the __________ documents ready. 秘書已將所有的相關資料準備好了。
(A) relevant 相關的
(B) possible 可能的
(C) feasible 可行的
(D) reliable 可靠的

◀ 解析 ▶
依照句意來看，秘書要準備「相關的」資料，故本題選 (A)。

130. This is the first time I have ever __________ to write such a long report.
這是我第一次要寫這麼長的報告。
(A) have
(B) had
(C) has
(D) having

◀ 解析 ▶
從 I have ever…，可看出使用現在完成式，空格中應該填入過去分詞，故本題選 (B)。

Part VI. ► Text Completion

Questions 131 - 134 refer to the following article.

A positive attitude is ___________ in today's business world, and your choice of words is essential in

131. (A) growing
(B) important
(C) normal
(D) attractive

creating the right attitude.

Now let's ___________ these two statements: "My jobs are boring." / "My jobs could be more exciting

132. (A) compare
(B) contradict
(C) translate
(D) develop

and my performance would be better if I could get more incentives." It is obvious ___________ the

133. (A) which
(B) that
(C) in which
(D) it

first statement is negative and reflects a passive attitude, whereas the second one is positive and reflects a desire to improve the situation.

Therefore, human resources department should develop strategies to motivate employees to think ___________ and work hard.

134. (A) unfortunately
(B) luckily
(C) negatively
(D) positively

正面思考的態度在現今的商業世界中是很重要的，遣詞用字更是表現正確態度的重要關鍵。現在讓我們比較以下兩句話：「我的工作好無聊。」/「若我可以得到更多鼓勵回饋，我的工作將會變得更有趣，表現也會更好。」很明顯地，第一句話很負面，而且反映出消極的態度。第二句話則是正面的，且反映出想改善現況的渴望。因此，人資部門應該規劃策略，來激勵員工正向思考和認真工作。

attitude (n.)：態度　incentive (n.)：鼓勵　reflect (v.)：反映　motivate (v.)：激發

131.
(A) growing 成長的
(B) important 重要的
(C) normal 正常的
(D) attractive 吸引人的

◀ 解析 ▶
從前後文意判斷，正面的態度是「重要的」，故選 (B)。

132.
(A) compare 比較
(B) contradict 反駁
(C) translate 翻譯
(D) develop 發展

◀ 解析 ▶
根據後段對兩個句子的解釋，可以推知此處是要「比較」兩個句子的表達方式，故選 (A)。

133.
(A) which
(B) that
(C) in which
(D) it

◀ 解析 ▶
此處並不需要用關係代名詞 which 或 in which，而是用 It is obvious that... 來表示「某事是顯而易見的」，故本題選 (B)。

134.
(A) unfortunately 不幸地
(B) luckily 幸運地
(C) negatively 負面地
(D) positively 正面地

◀ 解析 ▶
人資部門運用策略激勵員工，目的應該是讓員工擁有正面的思考，故本題選 (D)。

Questions 135 - 138 refer to the following letter.

Dear Mr. Chen,

Our current supplier of first-grade paper __________ recently informed us that they are discontinuing

135. (A) has
(B) has been
(C) have
(D) had being

their first-grade paper division. So our purchasing director will be __________ some first-grade

136. (A) visits
(B) visit
(C) visiting
(D) visited

paper manufacturers in your area next month.

Would it be possible for you to arrange a meeting and plant tour for us __________ the 2nd or 3rd of

137. (A) on
(B) in
(C) of
(D) for

next month?

Enclosed please find data on our projected need for paper, production schedules, and delivery requirements. I hope the information may be helpful to you in __________ our visit. Thank you.

138. (A) preparing on
(B) prepare with
(C) preparing for
(D) prepared to

Sincerely,
Lucy Hung

陳先生您好：
我們現有的優等紙張供應商最近通知我們，他們將裁撤優等紙張製造部門。因此我們的採購經理下個月會到當地去拜訪幾家優等紙張的製造商。您是否可以在下個月的二號或三號幫我們安排會議和工廠參觀的行程呢？我將我們預估的用紙需求、生產時程和運送要求的相關資料附在信中。我希望這些資料對您在安排行程上會有幫助。謝謝。

誠摯地，
洪露西

supplier (n.)：供應商　discontinue (v.)：停止　division (n.)：部門　enclosed (adj.)：附上的
requirement (n.)：要求

135.
(A) has
(B) has been
(C) have
(D) had being

◀ 解析 ▶
句中的 informed 為過去分詞，可推知此處是用現在完成式，主詞是 supplier，應搭配第三人稱單數的 has，故選 (A)。

136.
(A) visits
(B) visit
(C) visiting
(D) visited

◀ 解析 ▶
本題空格前是 will be，動詞應該使用 Ving，故本題選 (C)。

137.
(A) on
(B) in
(C) of
(D) for

◀ 解析 ▶
本題考的是日期的介系詞。下個月二號或三號，日期的介系詞應該用 on，故本題選 (A)。

138.
(A) preparing on
(B) prepare with
(C) preparing for
(D) prepared to

◀ 解析 ▶
空格前是介系詞 in，動詞應該用 Ving，故不選 (B)、(D)。一般用 prepare for... 來表示「為某事做準備」，故本題選 (C)。

Questions 139 - 142 refer to the following article.

In today's world of wanting things fast, customers don't want to call several different departments just to get a simple answer __________ the products they purchased.

139. (A) regarded
(B) regarding
(C) regards
(D) regard

Derma Corp., a leading cosmetic company, __________ this.

140. (A) respects
(B) memorizes
(C) remembers
(D) realizes

They are deploying a new system that will enable their customers to truly __________ a one call event

141. (A) experienced
(B) experience
(C) experiencing
(D) experiences

for all their questions.

Customers can simply make one call to place the order, check delivery, and handle other requests. This happens because Derma Corp. has an interactive database that links all of this information together __________ other divisions of the corporation.

142. (A) about
(B) to
(C) from
(D) since

在這個講求快速的世界裡，客戶並不想要打好幾通電話給公司的不同部門，只為了獲得與購買產品相關的簡單回覆。化妝品的領導品牌德瑪企業，完全了解這一點。他們正在配置新的系統，將讓客戶能真正體驗到，只要打一通電話就可以獲得所有答案的便利。客戶僅需打一通電話，就可以下訂單、查詢寄送進度和處理其他的需求，這是因為德瑪企業擁有一個互動式資料庫，可以將企業內部不同部門的資料都連結在一起。

cosmetic (n.)：化妝品　deploy (v.)：部署、配置　interactive (adj.)：互動的　database (n.)：資料庫
corporation (n.)：公司

139.
(A) regarded
(B) regarding
(C) regards
(D) regard

◀ 解析 ▶
此處是指與產品「相關」的訊息，可以用介系詞 regarding，故選 (B)。

140.
(A) respects 尊重
(B) memorizes 記憶
(C) remembers 記得
(D) realizes 了解

◀ 解析 ▶
依照前後文意推斷，應該是指 Derma 企業「了解」客戶不想花時間打電話的心理，故選 (D)。

141.
(A) experienced
(B) experience
(C) experiencing
(D) experiences

◀ 解析 ▶
此處的動詞結構是 enable sb. to + V，to 後面的動詞應為原形動詞，故選 (B)。

142.
(A) about 關於
(B) to 去
(C) from 從
(D) since 自從

◀ 解析 ▶
本句的意思是將資料「從」各個部門集結起來，此處缺乏的是介系詞 from，故選 (C)。

Questions 143 - 146 refer to the following article.

This report is about "Will the Internet kill our magazines?" Well, that's true that new technologies change many things. __________ does the Internet really change everything?

143. (A) If
(B) But
(C) And
(D) So

People may surf, search, shop online, but they still read magazines. Based on our research, readership of our Beauty Magazine has actually __________ over the past two years.

144. (A) increased
(B) reported
(C) accommodated
(D) realized

Even the 17-to-29 segment __________ to grow. Rather than being displaced by instant media,

145. (A) continue
(B) continued
(C) continues
(D) continuing

magazines are still prevalent in people's life. The explanation is fairly __________. Magazines

146. (A) skeptical
(B) pessimistic
(C) impersonal
(D) obvious

promote deeper connections. They create relationships. They engage people in ways distinct from digital media. Magazines do what the Internet doesn't.

這份報告是討論「網路是否會取代雜誌？」。新技術確實改變了很多事情。但是網路真的改變了一切嗎？人們可以在網路上瀏覽、搜尋、購物，但我們仍然會閱讀雜誌。根據我們的研究，「美麗雜誌」在過去兩年，讀者數量上還是有增加的。即便是 17 到 29 歲的年輕族群，也仍然在增加當中。雜誌依舊普遍存在於人們的生活裡，而非被網路所取代。原因很明顯，雜誌可使人們和文字有更深層的連結，能與人們建立關係。雜誌以不同於數位內容的方式吸引著人們，可以做到網路所無法達成的目標。

readership (n.)：（報章雜誌等的）讀者人數　segment (n.)：族群、部分　displace (v.)：取代
prevalent (adj.)：普遍的、流行的　engage (v.)：吸引住、使感興趣

143.
(A) If 如果
(B) But 但是
(C) And 以及
(D) So 因此

◀ 解析 ▶
此題空格根據前後的語意，應是「但是」較為合理，故本題選 (B)。

144.
(A) increased 增加
(B) reported 報告
(C) accommodated 容納
(D) realized 體認

◀ 解析 ▶
此空格之前看到 has，可判斷其後應接過去分詞，且根據語意應是「增加」較為合理，故選 (A)。

145.
(A) continue 連續
(B) continued 連續
(C) continues 連續
(D) continuing 連續的

◀ 解析 ▶
此空格之前看到主詞 segment 為單數，故判斷空格中的動詞應作單數形變化，故選 (C)。

146.
(A) skeptical 存疑的
(B) pessimistic 悲觀的
(C) impersonal 沒人情味的
(D) obvious 明顯的

◀ 解析 ▶
此題空格應填形容詞，且根據前後語意應是「明顯的」較為合理，故選 (D)。

Part VII. ▶ Reading Comprehension

Questions 147 - 148 refer to the following notice.

> **促成正向影響的途徑：投資馬來西亞**
>
> 馬來西亞投資網是一個線上微型貸款平台。我們相信，微型企業與小型企業擁有能夠提供工作機會與持續經濟成長的潛力。若想要參與並協助這些企業獲得成功，在馬來西亞進行投資是一個最好的方法。最低只要 15 元，您就可以開始進行投資！若您已準備好做出正向的改變，請上網站 www.invest-malaysia.com 或撥打 123-3727-3746 立即進行捐款。

microfinance (n.)：微型貸款　potential (n.)：潛力　sustainable (adj.)：能維持的、可持續的
contribute (v.)：貢獻

147. What is the main purpose of this message? 此訊息的主要目的為何？
    (A) To encourage investments in Malaysia 鼓勵在馬來西亞投資
    (B) To report Malaysia's economic situation 報告馬來西亞的經濟狀況
    (C) To attract travelers to visit Malaysia 吸引遊客到馬來西亞玩
    (D) To explain how to start a business in Malaysia 解釋如何在馬來西亞創業

◀ 解析 ▶
從第三句可知，此訊息主要目的為鼓勵在馬來西亞投資，以協助微型企業與小型企業成功，故選 (A)。

148. What can be inferred about Invest Malaysia from the message?
    由此訊息可推論出關於馬來西亞投資網的什麼事？
    (A) It's the largest marketing research firm in Malaysia. 它是馬來西亞最大的行銷研究公司。
    (B) It has approximately 300 employees worldwide. 它在全球大約有三百名員工。
    (C) It's an online donation platform. 它是一個線上的捐款平台。
    (D) It helps companies to expand market. 它協助企業拓展市場。

◀ 解析 ▶
訊息中僅提及馬來西亞投資網為一線上微型貸款平台，以及相關捐款方式等資訊，故本題選 (C)。

Questions 149 - 151 refer to the following advertisement.

> **別具野心？主動積極？**
>
> 您對錢永遠不夠用感到厭煩了嗎？
> 您想要找尋最快速的超越方式嗎？
> 現在就加入成為直銷公司的業務代表。
>
> 只要您精力充沛、熱情激昂，自備交通工具和電話，您就可以賺進四位、五位甚至於六位數字的收入。
>
> 沒有底薪，但會依照您談成的每個案子抽成，給予佣金！
>
> 請參考我們的網站 www.direct-sales.com 或撥打電話 123-3829-2382 洽詢。

ambitious (adj.)：野心勃勃的　self-starter (n.)：做事積極的人　commission (n.)：佣金　figure (n.)：數字

149. What is the main purpose of this advertisement? 此廣告的主要目的為何？
(A) To recruit new sales representatives 招募新的業務代表
(B) To attract new customers 吸引新的客戶
(C) To propose new business opportunities 提案新的交易機會
(D) To develop new product lines 開發新的產品線

◀ 解析 ▶
廣告中第三句提到，「現在就加入成為直銷公司的業務代表」，可知其目的為招募新的業務代表，故選 (A)。

150. The word "passion" in paragraph 2, line 1, is closest in meaning to
第二段第一行的 "passion" 一字意思最接近於
(A) performance 表現
(B) management 管理
(C) enthusiasm 熱情
(D) localization 在地化

◀ 解析 ▶
passion 一字意思為「熱情」，與 enthusiasm 意思最相近，故選 (C)。

151. What does the salesperson need to prepare in advance? 業務人員需要事先準備的東西為何？
(A) A contract 一只合約
(B) A website 一個網站
(C) A car 一台車
(D) A laptop 一台手提電腦

◀ 解析 ▶
第二段提及業務人員除了需具備活力、熱情之外，還需要自備交通工具與電話，故本題選 (C)。

Questions 152 - 153 refer to the following text message chain.

卡蘿 早上 8:50
嗨，馬克。你現在有空嗎？我想請教你一件事情。[1]

馬克 早上 9:10
不好意思，卡蘿。我剛回到座位上。有什麼事嗎？[2]

卡蘿 早上 9:11
沒關係。我想問要怎麼請年假，你知道嗎？

馬克 早上 9:12
你要將「請假單」填好交給人資部門。所以你要請假嗎？

卡蘿 早上 9:15
是呀，孩子們七月放暑假，我要休假一週。[3]

馬克 早上 9:16
瞭解。你一直很賣力工作，是該休假去放鬆一下。不管怎樣，若你對填假單還有疑問，可以再傳訊息給我。

卡蘿 早上 9:18
好的。[4] 非常謝謝你！

152. At 9:10 a.m., why did Mark reply "Sorry, Carol. I just returned to my seat"?
早上 9:10 時，為何馬克回應「不好意思，卡蘿。我剛回到座位上」？
(A) To complain how busy he was 抱怨他有多麼忙
(B) To explain the reason why he didn't reply earlier 解釋他沒有早點回應的原因
(C) To inform Carol that he's lost a case 通知卡蘿他失去了一個案子
(D) To help Carol to get an absent request form 幫忙卡蘿拿取假單

◀ 解析 ▶
第一、二個訊息的時間相隔了二十分鐘之久，可知馬克的回應應是表達歉意，及解釋沒即時回覆的原因較為合理，故選 (B)。

153. In which of the positions marked [1], [2], [3], and [4] does the following sentence best belong?
"It's very kind of you."
下面的句子最適合放在文章中 [1] [2] [3] [4] 哪個位置？
「你人真好。」
(A) [1]
(B) [2]
(C) [3]
(D) [4]

◀ 解析 ▶
這句話通常是在對方提供協助之後，受協助的那方所說的，故此句應出現在最後女子接受完男子的協助後，再回應較為合理，故選 (D)。

Questions 154 - 156 refer to the following advertisement.

史金納外科診所

由國際知名的整形外科醫生親自主持整形手術。
恢復您的青春、美貌與自信。

★除去難看的疤痕★
★線條重塑★
★面部輪廓雕塑★

我們的客戶包括娛樂圈、政治界和商業界的知名人物。

欲索取印有「術前術後」比較照片和客戶現身說法的免費手冊，
請寄電子郵件至 info@skinner.com 或致電 123-3828-3284。

154. What is the purpose of the advertisement? 此廣告的目的為何？
(A) To encourage foreign investment 鼓勵外商投資
(B) To advertise a cosmetic clinic 宣傳美容診所
(C) To recommend a change in the law 建議變更立法
(D) To support cooperation with other clinics 支持跟其他診所合作

◀ 解析 ▶
本廣告內容介紹美容診所營業內容，以及索取資訊的方法，可知主要目的為宣傳，故本題選 (B)。

155. What is suggested about doing cosmetic surgery? 文中認為美容手術如何？
(A) It is a newly developed surgery. 是新發展出來的手術。
(B) It will increase your self-confidence. 可以增加你的自信心。
(C) It is not as costly as you expected. 並不如預期中的貴。
(D) It is limited to women only. 僅限於女性才能做。

◀ 解析 ▶
文中提到美容手術可以恢復青春、美貌與自信，並未提到價錢或對象限制，故本題選 (B)。

156. The word "testimonial" in the last paragraph, line 1, is closest in meaning to
最後一段第一行的 "testimonial" 一字意思最接近於
(A) innovation 創新
(B) management 管理
(C) endorsement 認可、背書
(D) education 教育

◀ 解析 ▶
testimonial 一字意思為「保證、推薦」，與 endorsement 意思最相近，故本題選 (C)。

Questions 157 - 159 refer to the following article.

改變的能力在商業環境中的重要性

——倍斯特系統公司的威廉博世先生獨家專訪

倍斯特系統公司是一家成功度過 90 年代末期，網際網路泡沫化危機的軟體公司。該公司的首席執行長，威廉博世回憶道：「早在那之前，我們公司的業務早已完成重新導向。我們將大部分注意力放在我們的目標市場上，並專注在特別在乎 IT 系統品質的企業客戶身上。」

「我們的任務至今仍然沒有改變。」 博世先生表示，「向來都是以協助企業降低 IT 問題與花費為理念，而進行開發、設計、行銷和販售軟體。」該公司歷經了數次的重大改變，首先是改變了做生意的方式，接著則是將重心轉移到新產品上，再來則是拓展全新的客戶群。

但博世先生認為，轉型成功的關鍵，是公司裡的所有員工。「最重要的是，要讓我們的員工對他們的工作感到驕傲，並相信他們的所作所為能夠為世界帶來影響。」

157. How did Best Systems survive the dot-com crash? 倍斯特系統公司是如何度過網路泡沫化危機的？
(A) They took on a new CEO. 他們請了一位新的執行長。
(B) They reduced the size of the company. 他們縮小公司規模。
(C) They changed direction before it happened. 他們在危機發生之前就改變方向了。
(D) They announced new product lines. 他們推出新的產品線。

◀ 解析 ▶
第一段第二句即提到，網路泡沫化危機之前，公司就已進行業務重新導向，故本題選 (C)。

158. What is Best Systems' main objective? 倍斯特系統公司的主要目標為何？
(A) To become the best market research firm 成為最佳的市場調查公司
(B) To diversify their product types 生產多樣化的產品
(C) To recruit the most ambitious employees 聘請最有野心的員工
(D) To make software products to improve customers' IT environments
生產軟體產品以改善客戶的 IT 環境

◀ 解析 ▶
第二段提到，公司開發、設計、銷售軟體，以協助企業改善 IT 問題，故本題選 (D)。

159. According to Mr. Bosch, what has motivated Best Systems' employees?
根據博世先生所提到的，倍斯特系統公司的員工都受到什麼因素的激勵？
(A) The highest pay in the industry 業內最高的薪水
(B) The way Best Systems' products are making a difference 公司產品帶來改變的方式
(C) The variety of hardware products they make 他們所生產的各式硬體產品
(D) The new lifestyle they are creating 他們創造的新生活方式

◀ 解析 ▶
最後一段提到，公司員工都相信他們的所作所為能夠為世界帶來影響，故本題選 (B)。

Questions 160 - 161 refer to the following letter.

親愛的艾弗林小姐：

我是在某大型國際經銷公司服務超過八年的業務專員。我於上個月造訪倫敦時，有幸參觀了幾間您的商店。我對於加盟 貴公司並在台北開設連鎖分店感到非常有興趣。

若您能夠寄一些 貴公司連鎖加盟的詳細資料給我，我會非常感激。請問您是否能針對以下幾個問題為我解答？

1. 創業基金的費用大致有哪些？我需要支付多少百分比的營業額給您？
2. 一間新的連鎖分店，平均大約需要多久的時間才能開始獲利？
3. 您是否能夠在創業初期提供行銷與宣傳素材的支援？

非常感謝您，並期待您的回音。

誠摯地，
楊喬登

franchise (n.)：經銷權　in terms of：就…方面而論　turnover (n.)：營業額　franchisee (n.)：經銷商
profit (n.)：利潤

160. What is the purpose of this letter? 此信件的主要目的為何？
  (A) To inquire about partnership opportunity 詢問關於合作的機會
  (B) To promote a new product 推廣一項新產品
  (C) To advertise a new organization 為新組織做宣傳
  (D) To recommend a change in marketing strategy 建議行銷策略應做的改變

◀ **解析** ▶
第一段的最後一句，男子表示自己有興趣加盟女子的商店，後續並詢問相關問題，由此可知本題應選 (A)。

161. The word "grateful" in paragraph 2, line 1, is closest in meaning to
  第二段第一行的 "grateful" 一字意思最接近於
  (A) thankful 感謝的
  (B) patient 有耐心的
  (C) automatic 自動的
  (D) demanding 要求高的

◀ **解析** ▶
grateful 一字意思為「感激的」，與 thankful 意思最相近，故本題選 (A)。

Questions 162 - 164 refer to the following notice.

7/25 ~ 7/29 於加州斯普林菲爾德市舉辦的網路高峰會，

現正報名中！

本次高峰會是規模最大的合作夥伴訓練會議，專門對網路工作模式解決方案進行討論，並以行動性、雲端網路與社群協同作業等內容為主。本活動將提供各式策略、密集訓練與全新工具，協助您在行動工作型態的市場空間裡，有效運用其中龐大的商業潛力。

了解 2018 年的全新內容！

免費的活動前訓練課程：於 7 月 10 日前支付高峰會報名費用的參與者，將能夠於 7 月 22 日獲得線上自我學習課程的登錄權限。

美麗的全新地點：享受加州的陽光風情和彩虹會議中心的典雅風格

預覽高峰會的內容：

分組會議將以三大主題進行討論：**行動通訊、雲端科技、網際網路**，所有會議內容皆已開放預覽。完整的會議目錄將於 5 月發布。

除了分組會議之外，本次高峰會議程也提供了各式豐富的活動，例如由納沃網路公司首席執行長約翰路易斯，與執行團隊所發表的專題演講，以及由帕特納解決方案中心展示資源、計畫與工具等內容。

請準備好在令人興奮的全新場地內，體驗各式技術訓練的活動規劃，以及活動開始之前就能享受的超值內容。

期待您加入本年度網路高峰會的行列。

summit (n.)：高峰會　premier (adj.)：首要的　encompass (v.)：圍繞　collaboration (n.)：合作
intensive (adj.)：密集的

162. What is this article about? 此文章是關於什麼？
 (A) A summit invitation 一場高峰會的邀請
 (B) A hotel reservation confirmation 飯店訂房的確認
 (C) An interview schedule 一個面談的時程表
 (D) A competition announcement 一場競賽的消息公告

◀ 解析 ▶
全文第一句即提到，高峰會已開始開放報名，後續更介紹高峰會的內容，由此可知本題為 (A)。

163. Why should participants pay registration fees by July 10th? 為什麼與會者需在 7 月 10 日之前繳費？

(A) To get a 10% discount 可得到九折優惠

(B) To get a free copy of the software 可獲得一套免費軟體

(C) To attend an online training 可參與線上學習課程

(D) To join a celebration party 可參加慶祝派對

◀ 解析 ▶

文中提到免費的活動前訓練課程，且只要在 7 月 10 日前報名，就可獲得線上課程的登錄權限，故本題選 (C)。

164. What is NOT mentioned as a main track of the summit? 此高峰會的主要講題不包括哪一項？

(A) Networking 網際網路

(B) Mobility 行動通訊

(C) Cloud 雲端科技

(D) Productivity 生產力

◀ 解析 ▶

本題問的是「不包括」哪一項主題。高峰會的分組會議，分為三個主要講題：行動通訊、雲端科技、網際網路，故本題選 (D)。

Questions 165 - 167 refer to the following letter.

親愛的先生、女士：

[1] 我想要透過這封信，應徵目前 貴公司網站上所張貼的亞洲客戶經理一職。

在附件的履歷表當中您可以看到，我本身擁有 USC 大學的企業管理碩士學位，並在香港的瑪可羅軟體公司擁有兩年行銷與業務的工作經驗。[2] 我目前的職位是香港暨台灣區的業務副理。

我之所以對 貴公司所張貼的職位感到興趣，是因為該職位非常合乎我正在尋找的機會：能夠進入大型的國際電腦產品製造公司，並獲得管理區域業務的經驗。

希望我的應徵信與履歷表能夠引起您的興趣。[3] 我隨時都能接受面試，目前的雇主也很樂意為我推薦。

感謝您撥冗閱讀，並期待很快就能接獲您的回音。

誠摯地，[4]
穆喬治
georgemu@outlook.com

CV：履歷表　obtain (v.)：獲得　region (n.)：地區　reference (n.)：推薦信

165. What does George Mu say about his job expectation? 穆喬治提到他對工作的期望為何？
(A) He would like to transfer to the US. 他想調職到美國去。
(B) He wants to lead a group of software developers. 他想帶領一批軟體開發人員。
(C) He would like to work in an international environment. 他想在國際化的環境工作。
(D) He wants to return to school for advanced courses. 他想重回學校修習進階課程。

◀ 解析 ▶
信中第三段提到，他認為新工作應該能帶來進入國際電腦產品製造公司的機會，並獲得管理區域業務的經驗，由此可知答案為 (C)。

166. What is being sent with the letter? 隨此信附上的文件為何？
(A) A design sample 一個設計樣本
(B) George Mu's resume 穆喬治的履歷表
(C) George Mu's diploma 穆喬治的畢業證書
(D) A reference letter 一封推薦函

◀ 解析 ▶
第二段提到隨信附上他的履歷表，故本題應選 (B)。

167. In which of the positions marked [1], [2], [3], and [4] does the following sentence best belong?
"I would like to meet you in person and demonstrate that I do have the ability to achieve company goals."
下面的句子最適合放在文章中 [1] [2] [3] [4] 哪個位置？
「我想要親自與您見面，並證明給您看我有能力達成公司目標。」
(A) [1]
(B) [2]
(C) [3]
(D) [4]

◀ 解析 ▶
此句內容為要求面談機會，再看到內文，僅有 [3] 的前後文有提到 "interview" 關鍵字，故本題應選 (C)。

Questions 168 - 171 refer to the following article.

造訪台北

台北 101 大樓

台北 101 大樓是世界上最高的摩天大樓之一。它位於台北的商業區，在地表之上有 101 層樓與 5 層地下樓層。整棟建築物被設計成能夠抵抗地震與颱風。它擁有全世界最快上升電梯的正式記錄。

夜市

台北的夜市能提供多樣化選擇且物美價廉的料理。來自世界各地的旅客，都會前往這裡品嚐令人垂涎三尺的美食。包羅萬象的美食小舖，自下午 4 點開始營業至凌晨 1 點或 2 點左右。

忠孝東路

忠孝東路以其受歡迎的娛樂圈與商圈聞名，多間購物商場與百貨公司幾乎沿著整條道路林立。它是台北最為時尚且流行的區域之一。旅客能夠在這條路上找到任何想要的商品。

skyscraper (n.)：摩天大樓　business district：商業區　withstand(v.)：抵擋　ascending (adj.)：上升的
mouth-watering (adj.)：美味的　stall (n.)：攤販　numerous (adj.)：許多的

168. Where would this piece of information most likely appear? 此資訊最有可能出現在何處？
   (A) In a user's manual 在使用者手冊裡
   (B) In a newspaper 在報紙上
   (C) In a Taiwan travel guide 在台灣旅遊手冊裡
   (D) On Zhong-Xiao E. Road 在忠孝東路上

◀ 解析 ▶
本資訊主題為「造訪台北」，內容介紹數個知名景點，可推知是台北的旅遊資訊，故選 (C)。

169. What is NOT mentioned about Taipei 101? 關於台北 101 大樓，何者沒被提及？
   (A) It's one of the skyscrapers in the world. 它是世界摩天大樓之一。
   (B) It's located in the business district. 它位於商業區。
   (C) There is a night market inside. 它當中有個夜市。
   (D) It's a 101-story building. 它是一棟有 101 層的大樓。

◀ 解析 ▶
第一段中提及數個台北 101 大樓的特點，其中並未提到的是 (C)。

170. What time do night markets usually open? 夜市通常幾點開始營業？
(A) 4 p.m. 下午四點
(B) 1 a.m. 清晨一點
(C) 2 p.m. 下午兩點
(D) 4 a.m. 清晨四點

◀ 解析 ▶
本題問的是夜市開始營業的時間，於第二段最後一句有提到，故選 (A)。

171. What is mentioned about Zhong-Xiao E. Road in the article? 文章中提及關於忠孝東路的什麼事？
(A) There are only a few shopping malls here. 在此處僅有少數幾家購物中心。
(B) It's a modern area of Taipei. 它是台北的時尚地區。
(C) People come here to eat inexpensive food. 人們到此處吃便宜的食物。
(D) This place is full of high-technology companies. 此處高科技公司林立。

◀ 解析 ▶
文中第三段提到忠孝東路是時尚流行的區域，故本題選 (B)。

Questions 172 - 175 refer to the following letter.

致：人資主管
來自：業務行銷組
主旨：回覆：訓練課程

卡森先生，您好：

所有業務行銷的員工在上完近期的「效率會議」訓練課程後，有部分員工針對訓練課程表達了不滿。我認為您需要了解其中主要的兩項原因。

首先，我們的員工認為課程內容與他們實際在工作時參與的會議之間沒有任何關連。相反的，整個訓練課程似乎只是在討論一般會議的標準流程。因此，有好幾名組員認為整個課程基本上並沒有任何幫助。

另外，課程並沒有規劃讓組員發問的時間。這也讓課程本身與實際的會議之間，更缺乏任何直接的關連。

我們認為提供員工符合他們需求的訓練課程才是最重要的，不是嗎？因此，我建議我們在未來可以邀請不同的訓練講師。新任的訓練講師，應該先提供我們課程大綱，讓我們能夠確保訓練課程可以確實滿足員工的需求。

若您有任何其他的想法或回應，請隨時撥打分機 111 聯絡我。感謝您。

張莉莉

dissatisfaction (n.)：不滿　solid (adj.)：堅固的　outline (n.)：大綱

172. Why does Lily Chang write this email? 張莉莉為什麼要寫此封電子郵件？
(A) To complain about a training course 抱怨一場訓練課程
(B) To thank the HR Director for his help 謝謝人資主管的協助
(C) To ask for more training information 要求更多訓練的資訊
(D) To request some product samples 索取一些產品試用

◀ 解析 ▶
文中第一段即表明，員工對於訓練課程表達了不滿，希望能讓人資主管了解原因，故選 (A)。

173. Who is most likely Lily Chang? 張莉莉最有可能是誰？
(A) Mr. Carson's assistant 卡森先生的助理
(B) HR Director 人資主管
(C) Marketing Manager 行銷經理
(D) Company CEO 公司執行長

◀ 解析 ▶
文中多以「我們的組員」來指稱所有一起參與訓練的業務行銷組員工，可見張莉莉應該是業務行銷組的領導階層，故選 (C)。

174. What problem does Lily mention about the training? 莉莉提到關於訓練的什麼問題？
(A) Employees still don't know how to hold meetings. 員工還是不知道要如何開會。
(B) Some team members were absent. 有些團隊成員缺席。
(C) It was a dull training. 那是一場枯燥的訓練課程。
(D) It is not relevant to the actual situation. 跟實際情況沒有關連。

◀ 解析 ▶
文中第二、三段敘述對課程不滿的兩個主因，主要在於訓練內容與實際情況沒有關連，故選 (D)。

175. What does Lily suggest? 莉莉建議要怎麼做？
(A) Ask team members to give more feedback. 請組員多給一些意見回饋。
(B) Give the current trainer another opportunity. 給現有的講師再一次機會。
(C) Change a new trainer next time. 下一次換個新的訓練講師。
(D) Call extension 111 for more suggestions. 打分機 111 尋求更多建議。

◀ 解析 ▶
文中最後提出的建議，是希望能夠更換訓練講師並提供課程大綱，故選 (C)。

Questions 176 - 180 refer to the following article and letter.

餐廳評鑑

好食多餐館的全新限時供應三明治的點子，源自於店內的餐廳。多年來，我們發現好食多的顧客時常會將牛排夾在起士吐司當中，或是將蝦子塞進餐包裡食用。從現在開始，好食多將會為顧客執行這項工作。

全新的三種三明治，將好食多餐館的招牌牛排、海鮮，以及雞肉餐點，直接送到顧客的手中。這些新上市的三明治，淋滿 BBQ 醬汁，佐以手工裹上麵包粉的酥炸洋蔥圈，皆以新鮮現做的法式圓麵包製成。

主廚東尼貝克表示：「三明治在消費者之間正逐漸流行起來。」「我們向來都是以牛排、海鮮，以及沙拉聞名。現在可能要改成以牛排、海鮮、沙拉，以及三明治聞名了。」

即日起，好食多餐館的全新三明治將在所有店面供應。

關於好食多餐館

從每日新鮮準備的上等牛排，到沙拉、湯品，以及烘焙麵包，所有好食多的餐點都是在廚房內用心製作，這也是為何好食多成為消費者心目中享用美味佳餚的最佳去處。最著名的是超過 30 種的開胃菜、湯品、沙拉，以及點心吧，用餐時間不受限制，讓顧客更能夠彈性地用餐，並享有服務人員親送餐點與清理餐桌的服務。

stack (v.)：堆放　signature (n.)：特色　popularity (n.)：普及、流行　pace (n.)：速度

親愛的編輯：

拜讀完你的好食多餐館評鑑之後，我與我的孩子們在上星期五晚上，決定也去試試看好食多的三明治，畢竟我們都是三明治的愛好者。好食多所供應的餐點確實非常美味，並超乎了我們的期待。雖然我們早在下午六點左右就抵達了餐廳，但是整間餐廳卻早已坐滿了人，並有許多人正在排隊。由於當時外面正在下雨，所以我們擠入店內加入排隊的行列，並被告知大約還需要再等 20 分鐘。餐廳的等候區非常的溫暖且舒適。才經過短短 5 分鐘，我們就被通知可以入座了，這讓我們非常高興。整個服務團隊都非常的友善和熱心。我們 4 個人非常享受品嚐彼此美味餐點的用餐體驗。我們點的所有餐點中，我認為最好吃的就是新推出的三明治，既爽口又美味。我們也很喜歡好食多的牛排、海鮮以及沙拉，就連咖啡與甜點也非常地好吃。我極力推薦好食多餐館，也一定會再次前往用餐！

溫蒂哈里斯

packed (adj.)：擁擠的　toasty (adj.)：暖和舒適的　cozy (adj.)：溫馨的　attentive (adj.)：體貼的
fabulous (adj.)：極好的

176. Where does the article most likely appear? 此文章最有可能出現在何處？
(A) In a magazine 在雜誌上
(B) In a dictionary 在字典上
(C) In a phone directory 在電話簿上
(D) In a textbook 在課本內

◀ 解析 ▶
1. 此篇為餐廳評鑑的文章，最有可能出現在報章雜誌上，故本題選 (A)。
2. directory (n.)：通訊錄、電話簿

177. What kind of food is NOT served in this restaurant? 此餐廳沒有提供的食物類型為何？
(A) Sandwiches 三明治
(B) Steak 牛排
(C) Salads 沙拉
(D) Beef noodles 牛肉麵

◀ 解析 ▶
文中提到此餐廳以牛排、海鮮、沙拉著名，也推出了全新的三明治，但並沒有供應牛肉麵，故選 (D)。

178. What is the main idea of the letter? 此信件的重點為何？
(A) Good-Diner is a high-end restaurant and very expensive. 好食多餐館是高檔餐廳且收費很貴。
(B) Good-Diner mainly serves pizza. 好食多主要提供比薩餐點。
(C) The restaurant is way too crowded. 餐廳實在是太擁擠了。
(D) Good-Diner is truly a restaurant worth trying. 好食多餐館確實是值得一試的餐廳。

◀ 解析 ▶
信中讀者看過餐廳評鑑後，決定親身一試，而結果也相當令人滿意，故選 (D)。

179. Who is Wendy Harris? 溫蒂哈里斯是誰？
(A) A satisfied customer of Good-Diner 對好食多餐館感到滿意的顧客
(B) A mother of four children 有四個小孩的媽媽
(C) A magazine editor 雜誌編輯
(D) A chef at Good-Diner 好食多餐館的主廚

◀ 解析 ▶
溫蒂哈里斯是一位雜誌讀者，信中提到她與小孩共四人用餐，也就是說她只有三個小孩，因此只有選項 (A) 敘述正確，故選 (A)。

180. How long did it take for Wendy to be seated? 溫蒂哈里斯等了多久之後才入座？

(A) 20 minutes 二十分鐘
(B) 5 minutes 五分鐘
(C) 10 minutes 十分鐘
(D) Half an hour 半小時

◀ 解析 ▶
雖然她一開始被告知需排隊 20 分鐘左右，但 5 分鐘後就被通知可以入座了，故選 (B)。

Questions 181 - 185 refer to the following letters.

2018 年 8 月 25 日

路克懷特
軟體科技有限公司
西達巷 1837 號
38282 維吉尼亞州 哈克尼市

懷特先生，您好：

我們對在虛擬化IT環境內使用的應用軟體很有興趣。貴公司是首屈一指的軟體廠商之一，因此我們很希望 貴公司可以提供更多資訊、產品型錄和價格表等，以更加瞭解 貴公司的軟體產品和虛擬化解決方案。請將這些資料寄到：

珍妮湯瑪斯收
ICS 股份有限公司
哈特街 1849 號
38389 維吉尼亞州 哈克尼市

在此先謝謝您，非常期望可以讀到您寄來的資料。

誠摯地，
珍妮湯瑪斯
技術召集人，ICS 股份有限公司

virtualization (n.)：**虛擬化**

2018 年 8 月 30 日

珍妮湯瑪斯小姐
ICS 股份有限公司
哈特街 1849號
38389 維吉尼亞州 哈克尼市

湯瑪斯小姐，您好：

感謝您對於本公司虛擬產品與解決方案表示興趣。我相信當您閱讀完本公司的簡介與資料後，對於我們所提供的解決方案，與我們產品所帶來的優勢，會感到相當滿意。

請容我向您介紹幾點您應該會相當有興趣的特色。

本公司提供企業執行行動性：我們的虛擬解決方案，能夠讓您的員工隨時隨地運用最新裝置，與他人進行互動、處理資料，以及開啟應用程式執行工作。

員工可以在最新的「使用自己的裝置」模式下工作：本公司的產品能夠使高階主管擁有個人化、授予員工自主權，以及簡化 IT 基礎設施。

我們同時確保各種裝置使用上的安全性與相容性：藉由本公司的解決方案，企業能夠在維護業務機密性的同時，最大限度地提升存取性與合作性。

我很樂意針對您的任何問題或疑慮做出回應。若有任何我能夠為您服務的地方，歡迎撥打 123-2374-3828 與我聯繫。

感謝您。

誠摯地，
路克懷特

device (n.)：設備　infrastructure (n.)：基礎設施　compatibility (n.)：相容性　confidential (adj.)：機密的

181. What is the purpose of Jenny Thomas letter? 珍妮湯瑪斯寫信的目的為何？

(A) To request more information about an IT solution 要求關於 IT 解決方案的資訊

(B) To apply for a technical support engineer position 應徵一個技術支援工程師的職位

(C) To poach talents from Luke White's company 從路克懷特的公司挖角人才

(D) To invite Luke White to attend an IT seminar 邀請路克懷特參加一場資訊科技研討會

◀ 解析 ▶

從信中可推知珍妮湯瑪斯寫信給懷特先生的原因，是為了尋求更多關於軟體產品和虛擬化解決方案的資訊，故選 (A)。

182. What can be inferred about Soft-Tech Co.? 從文中可推論關於軟體科技公司的什麼事？

(A) It's a newly established company. 是一間新創辦的公司。

(B) Its stock price is very high. 公司股價很高。

(C) It's a leading company providing virtualization solutions. 是提供虛擬化解決方案的領導廠商。

(D) Its CEO is going to retire soon. 公司的執行長很快要退休了。

◀ 解析 ▶

懷特先生任職的軟體科技公司，從信中可看出是首屈一指的軟體廠商，故選 (C)。

183. What is probably being sent with the second letter? 什麼東西可能會隨著第二封信件寄出？

(A) A meeting agenda 會議議程

(B) Soft-Tech's product brochure 軟體科技公司的產品型錄

(C) Successful customer stories 成功的客戶案例

(D) A conference invitation 研討會邀請函

◀ 解析 ▶

第二封信件是懷特先生寄出的信，為了回應湯瑪斯小姐的要求，可推斷簡介與相關資料會一併寄出，故選 (B)。

184. What is NOT mentioned in Luke White's letter as a product feature?
路克懷特的信中沒有提到哪一項產品特性？

(A) Mobility 行動性

(B) BYOD model 「使用自己的裝置」模式

(C) Security 安全性

(D) Low prices 便宜的價格

◀ 解析 ▶

懷特先生的信中提到三項特點，其中並不包含價格便宜這一項，故選 (D)。

185. What should Jenny Thomas do if she has more questions? 珍妮湯瑪斯若有疑問應該怎麼做？
(A) Call Luke White 打電話給路克懷特
(B) Check on the website 上網站查詢
(C) Do more research 做更多研究
(D) Read some manuals 讀一些手冊

◀ 解析 ▶
第二封信的最後，懷特先生提到，若有任何疑問都可以打電話與他聯繫，並留下自己的電話號碼，故選 (A)。

Questions 186 - 190 refer to the following website, notice, and table.

葛瑞西爾軟體年度使用者會議

報名註冊

報名規定　　現場登記　　飯店住宿

葛瑞西爾軟體使用者會議今年將讓您獲得全面性學習與交流機會

- 實作課程：由產業專家所領導的訓練課程
- 探索區：一個透過觸控螢幕互動學習、探索最新科技的地方
- 討論室：讓客戶可以安排與專家進行一對一的會談
- 客戶感謝活動：與同業進行交流的絕佳機會
- 領導人論壇：針對高階主管所舉辦的講習課程與活動，僅限受邀者參與

點此看「常見問答集」

hands-on (adj.)：親自動手的、實用的　peer (n.)：同輩、同事、同業

葛瑞西爾軟體年度使用者會議問與答

問題：　**是否需要成為葛瑞西爾軟體的使用者，才能參與會議？**

回答：　不需要。雖然會議上有針對科技發展的討論，不過那並非參與會議唯一的好處。任何對科技發展與軟體設計主題有興趣的人，都能夠從會議中的發表會與分組討論獲得益處。本會議是專門提供給葛瑞西爾軟體使用者與所有對科技發展有興趣的人。欲了解會議議程，請參閱下列表格。

問題：　**如果目前尚未使用葛瑞西爾軟體解決方案，但對該軟體有興趣，未來可能考慮使用呢？**

回答：　本會議是探索這套軟體的絕佳機會，可了解如何利用該軟體為您的公司帶來優勢。現在是把握葛瑞西爾軟體低價訓練課程的最佳時機（費用 100 元），我們也很樂意免費提供有意願的使用者一套試用版軟體（30 日試用許可），供您參與體驗並探索使用這套軟體。

問題：　**團體報名是否能享有優惠價格？**

回答：　是的。請來電到 123-3736-3846 或寄電郵至 lucy.graw@great-hill.com 聯繫露西葛羅，詢問有關單一機關團體報名的優惠價格。

問題：　**會議現場的服裝規定為何？**

回答：　請穿著商務休閒服參與活動。

prospective (adj.)：預期的、未來的　temporary (adj.)：暫時的、臨時的　multiple (adj.)：多人參加的

葛瑞西爾軟體年度使用者會議議程

2018 年 3 月 30 日星期五

07:30 AM – 08:30 AM	報到、早餐時段
08:30 AM – 08:45 AM	茱迪斯泰瑞博士 開場致詞
08:45 AM – 10:15 AM	金李，UC 大學電腦科技教授 未來科技發展
10:15 AM – 10:45 AM	中場休息
10:45 AM – 11:15 AM	喬治羅莎，葛瑞西爾軟體公司工程部副總 大數據分析
11:15 AM – 12:00 PM	泰瑞強森，EAU 公司策略顧問 科技與創新
12:00 PM – 01:00 PM	午餐時段
01:00 PM – 02:00 PM	A 場次：電腦網路操作體驗室
01:00 PM – 02:00 PM	B 場次：虛擬化解決方案
02:00 PM – 03:00 PM	專題討論：科技趨勢
03:00 PM – 03:30 PM	中場休息
03:30 PM – 04:15 PM	比爾湯姆森博士，泰國科技公司 成功案例分享
04:15 PM – 05:00 PM	艾伯特布萊克，葛瑞西爾軟體公司執行長 終場致詞

remark (n.)：評論　innovation (n.)：創新　hands-on (adj.)：親自動手做的　panel (n.)：專題討論小組

186. According to the webpage information, which is NOT mentioned as a session of the conference?
根據網頁內容，何者非會議的講習課程之一？
(A) Outdoor activities 戶外活動
(B) Hands-on labs 實作室
(C) 1:1 Discussion 一對一討論
(D) Appreciation party 感謝派對活動

◀ 解析 ▶
根據首篇的網頁內容，會議活動中除了「戶外活動」之外，其他的都有被提及， 故選 (A)。

187. What is the purpose of the FAQs? 此問與答的目的為何？
(A) To report on a competition for students 報告學生競賽訊息
(B) To list questions and answers that participants might have
列出會議參與者可能會有的問題與回答
(C) To announce an upcoming event 宣佈即將舉辦的活動
(D) To advertise a computer game show 宣傳電腦遊戲展

◀ 解析 ▶
FAQs 是 Frequently Asked Questions 的縮寫，此處則是針對有意參與會議者，列出可能的疑問與解答，故選 (B)。

188. For whom are these three pieces of information probably intended? 這三則訊息的讀者可能是誰？
(A) University professors 大學教授
(B) Conference participants 會議參與者
(C) Projector manufacturers 投影機製造商
(D) Conference organizers 會議安排者

◀ 解析 ▶
三則訊息分別為會議介紹的首頁、參與會議的問答集以及會議議程，可推斷讀者應該是參與此會議者，故選 (B)。

189. What can be inferred about Ms. Lucy Graw? 文中可推論關於露西葛羅小姐的什麼事？
(A) She is one of the speakers. 她是講者之一。
(B) She will arrange travels for attendees. 她會為參與者安排行程。
(C) She handles the group discount issue. 她負責處理團體優惠事宜。
(D) She is in charge of creating the event website. 她負責製作活動網頁。

◀ 解析 ▶
露西葛羅的名字出現在問答集中，可知她負責的是關於團體報名的優惠，故選 (C)。

190. According to the agenda, when can attendees choose between different topics?
根據議程內容，與會者可以選擇不同主題場次的時間為何？
(A) 1 p.m. 下午一點
(B) 2 p.m. 下午兩點
(C) 10 a.m. 早上十點
(D) 4 p.m. 下午四點

◀ 解析 ▶
同一時間要選擇不同場次，根據議程安排，下午一點有 A、B 兩個場次，分別為不同主題，故選 (A)。

Questions 191 - 195 refer to the following letters.

寄件人：Gina Lo [ginalo@mail.com]
收件人：Mark Wu [mark-wu@ilt.com]
主旨：行銷專員職位
日期：2018 年 7 月 6 日

親愛的吳先生，您好：

感謝您百忙當中抽出空檔，與我討論有關 貴公司要招募的「行銷專員」 一職。真的非常感謝您願意撥冗與我面談。

在與您和 貴單位同仁談論過之後，我相信自己便是此職位的最佳人選。除了我的教育背景和良好的英語溝通能力外，我的行銷技能與策略思考，更會對完成工作帶來加分的效果。

我非常期待能為您效勞，並希望在行銷專員一職有了最終決定之後，能立刻聽到您的正面回應。若您需要更多資訊，歡迎隨時與我聯繫。可撥打我的手機號碼 0948-383-3838，和我聯絡。

再次感謝您。

誠摯的，
羅吉娜

position (n.)：職位、職務、工作　candidate (n.)：求職應徵者、候選人　background (n.)：背景
strategic (adj.)：策略性的、戰略性的

2018 年 7 月 15 日

羅吉娜小姐
古德路 1128 號
104 台灣台北市

親愛的羅小姐：

我很榮幸能夠在 2018 年 6 月 17 日與您會面。我對於您的能力與技術感到非常欣賞。您的資歷完全符合本公司想尋找的人才，我們非常高興提供給您 ILT 行銷研究公司的「行銷專員」職位。我相信您對於此職位與本公司所提供的福利會感到相當地滿意。

請容我先簡述本公司對此職缺所提供的薪資條件。您每月的薪資為新台幣 45,000 元，年終獎金將按照部門的營收淨值計算。另外，您每年將有為期 3 週的假期時間，另外能夠請 10 天病假。我們希望您能夠在 8 月 15 日（週三）開始上班。

前兩週，您將會接受以下的訓練課程：
—了解客戶行為
—使用分析工具來解讀數據
—整合研究結果

請於 8 月 5 日之前聯繫我，讓我們確認您是否願意接受此職缺的各項條件。歡迎來到 ILT 行銷研究公司，我們非常期待與您一起工作。

誠摯地，
吳馬克

qualification (n.)：資格　division (n.)：部門　net (adj.)：淨利的　on board：此處指可開始工作
interpret (v.)：解釋、說明　consolidate (v.)：合併　acceptance (n.)：接受

2018 年 7 月 17 日

吳馬克先生
ILT 行銷研究公司
商業大道 4737 號
100 台灣台北市

吳先生，您好：

我很高興能擔任 貴單位的「行銷專員」一職。您信中所列出的訓練課程大綱，讓我感受到 貴公司的確為行銷人員提供絕佳的成長機會。

我瞭解我的起薪會是每月新台幣 45,000 元，然而我希望在我加入 貴團隊之後，我的直屬主管會再根據我的專業表現來考慮加薪。

開始上班日是 8 月 15 日，這一點我沒問題。我期待當天在辦公室見到您時，可以親自當面向您道謝。

誠摯地，
羅吉娜

convince (v.)：使確信、使信服　immediate supervisor：直屬上司

191. Why does Gina write the email to Mark Wu? 吉娜為何寄電郵給吳馬克？
(A) To sell him some new products 為賣給他一些新產品
(B) To follow up on her previous interview 為追蹤她之前面談的結果
(C) To invite Mark Wu for a lunch meeting 為邀請吳馬克參加午餐會議
(D) To arrange another interview with Mark Wu 為與吳馬克約另一次面談

◀ 解析 ▶
根據吉娜電郵中的首段兩句話，便可看出她已經面談過了，現在是要追蹤後續結果，故選 (B)。

192. What can be inferred about Gina Lo from these letters? 由這些信可推論關於羅吉娜的什麼事？
(A) She will start to work at ILT in a month. 她會在一個月後開始去 ILT 上班。
(B) She is a software developer. 她是一位軟體開發人員。
(C) She is not experienced enough for the job. 她對此工作資歷不足。
(D) She will relocate to a new branch in September. 她將在九月調去新的分公司。

◀ 解析 ▶
第二封信是 ILT 公司通知羅吉娜通過面試，獲得行銷專員的職位。第三封信是羅吉娜於 7 月 17 日回覆，確認 8 月 15 日可以開始上班，上班時間約在一個月後，故選 (A)。

193. In the second letter, the word “interpret” in paragraph 3, line 3, is closest in meaning to
第二封信內，第三段第三行的 “interpret” 一字意思最接近於
(A) continue 繼續
(B) terminate 終止
(C) communicate 溝通
(D) elucidate 闡釋、解讀

◀ 解析 ▶
interpret 一字意思為「解釋」，與 elucidate 意思最相近，故選 (D)。

194. What should Gina Lo do by August 5th? 羅吉娜在 8 月 5 日前應做什麼？
(A) Submit her application form 將申請表送出
(B) Contact Mark Wu to confirm the job offer 跟吳馬克聯絡並確認工作條件
(C) Schedule an interview with Mark Wu 跟吳馬克約面談時間
(D) Attend a training session 參與訓練講習

◀ 解析 ▶
第二封信的最後一段提到，希望吉娜在 8 月 5 日前與馬克聯繫，確認是否接受此項職務的條件，故選 (B)。

195. What does Gina Lo mention about ILT? 羅吉娜提到關於 ILT 的什麼事？
(A) They should expand their product line. 他們應該要拓展產品線。
(B) Their managers should give employees a pay raise. 他們的經理應該給員工加薪。
(C) They offer valuable training courses to help staff grow. 他們提供有用的訓練課程幫助員工成長。
(D) Their main entrance needs a facelift. 他們公司的門面需要整修。

◀ 解析 ▶
第三封信的第一段提到，吉娜認為 ILT 提供給新進員工的訓練課程，對行銷人員的成長很有幫助，故選 (C)。

Questions 196 - 200 refer to the following emails.

寄件人：薇薇安史密斯 [Vivian-s@ad-co.com]
收件人：傑克威爾森 [jack-w@ad-co.com]；卡蘿凱爾 [carol-k@ad-co.com]
副本：陳馬克 [mark-c@ad-co.com]
主旨：冬季節能
日期：2018 年 10 月 4 日

親愛的傑克和卡蘿，

我們都知道，在冬季進行節能是很多公司所關注的事，我們公司也不例外。今年冬天，我們的目標不僅是節約能源，為環境做出貢獻，而且還要降低公司的水電瓦斯費。維修部門的馬克和我已經討論出兩個減少能源消耗的方法：

1. 檢修有縫隙的窗戶。有縫隙的窗戶不僅會讓冷空氣流入室內，還會讓暖空氣流出室外。我們公司的窗戶都有些老舊了，但是我們沒有預算來全面更新。因此，目前我們會先使用可以緊密密封的塑料來將縫隙封填起來，直到我們有預算時再換新窗戶。

2. 解決不必要的外洩。冷空氣鑽進室內、暖空氣外流不只是透過門窗而已。管線及其周圍可能會產生暖氣外漏，而冷空氣也可能透過孔洞進入到室內。我們打算使用絕緣材料來密封這些有可能發生洩漏的地方。

希望你們也可以提出好的節能點子。謝謝。

薇薇安史密斯

conserve (v.)：節約　trim (v.)：削減、減少　utility bills：水電瓦斯費　consumption (n.)：消耗
drafty (adj.)：有縫隙風會吹入的、通風良好的　insulate (v.)：使隔離、使絕緣

寄件人：傑克威爾森 [jack-w@ad-co.com]
收件人：薇薇安史密斯 [Vivian-s@ad-co.com]；卡蘿凱爾 [carol-k@ad-co.com]
副本：陳馬克 [mark-c@ad-co.com]
主旨：回覆：冬季節能
日期：2018 年 10 月 5 日

大家好，

我建議我們可以使用淺色的辦公傢俱。輕盈色調的牆壁顏色和辦公傢俱，可以反射照進我們辦公室的陽光。如此可以協助我們減少對日光燈的依賴。另外，我們應該只在有使用的會議室內開暖氣，關閉沒在使用的空間裡的空調。在沒人使用的空間裡開暖氣本來就沒有意義。

這些是我的想法，若有需要我也很樂意與你們進一步討論。

傑克威爾森

furnishing (n.)：傢俱　light-hued (adj.)：淡色的　reliance (n.)：依賴　radiator (n.)：暖器

寄件人：卡蘿凱爾 [carol-k@ad-co.com]
收件人：薇薇安史密斯 [Vivian-s@ad-co.com]；傑克威爾森 [jack-w@ad-co.com]
副本：陳馬克 [mark-c@ad-co.com]
主旨：回覆：冬季節能
日期：2018 年 10 月 6 日

薇薇安、傑克，你們好：

你們都提供了非常有效的方式來減少能源消耗，而且也不會犧牲掉今年冬天辦公室內應有的舒適度。

其實，我認為我們先檢視所消耗的能源用量是更為重要的。這是評估我們辦公室消耗多少能源的第一步，而且能幫助我們衡量應採取哪些措施來讓辦公室更節能。我們可以聘請一名檢驗員來檢查辦公室，找出哪些地方可能造成能源損耗。經過檢驗之後，我們可以選擇看看是哪些維修或更新，最符合我們的預算和需求。

謝謝。

卡蘿凱爾

sacrifice (v.)：犧牲　conduct (v.)：進行　energy audit：能源審核　assess (v.)：評估
modification (n.)：改變、修改　budget (n.)：預算

196. In the first email, the word "conserve" in paragraph 1, line 1, is closest in meaning to
第一封電郵裡，第一段第一行的 "conserve" 一字意思最接近於
(A) discuss 討論
(B) sustain 保留、維持住
(C) squander 揮霍、浪費掉
(D) consume 消耗

◀ 解析 ▶
conserve 一字意思為「保存」，與 sustain 意思最接近，故本題選 (B)。

197. Why does Vivian write the email to other colleagues? 薇薇安寫電郵給其他同事的目的為何？
(A) To ask them to submit sales reports 請他們交業務報告
(B) To discuss the progress of a project 討論專案進度
(C) To inform them of an event in winter 通知他們冬季舉辦的活動
(D) To discuss some energy-saving ideas 討論節能的點子

◀ 解析 ▶
根據薇薇安史密斯寫給其他人的電郵內容之前兩句，可看出是冬天將至，她想要問大家有無可以節能並減少電費消耗的點子，故本題答案選 (D)。

198. What is Jack's proposal? 傑克提出什麼建議？
(A) To use light-colored furnishings 使用淺色的辦公傢俱
(B) To replace all the old windows 汰換所有舊窗戶
(C) To turn on air conditioners 打開冷氣
(D) To recycle plastic bottles 回收塑膠罐

◀ 解析 ▶
根據第二封的電郵內容，可知傑克認為要採用淺色系的辦公室傢俱，故本題選 (A)。

199. What does Carol propose doing first? 卡蘿提議先做什麼事？
(A) Hold a meeting to discuss tomorrow 明天開會議討論
(B) Prepare marketing materials earlier 提早準備行銷資料
(C) Conduct an energy audit in advance 預先檢測能源消耗
(D) Hire more sales reps first 先招募更多業務代表

◀ 解析 ▶
根據第三封卡蘿寫的電郵，可知她認為要先檢視所消耗的能源用量，故本題答案選 (C)。

200. Which is NOT mentioned as a way to conserve energy in these emails?

這些電郵中，下列哪個節能方式沒被提及？

(A) Seal windows tightly 將窗戶緊密封好

(B) Resolve leaking problems 解決暖氣外漏的問題

(C) Turn off heaters in unused rooms 關閉沒在用的空間裡的暖氣

(D) Hold an energy-saving competition 舉辦節能競賽

◀ 解析 ▶

在所有的電郵裡，三人討論的節能點子中，並沒有提到「節能競賽」一事，故本題選 (D)。

© Caves Educational Training Co., Ltd.

考前準備系列 TP207

新多益一本通【試題解析】

出版及發行／師德文教股份有限公司
台北市忠孝西路一段 100 號 12 樓
TEL: (02) 2382-0961　FAX: (02) 2382-0841
http: //www.cet-taiwan.com

總 編 輯／邱靖媛
作　　者／文之勤
執行編輯／王清雪
文字編輯／林怡婷
美術編輯／林淑慧
封面設計／林雅蓁

總經銷／紅螞蟻圖書有限公司
台北市內湖區舊宗路二段 121 巷 19 號
TEL: (02) 2795-3656　FAX: (02) 2795-4100
E-mail: red0511@ms51.hinet.net
特約門市／敦煌書局全省連鎖門市

登記證／行政院新聞局局版臺業字第 288 號
印刷者／金瓚印刷事業有限公司
初版／2018 年 6 月　定價／新台幣 549 元

版權所有．翻印必究
購書時如有缺頁或破損，請寄回更換。謝謝！